I0823630

EVERYONE IS PERFECT HERE

Also by Jane Haseldine

The Julia Gooden Mysteries

THE LAST TIME SHE SAW HIM

DUPLICITY

WORTH KILLING FOR

YOU FIT THE PATTERN

EVERYONE IS PERFECT HERE

Jane Haseldine

SEVERN
HOUSE

First world edition published in Great Britain and the USA in 2026
by Severn House, an imprint of Canongate Books Ltd,
14 High Street, Edinburgh EH1 1TE.

severnhouse.com

Cover and jacket design by dholmesgraphic

British Library Cataloguing-in-Publication Data
A CIP catalogue record for this title is available from the British Library.

ISBN-13: 978-1-4483-2011-0 (cased)
ISBN-13: 978-1-4483-2013-4 (paper)
ISBN-13: 978-1-4483-2012-7 (e-book)

All Severn House titles are printed on acid-free paper.

Typeset by Palimpsest Book Production Ltd., Falkirk, Stirlingshire, Scotland.
Printed and bound in Great Britain by TJ Books, Padstow, Cornwall.

The manufacturer's authorised representative in the EU for product safety is Authorised Rep Compliance Ltd, 71 Lower Baggot Street, Dublin D02 P593 Ireland (arccompliance.com)

Praise for the Julia Gooden Mysteries

"An action-packed, highly believable suspenser starring a tough and determined journalist"
Kirkus Reviews on *You Fit the Pattern*

"Alluring . . . Fans are certain to enjoy the complex plot and Julia and Ray's evolving relationship"
Publishers Weekly on *Worth Killing For*

"Haseldine has a gift for atmosphere, setting and suspense and the many twists and turns will keep readers guessing"
Library Journal on *Duplicity*

"A sharp, breathless thriller. From the opening scene to the last, *The Last Time She Saw Him* kept me flipping the pages. I loved it! Jane Haseldine is one to watch!"
Lisa Jackson, #1 *New York Times* bestselling author, on *The Last Time She Saw Him*

"A gripping story that I read in one night—I could not put it down"
Debbie Howells, author of *The Bones of You*, on *The Last Time She Saw Him*

"Journalist Jane Haseldine's debut novel rings with authenticity as she, like Julia, is a former crime reporter. This is a harrowing read"
BookPage on *The Last Time She Saw Him*

About the author

Jane Haseldine is a journalist, former crime reporter, columnist, newspaper editor, magazine writer, and deputy director of communications for a governor. Jane writes the Julia Gooden mystery series, including *The Last Time She Saw Him*, *Duplicity*, *Worth Killing For*, and *You Fit the Pattern.*

janehaseldine.com

To Nash and Beck,
My perfect sons who light up the world. Always.

ONE
Carly Bennett

Present Day, Los Angeles

Light blue on dirty blonde.

Creative writing professor Carly Bennett did a quick scan of her face from its reflection in the window that overlooked the University of Southern California quad and smoothed a crease in her pencil skirt.

If Carly had known that the dean of the English department would schedule a last-minute meeting with her, she would've picked a better outfit than one that screamed, "I had no time to take this to the cleaner, so I ran a fast iron over it. But thank God the skirt is black so no one can see the stain from when my coffee cup lid jimmied its way free this morning."

Nothing like near first-degree burns on your thigh from an errant Starbucks Pike to jolt a person awake during LA's slog of a commute.

No matter. Here she was.

And she'd be ready. Even though she needed to master her prep on the fly.

Carly turned the corner to the English department's Office of the Dean and forged through her speaking points that she'd deliver to her boss, Bert Scanlon.

"Making the LA Times*'s 'Thirty-Under-Thirty' list was a complete surprise, but I'm so happy that the article will shine a spotlight on the great work our team is doing under your leadership."*

Ack. Too mealy-mouthed. Plus, it made her sound like a big-headed brown-noser. And nobody likes that person.

"Thank you for the kind words. Please know how much I

appreciate that you believe in me, and I swear, I won't let you down."

Better, and that sentiment was from the heart.

Carly pictured her face, front and center on the page when she'd pulled up the *LA Times* story that morning and hoped that the people she used to know from her early Malibu days saw it too.

Elitist jerks.

As for herself, Carly had read the write-up, over and over, until she could now recite it in perpetuity.

Carly passed by the USC English department's wall of fame, which showcased its students' esteemed awards through the years. She paused when she saw her name, capturing a moment in time from freshman year. Her: scared to near speechlessness among the far cooler co-eds but finding strength behind her pen.

Winner of the 2018 Undergraduate Writing Prize—
First Place: Carly Bennett

Had she really come this far? Most would've marked her a losing bet at age twelve, her personal line of demarcation, but sometimes, even dark horses can come from behind and win the whole damn thing.

Four. Three. Two. One.

"You got this," Carly whispered.

She reached for the security of her inhaler in her briefcase and entered Scanlon's office.

Gretchyn Olson, a middle-aged woman with salt-and-pepper hair was working the phone with precision. She held up a single finger when she saw Carly.

While she waited, Carly continued to clutch her briefcase in one hand and placed the other behind her back, where she dug a fingernail into a stray cuticle.

After a beat, Scanlon's assistant put the call on hold.

"They're waiting for you," Gretchyn said. "Hang in there, kid. Sometimes, you need to play the game."

They? And what game was she talking about?

Carly's neck felt hot, but she made certain she was smiling

when she entered the office, where she locked eyes with Scanlon, who rose to greet her. Scanlon had a Mr. Clean, shiny bald head, and his stomach struggled to stay behind the confines of the clasped gold buttons of his tweed coat.

Seated across from the dean of the English department was an unfamiliar male, who was well dressed, neatly manicured, and appeared to be in his early fifties.

Carly shot the stranger an equally polite smile. Who was this guy?

"Miss Bennett, thank you for taking time to swing by under such short notice," Scanlon said.

"Of course, sir."

Maybe the man was another reporter from the paper who covered the education beat and was writing a follow-up article on the English department.

"I don't believe you've met Franklin Yeager. You taught Frank's son, Landon, last semester."

In that moment, Carly felt like someone had jabbed an ice pick into her high-flying helium balloon.

The room became very still as Carly struggled to find the appropriate response.

"In all due respect, if this is about my former student, I think any further discussion should be held in private and between the administration, but I was under the impression the incident and disciplinary action had been decided," Carly said.

A robotic delivery, but at least she got the words out.

"There've been some developments that have been brought to my attention. I asked Frank to come in so we could clear the air, so to speak," Scanlon said. "Please, sit, Miss Bennett."

Carly kept her place, arms folded, standing above the men, but when Scanlon cleared his throat, she acquiesced and found a seat next to her former student's father.

"Landon didn't plagiarize the paper," Yeager said.

Yes, he did! Carly wanted to scream. Instead, she slipped her hands underneath her legs, in case her palms started to sweat.

"If my son did cheat, I'd be the first to request that USC boot him out the door on his fanny," Yeager continued. "But I know my kid, and I also know a liar, and Landon is beside himself over this false accusation. I'll be honest with you, when Landon first told me about the whole mess, I was ready to call my lawyer, but since Bert is an old friend, I thought, why not try and hash things out man-to-man first."

She had to respond. The words were there, ready to make her point, if only she could find the ability and the guts to say them.

"But he did ch-ch-cheat," Carly said, despising the catch in her voice.

When was the last time she'd stuttered? Probably a year ago, during her annual review with Scanlon. She wondered if the universe would grant her a reprieve, and somehow the two men hadn't picked up on her residual speech impediment, which still ambushed her in the worst possible moments, rising like an unkillable weed despite all her years of work to get rid of it.

She shot a glance at Yeager, whose mouth had turned up into a bow that resembled a smirk or, worse, pity.

If she were going down, at least she had to throw a punch.

"I want all my students to excel, and if they need extra time on an assignment, they know I'll give it to them, and my door is always open if they need additional help. But the paper Landon wrote was a complete replica of one I received from a different student last year. We're talking down to the semicolon."

Carly looked to Scanlon, hoping for some back up, but the dean kept his focus on Yeager.

"Then it wasn't a case of cheating but purely accidental on Landon's part," Yeager said. "Or is the word coincidental? You're the English whizzes in here, and I'm a businessman who wouldn't know a semicolon from a hyphen, but I do know mistakes can be made, even by well-meaning young professors. How long have you been a teacher? You look more like a co-ed than a professor, and I mean that in the most complimentary of ways."

Yeager chuckled, sounding to Carly like the laugh was cover so he wouldn't sound like a creep.

Too late.

Carly fought to speak up and defend herself. But she remained still and silent, stuck between two powerful, rich males who were doing a very fine job of reeling in the young, errant female who didn't know her place.

"This is my second year at USC."

"Miss Bennett is still relatively new to our school as a professor, but she's a rising star in our English department and did quite well as a student here before joining our professional fold."

The heat that Carly had felt in her neck earlier had now exploded into a full-blown, five-alarm inferno, despite Scanlon throwing her a pseudo-bone.

Carly had crossed her legs and put a hand to her throat to try and cover her growing rash when she noticed Yeager was staring at something on the bottom of her black high heel. Whatever it was seemed to give him great satisfaction.

"Mr. Scanlon . . ." Carly pleaded, but the dean interrupted.

"I appreciate that you hold your students to the highest of standards, as you should, but since Frank is a trusted friend to the school, this time, we'll expunge the previous disciplinary action and wipe the slate clean. Landon can resubmit the assignment and finish up the course through independent study, so he won't lose credit. I have your word that Landon will be more careful in his work going forward, Frank?"

"You bet. My kid is a good boy, and I knew we could wrangle this problem to the ground. You have my word on my kid and on my continued support. Generations of Yeagers have supported this school, and we'll continue the tradition. "*Fight on for ol' SC, our men fight on to victory!*" Yeager warbled, hitting the notes of the USC fight song slightly off-key but with great confidence in his delivery.

When Yeager stood to shake the dean's hand, Carly looked to the bottom of her high heel and saw a Macy's close-out sale sticker still affixed to its outsole.

Her previous high-flying balloon was now bits of spent plastic that an entitled rich boy and his adult minions had tossed into the dumpster.

"No hard feelings, OK? New teachers can make mistakes with the best of them," Yeager said.

He extended his hand to Carly.

You sold your integrity for a buck, and to a total cheese bag when you know I'm right! Carly wanted to scream to Scanlon.

Instead, Carly remained quiet and stared at Yeager's outstretched hand.

Scanlon cleared his throat again.

"Miss Bennett, the matter has been settled," Scanlon answered.

The dean's eyes narrowed, and Carly followed his cue.

She reached for Yeager's hand, gave it a quick shake, and regretted it the second her skin touched Yeager's.

"That will be all, Miss Bennett."

This was so unfair. She had to stand her ground.

"Is there something else you wanted to say?" Scanlon pressed.

Carly paused, searching for the words. They were right there, but when she jumped from the platform to catch the brass ring, she missed and spiraled into freefall.

"Miss Bennett?" Scanlon asked.

"Th–th–th–thank you, sir."

She couldn't remember leaving the office, but there she was, back in the lobby. Carly hurried past Gretchyn, and by the time she reached the corridor, she was certain that she heard the two men laughing from behind the office door.

"HA! HA! HA! HA! HA!"

After escaping the humiliation-fest in Scanlon's office, Carly lowered her head so she wouldn't have to make eye contact, or worse, engage in fake, idle chitchat after her fall, and continued her fast walk to the USC faculty bathroom. She had ten minutes until her advanced creative writing class started, which was threading the needle a bit, but the familiar vice was constricting her chest, and if she didn't take a pull from her inhaler soon, she'd be in the throes of a full-fledged, not to mention very public, asthma attack.

She struggled for air and rushed into an open stall. Once inside, she slammed the door, snatched her inhaler from her briefcase, and gave it a quick shake. She heard the familiar whistling sound coming from her throat and shoved her rescue inhaler into her mouth.

Feeling like a five-hundred-pound man was now sitting on her chest, Carly fought to stay calm. She closed her eyes, forced herself to hold her breath for the requisite ten seconds between puffs and prayed for the corticosteroid to kick in.

When the tightness in her lungs loosened, she could see, plain as day, her old practice phrase, the one she'd started reciting at boarding school to help conquer her stutter.

When her breathing steadied to a normal inhale-in, exhale-out, she whispered the words aloud to find her center.

"The girl wore her hair in two braids, tied with two blue bows."

Not bad. Her voice was clear and strong this time, unlike her herky-jerky performance earlier.

How had she let herself choke, and on such an epic scale?

Feeling like she was no longer dry-drowning from her asthma attack, Carly took one more hit of her inhaler. She squeezed the metal canister and pictured Scanlon's and Yeager's mugs, having a big old chuckle at her expense.

"Never again," Carly whispered, not quite believing it, but at least it was a start.

She rose from crouching position in the stall, straightened her shoulders, and then shot her middle finger in the air.

"That's bravery right there, giving the bird to a restroom door instead of standing up for yourself. Next time will be different."

Carly exited the stall and was relieved to see the faculty bathroom was still empty.

She splashed cold water from the sink onto her face, then patted her sticky armpits with a wad of paper towels from the dispenser on the wall. A poor girl's spa day.

Having no idea how much time had passed since the start of her asthma attack, Carly worried that she was late for her next class. She grabbed her phone from her briefcase to check the time and gasped.

On the home screen was a photo memory, which captured a hoped-for promise never to come.

Carly ran her finger over the image of her mother and studied her twelve-year-old self. The photo had been taken by her then soon-to-be stepbrother Julien, on the day she'd met him and the rest of the Whites.

A pang of melancholy cut through her. Everybody would've believed her if she were a rich boy.

TWO
Carly

Fifteen Years Earlier, San Francisco, Chatham Prep School for Girls

Twelve-year-old Carly Bennett sat on the cold metal chair in the office of Chatham's headmistress, Laverne Lusk, a reed-thin woman in her early sixties, with deep creases that lined the corners of her mouth.

Mrs. Lusk stood in the doorway while the police officer who'd driven all the way to San Francisco from Malibu loomed over her.

Carly looked way up at the officer, who had a slight paunch, thick sideburns, and a receding hairline. She was certain he'd told her his name after she was summoned over the P.A. system to come to the headmistress's office, but the sheer shock of being called to Mrs. Lusk's office twice in two days had caused her to forget the man's name.

She wondered if a person could perish from heartbreak and fright, while squinting at the officer's nametag that the front office required all visitors to wear.

Detective George Halloran of the Malibu Police department.

"Do you know why I'm here, Carly?" Halloran asked.

Carly tried to look at the officer, but instead, pictured only her mother, Emily, holding her hand on the return walk from their neighbor's house after Emily got off work from her job as a bank teller in the Valley. A precious time, when it was still only the two of them. Carly could recall the subtle smell of freesia from her mother's perfume, how pretty she thought her mom looked in her new dress, but most of all, how safe she felt with her mother by her side.

She trembled, wiped away a tear, and tried to accept her new reality.

"I already know what you're thinking," Halloran answered and pulled out a pink diary, *her pink diary*, from his jacket pocket. "I found this under your dorm room bed."

Halloran started reading the first page.

"*My name is Carly Bennett. I'm twelve. And I live in San Francisco now. Sorry if this all sounds lame already. I've never had a diary before. This is my first entry, so hang with me, please. I need all the friends that I can get. Right now, I don't have any. I hate being the new kid. And I miss my mom.*"

"Mrs. Lusk, that's mine!" Carly cried.

"Don't be an ass," Mrs. Lusk snapped, and then snatched the diary from the officer's hand. "The girl's gone through a terrible trauma. Since Carly has agreed to this interview, let me remind you that she's a minor without a parent present, and I'll be her surrogate guardian throughout. So, I'd suggest you check yourself before I shut this down."

Carly looked at Mrs. Lusk with wide eyes and appreciation and wanted to rush into her arms, but the headmistress gave Carly a slight nod, as if to say, "We'll play the game until we won't, but compose yourself so the bastards won't win."

Carly gave Mrs. Lusk a slight nod back, letting her know that she understood, and then answered.

Her mom would've expected Carly to be a good girl in the current situation, no matter what.

"I know you're here about my mom, but you shouldn't take a person's diary," Carly said.

"You're right, and I'm sorry. We got off to a bad start, but I promise, I'll do better. I'm trying to figure out what happened, and I think you can help me. Will you do that?"

Carly closed her eyes and envisioned her mother sitting beside her.

"OK," Carly answered in a small voice.

Halloran squatted down so he was at eye level with Carly. "Can you tell me about your homelife before you were sent here?"

A million brittle memories, like sharp pieces of glass, pulsed through Carly's memory, but she settled on the banal to be safe. "It was regular, I guess."

"I spoke to your stepfather and stepbrothers already, so I know that isn't true," Halloran answered. "Mrs. Lusk verified that you were on campus the night of the event, but you'd left your dorm and were found sleeping in a maintenance shed on the grounds."

"I'm the new girl, and I don't think my roommates like me," Carly explained. That part was the truth.

"The preteen and teen years can be a rough ride," Halloran continued. He was still eye level with Carly and leaned in closer. "Are you trying to protect yourself, or maybe someone else?"

Carly scooted her chair back while she tried to find her voice.

"No. Of course n–n–n–not."

Now she'd done it. Not only did she sound like a total dork, but the detective would think she was guilty as anything because of her stupid speech impediment. Carly had watched enough *Veronica Mars* episodes to know police got suspicious when a perp got fidgety or acted weird, and her stutter was about as weird as a person could get.

"That stutter of yours, did you always have it?" Halloran asked.

"What in the world does this have to do with what happened to her mother?" Mrs. Lusk interjected.

"I never had a s–s–s–stutter until this year," Carly answered.

Great. She was on a roll with stutter number two. It was as if her mouth operated independently from her body, dropping a trail of stupid girl breadcrumbs along the way.

"Trauma manifests itself in different ways, especially during stress. I'm not here to jam you up or cause you any more pain. But it would help if you could paint a picture of what was going on at the Whites' before you left. Do you think you can do that?" Halloran asked.

Mrs. Lusk nodded at Carly again, giving Carly the courage that she needed.

Carly looked out the window to the campus quad, where the young girls of Chatham Prep School hung with their groups. The sporty ones kicked a soccer ball; the girly girls huddled together in a circle, trying on each other's new lipsticks; and the brainiac nerds sat under a tree, debating whether Sylvia Plath or Virginia Woolf was the better writer.

A year ago, before the whole mess started, Carly would've fit right in with any of the cliques.

Missing the girl that she used to be, a self that had blossomed under her mother's care, Carly found her voice.

"I'll tell you what happened," Carly said.

"When was this?" Halloran asked.

"Two months ago."

Carly returned to looking out the window at her classmates, all going on with their normal day. How she envied their carefree lives.

She recounted the story.

The sudden jolt of pain was so sharp, Carly wanted to clutch her stomach, as if touching her recent source of misery would somehow make it better. Instead, the sixth grader remained still. She didn't want her mother to give her another strange look.

The two sat in Emily's new BMW. The car was idling in the driveway of the Whites' estate, a place mother and daughter had called home for the past seven months.

"There's nothing wrong with you, Carly," Emily said, breaking the silence that had lingered since they left Cedar Sinai Hospital.

"What do you mean?" Carly asked.

"The doctor ran all the tests. There's absolutely nothing wrong with you, besides your asthma, but you've had that since you were a baby, and we have that under control."

"My stomach hurts bad, I swear."

"I'm not saying you're lying. The doctor said you have a psychosomatic disorder. Essentially you think you feel pain, but it's caused by emotional stress. You think you're sick because you're unhappy. It's normal for a child to crave attention when a parent remarries, but Christopher and I have done everything to make you feel like we're a family. When you were little, you got extra attention from me when you had an asthma attack, so it would make sense for you to make up a story about your stomach hurting to regain my attention."

"I am happy, and I'm not a baby."

"I think you need some counseling. There's no shame in that. But you should've told me how you felt," Emily said. "You know I always love you, no matter what. Of course, money isn't an issue, but your stepfather arranged for you to see so many specialists. At least now we found the root of the problem."

Carly thought her mother was reaching for her hand. Instead, Emily picked up her ringing cell phone from the car's console.

"Let's hold the conversation, it's your school," Emily said before she answered.

Emily didn't say much during the call except for, "I see," and "I'm so sorry," before she hung up.

"What did the school want?" Carly asked. "If my teachers are mad about me missing classes, I'll make up the work, you know I will, and I'll nail an 'A' in all my subjects. Why won't you look at me?"

Without turning around, Emily gave her directive.

"Go inside. I need some time to process this."

"Process what? You're the one who's acting strange now, not me."

Carly raced out of the car before Emily could answer, and then up the staircase and to her room, where she face-planted on her bed.

Why was her mom acting so weird?

"Adults never believe kids, but don't worry. I know you're sick."

Carly bolted up from the bed to see Julien had entered her room.

He stood in the doorway with a cup of tea and one of his father's thick medical books tucked underneath his arm.

Julien was her stepfather Christopher's son.

He was seventeen, president of his prep school's debate club, and looked like a model in a Calvin Klein ad, like the ones she'd seen in a few of her stepfather's magazines, which always stank of old-man cologne.

"We're going to figure out what's wrong with you and then that stupid doctor you saw today is going to feel like an idiot."

"I'm sick of seeing doctors. They act nice enough to my face, but I know they think I'm a liar."

"Our dad's been making Julien see a boatload of shrinks since he was thirteen."

Julien's younger brother, Victor, was now inside the bedroom, bouncing from one foot to the other, as if it might kill him to stand still. Victor was fifteen and shared Julien's jet-black hair, green eyes, and bone structure, except his future chiseled features were currently hidden behind a pubescent, fleshy face. Whereas Julien was tall and sinewy, Victor was short and plump, with small mounds of boyish breasts visible underneath his Eminem T-shirt.

"Parents don't want to deal with teenage drama, so they shuttle their kids off to psychiatrists to do the heavy lifting," Victor continued. "If Chris doesn't like what the latest shrink says about Julien, he cuts them loose and hires another one. Isn't that right, Jules?"

"This isn't about me," Julien answered. "Are you eavesdropping again?"

"The door was open, and in case you forgot, I live here too. Yo, yo, yo, I just came up with the perfect rap for this situation," Victor said.

"Don't," Julien warned. "Just because you're wearing that shirt doesn't make you Eminem."

"No, dude, that's where you're wrong. I've been practicing. When I get a deal with Aftermath records, who'll be crying? Check this out.

Carly and Em came to town,
Cool and sweet 'til big money came 'round,
Now Em's all up in the Malibu scene.
And Chris is AWOL, he so mean.
Adults too busy and say Carly's lyin',
About her pain, but she keeps on tryin',
To convince them what she feels is real.
But it's up to the White boys to close the deal."

When Victor finished, the room fell silent, except for the sound of Victor's black Converse sneakers, tap, tap, tapping, on the hardwood floor.

Carly tried to smile a thank you for Victor's effort, but instead, she turned her face away so her stepbrothers wouldn't see how upset she was.

"For Christ's sake, shut it, Thunder," Julien snapped. "This is serious. Carly is sick, and Christopher and Em don't believe her."

"Knock it off with the Thunder stuff, OK?" Victor asked. Quieter this time.

"Isn't there a play rehearsal you need to go to?" Julien said. "And don't get pissy about me calling you Thunder. You deserved it."

"What did I do?" Victor begged.

"You've torpedoed a lousy situation further down the can by bringing up Em and making Carly feel worse," Julien said.

"You promised, and now you went and broke it."

Victor's face crumpled, and Carly thought her stepbrother was going to be the one in the room to break first.

"That was out of line. Sorry, bro, I know you mean well, but we need to help our girl out of this mess," Julien said, and then turned his attention to Carly. "It's never the kids. It's the parents who are the biggest disappointments. Don't worry, though. I'll take care of everything."

When Julien left, Victor plopped down next to Carly on her canopy bed and cupped her hand in his.

"Sorry if I was an idiot."

"I liked your rap," Carly said. "It was cool."

"My rap was lousy, and it was a lousier thing I did to bring up Em. I like her, I do, but money always screws with people's heads."

"Especially if they never had it before," Carly answered.

"You're wicked smart, but I'm guessing you learned that the hard way. People who are born filthy rich are equally screwed, you can trust me on that. And there I go again, making you feel worse. The Community Theater director says I always talk before I think. He calls me 'No Filter Vic.' I guess he's right. The director always has this big smile on his face when he calls me that, like I'm in on the joke, but I think I annoy him. I have that way with people."

"Don't say that about yourself. You and Julien are trying to help me," Carly said.

She sighed and rested her head on Victor's shoulder. "Why does Julien call you Thunder?"

"It's no big deal."

"It is a big deal by the way you reacted. Tell me."

"You swear you won't think less of me?"

"Cross my heart," Carly said and drew an "X" across her chest with her index finger.

"Don't tell anyone else, OK? Julien brought one of his friends to the house last summer. I was in the pool, and Julien told me to get out, since he and his buddy wanted to swim. When I did, his friend pointed at my legs and started laughing so hard, like I was the funniest thing he'd ever seen, kind of like I looked like the Elephant Man or something. Then he called me 'Thighs of Mighty Thunder,' over and over. I pretended to laugh it off, you know? Like what he was saying didn't bother me, but I swear, I wanted to die right there. Death by humiliation. Say, that's not bad. I can make that the lead track on my first album. Anyway, Julien knew how I felt, and I gotta give him credit. He told his friend to shut the eff up, and I thought Julien was going to beat the crap out of the kid. And to Jules's credit, he ghosted the jerk after that. But Jules still pulls that name out when he's pissed at me."

"I'll talk to him."

"Nah, Jules and I are solid, and I probably deserved it this time. Besides, if anyone can convince Em and my dad that you're sick, it's my brother. I'm pretty sure Julien could convince God to let the Devil return to angel duty."

"I always wanted a sibling. You're lucky."

"You have two now, and don't forget it. Julien and I will always have your back."

The following afternoon, Carly entered Principal Alfred Rooney's office, hoping he was going to break the good news that she'd won the school's patriotic essay contest. Her fantasy crashed and burned when she saw her mom and Christopher, looking pale and stoic. They sat on a bench across from the principal's desk.

"Miss Bennett, please take a seat," Principal Rooney instructed.

Carly found a spot between her parents and turned to her

mother for answers, but Emily continued to look straight ahead.

"You've been an exemplary student since you arrived here six months ago," Rooney said.

"Thank you, Mr. Rooney," Carly answered. "I really like it here. I'm thinking about running for class president next year."

Instead of encouragement, Rooney shuffled through some papers on his desk and didn't make eye contact with her. "Your disciplinary record was spotless before this, so this comes as a shock to everyone involved."

"I don't understand," Carly said.

Carly tugged at her mom's shirt, so Emily could explain why they were in this upside-down world, but her mom kept looking at Rooney.

Across his mahogany desk, Rooney slid three pieces of paper, each a threatening letter to Carly's English teacher.

In her head, Carly started to read the first note.

Dear Mrs. Ogan,

You are an evil witch, and everyone hates you. The C- you gave me on my Greek God essay was bogus, and you know it. If you don't fix my grade, I'm going to come to your house when you're sleeping and cut you open with a butcher knife. This is your fault for being a terrible teacher. You deserve to die . . .

Carly's entire body shook when she read the other two letters, which were equally as violent. The handwriting in the notes looked exactly like her own, down to the signature.

"I didn't write the letters," Carly protested. "I'd never do anything crazy like that."

"Threatening bodily harm to a teacher regarding a disappointing grade is completely unacceptable," Rooney continued.

"I can't tell you how appreciative I am that you didn't call the police," Emily said.

"This is still an egregious act, and our school can't condone violence in threat or in action," Rooney continued. "Has she exhibited similar behavior in the past?"

"Carly had some issues recently, mostly acting out to get attention, but I arranged for a counselor at my practice to help her work through it," Christopher answered.

"Someone set me up. I never wrote those letters, and I'm not an unstable whacko like you're saying," Carly shot back.

"That will be quite enough," Emily warned. "You apologize to your stepfather right now."

"I'm sorry that I was disrespectful," Carly said.

The shame, coupled with the fact that everyone now thought she was a violent, psycho freak, was too much. Carly covered her face with her hands, so she wouldn't have to see the judgment anymore.

"I'm glad your daughter will be getting support. Regardless, I have no choice but to expel her. It's a shame, because she seemed to hold great promise when she first walked through our doors, but perhaps this painful lesson will be a good one for her in the end."

Carly felt dissociated from her body, like she was floating above the scene, during the entire walk of shame out of the school and into the parking lot, where Christopher's Bentley was parked.

"I'm so disappointed in you, and quite honestly, I'm in shock," Emily said to Carly. "You were always my good girl."

"I s–s–s–swear . . . I didn't write those letters," Carly stuttered, surprised to hear the odd hiccup in her voice.

"You can't duck responsibility for this one," Christopher said.

"I promise, I didn't do the horrible things the principal said. I don't need to see a counselor, but I'll go if that will make everyone happy."

"It's too late for that," Emily said. "Christopher and I discussed this last night. There's an all-girls' boarding school in San Francisco."

"You're sending me away?" Carly asked. "You can't do that."

"Consider yourself the luckiest girl in the world. My grandmother went to Chatham, and so did my mother," Christopher answered. "It's a prestigious school, and they have a special program for girls with behavioral problems. With the right amount of counseling, I believe Chatham can get you back on track."

THREE
Carly

As Carly's students filtered out of her "Writers in the Word: Text and Context" class, she erased her lecture title, "The Strange Case of Dr. Jekyll and Mr. Hyde: Do the Worst Villains Exist Inside of Us?"

She picked up a stack of ungraded papers on her desk when her graduate assistant, Rebecca Hunter, ran down the aisle in her direction. Rebecca was in her mid-twenties with waist-length dark hair, a nose ring, and a tattoo of an elephant on her inner wrist.

"Sorry I'm late," Rebecca said in a breathless rush. "I wanted to sit in on your class, but I got caught in a killer line at the pharmacy. I picked up your new asthma medicine and left it in your office. How was your day so far?"

Her visit with Scanlon and the wealthy donor still seared in her mind, Carly rolled her eyes.

"A train wreck. A dumpster fire. Insert any appropriate disaster word you like. But, still, we persevere," Carly said. "As for missing my class, you'd be bored out of your wits listening to a sophomore lecture. And no running personal errands for me. That's not part of your job."

Carly slid her tortoiseshell reading glasses up the bridge of her nose and focused on the paper Rebecca was clutching in her hand.

"The printout is your schedule over the next few days. There's a USC faculty party meeting Monday, and you have a mixer with the creative writing grad students tonight. I'll be there for that one."

"I'll let you run the show at the grad party then," Carly said. "I have dinner plans."

"Like a date?"

"I guess you can call it that. I'm meeting someone at Nobu."

"That's awesome. If I looked like you, I'd be dating a new guy every night of the week, including Sunday, because who needs a night off, right?" Rebecca joked. "But that makes you even more amazing because you never flaunt it. What time is your reservation? Forgive me for my OCD brain, but I keep a master list of all your meetings on my phone, and if I don't change it, I'll be obsessing for hours. I'd be wrecked if I messed up something for you."

"Dinner is at six."

Rebecca updated Carly's schedule. "Added. You know, I met someone too. His name is David Ramsey. He's a terrible dresser. But underneath the awful clothes, he's gorgeous and doesn't even know it. He's a big fan of holistic healing and even does Reiki. I don't usually admit to being a fan of Reiki because that pushes you over the edge into full-blown New Age weirdo with most people. You can be health-conscious, and even raw vegan is mainstream now, but if you admit you're into Reiki, people give you this look, like you're some sort of freak. We've only been on a few dates, but I think he could be the one. He works at a vegan health food store downtown, but he started his own online company that sells vitamins and health care supplements. I think he's a real go-getter . . ."

Rebecca stopped, and looked toward the door. "It's GI janitor," she whispered. "I know he likes you. I see him following you around, and believe you me, he's crossing the threshold into full-blown creeper."

Rebecca rolled her eyes.

"Sorry, but I don't want to deal with his middle-aged pervy vibes. Am I free to go?" Rebecca asked.

"Ed Russo isn't a bad guy, but if you want to head out, I won't stop you."

Rebecca popped in her ear buds and then cut across the room to the adjacent aisle where she made her escape out of the lecture hall.

Russo, a longtime USC janitor, smiled his apologies for interrupting and pushed his mop cart into the room. Russo was a short, well-built man in his early forties with a square jaw and a tight blond crewcut.

"How are you doing, Miss Bennett?" Russo said in gravelly bass laced with the rough edges of a Revere, Massachusetts accent.

Class was dismissed for the day; how merciful was that after the earlier doozy with Sclanon? But Ed Russo saved her job once, so she owed him at least a bit of polite conversation.

Russo strode down the remainder of the aisle until he was a few feet away from her.

"I'm glad I ran into you. I wanted to thank you for recommending 'Into the Wild.' I'm not much of a reader unless it's the sports page, but I liked the story. I was thinking, maybe if you don't have plans later, we could get a coffee."

Russo was standing so close now, Carly could see the small crescent-shaped scar on his chin. When he reached for Carly's hand, she took a step back in surprise.

"Thanks for the invite, but I already have plans with someone."

"Oh man, I just made the weirdness between us even weirder now. I was hoping we'd have a chance to talk. I like you, Carly, I really do."

"I'm flattered, but I don't date people from work." The lie wasn't a complete lie, and seemed genuine enough that Carly hoped it would do the trick and not hurt Russo's feelings.

"I understand. A classy girl like you wouldn't go out with a janitor."

"That's not it, Ed, I swear. You're one of the good ones, and any girl would be lucky to go on a date with you."

"I almost believe you, but you master the bob and weave from the truth like I did during my drinking days, you can tell a lie, even a harmless white one, almost as soon as it comes out of a person's mouth. I don't want anything to happen to you, is all."

"What do you mean by that?" Carly asked.

Not one part of her liked where this was heading.

"It would be a shame if anyone in the English department, let alone the dean, found out what you did last month. You're a nice girl, and a shooting star in the department, so I'd hate to see you get in trouble."

"Is that a threat?"

"I wasn't always a janitor. I wanted to tell you more about that part of my life. But I get it," Russo said and retreated to his janitor's cart.

Carly tried to temper her breathing and felt for her inhaler.

Smiley, nice guy Ed was no nice guy after all. She'd been a sucker to think otherwise. But Carly had to massage Ed's ego enough to salvage the situation and her future at the school.

"I'd like to hear more about your life. But it's best that we keep our relationship professional. I hope that you'll keep my secret," Carly said. "It was a stupid, one-time mistake I made, and I regret it every day. Ed, are you listening?"

Ed's back was to Carly. He dragged his mop across the aisle and began to whistle, like she wasn't there.

"Ed?"

When he didn't respond, Carly snatched up her briefcase and headed out of the lecture hall to the faculty parking lot.

Never more relieved to end a school day, Carly got inside her Jeep.

Once she was alone, once she felt safe, she took in her reflection in her rearview mirror.

The person who looked back at her was Carly Bennett, the young, rising professional.

She tried to take comfort in that, but Ed's warning niggled in the back of her head.

Carly leaned in closer. The confident girl was now gone. Her eyes looked wide and filled with worry. She twisted the mirror to the side so she wouldn't have to see herself anymore and hoped to God what happened when she was at the Whites' hadn't made her a monster.

FOUR
Carly

March 2010, San Francisco, Chatham Prep School for Girls

Detective Halloran rubbed a hand over his face and then looked to the clock above Mrs. Lusk's desk.

Twenty minutes and counting since Halloran started the interview, and Carly could tell she wasn't giving the detective the answers he wanted. She felt like she was getting smaller and smaller in the chair as each minute ticked away. Maybe it would be better if she continued shrinking until she disappeared. At least she wouldn't hurt so much. Things were bad enough when she'd first been sent away, but nothing could have prepared her for what came next.

"You were upset your mother didn't believe you?" the detective asked.

"Tread lightly," Mrs. Lusk warned. She sat behind her desk, arms folded, like a sentry.

"My mom always believed me before, but she changed when we moved in with Christopher and his family," Carly said.

"Did you hate your mother because she sent you away? No one could blame a kid for feeling that way," the detective pressed.

Mrs. Lusk shot up from her chair, but Carly continued. "No," she whispered.

"Speak up, please. I can't hear you," Detective Halloran said.

"No! I never hated my mom. I loved her!"

No matter what happened, she shouldn't have yelled. Her mom would've been so disappointed in her.

"That will be enough for the day," Mrs. Lusk said.

"I'm trying to find out what happened. Don't you want that, Carly?" the detective asked.

"I'm sorry if I sounded disrespectful. I could never hate my mom. There was someone else at the house I hated. He tricked me."

Detective Halloran raised an eyebrow, as if at last, Carly had said something of interest. "What did this person do to you to make you hate them?"

"The child is already suffering, and I don't like your questions, not one bit," the headmistress said.

"Thanks, Mrs. Lusk, but maybe if I say it all out loud, it might make me feel better."

Carly watched the second hand tick its way across Mrs. Lusk's clock and told the adults about her final hours at the Whites' estate.

Carly swung her legs as hard as she could against the footboard of her canopy bed and wished she could forget what was coming for her.

She picked up the stub of a dried rose from her dresser, the remnant of a bouquet that Christopher gave her as a welcome gift on move-in day six months earlier. Carly wished she'd hugged Christopher back when he gave her the present, a dozen pale pink stems for her and matching red ones for Emily.

Had she even thanked her new stepfather for the gift? All she could remember was standing on the front steps of the property that looked more like a museum than a place where regular people lived and feeling awkward under Christopher's embrace and promise this was her home too.

Everything had happened so quickly, and no one had asked if she wanted this new life.

It wouldn't have mattered. Kids were always forced to go along on their parents' ride.

The black-and-white suitcase lay open and empty next to her on the bed, and Carly knew what she had to do.

She opened the outside zipper of her suitcase and slipped in the framed picture of her and Emily when the two still lived in the little ranch house. Sure, on paper, the place was a fixer-upper on a good day, with a sagging roof and chipped linoleum floors in the kitchen, but Carly loved it. She always looked forward to their lazy Sundays when mother and daughter wore their pajamas all day, ate Saltines spread generously with grape jelly, and painted each other's fingernails while old John Hughes movies played in the background.

Carly peered through the gauzy curtain that covered her bedroom window and felt a momentary reprieve.

The car wasn't in the driveway yet.

She looked for her treasured silver ballerina jewelry box that was usually on her dresser and caught her reflection in the mirror. She was tall for her age, with dark blonde hair like her mother's and large blue eyes that looked back at her with dread. She thought about running away and leaving behind a note, telling anyone who'd read it she wasn't a liar.

Instead, Carly took a puff from her asthma inhaler, just in case. She then piled hair ribbons and a trophy her soccer team had earned the previous year in the suitcase. She opened her nightstand drawer and found herself laughing over the irony of it all. But the awkward laughter turned into a whimper when Carly saw the card that Christopher and Emily had given to her the day they got married.

Welcome to our beautiful new life, precious girl, they wrote.

A series of hard, persistent knocks sounded on the other side of the door. She was sure it was her mother, telling her it was time, but Carly was relieved to hear Julien's voice and nearly fell into his arms when she let him inside.

"This is a wretched thing they're doing to you," Julien said.

"You still believe me, right?" Carly asked. "I'm sick, I swear. And I never wrote that letter."

"Of course, I do. If anyone's to blame, it's those idiot doctors who couldn't figure it out. When Christopher and Em come to their senses, they should file a big malpractice suit against the whole lot of them."

Julien picked up an ivory-colored figurine of a lady in a bonnet and long dress from the bedside table and closed it in his hand. Her mother had given her the figurine of the lady-in-waiting before Emily met Christopher and everything changed.

"The figurine is important to me. B–b–b–be careful," Carly

stuttered. The stupid hitch in her voice that seemed to come out of nowhere would probably be the last thing Julien remembered about her.

Julien cocked his head to the side. "Don't worry about the stutter. A buddy of mine at school used to have one, but now he's a hell of a debater and almost beat me at a recent school competition," Julien said. "As for doctors, they think they're smarter than everybody, but they're not. You need to be clever enough to outsmart them."

Julien returned the figurine to the dresser but laid it on its side instead of upright.

From the window, Carly saw her mother now on the front steps of the house. Emily blocked the sun from her eyes and looked down the road that led to the estate.

"I know you must be scared, anyone in your position would feel the same way, but if you have any problems, I'll fly to San Francisco in an instant. I ditched a lacrosse play-off game today, and my teammates were pretty teed off about it, but there's no way I'd miss being here. Christopher didn't even have the decency to leave work to see you off."

"Mom said he's doing rounds at the hospital."

"And there you go, making excuses for people who've let you down. You can't be so decent anymore or you'll never survive. Is there anything I can do?"

Carly looked back at the older boy, who seemed like he could bend any situation to his will. "Would you talk to my mom? She likes you a lot. If you can convince her that I didn't do it, maybe she'd change her mind."

"That's exactly what's going to happen. Jules is our only hope."

Victor nearly lunged inside the room, red-faced and sweaty. "I skipped theater practice early, but I couldn't get a ride, so I had to walk. I was worried I was going to be late, so I sprinted up the hill and nearly had a coronary about halfway up," Victor said, panting between words until he caught his breath. "We can't let this happen to Carly."

"I've already talked to Em and Christopher about this a million times, but if you guys want me to try again, I will."

Julien looked between his siblings, reticent and ready to take up the mantle, even if it was a lost cause.

Carly nodded, not wanting to speak, in fear she'd start stuttering in front of her stepbrothers. Instead, she took her asthma inhaler from her coat pocket and took another puff.

"Does that thing even help you?" Julien asked. "You carry it around like an accessory."

"I've got bad asthma. The inhaler is the only thing that saves me. I'm pretty sure I'd die without it."

"You're a perfect kid," Victor promised.

Julien patted her hand before he left.

Carly stood at the window, watching until she saw him exit the house and approach Emily.

"I think Jules has a pretty decent shot at this, but if he can't convince Em and Chris, let's run away. I have some money, not a ton, but enough. I have to wait until I'm eighteen to get my full trust fund, but if Julien can't close the deal, give me the word, and we can sneak out the back door and down the trail to the beach. All you need is your passport. We can hitchhike to the border and cross into Mexico at Tijuana. Julien and his buddies have done that a million times, so it can't be too hard."

"I don't have a passport. But if I run away, I won't be able to fix this."

"You're a good person, Carly Bennett. No matter what happens today, don't ever forget it."

The car appeared at the bottom of the hill, and Carly felt a chill down to her very bones.

Julien, who now stood alone at the driveway's edge, looked toward her room. He'd tried his best, she was sure of it, but Carly couldn't postpone her fate any longer.

She heard footsteps down the hallway and knew it was over. Carly had placed the figurine into her suitcase and zipped it shut when Emily spoke.

"Victor, please give us a minute."

Carly waited until her stepbrother left, and then rushed into her mother's arms, her one last Hail Mary to get Emily to believe her. At the very least, Carly hoped Emily would know she still loved her.

"Mom, please!" Carly cried and clung to her mother. If she dared let go of her mom, Carly feared she would disappear.

"I love you, little girl, more than you'll ever know."

When Emily kissed her forehead, Carly felt overjoyed and wondered if she'd somehow earned a last-minute reprieve.

When Emily pulled Carly close, Carly was certain her mom had changed her mind. But the spell broke when Emily gently pushed her away.

"The car is waiting. I know you don't believe me, but this is the best thing for you. I want you to get better."

"I don't have anything to get better from, except my stomach issues, and I'm not a liar. Please don't send me away, I'll be good, I promise."

"Chatham is a prestigious school. I hate that you'll be so far away, but I don't know what else to do at this point since you've left us no other option. Threatening violence is a serious thing. We're lucky the teacher didn't press charges."

"I'd never hurt anyone, you know that."

Emily went to the closet, pulled out a coat and handed it to her daughter.

"San Francisco is colder than LA, especially when the fog rolls in. I'll send you some warmer clothes to be sure you have enough to get you through the rest of the winter. I love you, little girl, with all my heart."

Emily picked up the suitcase.

Carly felt light-headed as she trailed behind her mother until they reached the front of the house, where Julien sat with his shoulders slumped on the first step. A single tear slipped down his cheek, and he jumped up when he saw her. He pulled Carly into a warm embrace, slipped a note in her pocket, and whispered, "Some things should stay the way they are."

Carly wanted to ask Julien what he meant, but she didn't want to seem stupid for not understanding what was probably so simple.

She looked up to her bedroom window to see Victor, staring back at her with a look of desperation. Victor pressed his palm to the glass, and Carly reached out her hand in his direction, but then he was gone.

No one could help her now.

The locks snapped into place as soon as Carly got into the backseat of the car. The woman in the front from the school turned around and gave Carly a firm smile and explained the rules of what was expected of her.

Carly nodded politely until the woman stopped talking and then stared at her mother, who had her arm around Julien's shoulder. Unable to help herself, Carly opened her window to say goodbye one last time.

Through the open window, Carly could hear Emily say to Julien, "You were right about everything."

She wanted to call out to her mother, but her escort from Chatham shut Carly's window. The tears came hard and fast, and Carly slipped her hand inside her coat for a tissue but instead found Julien's note.

Carly opened the piece of paper and started to read.

In what looked almost identical to her own handwriting, Julien had written, "*I won.*"

FIVE
Rebecca

Rebecca Hunter was certain her boss saved her life, or at the very least, spared her from eviction in LA's absurdly high-priced real-estate market.

She sat at a table in the USC library, but instead of working on edits for her English assignment, Rebecca's thoughts focused on Carly.

Rebecca knew Carly didn't need an assistant, but Rebecca's mentor and former creative writing teacher from her undergraduate days at USC was too nice not to help. A lesser person would've handed her a tissue and offered fake assurances that Rebecca's heart would mend, but not Carly.

Rebecca had been red-nosed and blubbering, like she had just been told all her family members had perished in a plane crash, when Carly jumped in to help.

Rebecca had unloaded how her boyfriend of two years, Nathan, broke up with her and moved out of their one-bedroom apartment.

Carly's thin story about needing an assistant was made up on the spot, but you had to love her.

In the back of her mind, Rebecca knew she had put on a few pounds. At first, she thought her clothes shrank in the dryer, but Nathan had a hand in it. He was the one with the terrible eating habits that worked their way into her own, like bad osmosis when two people were around each other too much.

Overeating had been like muscle memory she easily returned to without a thought. Rebecca had been the chubby girl from kindergarten until she graduated from her high school in a suburban wasteland outside of Toledo, where weekend excitement consisted of watching *Jeopardy!* with her grandparents on Saturday nights.

The summer before she left for USC, Rebecca decided change was critical. For three months, she existed on barely more than a head of iceberg lettuce a day, and when she wasn't running laps around her backyard so no one would see her cellulite bouncing on her pale, jiggly thighs, she burned off the rest of the unwanted weight by sitting in her dad's parked Buick with the windows closed and the sun beating down in her self-created hotbox.

She'd only passed out once from the unhealthy practice, but she'd lost fifty pounds by the end of summer, and decided when she arrived in Los Angeles, she'd be a new person who no longer had frizzy hair and the handful of acquaintances from church and the school band where she was fourth clarinet chair.

By September of her incoming freshman year at college, Becky Hupfeld underwent a metamorphosis from the Baby Fat Queen into the Bohemian English Major, Rebecca Hunter, and she never once looked back until Nathan told her he was leaving because she had "let herself go."

In all her twenty-four years, Rebecca knew a few things about the world, and this was close to number one: If you were a man who carried around a few extra pounds, you were still OK. But, if you were a woman who was even a bit overweight by society's standards, you might as well have killed someone.

In hindsight, Rebecca wished she'd stood up for herself with Nathan, but instead, she responded with a meek, "OK," as if her beau's callous assessment of her looks was something she believed too.

Somewhere amid the heartache, Rebecca realized she was somehow going to have to scrape together the entirety of the rent.

That's when her mentor in shining armor swept in. Carly insisted she was swamped and desperately needed her help, and the pay happened to be five hundred dollars a week, which would more than cover the rent.

Working for Carly was the best job she ever had.

Carly was so pretty. Sometimes Rebecca caught herself

looking a little too long at Carly's face, like she was studying the angles and light of a portrait on display at the Getty Museum.

Nathan would have never told Carly she was letting herself go.

The judgmental voice in the back of Rebecca's head called out a reminder: *You're an ugly little mouse, a drab, doughy girl who tries too hard to be a hippy so no one will discover how dull you are.*

The memories of the last few weeks rushed back then and buoyed her spirits. The new man in her life actually told Rebecca she was beautiful. Granted, they were having sex at the time, but no one ever called Rebecca beautiful before. "Cute" was the only title Becky Hupfeld from the outskirts of Toledo ever got, and the only people who called her that were either relatives, friends of her parents, or the token drunk high-school boy who considered Rebecca his last resort after all the pretty girls left the party. After the one instance with the upper classman, Rebecca showed up at school the following Monday, feeling like her stock might've changed, but when she passed the boy in the hall, he ignored her, as if his time on top of her, sweating and grunting in the backseat of his father's car, hadn't registered. No one wanted to admit they'd screwed a fat girl.

But David Ramsey, the man she met two weeks earlier, loved her curves. In fact, he seemed to appreciate every single inch of her.

Besides David, Carly was the only other true person in her life, not like the fakey fake grad students who pretended to care about her and her writing with their "helpful" classroom critiques, when what they really wanted was to see her fail.

Rebecca remembered how Carly mentioned she'd had a terrible morning, and then GI Janitor showed up to stalk her.

Who needed that guy around?

An image came to her of the Maumee River in Toledo that used to freeze over in winter. Rebecca recalled her father holding her mittened hand when the two ventured to the city for a special father-daughter excursion.

"See how peaceful the lake looks, Becky? Smooth as glass. That's how you want your life to be."

Rebecca had been curious about what happened to the fish and every other living thing trapped beneath the surface of the frozen lake, but never asked her dad so as not to spoil the vibe.

She decided to stop procrastinating on her schoolwork, but then the realization hit. Her responsibility was to make sure Carly's life was as smooth as glass. And if anything got in the way, it was her duty to trap it and make sure it stayed hidden beneath the surface, as if it never existed.

SIX
Carly

Carly followed the Chinatown exit and the unfamiliar address her best friend Ava Patel had given her. She parked on a neighboring alley to the Chinatown Metro Station and searched for the signature van with "Ava's Bail Recovery" logo on its back doors. Instead, Carly spotted Ava's blue Nissan parked across the street. She must have needed discretion with whatever business brought her to the neighborhood.

She retrieved Ava's birthday gift and took a squeaky elevator that looked like it was built circa 1908 down to the basement level of a squat old building that seemed likely to collapse if the Santa Ana Winds picked up.

"You're not supposed to really hit him!"

Carly exited the elevator and followed the sound of her childhood friend's voice to a door at the end of a hallway that smelled like a rank combination of urine and mildew.

The door was halfway open, so Carly entered what appeared to be a long and narrow warehouse. The space was badly lit and mainly empty, with a few cheap folding chairs and a metal table in the corner piled high with water bottles and empty pizza boxes.

In the center of the room, Carly spotted Ava, dressed in a pair of pink bicycle shorts and a snug white T-shirt that stretched tight against her jacked biceps. Ava, who was petite but well built, knelt next to a shirtless man with an icepack pressed against one eye.

"Sorry to crash your early birthday party," Carly said as she tried to piece together the scene, which included about a dozen or so other shirtless men, all about thirty, who appeared oiled-up and overly exercised. "What's happening here exactly?"

"It's a dress rehearsal gone wrong," Ava answered in a pristine British accent undermined with hints of SoCal Valley. "The real deal is tomorrow, but my buddy Joe, he forgot he wasn't supposed to throw a real punch."

Ava moved away from the injured bodybuilder with the ice pack, and all five feet two of her got in the face of another man who looked like a piece of granite. "If he sues, it's on you."

"It was the heat of the moment. I'm sorry. Please, I won't do it again," answered the man Carly assumed was Joe.

"You get one more chance and that's it. All right, everyone, take five. Follow me, Carls," Ava said. She hooked her arm around Carly's and led her to the alley.

"Sorry to drag you to this dump," Ava said. She eyed the present under Carly's arm. "You didn't have to get me anything."

"Happy almost birthday, but you don't get the present until you tell me what's going on in there."

"You with your early birthday biz. OK, so here's the skinny. I've been working for weeks to pick up a bail jumper. The guy, he used to be a big dog in the MMA world in the LA circuit, but then he started hitting the Jack bottle and lost everything. The man's stage name in the ring was Big Ginger Watson when he was somebody, but his real name is Neil McNamara. He got busted for putting a man in the hospital after a bar fight, and McNamara skated on his court date. I got intel he was crashing with a girl, so I called her and made up a story that Big Ginger could make three grand at a pop-up, no-rules MMA underground match in Chinatown."

"They actually have pop-up MMA matches?"

"I have no idea. But McNamara needs cash to blow out of town, so I'm pretending to be a promoter for a fight. I have an acquaintance who used to work parole with me, whose dad owns this building, and they agreed to let me use it for the bust. I paid some gym buddies to show up, take their shirts off and look like they want to kill somebody. McNamara is supposed to come here tomorrow for the fake match, so today was the dry run. Everything was going well until Joe screwed up and decided to do some method acting."

"What if McNamara doesn't show up?"

"People will do anything for money."

Ava steepled her fingers against her temples and focused on Carly. "I swear, those dimwits in there are giving me a headache, but enough about my business. Are you ready for your big date? It's about time you socialized, Carls. Who's the guy again?"

"Sebastian Foster. He's a ginger, and a restoration architect. I ran into him at the library. He was checking out a book on the history of LA architecture, and I had a fresh stash of Brontë novels."

Ava patted her mouth and pretended to yawn. "If you and old Sebastian make a go of things, I promise I'll save your kids from being complete geeks and freaks."

Carly made her goodbyes and headed to her car to head to Malibu and her date.

Ten minutes on the freeway, Russo's threat came back to her, his words feeling like a crow's steely beak steadily pecking away at her façade.

She'd screwed up a month earlier, sure. But it was supposed to be their secret.

It had been a foolish slip on her part, not even a slip really, since there was no set bar for her to slip from, just an anomaly in an otherwise normal adult life. Looking back, she realized how foolish she was and how close she had come to losing everything she'd worked so hard to accomplish.

The image of Emily and her that popped up on her phone earlier that morning burned bright, and Carly knew she couldn't risk losing everything again.

She'd been selective in her truth-telling with the detective all those years earlier to protect herself, an instinct that she didn't know she possessed at the time.

In an about-face, Carly sped across four lanes of traffic to make the exit that would take her back to the city.

She drove on mental autopilot while memories from the day that changed her life forever returned.

The hammer had dropped twenty-four hours before Detective Halloran showed up to question her.

It still killed her that she couldn't remember the ending.

SEVEN
Carly

The Day Before the Sheriff Interview, Chatham Prep School for Girls

Two months after her arrival at Chatham, Carly was in the headmistress's office for the first time, and certain Mrs. Lusk was going to suspend her.

She sat across the desk from the headmistress and kept her head lowered when she responded.

"I'm sorry I ran away, Mrs. Lusk. I promise, I'll never do it again. Please don't tell my mom, because she'll worry, and I don't want to make her mad. I swear, I'll do better at school."

Carly tried to give Mrs. Lusk her best pleading look, but her head was pounding, and she worried she might throw up on the headmistress's floor.

"Where were you, Miss Bennett?"

Carly closed her eyes and remembered feeling comforted by the coolness of the bus window when she'd pressed her cheek against it.

"I went to Golden Gate Park," Carly lied. "There was a penguin exhibit at the zoo, and I wanted to see it."

"You were gone for several hours."

"I know, and I'm sorry, but I didn't know the rules."

Carly raised her head for the first time since she entered the room. She held Mrs. Lusk's gaze and hoped the fact that she was looking Mrs. Lusk in the eyes for once would make the headmistress believe her.

"Underclassmen aren't permitted to leave campus unless they're accompanied by, or have permission from a guardian, even on the weekend."

Mrs. Lusk sighed and clasped her hands in front of her.

"I'm sorry, and I know you don't believe me, but I went to the zoo. I was gone so long because I didn't want to come back here. No offense, but I'm having a hard time fitting in because I'm new. I planned to spend the night at the park and sleep on a bench, but when it got dark, I chickened out and took a taxi back to campus. My mom sends me an allowance every month. I've never spent any of it, but I used a little to pay the fare. Anyway, it was late, and I realized I'd lost my key. I didn't want to get in trouble, so I walked around campus for a while. I found a building that was unlocked, and I fell asleep on the floor."

"The specifics of your truancy are a conversation for another time, but one of our employees confirmed that he found you in a maintenance building, asleep," Mrs. Lusk answered.

Carly thought the headmistress was going to let her have it, but was surprised when the older woman gave her a kind look. "Has anyone in your family contacted you?"

"No. After the security guard found me, I went back to my dorm, and I saw the message that I needed to come to your office. I figured I was in trouble for what I did."

"I received a call from your stepfather's lawyer an hour ago."

"I'm not following," Carly said.

"There was a break-in at your family's home."

"Is my mom OK?"

"I'm very sorry for your loss, Miss Bennett, but your mother was killed during the burglary."

The room around Carly seemed to get smaller, like she was in a carnival funhouse where size and shape were distorted, and Carly was sure she would be crushed alive from the walls that continued to press closer.

Carly's breath was coming too fast, and she felt she would stop breathing if she was forced to stay another second in the room.

"Are you all right?" Mrs. Lusk asked. "I realize this is a great deal to take in."

Carly scrambled to find her inhaler in her Chatham blazer pocket. Out of the corner of her eye, Carly could see Mrs. Lusk reach for the rotary phone on the desk.

"I have a student who needs help. I think she's hyperventilating," Mrs. Rusk said into the receiver.

Carly leapt from her chair and ran for the door. When she found it was locked, Carly pounded on the glass.

"Miss Bennett, stop!" Mrs. Lusk insisted.

"I can't breathe." Carly gasped.

Before the school administrator could reach her, Carly struck the door's window with such force, the glass shattered, and her hand came away bloodied.

She heard a whooshing sound in her ears and realized she was on the floor with a group of adults now standing over her.

"Get the Bennett girl to the infirmary," Mrs. Lusk said. "I want her closely monitored for the next twenty-four hours. The girl's mother died. It's a tragedy, but I fear the child could be a danger to herself."

EIGHT
Ed Russo

Ed Russo knew he was a pure, unadulterated, chicken-fried idiot.

He thought about dumping the flowers he'd spent forty-five minutes trying to pick out at the florist section of the grocery store into the garbage can by the entrance to the English department building.

Low-class yellow daisies for a high-class girl. What was he thinking?

He should've never asked her out, and then he was trying to apologize with semi-wilted daisies from Safeway.

At the time, he knew darn well his innuendo, "It would be a shame if anyone found out what you did," was a blatant threat. The fact that he knew about Carly's secret enabled him to regain some power over her rejection.

But now, all Ed Russo felt was small for being so mean.

One month earlier, he'd unlocked Carly's office since she'd lost her keys, and could smell alcohol on her breath, barely hidden underneath what was likely half a bottle of mouthwash.

There was cool Carly, acting like everything was normal, and she hadn't had a glass of wine to settle her jangled nerves before her review with the bloated old toad, Dean Scanlon.

His advice for her to go home and claim that she was sick came from the purest place of his heart. As for Carly, she was humiliated, apologetic, swearing she'd never in her life done anything like that before, and grateful for his help, not to mention his silence.

Carly would never believe him anymore, but at least, he owed her an apology that he'd offered up in a card that he'd leave on her desk, sans the sad-sack flowers.

He'd talk to his sponsor later to get advice on how he'd handled the whole mess with Carly. The cost to date for his drinking included one wife, a golden retriever, and his job as a radio host and play-by-play announcer at Dodger's Stadium.

He'd been the master of disguise as a functioning alcoholic for years, showing up to work with three beers under his belt and still being able to call the games like a pro.

His smoke and mirrors had been a good suit, never drinking past his manageable three-beer limit before a work gig, and brushing his teeth four times before he finished with half a bottle of mouthwash.

The latter teed up his suspicion of Carly, when he'd opened her office for her last month, before her review.

Ed's personal crash and burn happened after a lunch at a local steakhouse with an Army friend to mark his official divorce. After one celebratory highball martini, followed by a shared bottle of wine and then two after-dessert drinks, Ed had to close one eye to stop seeing eight lanes of traffic instead of the usual four, as he drove the 101 to call the Dodgers' game against the Cincinnati Reds.

His slurred performance had made him a one-hit wonder on social media, where for a single humiliating day, Edward Russo, otherwise known as "Big R in the Morning," was the cautionary poster child for what happened if you drank on the job.

After hitting rock bottom, he'd learned nothing changes if nothing changes.

Ed felt for his three-year AA medallion in his windbreaker pocket and turned the corner to Carly's office.

The building was empty, as expected, considering it was a Friday night and the start of a long weekend.

"Miss Bennett?" Ed called out before he knocked on the professor's door.

Ed hoped she wasn't inside, because God knows, he wanted to drop off his "I'm sorry" card and run.

Ed rubbed his medallion between his index finger and thumb when he heard the sound of something crash on the other side of the door.

"Carly, are you OK?"

Ed knocked harder this time, but when there was still no answer, he reached into his duffel bag for his set of master keys.

After fitting the key into the lock, he expected to see the professor inside, grading papers.

Instead, the room appeared to be empty.

Ed flicked on the lights and felt his stomach knot when he saw what was spilled across Carly's desk.

He entered further into the room to take a closer look when he felt something solid wedge against his spine.

"Don't move," a voice whispered from behind.

Before Ed could turn around, his body jerked violently, and he felt like a million stinging hornets were crawling underneath his skin.

Ed collapsed on the floor, unable to move, and whimpered when a figure emerged from the shadows.

NINE
Carly

Carly sat alone at a table for two at Nobu and nursed the remains of her wine.

Sebastian was officially thirty minutes late.

She checked her phone again to see the same result. The last message she received from Sebastian was four hours earlier when he confirmed their dinner date for that evening.

Her waiter, a middle-aged male with a pencil-thin mustache, approached her table. “Can I get you another glass of Sauvignon Blanc or an appetizer to start while you’re waiting for your guest, miss?”

“I’ll hold off until my friend arrives. I’m sure he’s stuck in traffic.”

When the waiter left, Carly rescanned her phone. No new messages.

She’d wait a smidge longer before she left. If he were a no-show, at least she’d have her pride intact, and she could go home or enjoy dinner in the company of herself.

Her phone buzzed on the table and Carly grabbed it.

The one-word message was from Ava.

So?

Decision made. Carly raised her hand to get her waiter’s attention. “Can I get the check, please? My friend had a last-minute emergency and couldn’t join me.”

Carly smiled at the waiter, as if everything were just peachy keen and she hadn’t been stood up by some well-dressed man who chatted her up while in line to check out books at the LA Public Library.

Sure, it was possible that Sebastian had got stuck in the horror that was LA traffic, but most people with even a shred of politeness would call to say they were running late.

She signed the check, and when the valet brought her car around, Carly slid inside and placed her Jeep in gear, ready to leave the terrible date that wasn't in her rearview mirror, when a hand rapped on her front passenger window.

"Carly, I'm sorry."

Sebastian, the thirty-something restoration architect with ginger hair and a matching well-kept beard had a sheepish look on his face.

"I got caught in traffic on the 405, and I couldn't get phone reception. If I haven't totally blown it, can we still have dinner?"

Carly lowered the window halfway.

"I know traffic is a bear at rush hour, so don't sweat it, but I'm sure they gave our table away by now. Why don't we try and get together another time? It's been a long day, and I probably wouldn't be very good company. Let's stay in touch about a do-over."

Carly tried to close the window so she could go home to a book and a pair of her baggiest sweatpants, but Sebastian leaned into the open space before she could.

"I lied."

"I don't understand," Carly answered.

"If you want to leave, I get it, but I need to tell you something first. I wasn't stuck in traffic. I was sitting in my car about a half-mile down the road for the past hour, trying to get the guts to meet you for our date."

"You don't need to explain . . ."

"But I want to. If you never want to see me after, I get it. My wife died a year ago, and I haven't been on a date since. When I met you at the library, I was blown away. I mean, who meets a wonderful woman while you're waiting in line to check out a library book? The next thing I knew, I was asking you out. This morning, I had butterflies in my stomach because I was excited about our date, but right before I got to the restaurant, I panicked. I'm sorry I blew it, but I still think you're great."

Carly watched Sebastian looking like a sad sack with his shoulders caved inward as he walked toward a restored vintage Volkswagen Karmann Ghia with Nevada plates that was parked with its nose facing her.

It wouldn't kill her to be kind to the widower.

"Wait," Carly called out. "Do you want to take a walk on the beach? Zuma isn't too far from here."

Before he reached his car, Sebastian turned around with a relieved smile.

"I'd love to. How about I drive? You wouldn't believe how well my little Karmann Ghia handles on mountain roads."

Carly weighed her decision. Sebastian seemed as harmless as a stray puppy. She wasn't a fan of being in a car with a stranger unless it was an Uber driver, but Sebastian recently lost his wife and had almost been too terrified to meet her because of his grief.

Yet he had the guts to follow through.

She could throw him a bone.

"Hop in," Carly said.

Carly took a deep breath of the ocean air, feeling relaxed for the first time all day, and looked toward the ocean. The section of Zuma Beach that Sebastian suggested was sparsely populated with a single family—only a small spot on the horizon—packing up for the day, and a lone female runner in a baseball cap jogging in her direction on the right.

Carly sat barefoot on the sand with Sebastian's grey sportscoat underneath her.

"Your chivalry is impressive, but you're going to find sand in this coat for years to come."

"It'll be my pound of flesh for almost messing up the date, my lady."

Sebastian grimaced and shook his head as soon as the words came out of his mouth.

"Oh man, I was trying to be smooth with that line, but I'm pretty sure that was the corniest thing I've ever said. I'm a little rusty at this whole first-date experience, so let me try again. A girl like you deserves the best. How was that?"

"Better, but your line was OK, just a little Elizabethan."

She searched for the next line of small talk and remembered the Karmann Ghia and its out-of-state license plate.

"I'm guessing you're a California transplant."

Sebastian cocked his head to the side. "Are you psychic or did I tell you that already?"

"I saw the license plate on your car. That Karmann Ghia is a beauty."

"Thank you. She was a tired old girl when I found her in a scrapyard in Reno, but I brought her back to life and restored her to what she looked like when her model was debuted on the showroom floor in 1974. I grew up outside of the city and my dad was a carpenter, who taught me the importance of restoring things and how to do it. No one should underestimate the power of the hammer and nail. Are you hungry?"

"Starving, but besides dried-up seaweed and a few wizened fries that even the seagulls didn't want, I think we're out of options."

"That's where you're wrong. I'll be right back."

Sebastian, barefoot and with the cuffs of his pants rolled up, jogged to the lip of the parking lot where an ice-cream vendor had set up momentary shop.

"Do you prefer fruit punch or cotton candy?" Sebastian asked. He held out two ice pops in his hands with a picture of SpongeBob SquarePants on the wrappers.

"Tough choice, but I'll take cotton candy."

"Cheers," Sebastian said and tapped his ice cream against Carly's. "Thank you for being a good sport about everything. But since I told you something about myself, it's only fair that you do the same."

"That I can't do. I'm sorry to be a buzzkill, but I lead a boring life. People who watch paint dry for a living probably have more exciting stories to tell."

"A young, beautiful, USC English professor leads a boring life? I doubt it. Come on, you've got to share some little thing about yourself with me. Here's an easy one. What's your family like?"

"That's tricky. I guess you could say that I'm an orphan. I have no idea where my biological father is, and my mom passed when I was a kid."

"That's terrible, but I hope you have some good people in your life; otherwise, that would be the saddest story ever told."

"No need to feel sorry for me in the family department. My family is my best friend, Ava. She's a bail bondswoman, and she's always had my back, ever since we were kids. Her parents are about the nicest people you could ever meet, and they took me in as their own when Ava and I were at boarding school."

"What about your stepdad?"

Carly did a mental inventory of her conversation with Sebastian at the library and the few texts they'd shared before their date. There's no way she would've mentioned anything about her past with a stranger, let alone revealed any info about Christopher.

"What about my stepdad? I don't think I mentioned him."

"My mistake. A colleague of mine at Kaplan Chan was blathering on about her dysfunctional blended family this morning at work, so it must've stuck in my head. Your family must've been rich if you went to boarding school."

"I'm not a fan of talking about my past. Let's move on, please," Carly answered.

"Foot, please meet mouth. I'm on a roll here with my idiot questions, so let me try and make up for it."

Sebastian reached for Carly's hand and gave it a soft kiss.

Startled, Carly pulled her hand away. Grieving widower or not, the date was over.

She debated whether it would be rude to call Sebastian an Uber, when she noticed the female runner from before, closer now and staring directly at her with laser focus.

"The kiss was a terrible idea. I'm sorry," he said.

Sebastian paused, looked out to the horizon, and then pointed to the female runner. "Do you know her? She keeps staring at you."

"I don't think so. We're the only people left on the beach, so she might be curious or cautious. Women can never be too careful when they're alone."

That's why she needed to end this thing. After she dropped Sebastian off at the restaurant, she'd never see him again.

Sebastian's phone buzzed in his pocket. He took a quick scan of the screen and tapped out a message.

"Sorry for the distraction. It's work. If you aren't tired of me yet, how about we take a drive to Malibu State Park? I know the best spot to watch the sunset there. And not to sound like a total dork, but I have a sunset tracker on my phone. We've got twenty minutes and counting. What do you say?"

"I say thanks for the offer, but I'll drive you back to the restaurant. I have plans with my best friend later," Carly lied. "It's her birthday, so I can't be a schmuck and miss her big day."

"Sure, I understand."

Carly followed the speed limit up the two-lane mountain road back to the park and shifted the car to low gear. Las Virgenes Road cut through the Santa Monica Mountains and back to the restaurant. Las Virgenes' winding stretch through Malibu was especially tricky. The road coiled like a long, twisting Garter snake with no shoulder and nothing but a guardrail on one side to separate vehicles from its 3,100-foot drop below.

"Since you're driving, I'll be in charge of music," Sebastian said.

Carly looked at the time on the dashboard clock. Fifteen minutes until she returned Sebastian to his car. She regretted her decision to drive him to the beach, but at least the date was almost over.

"I'm feeling a lot of pressure here. If I pick smooth jazz or yacht music, then I'm a bore. Heavy metal would make you think I've got a dark side. Pop is almost a safe choice, but then you might think I'm vapid. That's it. Coffeehouse acoustic it is."

Sebastian selected the station, and a melancholy Taylor Swift song filled the car.

He closed his eyes and sang along in an off-key tenor. "I'm killing it, right?"

God, how she couldn't wait for this date to end. Carly looked at the time on the dash, but gripped the steering wheel when she noticed a fast-approaching SUV in her rearview mirror.

She anticipated an upcoming hard turn a quarter-mile ahead, changed gears, and hit the accelerator to create some distance between her sedan and the other car before she reached the bend, but the SUV followed pace until it was locked inches away from her bumper.

When she came out of the turn, Carly shot a nervous glance in the rearview mirror and punched the gas, but the SUV was right behind her and flashed its lights as a warning.

Her eyes ticked back to the road and then to the image of the vehicle in the mirror. The SUV was dark-colored and had tinted windows, leaving Carly unable to see the driver, who was doing a very good job of trying to scare her.

"What a jerk. There's a lookout ahead where you should pull off," Sebastian said.

Carly calculated her next move and tracked her speedometer. She was driving seventy, but she accelerated as the SUV swerved into the other lane and blew past her.

"LA drivers are the worst. They're too obsessed with their cars and think they're gods behind the wheel and everyone should get out of their way," Sebastian said. "Still, let's pull over for a second at the lookout. Your hands are shaking. You could use a minute to gather your nerves."

Carly loosened her death grip on the steering wheel and decelerated before she made the last sharp turn of the steep grade, as Sebastian busied himself with his phone.

"I found it. I have a picture of a historical building I restored, and I'd love to show it off."

Sebastian moved closer with cell phone in hand and a picture on the screen.

Carly turned to take a quick look but caught something out of the corner of her eye.

She focused back on the road and the curve ahead. When she came out of the bend, the SUV was now in her lane and driving toward her at high speed.

"H–hold on!" Carly cried. Her hands windmilled across the steering wheel as she maneuvered her car into the other lane.

"What the hell?" Sebastian shouted.

Carly heard Sebastian scream when she lost control and the car spun three times before it came to an abrupt stop, just inches away from the guardrail and canyon below.

The sound of an engine speeding away cut through the sudden stillness.

Carly looked through her windshield for the SUV, but it was gone.

TEN
Julien White

"You're here. Dennis Hebert is already inside for his appointment, and he's in rare form tonight."

Julien White didn't respond to his receptionist but instead studied a small brown box that was sitting atop her desk.

Like the reception area, the rest of Julien's office was bathed in shades of blue. The monotone color selection was courtesy of the American Psychological Association's recommendation, since it was supposed to promote calmness.

Certainly not Julien's personal aesthetic.

"That's the package you were waiting for," Talia Chen continued. "Did your meeting run late? Mr. Hebert is anxious to see you."

"I don't welcome lectures about my punctuality. Am I clear, Miss Chen?" Julien snapped, but then eased off his brusque tone when the young woman cast her eyes to her lap where she kneaded her hands together.

The twenty-five-year-old had held the receptionist position at Julien's solo psychiatry practice for the last three months. Julien passed over some older, more experienced secretaries and decided on Talia since he liked her intellect, and he was certain his shy new hire would be submissive. Add to the fact, Julien pegged Talia, whose body resembled that of a fragile ten-year-old boy, as someone who would do her job without fuss or drama.

This was his practice, after all.

"I've upset you, haven't I?" Julien asked. "I'm sorry I was an ass. I was stuck in a first-rate boring meeting at Cedars-Sinai, but I shouldn't have taken it out on you. Will you forgive me?"

Julien gave his employee his best penitent look, and Ms. Chen smiled demurely.

"I'm truly sorry," Julien said.

"You don't need to apologize. I'm sorry if it seemed I was lecturing you for being a few minutes late. I know you've been under tremendous stress lately over your father," Talia said. "I picked up a sandwich for you from Cantor's Deli during my dinner break. It's corn beef on rye with spicy mustard. I know it's a small gesture, but my grandmother used to tell me tiny slivers of joy can cut through the dark times."

Julien kept smiling at his employee, but her feel-good message belonged on a knock-off Hallmark card, along the lines of other ersatz platitudes like the dreaded, "Everything happens for a reason." Instead, Julien kept his true feelings to himself.

"You are wonderful," Julien said, and as expected, his compliment made Talia perk up, like a wilted flower scorched from the heat come back to life after it was watered.

The psychiatrist headed to his office, where his regular Friday-night appointment waited for him, but before he went inside, Julien placed his index and middle fingers of one hand against the side of his neck until he calculated his pulse rate; he was pleased it clocked in at forty-five beats per minute.

Julien took a deep cleansing breath and opened the door, where his doughy patient with the bad bowl haircut sat on the couch. Dennis Hebert was tensely coiled and looked like he was about to spring up from his seat when he saw his therapist.

"Mr. Hebert, how are you feeling this evening?" Julien asked.

"Terrible. I'm getting trolled on social media again. The trial ended three months ago. When are people going to leave me alone? It was an accident, for Christ's sake."

Dennis Hebert was thirty-one and had dodged a major legal bullet after being acquitted of manslaughter. The dead person was his child, a two-year-old boy named Dylan, who Dennis left to die in a hot car while he had sex with a colleague who wasn't his wife. The woman in question, Dennis told him during their very first therapy session, was a twenty-three-year-old named Ashley who gave crazy good blowjobs; so phenomenal, in fact, that Dennis forgot his son was cooking inside his car that was parked outside of Ashley's apartment.

Julien had carefully read the news reports and followed with great interest the social media annihilation of Dennis. After the child killer was acquitted by a hung jury three months earlier, Dennis's father, Joe, had reached out and begged Julien to take his son's case, which he did at no charge. And wasn't Joe beyond grateful after the esteemed psychiatrist, the very one whom Joe had seen on a TV news show sharing his expertise about depression, agreed to treat his child.

It wasn't an abundance of empathy that made Julien agree to see Dennis. He was curious as to what kind of person would leave his child to bake to death in a hot car.

During the first few sessions with Dennis, Julien heard the usual blah, blah, blah about how his patient suffered through a terrible childhood and then was saddled with an overbearing wife.

Despite the cool temperature of the room, always set to a crisp sixty-five degrees, Dennis's forehead looked damp, and his polo shirt appeared tacky against his skin. Julien didn't care for his patient's disheveled appearance, but more so, he was tired of Dennis's constant weakness.

The man was clearly not smart enough to lie his way out of his terrible deed, or strong enough to accept responsibility for his actions.

"In order to get past the pain that you're feeling, you need to talk about what happened. I mean *really* talk about it this time, Dennis. Do you think you can do that?"

"I do want to feel better, but sometimes, I feel like the world is still judging me on one single act. It's not like I'm the only person who's ever made a mistake. Have you ever done something you regret?"

"Everyone has regrets. Tell me what you were doing when Dylan died," Julien said.

"Christ, I've told you this before. Ashley texted me and said we should meet up at her place during her lunch break. I had the day off, and since my wife was working, I had Dylan. I fed him lunch and changed his diaper, so it wasn't like I was neglecting him."

"Before this happened, did you consider yourself a good father?" Julien asked.

"Yes, I swear. I never hit him. People hit their kids and they haven't gone through half the backlash that I have. The press crucified me, and I'm never going to be able to get a job because of all the negative things they wrote. The media painted me out to be the devil. Do you know how many times my life has been threatened? I was a hashtag on Twitter, for Christ's sake. It's unfair the way I've been treated. No one is asking how I feel after all this."

"Tell me about a good memory you had with Dylan," Julien said.

"When he was a baby, I used to read Dylan this 'Twinkle, Twinkle, Little Star' book every night before bed. Little boys gravitate toward their dads, and I could tell Dylan loved me more than his mom. I'm pretty sure my wife got jealous of my relationship with Dylan, because the book disappeared, and I think she hid it. She was selfish that way."

"What did you dress your son in the day he died?"

"Why is that important?"

"Answer the question, please."

Dennis let out a deep sigh but continued. "Dylan, he loved baseball, so I dressed him in a Dodgers jersey and a blue pair of shorts."

"Was he awake when you left him in the car?"

"Yes, but I gave him a book and some stuffed animals to play with, and I told him I'd be right back."

"But you didn't come right back."

"No, of course not! Why are you asking me questions when you already know the answer?"

"Did you often make promises to your son that you didn't keep?"

"Why does this sound like an inquisition? You're supposed to be helping me!"

"Did Dylan say anything to you before you left? You're in a safe place here. I promise, it will make you feel better to get it out in the open."

"God, why are you making me do this?"

"Unless you allow me to dig deeper, I'll never be able to help you. What did Dylan say before you left him?"

Something shifted in Dennis's face, and for the first time since Julien started seeing him, his patient seemed to fully grasp the enormity of what he'd done. "My boy said, 'I love you, Daddy.'"

Julien remained silent and allowed the heavy weight in the room to fully descend upon his patient.

"I killed my child. I don't want to live anymore. I deserve to die," Dennis cried.

During his studies at Berkeley and later Brown, Julien learned many prompts on how to bring possibly suicidal patients back from the brink. But in this instance, Julien thought his expertise would be wasted on the man. After all, Dennis had left his child to boil to death in a hot car so he could hook up with his cheap mistress.

That showed unbearable weakness.

Weakness was something he couldn't tolerate.

Julien thought about his mother, who took her own life because of circumstances she couldn't control. Dennis was a basic asshole who was too interested in sticking his dick into something warm without an ounce of concern that his baby was frying in the car.

"Are you sure that's what you want to do?" Julien asked. He looked out at the view of LA's night skyline from the window of his eleventh-floor high-rise and waited for his patient's response.

"No, but I don't want to carry around this pain anymore," Dennis answered. "No one is ever going to forgive me for what I did. Do you think I deserve forgiveness?"

"The way I feel doesn't matter. The question is whether you think you deserve to be forgiven," Julien said. His back was still turned to his patient, and he took a quick scan of his watch. "We're out of time. We'll continue talking about this next week. Ms. Chen can confirm your appointment."

Before Julien could turn around, Dennis had left the office.

Now alone, Julien considered his patient's query about regrets and forgiveness, and pictured his stepsister fumbling for the right words to say when she'd first arrived at his home.

Had anyone known the truth about his role in getting the girl sent away, they would say Julien did a terrible thing, but—looking at the bigger picture—he'd saved Carly from a much worse fate at the time. Now, he wondered if Vic believed that too.

A light rapping sounded on the door, and the receptionist poked her head inside.

"Is it all right if I go home?"

"By all means, it's late. Have a lovely evening."

Julien waited until Talia left, and then opened the package she'd given him earlier. Once it was out of its brown wrapper, he inspected the logo on the front of the small box and slid it inside his briefcase, snapping the locks in place.

Before he left for the evening, he had one more task at hand. Julien opened his top desk drawer and studied the weathered photograph he'd found in a dusty old box in his father's garage during his final visit with the dying old man.

In the picture, Carly sat next to him on the deck of his father's Malibu estate. His stepsister's eyes were downcast, while Julien stared ahead, smiling brilliantly at the camera. Victor stood behind the pair, photo-bombing the shot, with his arms held out wide at his side and his mouth open in an exaggerated expression. Good old Vic, always the comic relief.

In his recollection, Emily had snapped the photo a few weeks before Carly was sent off to boarding school.

Julien pocketed the photograph before he turned off the lights and ran his index finger over its smooth matte edge until the elevator arrived. He'd made his share of selfish acts, but in the end, he had tried to help the girl, after all.

The idea to call his brother came to him. Julien pulled out his phone from the breast pocket of his suitcoat. But then he thought better of it.

Family, he knew, was every man's eternal source of pain.

The picture prompted a memory of his time with Carly. And the aftermath. The balding detective with the paunch from so many years ago flashed in his mind's eye. What was his name?

Halloran, that was it, the Malibu cop who'd drilled Christopher, Vic and him for hours the day after Em was killed.

Julien headed to the elevator, all the while recalling snapshots of what he'd told the detective. And what he'd left out.

ELEVEN
Dr. Brian Whittaker, Julien's psychiatrist

March 2010, Santa Monica

Julien insisted he needed to talk to Carly. Immediately.

Dr. Brian Whittaker knew Julien was riled up to an emotional level of a ten, and allowed the teenager to continue their session outside his Santa Monica office, several blocks down from the confines of his high-rise. They now sat on a park bench in Palisades Park. This was a rare exception the child psychologist allowed when his longtime patient was especially agitated. And today, Julien was more upset than Dr. Whittaker had ever seen.

Every part of Julien's body was in motion. Head nodding as if Julien finally understood something. Feet rattling beneath him, like the boy was ready to run.

Julien rubbed his hands together on repeat and stared back at Dr. Whittaker, unblinking.

"You were right about everything. I'm sorry I blocked you out for so long, but it was hard after my mother died. I've always been a jerk to you."

"Stop worrying about how I feel, Julien."

"I can't. I was a first-rate prick to you, and you didn't deserve that," Julien answered. He reached over and laid his hand on top of Dr. Whittaker's.

The child psychiatrist's instinct was to pull away, but he didn't, not wanting to upset Julien any further. Dr. Whittaker, who was in his early thirties, realized the parents who ushered their children into his office each week thought he was close to being a kid himself. But his youth was an asset, helping the children he counseled to feel like their doctor was relatable, and not a stuffy older man passing judgment. At least he hoped it gave him an opening with the kids, especially with the difficult cases like Julien.

Dr. Whittaker waited a moment and then pulled his hand from underneath Julien's, patting the boy on the shoulder so as not to make Julien feel he was being rejected, especially now, when Julien was on the cusp of a breakthrough. His apology alone was a huge step, since it was the first time Julien had taken any accountability for his actions in the entire four years since they started working together.

"You mentioned your mother. Are you thinking about her now?" Dr. Whittaker asked.

"I always do."

"That's understandable. But you're not responsible for your mother's suicide."

"Don't try to cover for me. It was my fault."

"I've told you before, you can call me Brian if you like. Tell me how you're feeling."

"Like a self-centered jerk. I knew my mom was in one of her moods the morning she died. She'd locked herself in the bathroom the night before and wouldn't come out. But my dad didn't care. I called him at work, and he told me to leave her alone and she'd come out eventually. The next morning, I found her asleep at the bottom of my bed. She opened her eyes and smiled at me, but I was angry because I had a calculus exam that day. I was up most of the night, banging on the bathroom door, begging her to come out. I was afraid she was going to hurt herself. My brother Vic slept through most of it. As the big brother, it was my duty to handle the situation. I said something to her. I wish I could take it back."

"What did you say?"

Julien pulled his knees to his chest like he was trying to comfort himself.

"I said I hated her, and she was the most terrible person who ever lived. But then I said something a million times worse."

"You're in a safe place. What did you say?"

"Please don't make me . . ." Julien started.

"I'm not going to make you do anything."

"Promise you won't hate me."

"I won't hate you," Dr. Whittaker promised.

Julien started to cry, loud, wracking sobs that seemed like they would consume him whole.

"I told my mother, 'I wish you were dead.'"

At that moment, none of the psych lectures Dr. Whittaker heard at Princeton mattered. As a student, it had been engrained in him that a successful psychiatrist must create a connection with the patient while simultaneously not crossing any physical boundaries. His patients weren't his friends.

But Julien was hurting, and if he didn't try and comfort the boy, he ran the risk of Julien retreating back to the cavalier, mean boy who had been frequenting his office.

Dr. Whittaker wrapped his arm around the younger man's shoulder.

"I'm so sorry," Julien said.

"Your mother was depressed. And from what you've described, I believe she suffered from some significant mental health issues that weren't resolved. For some, it's too overwhelming to continue in this life. Her death was in no way your fault."

Julien stopped crying and looked at Dr. Whittaker like a fretful child.

"You told me to be accountable, and I will be for once, but I'm scared of what I might do to myself."

"Do you feel suicidal?"

The handsome teenage boy with the jet-black hair shot up from the bench. "I screwed up. I was hurt and jealous. God, I'm sorry. I can't believe I did those terrible things."

"Is this about your stepsister?"

"You know me better than anybody. I'm sorry for always making things hard for you, but please know you've helped me immensely. I don't think I've ever thanked you. God, I'm such an ass. I bet you think I'm a self-absorbed trust-fund kid. Do you hate me? I don't blame you if you do."

"Of course, I don't hate you. But don't worry about how I feel."

"I need to talk to my stepsister. It was all my doing, and I got her sent away. Granted, Carly has some mental problems, but she didn't deserve what I did to her."

"Let's focus on you," Whittaker said.

"Carly is my focus right now," Julien said. "Don't you get it?"

"What problems do you think Carly has?"

"I shouldn't have said anything bad about her. Carly's a good kid, but she makes up things that aren't real. There was this whole big deal where she thought she was sick, but she was making it up for attention."

"Do you think she's delusional?" Whittaker asked.

"You're the expert."

"I can't diagnose Carly without seeing her. You said it was your fault your stepsister got sent away. When did this happen?"

"Two months ago. It's been eating me up inside ever since. I need to call the boarding school right now, or otherwise, I'll lose my courage. I need to do one thing right," Julien said.

He reached into his back pocket and turned to Dr. Whittaker with a look of panic when he came up empty. "I left my phone in your office. I need to call Carly. Can I borrow yours?"

Dr. Whittaker thought about Julien's request. If he forced Julien to walk the four blocks back to his office to retrieve the phone, Julien might change his mind. And that would pose a significant regression when they were so close to a breakthrough.

"I'll make an exception but just this once," Dr. Whittaker said, and handed Julien his cell phone. "What are you going to say to Carly?"

"I'm going to beg for her forgiveness. I was a monster to her, but I'm ready to make it right. She always liked my brother better, I could tell, and I guess that made me even more jealous. It's embarrassing to say that out loud."

Julien walked from the bench and to the edge of the bike path, keeping his back to the psychiatrist.

Dr. Whittaker could see Julien pull out a piece of paper from his pocket and then tap his index finger on the cell phone's keypad.

He wondered if Julien was sending a text, but dismissed the thought when Julien put the phone to his ear.

"Good job." Dr. Whittaker looked at the boy in the distance. "Good job, son."

Julien looked back at Whittaker and mustered a slight smile.

Five minutes later, Julien wiped a tear from his eye and handed the phone back to Whittaker.

Dr. Whittaker looked to the bike path, where he saw a young teenager wearing a Viking helmet, cruising with precision down the concrete strip on a skateboard in his direction.

"Yo, Jules, what are you on, like a field trip or something? Dad is in the car, and he's plenty pissed."

"You must be Julien's brother. It's nice to meet you," Dr. Whittaker said.

Dr. Whittaker extended his hand, but Victor didn't venture closer or reciprocate his formality, but kept standing on the bike path, with skateboard in hand.

"Julien needs to get going, ASAP. My dad sent me to find him since your receptionist said you took a walk or something. Jules, are you done?"

"We just finished. Please tell your father that I'm sorry for any confusion. We went a few minutes over this time, and Julien wanted to hold the session outside. During intake, your father approved outside sessions on occasion," Dr. Whittaker said. "I like your hat, by the way."

"That sounds like Chris, forgetting something he agreed to earlier. My dad likes to change the rules when they don't work for him anymore. And thanks for the compliment. I snitched this from my theater company's prop closet. What does a Viking helmet say about my personality, doc?"

"Many things, it could say. Or nothing at all, it could say too," Julien answered for Dr. Whittaker.

"Dude, that's so Yoda," Victor said.

"Digging into your psyche is just a riddle, after all," Julien replied. "But Dr. Whittaker is a master at solving puzzles. He's way smarter than you or I will ever be."

TWELVE

Ava

Who almost gets run off the road during a first date with some boring architect from the library? Ava cut through the yard of Carly's Echo Park bungalow following her best friend's call with the news she was almost in a severe accident.

Through the window, Ava saw Carly sitting barefoot on the living-room floor. Carly was wearing an enormous pair of shapeless grey sweat clothes and had two dark smudges of mascara under her eyes.

An incoming call from the Valley flashed on her phone, but Ava ignored the familiar number. Her cell then beeped an alert that Ava's mother, Kyra Patel, had just left a guilt-laden message. Ava didn't need to play it. She could already hear Kyra's voice dripping with polite anger about how she spent all day cooking dinner for her daughter, only for her eldest child to run out the door before dessert was served the second Carly rang her.

Ava let herself into Carly's house where she was struck by a horrific odor that smelled like a cross between mildew and roadkill.

She looked down at Carly, still sitting on the floor.

"How are you doing, sunshine?" Ava asked. "I'm not sure what you have brewing on the stove, but it smells like something died in here. Are you boiling mothballs and an old woman's fur coat?"

Rebecca popped her head outside of Carly's kitchen and gave Ava an awkward wave. "Sorry about the smell. I'm making Carly a special tea to help her relax."

Fabulous. The loopy-loo assistant was there.

"A smell like that isn't going to make anybody relax. You're going to kill us all."

"It's powerful at first, but once the tea steeps, the bitter smell should go away. Would you like a cup?" Rebecca asked.

Ava raised a single, pointed eyebrow as a response to Rebecca, who retreated to the kitchen.

"Did you get the make and model of the SUV that almost hit you?" Ava asked.

Carly rose to her feet, rushed to Ava's side, and gave her friend a tight bear hug.

"Easy there. You're OK, Bennett," Ava reassured.

"Thank God you're here," Carly said. "I think the car was blue. Or maybe black. It could've been a Ford or Chevy. I was just trying to stay on the road. I remember, the windows were tinted because I couldn't see the driver."

"Are you sure the same vehicle that followed you tried to hit you head-on?" Ava said.

"I'm positive about that."

"Why didn't you call the police?" Ava pressed.

"It seemed like a waste of time. The SUV took off, and I didn't get the license plate or see the driver."

Rebecca reappeared in the living room, carrying a tray and wearing an apron, like Susie Homemaker ready to save the day with a sunny smile and fresh baked goods.

Ava never got chicks like that. But if Rebecca's presence helped Carly, who was she to judge?

"What happened to you sounds terrifying. You could've been killed," Rebecca said. In front of Carly, she placed a plate of cookies and a cup of hot water crested with a half-dozen small, colorful balls floating on top. "No more terrible smell, and the tea is beautiful, don't you think?"

"It looks like a tiny Japanese garden in a cup," Carly said.

"This tea is almost impossible to find in the U.S. It's not only rare, but it also has therapeutic benefits. The balls are silver needles and marigold flowers that bloom when you put them in hot water. You can usually only find the tea in Japan, but the man I'm dating sells holistic products, and he recommended it to help you relax."

Without warning, Carly cupped her hands over her nose and mouth and wheezed.

Ava knew her friend was about to launch into a full-fledged asthma attack.

"I told you the smell was going to kill somebody. Where's your inhaler, Carls?" Ava asked.

Carly, still wheezing, flung a hand toward the hallway bathroom.

Ava sprinted to the bathroom, snatched the rescue inhaler from the shelf, and gave it a few hard shakes, like she'd seen Carly do on repeat through the years.

She ran back to the living room and kneeled, so she was at eye level with her friend.

"You got this, Carly. Ten's our magic number. If you get to ten puffs and you're still struggling, I'm taking you to the hospital," Ava said.

Ava held her friend's shoulders, while Carly beat her bare feet on the floor and took hits from the metal canister.

When Carly's breathing steadied, she gave a thumbs up. "I'm OK now. Sorry for all the drama."

"This is all my fault," Rebecca cried. "I picked up your new asthma medication from the drugstore, but I left it in your office."

"I'm going to campus," Ava said.

"No one's to blame or no one's going anywhere. The stress from earlier triggered me, but I'm fine. If the tea will help me relax, I'm game."

Carly took a sip from the cup but winced. "The presentation is a ten, but the taste is . . . well . . . interesting."

"Translation, Carly's just being nice. What she means is the tea tastes vile," Ava said.

Rebecca's face reddened, and Ava regretted being a mean girl. "Listen, kid, that was a nice thing you did for Carly. It's getting late, so if you want to go, I've got it covered. I'll make sure Carly is OK."

"You go enjoy yourself. My lungs are jacked with corticosteroids, and Ava's here if I need anything," Carly promised.

Ava waited until Rebecca left and then dumped the tea down

the kitchen sink. When she returned to the living room, Carly was staring out the window and clutching her inhaler.

"Is your assistant on meds or what?" Ava asked.

"Of course not. Stop being so judgmental."

"I will as soon as she stops being so awkward. I'm down with hippy chicks, but there's a question mark around that girl," Ava answered. "Depending on if you're up for it, we can try and reach Sebastian to see if he can remember anything about the SUV that tried to run you off the road."

Carly retrieved her cell phone from her sweatpants pocket. She then tapped Sebastian's number on the screen and put the call on speaker.

Instead of a ringing sound indicating the call was going through, a computerized voice came on the line.

"*The number you have dialed has been disconnected or is no longer in service.*"

"That's weird. I just spoke to Sebastian this morning," Carly said.

"Either you freaked your date out so much, he cut and ran out of SoCal, or you got scammed. My money's on the latter. I taught you well, but here's hoping he didn't rifle through your purse when you weren't looking any and lift your credit card info. Please tell me that didn't happen."

"I'm not an idiot, but this doesn't make sense."

"What do you know about this Sebastian person?"

"His wife died last year, and he works as a restoration architect at a place called Kaplan Chan in the city."

"I'll trace the number and see what I can find. If it's a burner phone or a prepaid one, we're going to hit a wall. I'll call you as soon as I get intel. Is there anything else you remember about Sebastian?"

"He had a nice car, a restored Karmann Ghia. I think it was a seventies model. It had Nevada plates. Sebastian said he was originally from somewhere outside of Reno. Do you think he could be tied to the SUV that tried to run me off the road?"

"For all we know, he didn't pay his phone bill. But in this world, if you don't lead with suspicion, you're nothing more than a sucker in training."

Ava headed to the door when she noticed Carly was right behind her. "Where are you going at this time of night?"

"Campus. My doctor prescribed me a new corticosteroid to use only in the case of emergencies. I think it's safe to say, this is an emergency."

THIRTEEN
Carly

It was nearly midnight when Carly let herself into the USC English Building. She fast-walked down the hallway to her office, all the while ruminating about her strange date and how Sebastian seemed to have suddenly gone AWOL.

Carly turned on her cell-phone light to help her see, when she noticed her office door was ajar.

Odd, but Rebecca must've forgotten to lock it when she dropped off her new asthma medicine. Holding the light in front of her, she swung open the door and panned the room.

She screamed when she saw the body.

Her piercing cry echoed down the empty English department wing.

Curled on the floor in a fetal position was the body of Ed Russo, who had a plastic bag sealed around his head, and a red Sharpie clutched in his right hand.

Next to his torso, the word, "Carly," was scrawled on the cement floor.

FOURTEEN
Carly

Two hours later, from inside the reception area of LAPD's Rampart Station, Carly rattled off as much information into the phone as she could before the cops returned to question her.

"Slow down. You're where?" Ava asked.

"Something terrible happened. I'm at the police station on Sixth Street. I drove to campus to get my asthma medicine. I found a dead man inside my office with a plastic bag over his head."

"Do you know him?"

"His name is Ed Russo. He's our school janitor. We're friendly, but he had something on me. Last month, I was nervous before my annual review with the dean, and I went home and had a drink before I went back to campus. I couldn't find the keys to my office, so Ed showed up to let me in, but he could smell liquor on my breath. He told me to go home. The last time I saw him alive was this morning, and he asked me out. When I told him no, he dropped a big enough hint that he was going to turn me in for what I did."

"That gives you motive. Is there anything else I should know?"

"Ed wrote my name in a red Sharpie next to his body before he died."

Carly looked toward the double glass doors to the inside of the precinct where the police officers who picked her up were probably plotting her imminent arrest.

"You've gutted, fileted, and deboned me all in one sentence. Don't say a word to the police, do you hear me? Keep your mouth shut until I can get you a lawyer on the fly, if I don't get there first. I'm in the Valley at my parents' house, but I know someone who can probably get there faster. I'll reach out to Sean now."

"I'm the one who called the cops, and I came to the station on my own volition. Plus, it's too late for me not to talk to the police at this point, or they'll think I'm a suspect, if they don't already."

"For now, keep it zipped until I can get myself or a surrogate there."

The thick glass door to the precinct buzzed open, and Carly followed LAPD Officer Lila Rodriguez into the confines of the building. The Robbery-Homicide detective was in her mid-forties. Carly focused on the woman's long black ponytail, which swayed back and forth across her taut uniform shirt, until they reached an interview room, where Rodriguez's partner, Detective Zachary Smith, sat on the opposite side of a rectangular table, facing the door.

Smith was a few decades younger than his partner and, without a word, emanated a sense of unbridled arrogance that reminded Carly of Julien and his rich, entitled prep-school friends.

"Thank you for agreeing to speak to us, Miss Bennett. Please take a seat," Rodriguez said, and kept her position of dominance and stayed standing with her arms folded across her chest. "Just so I understand, why were you on campus after hours?"

Carly flashed to the image of Ed Russo's face masked behind the plastic, and how the bag puckered inward toward his mouth in his final death pose. She imagined Russo's last moments as he struggled to breathe.

"I left a prescription in my office that I needed for the night. I'm a severe asthmatic, and my doctor can confirm that."

Carly reached into her bag, retrieved her inhaler, and took a dry puff for reassurance. "How did you know Mr. Russo?" Rodriguez asked.

"Through work. We exchanged pleasantries when we crossed paths, like, 'How's your day going, Ed?' or 'Can you believe how hot it is today?' That kind of small talk. But we weren't friends."

"When was the last time you saw Mr. Russo?" Rodriguez asked.

"This morning. I recommended a book to him. Ed said he liked the story."

"Did you know Mr. Russo socially?" Smith asked.

"Socially? Are you asking if we hung out after work?"

"You're an attractive female, and you seemed on friendly enough terms with Mr. Russo, so maybe the two of you met up outside of school hours," Smith suggested, and leaned across the table toward Carly. "He's older, but maybe that doesn't bother you."

Carly wondered what Smith's childhood was like to make him such a jerk, and answered without thinking.

"Gross, no! Let me say that again," Carly said, catching herself. "Ed wasn't gross, but we didn't have a romantic relationship. With all due respect, I've had a heck of a day, and our current meet-and-greet is the topper on my magical maggot sundae."

"I realize finding Mr. Russo's body must've been traumatic for you. We're trying to get a sense of how well you knew Mr. Russo," Rodriguez said.

"I never slept with Ed, and we never socialized after school. Ed seemed like a good man who was trying to pull his life together after some personal troubles."

"What 'personal troubles' are we talking about here?" Smith pressed.

Carly shot a quick glance at what she assumed was a two-way mirror, and scrambled for a response. "I don't want to speak badly of Ed or his struggles. People go through difficulties, including present company, unless you officers have been blessed with a charmed life."

Smith rose from his chair, and leaned his body against the table, so he was positioned above her. "I spoke to his ex. We know Russo had alcohol issues."

"You ask a lot of questions when you already know the answers."

"Where were you at seven thirty last night? Rodriguez asked.

"I was at Zuma. I was supposed to have dinner with someone at Nobu, but he showed up late, so we decided to watch the sunset at the beach."

"Can this someone vouch for your whereabouts?" Smith asked. "Ed Russo's ex-wife can place him at USC at seven thirty. He called her from the parking lot and told her that he had an issue with an English professor that he needed to clear up. The security cameras in the front of the English building were on the fritz, but his wife can place him at the school then."

An issue with an English professor? This was bad—very, very bad. Even a junior detective would home in on her as the lead suspect since Ed, in what was probably his last act, had written her name on the floor of her very own English department office.

Carly ran a nervous hand through her hair and prayed she wouldn't stutter. She waited a beat to respond and mentally worked through her practice phrase. The cops likely thought she was a loon for doing dry hits on an asthma inhaler, so if she came out stuttering, she'd be cuffed and booked into Century Regional Detention Center in no time.

"I'll see if I can reach my friend. His name is Sebastian Foster, and he's an architect in town. Sebastian and I were almost in a car accident. An SUV that was following us nearly ran my Jeep off the road."

"Sounds like you did have quite a traumatic day. Any chance you got the plate or the make and model of the vehicle?" Rodriguez asked.

"I didn't. Everything happened so fast."

"Do you have a number where we can reach this Sebastian?" Smith asked.

"That's the thing. I tried to call him after our date, but his phone is disconnected."

"Uh-huh. One more thing," Smith said. "I smelled alcohol on your breath when we responded to the call. Maybe you and Russo used to be drinking buddies, he cleaned up his act, but you fell off the wagon. He confronted you about it, and you felt threatened."

"I had a glass of wine when I was at Nobu. The story you're spinning is pure fiction."

"What time were you at Nobu?" Smith continued.

"My reservation was at six, and I left around six forty-five. I went to the beach after with Sebastian. I realize no one can place me at the restaurant with Sebastian since we met up in the parking lot later, but I'm sure I can find him if you need to verify my story."

"Regarding your timeline, you claimed that you left the restaurant at six forty-five. That would've given you plenty of time to get back to USC to settle any scores with Mr. Russo," Smith said. "And without an alibi for the lost time, your account is thin, unless anyone else can place you at Zuma Beach during your lost hours."

The interview room door opened, and an older, stocky bald man with a thick white beard poked his head inside, gave Carly a hard stare and then left without a word.

"Who was that? Carly asked. "I came here because I wanted to help you find out who killed Ed, but it's clear that you think I'm involved. I wanted to play nice, but you didn't, so I'm not talking any more until I get a lawyer."

Carly stood to leave when the older officer with the white beard reentered the room.

Great. More cops invited to her downfall.

"Miss Bennett, I'm Sergeant George Halloran. I thought your name sounded familiar. Do you remember me?"

The first fingers of a headache pounded in her temples. Of course, she remembered him.

"You interviewed me about my mother's death when I was at Chatham. What is this about?"

Before Halloran could answer, the interview door banged open, and a lanky, raven-haired male with pale blue eyes stormed inside.

Carly rose from her chair to greet Ava's ex, but Sean Murphy waved a hand for her to sit down.

"I'm Miss Bennett's attorney. Three officers drilling one witness, what will the LAPD think of next? I thought you folks tried to destroy innocent lives by working in pairs," said Sean, who delivered his warning with a steel point conditioned from a childhood growing up with a gang of other poor boys in Belfast, Ireland.

"Mr. Murphy, I've seen your name on a few case files from the public defender's office," Smith said. "I'm surprised the professor would hire someone of your pedigree to represent her."

Sean's eyes flashed. He took a step in Smith's direction, before grabbing Carly's arm and steering her toward the door.

"Mr. Murphy, before you go, it would be in Miss Bennett's best interest if you heard this," Halloran said. "I work juvenile crimes now for the LAPD, but when I was with the LA County Sheriff's department, I handled her mom's homicide with my partner. I interviewed Ms. Bennett at the time, and all these years later, something about her story didn't add up. I still work with kids, and I've sharpened my instincts about when they're not telling the whole truth."

"Get to your point if you have one. And since you work in the juvenile division, let me remind you, Ed Russo was far above the age of eighteen, so this isn't your case," Murphy answered.

Halloran glowered at Murphy and continued.

"I heard Miss Bennett was picked up for questioning in Russo's murder, and I wanted to give an assist to my colleagues in Robbery-Homicide when I recognized her name," Halloran answered. "I've got historical knowledge about Emily Bennett's death, and I find it more than curious that both Ed Russo and Emily Bennett died in similar ways."

"This is absurd," Carly protested.

"Where did your mother die?" Sean asked Carly.

"Malibu."

"Emily Bennett's case is no longer under your jurisdiction then, or anyone else in this room, plain and simple. The fact that you're obviously trying to link my client to both cases is laughable at best. Roll up your sleeves and do some real detective work to find out who killed Russo."

Sean peeled off three business cards, handed them to the officers and then shuttled Carly out of the station and to his waiting car.

"Thanks a million, Sean. You were brilliant."

"Sorry, but I'm so pissed right now, I need a smoke," Sean said. He opened his window and pulled a Camel from a nearly empty hardpack on the dashboard. "How much did you tell the cops?"

"Not much. I didn't know Ed all that well, and I don't know who'd want to kill him."

Ava's ex-husband exhaled two perfect smoke rings and then batted them toward the open window.

"Ava gave me a broad-brush briefing on the case, and now with this potential connection with your mother, the situation could turn bad, and quick. Tell me everything you know about Russo and every single detail you know about your mother's murder."

FIFTEEN
Emily

March 2010, Malibu, the Whites' Estate

Emily slipped on her ivory-colored silk nightgown and sat on the edge of the bed with her cell phone in hand and a picture of her little girl on her lap. She stroked Carly's face in the picture and then punched in the first five numbers to Carly's school, but stopped when she worried it was too late to call.

Emily sighed and placed her phone on her dresser. She'd wait until tomorrow to phone Carly with the news. Or perhaps she'd surprise her daughter and show up at her school unannounced.

Whatever she decided, Emily would need input from Chatham on a path forward for Carly once she came home.

Emily's heart ached when she looked at her daughter's large blue eyes in the photograph, still filled with a child's joy and innocence. Emily had taken the photo six months before they met the Whites.

In less than a year, what Emily thought she knew about her child had been upended.

Carly was acting out in such a disturbing way that Emily barely recognized her anymore. And Chatham had a sterling reputation, so it made perfect sense to send her daughter there.

A period of homesickness was inevitable, but the way Carly was spiraling was something different. In the seventy-five days since she had left, Carly had been beyond miserable and borderline catatonic, to the point Emily dreaded going to the mailbox where she'd find another heart-wrenching letter from her daughter, professing her innocence and begging Emily to bring her home.

Chatham was one of the most prestigious private girls' schools in the country. After the unconscionable stunt that Carly pulled on her English teacher, Julien, followed by Christopher, convinced Emily it would be best for her twelve-year-old daughter to leave her.

Think of the Ivy League college opportunities that would await her, Emily!

Imagine the world-class education Carly would receive, Emily!

Thank heavens for our family's connections and annual donations to Chatham, Emily!

She clenched her hands into fists and felt ashamed over what she'd done. Her decision caused her already fragile daughter even more distress. If she didn't bring Carly home, her daughter could be ruined beyond repair.

If that weren't enough, now her marriage was slipping away too.

Emily twisted her large diamond wedding band around her finger and nearly laughed aloud when she pictured herself in the tan polyester suit she had been wearing when she first met Christopher at the bank.

A few of the other female tellers teased Emily that the handsome, well-dressed man was offering other customers the chance to go ahead in line so Emily would be the one to wait on him.

After his fourth visit, Emily struck up the courage to ask why Christopher was visiting her branch when his home address was an hour away.

Christopher looked flustered by her boldness and promised he'd explain his reasoning if she agreed to go out with him.

Their first date was on Christopher's sailboat, where Christopher admitted he happened by her branch by accident. Christopher took her hand and explained he was awestruck by Emily's ethereal beauty and continued to find excuses to return to the bank.

On their fourth date, when Emily boarded Christopher's private plane to San Francisco for the weekend, the two consummated their relationship. Christopher was almost fifty, and a good fifteen years older, but Emily imagined he'd be a passionate lover despite their age difference.

Her assumption had been wrong.

Their sex life wasn't horrible, but each encounter was quick, rote, and predictable. After he proposed, Emily considered making gentle suggestions about what she liked, but by then, too much time had passed.

Sex was one small part of a happy marriage, and she already knew the tradeoff of being in a miserable, yet passionate one.

Her ex-husband was a fall-down, blackout drunk. As a single mother, Emily would lie in bed at night, wishing more than anything she could give Carly the world.

When Christopher swept into their lives, he gave them just that.

Emily looked out her bedroom window for Christopher's car and remembered how her friends joked she was marrying Christopher for his money. Emily knew he made a good living as a doctor, but she had no idea how wealthy Christopher was.

She'd trade every penny if he'd only come home.

Emily caught her reflection in the dresser's mirror and thought how haggard she looked. She pinched her cheeks to give her face some color when her cell phone rang.

It was Christopher.

"I'm almost done at the hospital. Can I come by? I don't want to pressure you, but I'd love the chance to apologize. I was a jealous ass. I hope you can forgive me."

"Oh, Christopher. What you thought you saw . . ."

"You don't need to explain. The only thing I know is that I'm miserable without you."

In the mirror's reflection, Emily saw herself smiling.

"I feel the same, but I need to make things right for Carly first. I'm flying to San Francisco tomorrow to bring her home."

"I fully support your decision. We'll come together as a family and make sure Carly has the tools she needs to heal."

"I can't tell you how much that means to me. When will you be home?"

"In a few hours. I can't wait to see you."

The weight that she'd been carrying around for weeks had

lifted. Emily pulled her suitcase from the closet in preparation for her San Francisco trip and then answered her ringing cell phone, assuming it was Christopher, calling back to say he loved her.

"Mrs. White?" said a strange male voice.

"Yes, who is this?"

"Dr. Brian Whittaker, Julien's former psychiatrist. I'm sorry I'm calling so late, but I've been worried about Julien. I wanted to be sure he's OK."

"My husband told you never to bother us again. This is inappropriate."

"I'm sorry, but please hear me out. Julien was making significant progress before your husband refused to let your son see me anymore. I'm not asking you to have him continue his counseling with me. I hope you've arranged for Julien to see someone else."

"Any decisions regarding Julien are of no concern to you. My husband told me what you did."

"None of that was true. I'd never do anything to Julien or another child. Julien and I spoke earlier. We both agreed it was a big misunderstanding."

"You called Julien?"

"No, he called me. Julien was upset over how his father reacted. Julien thought the whole misunderstanding was his fault. I'm concerned, because when Julien thinks he's done something wrong, he acts out. That's why I'm hoping he's still in counseling."

"What my husband and I decide is best for Julien is none of your business. Don't bother my family again."

When Emily hung up, her hands were shaking. She'd tell Christopher about the psychiatrist's call when he arrived home. Christopher would handle it.

Emily tried to put the call out of her mind when her phone buzzed again.

She answered when she saw it was Julien.

"Hey, Em. I tried to call earlier. Do you know where my dad is? I tried his cell, but it went straight to voicemail. And Vic's not picking up either."

"Sorry I didn't answer. I got tied up with some unexpected

calls. Christopher is at work and won't be home for a few hours, and Victor is with his friend Bodie again. I swear, that boy is spending more time at the Andersons' pool house than he's at home these days. Hold on, I can barely hear you. I'm hoping you're not at a bar. The agreement was you could go on your class trip if you promised to follow the rules."

"I haven't done anything wrong. Dad said I could use my credit card if I had an emergency."

"Are you in trouble?"

"I'm not, but my hotel-mate is having some problems. He's been drinking pretty much the entire trip. He got back to our room with a couple buddies and now they're doing shots. I can't handle another night like last one."

"What happened?"

"Between us? He snuck out after curfew. When he came back, he was incoherent and threw up pretty much until morning. I stayed with him in the bathroom the whole time to make sure he was OK. I don't think I've slept in twenty-four hours."

"The parent chaperone for the trip is Kyle's dad, right? Do you want me to call him?"

"Thanks, but I don't want to get my roommate in trouble. He's not a bad kid."

"Who is it?" Emily asked.

"I trust you, but I can't tell you. If the school finds out, he'll get expelled, and graduation is only a few months away. I'm going to ask the front desk if they have another room for me, if that's OK by you."

"Of course. I'll cover for you with your dad if he asks."

"You're a lifesaver, Mom."

Emily hung up the phone, and her eyes filled over the fact Julien called her "Mom." A first for him and a reward she'd never received from Victor yet.

She climbed into her four-poster king bed and wrapped a thick down comforter around her.

She decided to sleep for an hour, to be refreshed when Christopher got home.

Sleep came quickly.

* * *

In the dream, Emily walked through the gates of the boarding school, where Carly leapt into her arms. Her daughter looked angelic and not unhappy anymore as Carly led Emily by the hand to her room.

Emily felt as if she'd burst with joy until the hallway became dark. It was becoming harder and harder to breathe.

When they reached her room, Carly instructed Emily to lie on her twin bed and close her eyes. Emily took off her shoes and did as she was told but coughed violently.

Something was pressing down hard against her face.

"You can open your eyes after I count to ten. Ready?" Carly asked. "I love you so much, Mommy."

Emily tried to tell her daughter she loved her too. But she couldn't breathe.

She reached for Carly's hand and squeezed it as hard as she could.

She awoke then to a strange and horrible sensation. Something was sealed against her face, making it impossible to open her eyes or take a single breath. Emily's feet beat hard against the mattress as she clawed at her attacker's arms and felt the weight of someone straddling and holding her down like an anchor on the bed.

After two minutes, it was over.

The coroner's report would list Emily White's time of death as 12:07 a.m.

In small square letters, the coroner wrote:

> Case number 202, Emily White, a thirty-five-year-old Caucasian female. Based on the levels of carbon dioxide in the deceased's blood serum and the recurrent presence of small, red and purple spots caused by hemorrhaging in the subject's eyes, the victim's cause of death is believed to be a homicide. The medical data indicates Mrs. White was smothered to death in her sleep.

SIXTEEN
Ava

Eight a.m.

Ava cut across Sixth Street and passed the trendy buildings that lined either side of the city's Arts District and headed toward Kaplan Chan, which was located on the ground floor of a pastel yellow and turquoise striped building.

Ava turned up the collar of her leather jacket, leaned in heavy on her British accent, and entered the lobby, where a twenty-something male with wire-framed glasses and a shock of dyed black hair was manning the reception desk. A nametag on the desk listed his name as "Mychael."

She put a leash on her edge and ramped up the charm to a ten. Or really an eight-point-five, because a ten would be pushing her limit.

"Hello, Mychael. I fancy how you spell your name. Would you be a love and ring Sebastian for me? I'm Ari Jones," Ava said, pulling her made-up alias out of the air. "Sebastian and I have been playing a maddening game of phone tag. My Grandma Mahu left me her home in Sherman Oaks, you see. Grandma Mahu passed recently, but before she died, she made me promise that I'd restore her home back to how it looked when she was a child. Sebastian said your firm could take on the project."

"I'm sorry for your loss, but we don't have a Sebastian here," Mychael answered.

"My mistake then. I may be wrong on his first name, but I'm sure he said his last name was Foster."

"We don't have a Foster or a Sebastian here. I'd be happy to connect you with another member of our staff . . ."

Ava was out the door and back on the street before Mychael, whom Ava was certain added the pretentious "y" to his name just because, could finish his sentence.

Back in her truck, Ava considered the slim details she knew about Sebastian Foster, or whoever he really was, when her cell phone rang. She picked up when she saw Sean's number.

"How bad is my girl's situation?" Ava asked. "I went back to her house last night when the LAPD cut her loose, but from what I can tell, she's got zero chance of anyone backing up her alibi, including the fake douche, Sebastian the architect."

"As expected, her prints were all over her office, but the plastic bag around Russo's head, it came back clean. USC has cameras around the perimeter of campus, but there's no direct CCTV footage of the English building."

"What about cars coming in and out of the school?"

"The LAPD is combing through its license-plate recognition camera pix now, but if Russo's killer entered on foot, that's going to be harder, if not impossible, to track."

"How about Sebastian's phone, were you able to trace it? And what about the car?"

Ava drummed her fingers on the truck's dash, waiting but doubtful for a break.

"The phone was a burner. I'm working on the car."

"The story Sebastian told Carly about working at Kaplan Chan was a front," Ava said.

"Do you know for sure Carly met this Sebastian person?"

"It's early, and maybe I only slept for twenty minutes last night, but what are you asking me exactly?"

"I know you don't want to hear this, but are you sure Carly didn't do it? I know the two of you have been friends forever, but Russo's body was found in her office, and he wrote her name on the floor while he was dying. That's a dead giveaway to me. And the cops are sniffing around whether she had anything to do with her mother's murder."

Ava peeled her truck out of the parking space, unmoved when a car blasted its horn behind her.

She slipped on her aviator sunglasses and punched the gas harder.

"That's a load of bunk. Carly didn't kill anyone. I appreciate your help, but being a first-rate ass doesn't look good on you."

SEVENTEEN
Carly

Carly lay in bed with a pillow draped over her face to block the mid-morning sun that cut its way through her curtains.

She groaned, looked at the alarm clock. It was ten a.m.

A strange sensation stirred in her stomach. She rose to go to the bathroom, but the feeling subsided when she stood. Her sudden nausea must have been a byproduct of all the trauma from the previous day.

Sleep was futile at this point. Carly headed to her spare bedroom, which was a catchall of books, clutter from school and sparse keepsakes saved through the years.

She reached up to the highest shelf of her bookcase for her prized possession: An ivory-colored figurine.

A coat of dust covered the old-fashioned statue of a beautiful woman wearing a long, billowy dress and holding a parasol over her head. Carly held it in the palm of her hand, like she'd done when she was ten. She'd first discovered the prize sitting atop her place setting at the kitchen table in the little ranch house she shared with her mother. At the time, Emily was making eggs and was hurrying to prepare Carly breakfast before she left for work.

"*Good morning, sleepy head. I hope you like your present. I was taking a walk on my lunch break yesterday, and I found an adorable craft store. I could've spent my entire paycheck buying things for you there, but the figurine spoke to me. I couldn't leave until I bought her for you. She's called the 'Vivienne Lady.' I think she's going to bring us luck.*"

"*She's beautiful, Mommy. I'll keep her forever, I promise.*"

Carly put the figurine into her pocket and sifted through the clothes hanging in her closet until she found her old school blazer from Chatham.

She pulled the blazer from the hanger and worked her fingers along the inner lining until she felt it. She snatched a pair of scissors from her desk, snipped the satin burgundy lining until she'd made a three-inch incision and then extracted the rectangular stub from its hiding place.

The bus ticket was faded now. Its computerized block lettering chronicled her journey fifteen years earlier: Greyhound Bus Number 205, departing from San Francisco at nine a.m. on March 4th, 2010, and arriving in Los Angeles at five in the afternoon the same day, with a connecting, last stop that would take her to Malibu.

To cover her tracks, Carly had sewn the stub into the lining of her blazer, so no one would find it. Most people would've thrown the thing away. Carly hung onto the bus ticket as a reminder of what she did.

The odd sensation in her stomach returned, but now it felt like someone had jabbed a knife into her and then twisted the handle. Her face felt hot and then a second wave of nausea came over her. Carly clutched her stomach and was ready to run to the bathroom, but as quickly as the feeling came, it was gone.

The stress was going to ruin her if she let it.

Carly stuffed the ticket inside the fresh hole in the blazer's lining and hung the jacket up in the farthest reach of her closet.

Her cell phone rang.

The caller ID read Bert Scanlon.

She clutched the Vivienne Lady for courage and answered.

"Miss Bennett, I trust you are doing well, considering the circumstances," her boss said.

"Thanks for checking in. It's horrible what happened to Ed."

"About that, if you get any calls from the press, refer them to the school's public relations department. You're not to say a word to the media."

"I understand. I'd like to take some time off, if that would be OK."

"The school has grief counselors available, and classes will be canceled for a few days. That should give you enough time to regroup. The school president and I have been able to keep a lid on most of the details surrounding Mr. Russo's death, including the fact that you found the body."

"What if students ask questions about Ed's death?"

"You tell them it was a terrible thing and that you aren't privy to any details. Refer them to the counseling department on an as-needed basis. I trust that you didn't know the janitor well."

"Ed was a p–passing acquaintance."

Carly clapped a hand over her stupid, stuttering mouth.

After thirty seconds of dead air, Scanlon responded.

"Are you all right, Miss Bennett? When classes resume, the administration will need you to act with the professionalism and composure we expect of all our professors."

Carly worked her practice phrase in her head. "*The girl wore her hair in two braids, tied with two blue bows.*"

When her tongue felt as though it had lost its uncontrollable tic, she answered.

"Of course, sir. I do have one request, though. I want my office moved, considering what happened."

"Ronnie McVeigh retired, so you can have his old space. Someone from maintenance can move your belongings. We'll see you on campus bright and refreshed in a few days."

Carly hung up and stumbled to the bathroom, where she grabbed the sink with both hands and stared at her pale complexion in the mirror.

A strange thought clicked into place.

Stumbling into a crime scene with Ed Russo's dead body, along with the resurrection of the bus ticket followed by Scanlon's call, had caused her phantom childhood stomachaches to return.

Carly lay on the floor until the pain worked its way through her. After twenty minutes, she crawled back into bed and prayed for sleep.

In between consciousness and dreams, Carly envisioned her life at Chatham playing out in real time, as if she were still there.

She shivered under her blanket, recalling Detective Halloran's interview with her at the boarding school.

He'd asked if Carly had any friends. She'd said no.

That had been one of the few truths she'd told him.

But things changed, and she'd learned one true friend was all she'd ever need.

EIGHTEEN
Carly

March 2010, San Francisco, Chatham School for Girls

Two weeks after her meltdown in the headmistress's office where she heard the news about her mother's death, Carly hid inside the bathroom stall in the academic building at Chatham and willed the universe as hard as she could that the other students would leave.

"The new girl is creepy. She runs through the hallways with her head down, like some kind of bent-over hobbit."

Carly bit her lip as the chorus of haters continued to peck away at her.

"One of her roommates swears she can't speak. I'm betting the administration stuck an idiot mute in here, to make us suffer."

A stall door banged open. Carly peered underneath her own to see a pair of combat boots thump across the acrylic floor tiles.

"You better watch your ass around the new girl. She killed someone, swear to God. It was some perv gardener who tried to come on to her little sister," the owner of the combat boots said.

"Freak girl is a killer? No way!"

"Bennett is one hundred percent certifiable. I got the intel from an excellent source."

The girl in the combat boots had a British accent.

"Rusk told you?"

"Even if she did, I wouldn't tell you. I'm not going to rat anyone out, but I know as a fact, the Bennett girl hacked the perv to death with his own garden hoe."

"You're lying, Ava. She'd be in jail if she killed somebody."

The collective shuffle of shoes moved closer, and Carly feared her classmates had discovered her hiding place.

"I think a stupid little girl called me a liar."

Carly peeked through the crack in the door at the pair of black leather combat boots that took menacing steps toward the semicircle of plaid skirts and loafers.

"Sorry. I didn't mean it."

"Check your mouth next time, or I'll check it for you. The jury didn't convict the Bennett kid because they thought she was insane. That's why they put her in here with us. If I were you, I'd watch my back, especially when you're sleeping."

Carly wanted to scream her innocence, but then she'd have to confront the girl with the intimidating shoes and the accent.

Instead, the bell rang, and the girls scattered, except for Miss Combat Boots.

Carly felt like she was plummeting. Her life was so horrible already, and now she was being labeled a killer. But there was no way she was going to get into a fight. Carly exited the stall and kept her eyes on the white tile floor with the plan of trying to get out of there with her limbs still intact.

"Hey, you're Carly Bennett, right?"

A firm hand clutched her shoulder when she tried to pass, and Carly feared she was about to get pulverized. She took in what she thought would be her last image on the earth, a striking girl with lustrous light brown skin and a shiny black Mohawk.

"I didn't k–kill anyone," Carly stammered.

"I knew those idiot girls were wrong about you not being able to speak," the classmate said and smiled. "I did you a favor. If everyone thinks you're crazy, they won't bother you. Let me give you two pieces of advice to help you survive this hellhole. Number one, the school's dress code owns you except for your hair and shoes. Number two . . . and pay attention, Sunshine . . . never let anyone see your fear because otherwise, you'll be screwed. I'm Ava, by the way. Ava Patel."

The second bell rang its warning, and Carly rushed out of the bathroom to her English class. The period was her favorite, but during the teacher's discussion about Tom Joad's existential struggles in *The Grapes of Wrath*, she found her thoughts wandering back to Ava and how she stood up for Carly for no good reason.

That night, sleep was impossible, so she stole out of their shared dormitory space and headed to the showers.

Carly positioned herself underneath the freezing cold spray until she shivered, and her lips turned blue. She closed her eyes and pictured herself a few weeks earlier, getting off the bus at LA's Greyhound station, the faded liquor store sign across the street, and the construction worker who offered her a ride the rest of the way to Malibu.

Carly rested her forehead against the cement shower wall when a voice called from behind.

"You're going to freeze to death."

Carly covered her bare chest when she saw the girl with the Mohawk.

Ava threw Carly a towel and turned away. "Don't worry. I wasn't here for a peep show. I came in for a smoke and saw you were about to turn into a Popsicle. Do you want my two cents?"

Carly wrapped the towel around her and tried to temper the mixture of humiliation and anger of being caught in a private moment.

"No th–th–thank you."

"I'll give it to you anyway. I heard your mom died. She was murdered, right?"

The strange girl was now treading on what was hers.

"That's none of your business," Carly answered, with flint in her voice this time.

"Good, you should be mad. Feel whatever you need to feel, but at some point, you have to let it go. If you hang on too long to the things that hurt you, it's like you're holding on to broken glass. You can't let the bad thing that happened destroy you."

Carly thought the other girl was baiting her, trying to gain her trust only to humiliate her at a time of her choosing. And she'd stuttered after all, which solidified the terrible fact that she was a big fat zero. Carly stared back at Ava, doing her best to hold her ground.

Ava laughed and gave Carly a wink.

"I stuck a bottle top in the door to the roof earlier, so we can go up there if you like," Ava said. "I won't run the risk of setting off the fire alarm with my smokes up there. Come on, I don't bite, I swear."

Curious, Carly dressed and followed Ava through the dark hallways and up the stairs until they reached the roof.

Carly breathed in the crisp night air and took in the wonder of the stars that shined with promise overhead.

Maybe it was the wonder of the universe that caused her to put her guard down.

"Do you think if a person is good at their core, they should be forgiven for doing one bad thing?" Carly asked.

Ava took a drag of her cigarette and raised an eyebrow, as if Carly were a strange and possibly dangerous creature caught under the lights of the circus big top.

"You're an interesting one. Sure, decent people can make bad mistakes, but if their motives are pure, then that changes the equation. Are you asking for yourself?"

"No, it was a stupid thing to say. I bet you think I'm weird now t–t–too."

Carly cast her head down and pivoted to leave. The older girl would now turn on her too, but Ava grasped the back of Carly's Chatham sweatshirt and reeled her back.

"I think you're a lot more interesting than the morons who go here. I hate stupid girls. You stutter, right?"

"Why are you asking a question when you know the answer?"

"Good point. Don't be embarrassed about it. My little brother Narun has a lisp. He's a good kid but super shy. I was his full-time bodyguard until my parents shipped me off to this hell-hugger to pick up some lessons on how to be a proper lady. As you can see, it hasn't worked out for them so far." Ava did a mock curtsey and stuck out her tongue.

"You must miss your brother."

"You have no idea. I used to go to his speech therapy visits. For homework, his teacher gave Narun some sentences to practice that were supposed to help him not talk funny anymore. Have you ever tried that?"

"I haven't tried anything. The stutter is new and only comes out when I'm anxious."

"If you didn't stutter before, you should be able to fix it yourself. I can help you," Ava said. "The girl wore her hair in two braids, tied with two blue bows."

"What am I supposed to do with that?"

"Work with me here. That's a sentence my bro had to recite. I remember that one, because Narun hated it because it was about girls."

"The girl wore her hair in two braids, tied with two blue bows," Carly said.

"Nice. Just keep practicing, and you'll kick that stutter to the curb. Tell you what, if anyone gives you a hard time again, you tell me, and I'll take care of them. And one final piece of advice. The head nurse likes to give us 'problem' girls a boatload of meds to keep us in line. Is the nurse giving you pills?"

"Every day, but I don't take them."

"Good. The pills will suck the light out of you. Some girls sell them on the Chatham black market, but that's not my style. Swear you won't take them. I can't be friends with a junkie."

Ava extended her arm and clenched her hand into a fist.

"What am I supposed to do here?" Carly asked.

Ava shook her head and laughed.

"You've never done a fist bump before?"

"Not really," Carly answered.

"Unbelievable. If you promise, then tap your fist against mine. Easy as that."

Carly balled a hand into a fist and tapped it against Ava's.

"I swear," Carly said. "Cross my heart."

"You promise with your heart, I promise with my fist. Either way works, as long as you mean it. It's official then. You and me, Bennett, we're friends."

NINETEEN
Rebecca

Rebecca searched for her house key inside the jumble of her backpack, the slow burn still lingering over Ava's comments from the night before. Not only had Carly's best friend insulted the tea Rebecca took such care in preparing, but Ava had dropped a very clear suggestion that Rebecca should leave, as if Rebecca were back in high school and had the gall to sit at the popular girls' lunch table.

Instead of speaking up, Rebecca had stood there, slack-jawed and smiling, even when Ava referred to her as "Kid."

It was true she was only twenty-four. Carly and Ava were older, but Rebecca wasn't a child.

On the drive back to her duplex, Rebecca rattled off a stream of witty and barbed comments to an imaginary Ava, slaying the tough girl who frightened her with sharp, intelligent quips. During the monologue, Rebecca's voice got deeper and more serious when she mentioned the full-ride scholarship she earned to USC. Did Ava know she published her first short story in a renowned literary journal? Sure, the magazine wasn't actually "renowned," more like "fairly decent and rarely read," but the imaginary Ava wouldn't have known the difference.

Rebecca fished a loose key from her bag and attempted to fit it in the lock, but it wouldn't turn.

She took a closer look.

No wonder it wouldn't work. The key was for Carly's place.

Rebecca lifted the flowerpot next to her front door. Her ex had often lectured her about leaving a spare key in such a conspicuous place, and although she never admitted it to him, he had a point. Rebecca lived in the University Park neighborhood, which wasn't that far from Skid Row. Even though her place was close to USC, her area of the world had a high level of crime. Still, Rebecca felt if she kept good energy inside her home, it would help keep the bad things out. Plus, she slept with a baseball bat next to her bed, because a single girl living alone in a big city could never be too safe.

Rebecca reached under the flowerpot but panicked when the key wasn't there. That's when she noticed a light on in the back of the house. She grabbed pepper spray from her backpack, tried the front door, which opened, and crept down the hallway.

Music was playing from the kitchen, and the aroma of garlic sautéing in olive oil filled the space. Not the typical M.O. for a robber.

"You're not supposed to be here yet!"

Rebecca's new beau, decked out in a blue and white polka-dotted apron, stood in front of a boiling stockpot on the stove with wooden spoon in hand.

Rebecca hid the pepper spray behind her back.

"I'm sorry if I scared you," David Ramsey said. "I should've called to tell you I was going to drop by, but I wanted it to be a surprise. I knew you were dealing with a heavy situation with your friend, so I planned to sneak in, make you dinner, and then head out before you got home. You mentioned you kept a key by the door. I hope I didn't overstep my bounds. If you haven't noticed, I talk way too much when I'm nervous."

David's eyes were wide with worry, causing Rebecca to want to throw her arms around him and hug David as hard as she could, despite the fact he was wearing thick white socks with a pair of Birkenstock sandals, along with his usual sloppy man-bun and shaggy facial hair.

Working on his look would be her first task. The poor sweet boy. She likened her new man to a bedraggled puppy at a shelter, just needing a good wash and flea dip to unveil its true beautiful self.

"This is one of the best surprises ever. You did all this for me?"

"Of course, silly."

David took her in his arms then, and if Rebecca knew how

to swoon, she would. She closed her eyes and smelled the patchouli oil on David's skin. Rebecca waited for his kiss, but David hurried back to the stove.

"Hold that thought. I need to stir the garlic. I'll ruin your dinner if I let it burn. You're such a distraction."

David swirled the wooden spoon in the pan, drizzled some white wine inside and then poured Rebecca a glass.

She took a sip and recalled how she'd immediately liked David when they first met at an off-campus vegetarian restaurant a few weeks earlier. Rebecca had been alone at a table with a notebook and pen, jotting down an idea for a new story. She'd noticed David at the bar, but he looked older, a real adult with a good job and a mortgage; someone who didn't eat peanut butter sandwiches like she did every last Friday of the month to make ends meet.

Rebecca was well into the second page of her story, when David stood over her table. After two hours of talking, Rebecca discovered her new acquaintance had done mission work in Sri Lanka, and he liked her nose ring and new elephant tattoo. They met up later that night for dinner, and then Rebecca took him back to her place, where they had the best sex of her life. When she woke up, he was still there, sleeping with his arm around her shoulder.

"How's your friend?" David asked.

"She's still rattled, but who wouldn't be in her situation? Imagine, discovering a dead man with a plastic bag around his face in your office. I get chills every time I think about it," Rebecca said and shivered.

"Did you know the man who was killed?"

Rebecca shrugged and hoped her reaction didn't make her seem like an insensitive jerk. Sure, she felt bad if someone died, let alone get murdered. But Ed was a creeper.

"He was a school janitor. I think he showed up during my junior year. Ed had a slick voice like a gameshow host, and he tried to be cool and rub shoulders with the undergrads, especially the guys. He was always chatting up the male students about sports. I know this makes me sound mean, but Ed seemed desperate. He was an older guy past his prime, trying to be buddies with the students. Still, he didn't deserve what happened to him."

"Your friend must be traumatized. I hope the tea helped."

"You are the kindest person in the world," Rebecca said. "Please, at least let me pay for the tea."

"I won't take a penny. I know how important Cheryl is to you."

"My boss's name is Carly, not Cheryl."

"Sorry, well then Carly is very lucky she has you," David said.

"I'm the lucky one. I had a creative writing class with Carly my sophomore year. She was the only teacher who saw promise in my writing. Carly fought for me when one of my scholarships got cut. That's the thing about her. Carly will always fight for other people. But she's a dark horse. There's something about her I can't figure out; it's like she's hiding a secret."

"It sounds like your friend has issues."

"I don't want to come off like Carly is screwed up, because she's not."

"I'm sorry about your friend, but I don't want to talk about her anymore. My fixation for the rest of the night is you," David said. He turned off the stove and pinned Rebecca against the wall. "I don't think I can wait until after dinner."

"Wait for what?" Rebecca asked.

"For you. You have no idea how sexy you are."

David slid his hand up her skirt and, when she gasped with pleasure, Rebecca was certain she was the luckiest girl in the world.

TWENTY
Carly

Carly pulled into the faculty parking lot of the USC campus after spending her requisite few days off in bed, courtesy of the canceled classes. Three local TV news vans and a makeshift stage were set up in the park across the street, where the college president, along with the USC director of communications, huddled, rehearsing their spin.

With ten minutes to go before her "Introduction to Fiction Writing" class, Carly put on a pair of dark glasses and made a straight line to the English building.

She was halfway to her class when a female voice called from behind.

"Miss Bennett, do you have a minute?"

A red-headed young woman rushed to catch up to her.

"I was hoping I could talk to you," the girl said. "I'm Amelia Peterson."

Carly tried to place the student. Maybe Amelia was in one of her undergrad classes last year?

"I'm sorry, but I'm late for class. Feel free to stop by my office later if you'd like," Carly answered.

Carly picked up her pace and took several deep breaths before she went inside her classroom.

Scanlon wanted normal. She had no other choice but to play the game.

"Hello, my fellow writers. I know we were all recently impacted by a tragedy on campus. The school has counselors if anyone needs to talk, and remember, my door is always open too," Carly said.

Despite a few concerned faces, no student spoke up about

Russo's death, so Carly continued with her lesson for the third-year students in the jam-packed auditorium.

"This week, we're going to pivot from Tolstoy's classic tale of love and adultery to a writing assignment with a modern twist. Stories, my friends, are all around you, and woven into your everyday life, and that includes music. Today, we're going to listen to three songs. I realize this isn't a music class, and you're lucky, because no one would want to hear me sing."

A chorus of laughter filled the classroom.

"Lyrics, like poetry, can tell powerful stories. So, listen up and pay careful attention to the stories you're about to hear."

Carly sat on the edge of her desk as Bruce Springsteen's "Thunder Road," Kelly Clarkson's "Breakaway" and Eminem and Rihanna's "Love the Way You Lie" played. Most of the students scribbled down their thoughts, while a few stared at her as if looking for a cue on how the songs should make them feel.

Carly kept her smile intact until her face hurt, but fantasized what it would be like to jump on top of her desk and scream, "*I found the dead body of the English department's janitor in my office, but the school wants me to act like not a damn thing happened, and the cops think I did it. And by the way, kids, someone tried to run me off the road the other night and the man I was with at the time is on the lam, but keep on listening to the music, and don't mind me if I melt into a blubbering mess right in front of you.*"

Instead, Carly kept up the sappy grin and swayed her shoulders to the music until the songs ended, as if the last few days were peaches and cream.

"What do we think? I saw a few of you dancing," Carly said. "Can anyone tell me a common theme in all three songs?"

A hand shot up.

"Yes, Laura. I have to call on you since you're wearing that very cool Ramones T-shirt."

"The characters in the songs sound kind of screwed up, like they're in bad situations and they want to get out of them," the girl answered.

"Well said. The characters all want to escape from something. Maybe it's a place, maybe it's a relationship, maybe it's the past, and they can't truly be happy until they overcome whatever it is that's holding them back. Consider for a moment, what happens to characters when you put them in difficult situations? Do they fight their way out of the problem, or do they give up? What attributes do you arm them with in their battles? And who, or what, is the foe they need to overcome? Your assignment this week is to write a short story based on one of the songs you heard. But I want a resolution for the character at the end. Granted, the ending doesn't have to be happy, but realistic. Get inside your characters' heads and let the reader know how they feel. I want you to write a one-paragraph synopsis of your idea. Are there any questions?"

"Can we pick a different song? The three you played were pretty basic. Anyone with a pulse could figure out what they were about."

Enter the latest installment of the cocky kid Carly had every year for this class: Oliver Leiken. By week one of the semester, Oliver had told everyone, including Carly, he was going to write a bestselling novel, and seemed to delight in picking apart his classmates' work, to the point Carly had to console one girl who fled the room in tears after being on the receiving end of an Oliver critique.

Carly always supported her ambitious students, but she hated a bully.

"I think Bruce Springsteen, Kelly Clarkson and Eminem would disagree with your assessment of their lyrics. Is there a specific song you were thinking of instead, Mr. Leiken?"

After three years of teaching the course, Carly could predict with decent accuracy what Oliver would say next and made an internal wager between Billie Eilish, Twenty One Pilots and Leonard Cohen, when Oliver gave his answer.

"'Hallelujah.' It was written by Leonard Cohen."

"I'm familiar with the song. What do the lyrics mean to you, Mr. Leiken?"

"Well, the lyrics are complex and existential, so I don't think most people would understand. Plus, I don't want to give anything away in case someone else uses my song," Oliver said.

"If another song moves you more than the ones I played, go

for it. Start jotting down your thoughts and let me know if you want feedback."

After thirty minutes, Carly wrapped up the lecture and began erasing the whiteboard, when Laura with the Ramones T-shirt approached her.

"Hey, Miss Bennett, is it OK if I talk to you about something?"

"Sure, the floor is all yours."

"I heard a janitor at the school was killed, and his body was found somewhere in the English building. The dean sent a message about it to the students, and I saw a segment about the murder on the TV news, but no one is saying what happened. My mom called me, totally freaking out, so I wanted to know if you think we're safe at school."

"That was awful what happened, and I understand why your mom is worried, but I've been told that Mr. Russo's death, although tragic, was an isolated incident. That probably sounds like spin, but I don't think you have any reason to fear for your safety. If you want to talk to someone about how you're feeling, the school has counselors, and I'm always a cell-phone call or text away."

"Thank you, Miss Bennett. I'll let my mom know. She hears me talking about you all the time, so what you said will make her feel better. Have a great rest of your day!"

The remaining students filtered out of the auditorium, and Carly packed her briefcase. She nursed regrets over her fake assurances when something caught her eye.

Someone was sitting alone in the back row of the auditorium.

Carly tensed, worrying the person was a member of the press, waiting in the trenches to drill her about Russo's murder.

"Can I help you?" Carly asked.

She walked down the aisle toward the exit, getting closer to the stranger.

He was an adult male.

"If you're looking for a comment, I can't help you."

"Carly, it's me."

She froze in place and felt detached from her body, as if she could float away from the unexpected horror show playing out on the screen. There in front of her was Julien White, walking toward her with an outstretched hand.

He was older now, in his thirties, but still as beautiful, with the same dark hair, square jaw and the aura of unbridled confidence.

"Hello, Carly. I enjoyed your lecture. You look well."

"What are you doing h–h–h–here?"

"I'm sorry to barge in unannounced like this. I probably should've called first, but I wasn't sure you'd talk to me."

Carly waited to respond, and tried to untangle the mashed-up words in her mouth so she wouldn't stutter a second time, which would be a drip–drip–drip of blood in the water.

"You're right about that. What do you want?" Carly demanded.

"A chance to talk. I'd been planning to reach out to you for some time, but then I heard about the murder on campus. I wanted to be sure you were OK. I admit, I've googled your name through the years and knew you were a professor here. I also wanted a chance to apologize. If you give me a few minutes to explain myself, I promise I'll leave, and I'll never bother you again."

"Five minutes is all you have. Then I want you gone," Carly snapped.

The tough-girl talk sounded false in her ears, but it was the only decent card she had in her hand.

"Did you know the man who died?" Julien asked.

"Yes, but not well. I can't say anything more about it. I left some papers up front. I need a few minutes. You can meet me outside my office when I'm done," Carly lied to buy herself some time.

She had to regain her center.

"Of course. I can't tell you how happy I am to see you," Julien answered.

Carly watched Julien's confident walk as he left and jumped when she heard the door close with a bang behind him.

She closed her eyes and tried to recall the girl she used to be before Julien came into her life.

TWENTY-ONE
Carly

May 2009, Malibu

When she'd first arrived at the Whites' estate, Emily had kept Carly close, but Carly was too intrigued with Julien, all polish and cool confidence, and of course agreed when he offered to give her a personal tour of the property.

"You go to public school, right?" Julien asked. He walked ahead of Carly on the path through the woods behind the house, and Julien even held back some low-slung branches so Carly wouldn't get hurt when she passed. "My dad makes me go to this all-boys' prep school where almost everybody is a phony. I'm reading a book right now, *The Catcher in the Rye*. It's a classic."

Carly felt a strum go off inside her. She was right to think she and Julien had a connection.

"Sure, Holden Caulfield. I read it. He's in an all-boys' prep school, like you. I love books. My mom thinks I go to sleep right after she tucks me in, but my friend Gracie gave me this pen flashlight so I can read in the dark. Don't tell my mom though, OK? She worries a lot."

Julien turned on the path, and Carly felt electric when the older boy flashed her a perfect smile.

"I knew you were smart. I could tell right away when I first saw you. Yeah, Holden Caulfield is in prep school like me, and he thinks everyone there is a phony. He's a genius, but most people, they don't understand him. His parents' money doesn't help him either. You're better off that you don't have any money. Your mom works as a bank teller, right?"

"We're not exactly poor, if that's what you mean. My mom has to work. She doesn't get any money from my dad."

"Your father doesn't give you any money?" Julien asked, as though that were the strangest thing he'd ever heard. "Where's your dad?"

"Somewhere back east. I haven't seen him since I was little. He sounded like a jerk, from what my mom told me, so it's better he's not in our lives anymore, I guess."

"Sorry if you didn't get what I said about your family not having money. Let me say it another way. I think a kid is better off if his parents aren't super rich. Half of my friends at school, they're either in therapy or sneaking pills from their parents' medicine cabinets. You're simple and that's good."

"Simple doesn't sound like a compliment." Carly looked up at Julien, whose dark eyes stayed on her and didn't let go.

"Simple is the highest of compliments, and I like that you don't agree with everything I say. Most people do, and that makes them fake. I'm also glad you and your mom came here. I get the feeling you and I are going to be pretty good friends."

"Dude, are you going to hog the entire time we've got Carly? Nice to meet you!"

Victor White, now standing in front of them on the path, gave Carly a mock salute. "I'm Julien Junior."

"You wish," Julien added. "This is my little brother, Victor."

"Not so little, thank you very much. I'm only two years younger than Jules here. Did Julien tell you where the bodies are buried around here?" Victor asked.

"If there are bodies buried on the property, I want to know every detail," Carly answered, ready to play their game.

"Nah, I'm just pulling a funny," Victor said. He looped his arm around Carly's and guided her back in the direction of the house. "Jules was right. I think we're all going to be fast friends in no time."

TWENTY-TWO
Julien

Carly surprised him.

Julien had done his homework and found several pictures online of what Carly looked like now, yet she was much more attractive in person. She had blossomed into a lovely, delicate-looking woman, who carried herself with an elegant confidence in the classroom, at least until he showed up, and the poor thing defaulted to the speech impediment she developed during her short stint with his family.

Pity.

But there had also been a murder on campus. He couldn't discount the possibility that Carly might have been affected by the tragedy.

He enjoyed her lecture, but his favorite part was when his stepsister kept her cool after the pretentious little prick insulted her.

Julien had no patience for pretentious little pricks.

Carly had crossed his mind through the years. He'd often wondered how she fared and if he'd destroyed her. Still, Julien believed for a very long time that Carly was better off without him popping into her life to check in.

But things had changed, and here he was.

After spending forty-five minutes listening to her lecture from the other side of the open auditorium door, Julien learned one obvious tell about his stepsister: Carly was still fixated on him. It was all too clear by the songs she selected for the writing assignment.

Carly had every right to hate him, but Julien did try to make things better for the girl, even after he single-handedly executed her downfall.

Julien rounded the corner to Carly's office and spotted the obnoxious student who had been rude to his stepsister a few paces ahead of him.

Oliver Leiken's walk was quick and deliberate, his clothes trendy and expensive and his hair a ridiculous pompadour that screamed for people to notice him. Julien pegged the younger man as being well-off but either neglected or browbeaten at home by an overbearing mother, so he craved attention elsewhere and delighted in belittling women due to his misogynistic tendencies.

"Oliver," Julien called out with authority in his voice that made him sound as if the two were already acquainted.

Oliver Leiken turned with a slight smile, but his face soured when he saw the stranger.

"You were in Carly Bennett's class," Julien said.

"That's right. It sucked as usual."

"There's something I need to tell you," Julien said. He stood still and stared intently at the student.

"Yeah? What's that?"

Julien leaned in and spoke in an even, matter-of-fact tone. "You're a pretentious little prick, and very bad things happen to pretentious little pricks."

Oliver's face went ashen, and he took a hasty step back.

"Sorry? I . . . Do I know you?" Oliver stammered.

"Yes, you are sorry. Very, very sorry. That's exactly what you're going to say to Miss Bennett. But first, you're going to tell me what you are."

"I don't understand," Oliver said. There was a tremor in his voice, and Julien wondered if the terribly rude boy was going to piss himself.

"You are a pretentious little prick. Now say it back to me."

"Please, I . . ."

"Say it," Julien insisted.

"I'm a pretentious little prick."

"Good. Yes, that's exactly right. Now off you go. Apologize to your teacher. I hope you've learned a lesson here. Have you learned a lesson?"

"Yes, I have, sir. I was an ass to Miss Bennett, and I swear, I'll never do it again."

Julien smiled pleasantly at Oliver, who ran back down the hallway as fast as he could.

TWENTY-THREE
Carly

The snapping jaws of her demise were closing in.

As she tried to make sense of Julien's sudden reappearance in her life, the familiar dark cloud grew in her lungs. She wheezed, and then succumbed to a coughing fit. She snatched her emergency inhaler from her briefcase, sucked in two large puffs, and fought for air.

She gripped her desk with both hands until the medicine kicked in and the boa constrictor in her chest released its vice grip.

Carly wiped a bead of sweat from her temple, picked up her briefcase, and put on her professional mask.

At least Julien hadn't been there to see it.

The door to the lecture hall flung open. Oliver raced down the aisle in her direction. He was pale and rubbed his hands together in a nervous, jerky motion.

"Miss Bennett, I'm sorry I was such a jerk to you," her student said in a rush. "I liked the songs you played, but I tried to embarrass you so everyone would think I was smart."

"Don't worry about it. You can choose any song you want for the assignment. Is everything all right?"

"I was a pretentious little prick. You didn't deserve that."

"Don't say that about yourself."

"It's true. I was a pretentious little prick, and I swear, I'll never do that to you again."

Before she could answer, Oliver bolted up the aisle and out of the classroom, leaving as quickly as he came.

Unable to postpone the inevitable, Carly headed down the corridor of the English department.

When she rounded the bend, there was Julien, waiting outside her office door.

She wanted to scream at the universe and ask what sort of horrible surprise it had waiting for her next, but kept shambling toward her stepbrother. Her underarms felt sticky, and a hot mess would be a merciful way to describe her deteriorating appearance.

But Julien looked cosmopolitan and cool, like he could be sipping champagne on a yacht. He was dressed in a well-tailored suit and his skin was tan. Besides a few slight lines by his eyes, Julien could still be seventeen.

Carly let them inside her new office and remained standing while Julien took a seat across from her desk.

"Why did you come here?" Carly snapped.

"I realize you're angry."

Carly felt for her inhaler in her pocket and tried to channel Ava. "Don't patronize me. You destroyed my life, but you still had the nerve to come into my classroom like nothing happened."

Julien nodded. Understanding.

"You've done well for yourself, so it's natural that you'd feel protective of your career. I'm not here to undermine your accomplishments. I'm grateful for the chance to talk."

"Get to the point, if there is one," Carly said. "If you're still here after your five minutes are up, I'm calling security."

"I heard about the murder at USC. I came to check on you and to tell you how sorry I am."

"I find that hard to believe. If you were so worried about what you did to me, why did you wait so long to show up?"

"I wanted to reach out before, but I was ashamed. I hurt you in ways I'll never understand, and my actions have always stayed with me. I've never been able to forgive myself for how I treated you. When I heard about the incident on campus, I was worried about you. I realized I couldn't postpone seeing you any longer."

Carly steepled her fingers against her temples.

"Your lies make my head hurt. I said you had five minutes, but I'm cutting it short."

"My father died. Christopher passed away last week after a long illness. I was by his side until the end. My father suffered until his very last breath."

Carly stopped herself from reaching for Julien's hand.

"I'm sorry to hear about Christopher."

"That's very generous, considering how my father treated you," Julien said. "It's important that I explain myself. When you and your mother moved in with us, I liked you both, I really did. But when it seemed like my father was paying more attention to you, I was angry that you were taking him away from me. I realize how petty that sounds now."

Julien lowered his head, eyes cast down and away from Carly.

"I can't tell you how many times I've practiced what I'd say if I got the courage to confront you, but now that I'm here, everything that's coming out of my mouth sounds lame."

"You're right. Lots of parents remarry, but their children don't usually set traps to destroy their new stepsiblings. What you did to me was horrible."

"My mother died a few years before Christopher married Em. Lauren, my mom, killed herself when I was thirteen. I was there. I saw her jump off the roof of our house. I was devastated. We were very close, and I blamed myself for her death. Christopher was always distant when Vic and I were growing up. My dad spent most of his time at his practice or the hospital, but after my mother died, Christopher became present in our lives for the first time. We started spending more time together. Can I tell you a family secret?"

"Save your secret for someone who cares."

Still hanging to the tough-girl Ava façade with all her life.

"Well deserved again. But humor me. As a clinician, I know now that my mother had mental health issues. If I were to diagnose her today, I'd say she was likely bipolar or possibly schizophrenic. But my father never forced her to get help. I think my father ignored the seriousness of my mother's condition because he would've been humiliated if our family secret got out. But after Lauren died, my father worried I might have inherited her condition. I think that's why he sent me to so many shrinks. Not Vic though. Vic was brilliant, even back then. Most people overlooked Vic's brilliance, though, because he was such a loud, obnoxious kid. I guess my father thought his second son was smart enough to help himself, unlike me."

"I don't feel sorry for you. I'm sorry for your mom and

whatever personal demons she had that made her take her life. You wrecked me when I was a kid. Did you ever tell anyone about what you did to me?"

Julien looked up at Carly, eyes sorrowful as though desperate for her forgiveness.

"I told my dad and Vic after a counseling session with my shrink. We were driving back from Santa Monica. Victor was so pissed, he started pounding on the back of my seat. At one point, he screamed for my dad to stop the car. I still remember seeing Victor, running down the sidewalk, with both hands raised, giving me the finger. After that, he spent most of his time at his friend's house. He never forgave me."

"Your time is up. I'm not a fan of bullies who paint themselves as victims," Carly said.

"I understand." Julien rose but turned to address her one last time. "Before your mother died, she planned to bring you home. Em felt horrible about sending you away. She was going to fly to San Francisco to surprise you. After you left, Em always told me how much she missed you. She never stopped loving you."

"If you're lying, I s–s–swear, I'll make you regret it," Carly stuttered, unnerved yet elated over the possible revelation.

If Julien were telling the truth.

"I promise, that's exactly what happened. There's more I can tell you about your mom, but that's up to you. If you want to talk, give me a call. You might not believe it, but I'm not the same person."

"Do you still talk to Victor?" Carly asked.

"I wish. Like you, he's made a successful life for himself. He's a director at Paramount."

Julien pressed his business card into Carly's hand and left her office.

Carly leaned on the door and watched his retreat. When he exited the English building, Carly closed the door and snapped the lock in place.

Her fingers trembled as she studied the business card.

"Julien White, PhD, Clinical Psychiatrist and Expert on Human Behavior."

Those poor souls under her stepbrother's care.

TWENTY-FOUR
Carly

After Julien's Hiroshima bomb-drop in her life, Carly called Paramount Pictures and spoke to a receptionist. Carly listened to ten minutes of canned hold music until the receptionist returned and told her that Victor cleared his schedule for her and would be available to see Carly that afternoon.

Now inside the Hollywood studio's lobby, Carly killed time by googling her former stepbrother's professional ascent. She decided on an *LA Times* story from the previous year and clicked on the link.

From Riches to Rags and Back: Victor White Bleeds his Pain onto the Screen

Sure, she'd been curious about what happened to her stepbrothers, but out of self-preservation from snake-bite memories, Carly never crept around the corners of the Internet or her socials to find out how Victor fared.

A set of glass doors parted and a young male in a designer suit greeted her.

"Miss Bennett, please follow me. Mr. White is ready to see you."

After a five-minute walk, Carly was ushered into a large warehouse outside of the main studio that looked big enough to house a small fleet of commercial airplanes.

When her guide left, and still without Victor in sight, she did a quick scan of the array of items stored in the warehouse: a stuffed polar bear frozen on its haunches; a suite of video arcade games; a Mardi Gras float; a sleek, jet-black BMW; and rows of other items that lined the space.

Carly made her way to what appeared to be a rack of vintage guns, when a voice from long ago called out.

"Carly Bennett . . . You . . . are . . . perfect."

She did a quick pivot.

There was Victor, tall and still stocky, but thick muscle now replaced his once prepubescent baby fat. He wore a mustache and scruffy brown beard and was dressed in blue jeans and a denim shirt.

Carly's nerves eased.

Victor was beaming at her.

"Welcome to my playground. Unlike actors, props don't give you attitude," Victor said. "But before the tour, I'm going to hug you whether you like it or not."

Victor wrapped Carly in a tight bear hug.

Carly held her hands at her sides, stiff and wooden like a child's toy soldier. But Victor's embrace melted her awkwardness, and Carly hugged him back.

So much wasted time. She regretted the missed years between them.

Victor stepped back and gave Carly an appreciative once-over.

"Damn, Carly Bennett. You're a straight-up stunner. When my secretary told me you called, I was on set, but I kicked filming to my assistant director because there was nowhere else that I'd rather be. Tell me about yourself in under two minutes. And only the good stuff. I'll dig around with other questions as needed."

"I'm not good under pressure, but I'll try. I'm an English professor at USC. That sounds anticlimactic now that I said it. Let's start with that while I scramble to fill in the blanks."

"There's nothing wrong with being scripted. You were always bookish, so an English professor is the perfect career land for you."

"What about you, Mr. Hollywood?"

"You make me blush but keep it coming. Here's my, 'What have you been doing for the past fifteen years' highlights reel. My childhood dream of becoming an actor tanked. I wasn't leading-man handsome enough, and I never wanted to be a character actor. No bit parts for me. I went to UCLA for film school, landed a few lucky breaks, and now I get to be the boss with the vision. I'd love to produce one day, but that takes cash. I've been making mostly moody art films about dysfunctional families, but who wants to keep reliving a lousy childhood? Enough about me. Tell me more about yourself."

Carly reached into her vanilla playbook of speaking points about her life.

"I did OK, all things considered. I made a great friend at Chatham, and her family took me in. I went to college and grad school and then landed a job at USC. I'm still working my way up the ladder, but I found my calling. I love being a teacher."

"USC is a big deal and to make professor at such a young age. You were always the humble one and never the braggart, like old Jules," Victor said. "Now where are my manners? I haven't even given you a tour yet."

Victor took Carly's hand and led her to the BMW on the other side of the warehouse. With palms flat, he hoisted himself onto the hood, then patted the empty space next to him for Carly, who followed suit.

"I told you this place is my playground. It's our prop warehouse. Do you know that you're sitting on a car that was featured in last year's number one action flick at the box office?"

"I feel unworthy," Carly answered, with a laugh.

Victor reached for Carly's hand again, and this time, he didn't let go.

"Can we be real with each other? I love the polite catch-up, but let's get to the core of it. I always felt like crap about what Julien did to you when we were kids. I never expected you to write me back when you were at Chatham, but I hoped that you would. When I never heard back from you, I figured you decided the Whites were a poisoned package deal."

"What are you talking about? I never got any letters from you when I was at school."

"Then I was sabotaged. I wrote to you every week during that first year. And I took the train once to San Francisco to surprise you. It was right before Thanksgiving during your first year at school. I thought you were sore at me when you didn't write back, so I figured, I'd pop in out of the blue, since you were too nice of a kid to tell me to beat it in person. But some spinster chick in the front office said you'd gone home with a friend for the break. I left, feeling a little less glum, because I thought you'd moved on. I was happy for you."

Carly fought back tears. She hadn't been left to rot at Chatham without a single care.

"No one ever told me about your visit."

"I didn't tell the lady my name, only that I was a relative from LA, because I didn't want to make it weird for you. As for the letters, Chris probably had the housekeeper confiscate them from the mailbox. Julien and I were forbidden to ever contact you, but who needs rules? Chris's first excuse was that we had to give you space, so you could acclimate to your new school. Then, when Em died, Chris and his asshole lawyer thought it was best that we cut you free to reduce the family's liability."

"Liability of what?"

"That I don't know. I do remember that right after Em died, Julien went downtown with Chris for some big meet-and-greet with Chris's lawyer, Lawrence. I wasn't invited."

"You found out that Julien set me up."

Victor sighed and squeezed her hand tighter.

"I found out what that creep did to you. I'm trying to sound like a bigshot here, so let me start again. I'd love to tell you that I Nancy Drewed it and uncovered my brother's assholery. But I only found out because Julien told me. About a month after you left, Jules had an outdoor therapy session with his shrink, Dr. Whittaker I think his name was. I picked up Julien and when we were walking to Chris's car, Julien was all emotional, like Mr. Cool had lost his cool, and he was trembling. On the ride home, Jules blurted out his confessional in the front seat of Chris's Mercedes. I remember being so pissed, I wanted to reach over the seat and strangle him. Funny thing about it though, Chris didn't say a goddamn thing."

"Julien showed up in my classroom today. I haven't seen him in fifteen years," Carly said.

"What did Julien want?"

"He told me your dad died. I'm sorry."

"Mr. White, I'm not sure if Mr. Nowak was expecting you, but of course, he'll make an exception. I'll even work you in myself, no problem. I'm so sorry to hear about your father," the receptionist said.

"Thank you, but please call me Julien. I'm at an unfair disadvantage. You know my name, but I don't know yours."

"Anthony DiMatteo."

"I wasn't expecting an Italian surname from a fair-haired person."

"My family is originally from Sicily. There's a good amount of blond, blue-eyed people from that region. My grandparents are from a tiny town called Gela."

"I've been to Italy many times, but never Sicily. Have you been?"

Anthony's face reddened, as if he were embarrassed over his lack of worldliness and travel. "No, but I'd like to go there."

"Since I haven't gone to Sicily either, we'll have to visit there one day."

Julien dropped the comment for Anthony to wonder about his intention. Was it polite chitchat or had Julien extended an invitation to go to Europe with him?

Anthony's eyes shone. "You shouldn't make promises you don't intend to keep," he teased.

"I never do."

Lawrence came out of his office, pumped Julien's hand, and then patted him on the back.

Lawrence was in his mid-sixties with silver hair and the same Harvard class ring he'd worn since Julien first met him.

"What brings you here, my boy?" Lawrence asked.

"I had a bit of an issue come up. You're the only person who can help me."

Lawrence ushered Julien into his office and gestured him to sit. Julien took a spot in a brown leather chair across from Lawrence's giant mahogany desk while the lawyer went to his bar and poured a shot of scotch each into two crystal tumblers.

"Glenlivet. It used to be your father's favorite."

"It's only four in the afternoon but, considering the circumstance, I'll join you." Julien put the glass to his lips and pretended to take a drink.

"Do you have an issue with a patient again?"

"No, my visit is about a personal matter. Do you remember Carly, the daughter of my father's second wife, Emily?"

"Vaguely. Christopher cut her off when Emily died, as I recall, which I think was a smart move."

"About that, I went to see her today. I'd like to make up for something I did to her a long time ago. But I need some information first."

Lawrence sat back in his chair and sighed.

Fifteen minutes later, Julien left the office empty-handed. He passed by the reception desk, but when he didn't see Anthony, he left his business card for him and headed back down in the birdcage elevator to the street.

When Julien reached his car, he decided Lawrence was still a first-rate prick. If Julien hadn't intervened as a boy, the first-rate prick would've gladly finished off what Julien hadn't had the heart to do himself. Julien liked Carly too much to go for the kill.

"That's true about Chris," Victor answered. "Believe me, I felt bad when I heard the news from his lawyer, but Chris and I had been estranged for a long time. Do you believe people can snap, I mean good people who seemed otherwise normal, but something triggers them, or maybe it's a whole bunch of somethings that build up over the years, and then they lose it?"

"I think stress can make people act in ways that are outside of norm," Carly answered.

Victor's face broke into a wide grin, and he patted Carly on the knee.

"It's just like you to give a classy response. I asked because that's what happened to me. It was at my UCLA film school graduation party. Chris threw a big hoopla at his Malibu house, only because he thought it would make him look good. I was sitting by the pool, drink in hand and my feet in the water, and I looked around at everyone who was there. And you know what? Besides Julien and my buddy Bodie from high school, all the guests were Chris's friends and colleagues from work. He wasn't even pretending that he threw the party for me. I started to fixate on what happened to you and Em, and all the stuff he put me through as a kid. I snapped."

"What did you do?" Carly asked.

"I went blind with rage, so I don't remember everything, but Jules told me later that I tackled Chris from behind and threw him into the pool. Chris acted like it was a joke to save face, but the party was over after that, and so was our relationship. Chris cut me off, and when he died, he didn't leave me a penny."

Better off that way. Carly kept her thoughts to herself so as not to disrespect the dead.

"I'm sorry. But you should be proud of all you've accomplished. I read the story about you in the *LA Times*."

"You didn't come here to listen to my sob stories, and I don't want this to be all about me. I'm guessing you wanted to reconnect because of Julien crashing your class, and I was a safe entry point."

"I should've contacted you sooner."

"Ditto."

"When I didn't hear from you when I was at Chatham, I figured you didn't want anything to do with me. I always liked you. I wanted to reach out before, but I was afraid that you'd reject me again."

"We both were stupid, but now, here we are, and I couldn't be happier. What else did Julien tell you?"

"He said your dad's death hit him hard and made him do some soul-searching. Julien claimed he wants to make up for what he did to me."

Victor laughed a big belly laugh that echoed in the giant space.

"Do you believe him? I'm asking as one of Julien's cautionary tales," Victor said.

"I don't trust him, but Julien said he has information about my mom. He said she was going to bring me home and regretted her decision to send me away, but she never got the chance."

"I'm sorry about Em, and I liked her, although I never felt like she took to me. She always gravitated toward Julien, but who wouldn't? He of the good looks and movie-star charm. If he'd only been brilliant too, he'd be dangerous. I wish I could fill in the blanks for you, but after you got shoved off to boarding school, and Julien pissed out his confessional in the front seat of Chris's car, I wanted nothing to do with them anymore. I moved into the pool house of my buddy's family for the rest of high school. Chris didn't care, and Em was mucking it up with her new country club friends before she was killed. Sorry, that sounded cold about your mom, but all of it is the truth."

"Julien said you two had a falling-out."

Victor snorted and then launched off the hood of the car.

"Is that what he said? Typical Julien, making it sound like it was some mutual dustup. Tell you what, I'm hoping this isn't a one-and-done between us. Let's hold off on more dark tales of the Whites until I see you next," Victor said. "How about we take a minute from the heavy conversation, and I can give you a proper tour?"

Before she could answer, Victor was heading to the gun rack where he pulled a Winchester rifle from its mount.

"I saw you looking at the prop guns when I came in. Do you shoot?" he asked. "Don't worry, these guns are toys and are as harmless as Halloween costume chotchke. They look real enough but do no harm. This one is a personal favorite."

After securing the Winchester back in its place, Victor opened a bottom drawer in the rack and pointed to a small, silver revolver.

"Go on, it won't bite, that is, if you want to pretend that you're a righteous CIA agent kicking butt against the bad guys."

"How can I say no to that?"

An odd thrill moved through Carly when she removed the gun from the drawer and held it at her side.

"If you're going to play a part, you've got to be believable. Hand on the trigger and get in a wide, confident stance," Victor directed.

He stood behind Carly, raised her hands in front of her and kept his arms clasped around hers.

"I knew it. You're a natural," Victor said.

The excitement of holding the prop gun now gone, Carly placed the revolver back in the case.

"Now that we're done playing Hollywood, I guess we should get back to more serious topics. What did people tell you about Em's death?" Victor asked.

"I only heard the highlights, that she was killed in a home invasion. Were you home when it happened?"

"I was at my buddy Bodie's house, Chris was at work, and Jules was on a school trip. The cops were tripping all over themselves, trying to get us to alibi up before they cleared us. But they did. Can I tell you something I've never told anyone else before?" Victor asked.

"Of course."

"I always felt like if I'd been home more, I would've been able to save your mom."

"I have my own regrets."

"One thing I know for sure, Carly Bennett, I'll be here for you from here on out. Cross my heart, and I swear this time, my promise will last forever."

TWENTY-FIVE
Julien

Julien took the elevator to the twelfth floor and the office of his lawyer, Lawrence Nowak of Nowak, Miller and Hawkin, one of LA's most highly respected law firms, and considered his recent meet-up with his stepsister.

He looked vacantly at the ascending numbers as the elevator rose, pleased Carly was angry with him. Julien had wondered if she'd be weak, and at first, he assumed that was the case.

Bravo, Carly. He liked how she turned out. His stepsister was smart and attractive in a natural way, unlike the women who walked through the streets of LA like they were the cat's ass, when they were nothing but phonies.

Julien appreciated the original character of things, including the office building's vintage glass and steel birdcage elevator that hadn't changed since he was a boy. Julien estimated he rode the classic-style elevator up and down hundreds of times during trips to the city when Christopher met his lawyer and allowed Julien to tag along.

The last time he joined his father was when he stopped the idiot lawyer from ruining what was left of Carly's life.

The elevator chimed its arrival on the twelfth floor that was dedicated entirely to Nowak, Miller and Hawkin's bustling practice.

Julien exited and headed to the reception desk, where a blond man wearing a pair of trendy round glasses greeted him. The secretary was good looking in a preppy, blue-eyed, All-American kind of way. Julien, who was thirty-three, pegged the younger man as being in his late twenties and gay. Lawrence, who Julien suspected was still closeted about the true nature of his sexuality, likely hired the male receptionist because he was attracted to him. Perhaps the two were having an affair.

"Mr. White, I'm not sure if Mr. Nowak was expecting you, but of course, he'll make an exception. I'll even work you in myself, no problem. I'm so sorry to hear about your father," the receptionist said.

"Thank you, but please call me Julien. I'm at an unfair disadvantage. You know my name, but I don't know yours."

"Anthony DiMatteo."

"I wasn't expecting an Italian surname from a fair-haired person."

"My family is originally from Sicily. There's a good amount of blond, blue-eyed people from that region. My grandparents are from a tiny town called Gela."

"I've been to Italy many times, but never Sicily. Have you been?"

Anthony's face reddened, as if he were embarrassed over his lack of worldliness and travel. "No, but I'd like to go there."

"Since I haven't gone to Sicily either, we'll have to visit there one day."

Julien dropped the comment for Anthony to wonder about his intention. Was it polite chitchat or had Julien extended an invitation to go to Europe with him?

Anthony's eyes shone. "You shouldn't make promises you don't intend to keep," he teased.

"I never do."

Lawrence came out of his office, pumped Julien's hand, and then patted him on the back.

Lawrence was in his mid-sixties with silver hair and the same Harvard class ring he'd worn since Julien first met him.

"What brings you here, my boy?" Lawrence asked.

"I had a bit of an issue come up. You're the only person who can help me."

Lawrence ushered Julien into his office and gestured him to sit. Julien took a spot in a brown leather chair across from Lawrence's giant mahogany desk while the lawyer went to his bar and poured a shot of scotch each into two crystal tumblers.

"Glenlivet. It used to be your father's favorite."

"It's only four in the afternoon but, considering the circumstance, I'll join you." Julien put the glass to his lips and pretended to take a drink.

"Do you have an issue with a patient again?"

"No, my visit is about a personal matter. Do you remember Carly, the daughter of my father's second wife, Emily?"

"Vaguely. Christopher cut her off when Emily died, as I recall, which I think was a smart move."

"About that, I went to see her today. I'd like to make up for something I did to her a long time ago. But I need some information first."

Lawrence sat back in his chair and sighed.

Fifteen minutes later, Julien left the office empty-handed. He passed by the reception desk, but when he didn't see Anthony, he left his business card for him and headed back down in the birdcage elevator to the street.

When Julien reached his car, he decided Lawrence was still a first-rate prick. If Julien hadn't intervened as a boy, the first-rate prick would've gladly finished off what Julien hadn't had the heart to do himself. Julien liked Carly too much to go for the kill.

TWENTY-SIX
Julien

March 2010, the Office of Nowak, Miller, and Hawkin, Los Angeles

Seventeen-year-old Julien heard the two adult men blathering on about money, but he blocked out the noise, fixated on the horrible way Emily died.

Smothering was the cruelest, most awful way a person could be killed, especially in Emily's case. One minute, she was at her most vulnerable, sleeping in her bed. Then she awoke, with a pillow pressed against her face. Julien considered how Emily felt in those last few minutes of her life, claustrophobic, panicked, weak and desperate to breathe.

Since there was no bruising on her neck . . . in addition to the fact the authorities found a pillow on the floor next to her bed . . . it was a slam dunk for the police to decide his stepmother had been smothered to death with a king-sized, white goose-down pillow. The front door of the Whites' estate had been bashed in, and jewelry and computers were lifted from the house, leading police to believe the initial motive was robbery, and Emily became a casualty when the intruder, who likely thought the house was empty, discovered her sleeping in bed and had to dispose of the potential witness.

Poor Emily. If only she hadn't met his father and stayed in the Valley working her humdrum job as a bank teller, she'd still be alive. Julien looked out the window of the twelfth-floor office of Nowak, Miller and Hawkin.

Julien pursed his lips and figured the tragedy would topple what was left of Carly. Julien had lost his own mother when he was thirteen, but Carly was different. She didn't seem to have any fight in her, so the news about her mother could be her undoing.

Daddy Doctor Christopher was always working, so Lauren was the only constant presence in his early childhood.

When Christopher announced he wanted a divorce, Julien witnessed his mother's moods tailspin.

On the day after his thirteenth birthday, Julien got home from school, snuck a beer from his father's office and then dove into the pool in the backyard. He came out and cupped a hand over his eyes when he saw his mother, barefoot and teetering on the edge of the roof with her arms spread wide at her sides, as if she could fly. The only saving grace was that Victor was inside the house at the time, watching some boring old black-and-white movie.

In his last memory of her, Lauren looked down at her child and then jumped headfirst to her death.

Instead of running to her side, Julien told the housekeeper what happened, went to his room, and locked the door behind him.

He stayed there until his father came home. Christopher remained by his side after the funeral and even cut down his hours at his practice to be sure Julien was OK. Poor little Vic chased after Christopher, trying to get his attention after Lauren's death, but the patriarch only had it in him to focus on the son he thought needed help.

And that only lasted a cool minute.

The conversation between Christopher and his attorney debating the family's financial and ethical responsibility to Carly continued around him. Julien wished he could be the shot caller, since the adults in the room couldn't seem to make a decision to save their lives.

"I feel some sense of responsibility to take care of Emily's child," Christopher said to his lawyer, Lawrence.

Julien studied the older man's face. It was impossible to peg his age since Lawrence had some work done. Lawrence's skin was smooth but deeply tanned, and he wore an expensive dark suit and a pair of square glasses.

"The 'child' has a name. It's Carly," Julien answered.

"To be clear," Lawrence said, and leafed through a stack of papers on his desk, "does Emily's child . . . Carly . . . have any idea about your net worth?"

"I hate this. Do we have to decide right now? I lost my wife, for Christ's sake."

"I realize the timing isn't ideal, but this is critical. You need to wise up, protect your assets and consider whether the daughter will sue your estate. Carly could file a wrongful death suit because her mother died in your house. Thinking ahead, she could claim negligence on your part for sending her away. Any two-bit lawyer she hired could argue Carly might've been able to save her mother if she hadn't been removed from the family home. How old is Emily's kid?"

"Almost thirteen," Julien said.

"Is there any chance Carly killed her mother? Maybe she wanted revenge for getting banished from the family," Lawrence said. "I'm not a criminal attorney, but you have a lot at stake here, and that could be an option to consider. I know the chief of police. Give me the word, and I'll reach out to him. Usually, cops will lock onto a single suspect or theory, and since there were a few burglaries in your neighborhood before Emily died, they'll stick with that story. If the girl isn't stable, it would be easy to pin the death on her. Not a bad idea if you think she'd make trouble for you later. Or maybe Carly did it. Plenty of children murder their parents."

"What the hell are you suggesting? Framing a kid whose mom just died? That's downright evil, even for you," Julien said.

"Mind your language, but Lawrence could have a point," Christopher said.

The elder Mr. White leaned back in his chair and sipped his scotch.

"Carly was at school in San Francisco when Emily was killed," Julien said. "There's no way Carly would've slipped out. Plus, we're talking Emily's kid here. Carly made stuff up to get attention, but I don't think for a second that she'd have the skills to sneak out of school and find a way to Malibu. Let alone kill her mother. Both of you are first-rate jerks for suggesting it."

"Easy there," the lawyer said in a soothing tone. "Carly is a troubled child?"

Christopher shot Julien a look and continued. "She has behavioral issues to the point we felt it was best to remove her from the family home. It was ultimately Emily's choice. Granted, Carly went to one of the best boarding schools in the country."

"We could go at this in a few different ways," Lawrence said. "You could give Carly a lump sum with the condition she is under no circumstance to contact the family. This scenario could pose an issue. I've handled enough of these cases where once the gravy train dries up, she could show up again, asking for more. My suggestion is to pay for her schooling and other living expenses until she graduates, and then cut the cord. You said she's a troubled child."

"She wasn't invited to the funeral either, since you thought that would open up a can of worms too," Christopher said. "I'm still sick about that."

"I made the call because you couldn't."

"What do you think I should do, Julien?" Christopher asked.

Julien enjoyed the puzzled look the attorney gave his father, as if Lawrence didn't understand why Christopher was deferring to his son.

"Number one, don't tangle up Carly with what happened to her mother. Keep her at school, and then pay her bills until she graduates from college, if she goes that far. It would be better for all parties involved, including Carly, for her to no longer have contact with us," Julien said.

"Does Carly have other blood relatives we need to worry about?" Lawrence asked.

"Only a father who walked out when she was four," Christopher said. "Julien is right. I'll provide for Carly until she graduates from college."

"You and Emily were married less than a year, Chris. You don't owe the girl anything, but if that's the way you want to go, it's a generous financial compensation. I'll get the paperwork in play."

Relieved the messy business was over, Julien moved to the

window. He could see the attorney checking him out in the reflection of a large mirror that hung on the wall next to Lawrence's framed diplomas. Julien recognized the look. It wasn't appreciative or curious, but purely carnal. He turned to face the man, but Lawrence's game face was back on, and the respected lawyer smiled paternally at Julien.

He wasn't disgusted over the lawyer's lust for him. On the contrary, it made Julien feel powerful. The prospect of a sexual encounter with the older man repulsed him, but Lawrence's desire shifted something in his favor, and Julien liked that very much.

"You'd be a good lawyer. What are your plans after you graduate?" Lawrence asked.

"No offense, but I find law boring. I'm more interested in studying people."

"I'm sure you'd be good at that," Lawrence said. "Very good, indeed."

TWENTY-SEVEN
Carly

The wine was still there, tucked behind a box of Christmas ornaments.

When she got home from school following Julien's surprise appearance, Carly went straight to her garage and found the bottles, each with a cheery greeting written in festive gold or silver marker.

Merry Christmas, Miss Bennett!

Happy New Year, Carly!

To Our Most Promising New Professor. Cheers!

Thanks for Being a Great Neighbor!

The smooth curves of the Pinot Noir bottle she selected felt comforting in her hand. Carly didn't have a problem with alcohol, but it often did the trick if she was battling insecurities. Her first taste of liquor was when she was four. That was also one of the few memories she had left of her dad, Michael Bennett, an aspiring writer from England. She was sitting on the grass next to her father's chair in the backyard of their house, while Michael finished off the last of a cold six-pack of Newcastle Brown Ale that he pulled, one by one, from a Styrofoam cooler filled with ice.

Carly had finished eating her orange Popsicle and was fussing for another when her father offered an alternative.

"It's too hot and I'm too tired to get out of this chair to get you another sweet," her father said. "Try a little sip of this instead, love. It'll cool you down."

Carly could still feel the cool metal of the can against her fingers and the effervescent burst of liquid in her mouth when she took her first sip.

Her father had no idea Emily, who had returned home from

work, was watching the entire scene unfold from the kitchen window.

Carly recalled her mother snatching her up, the can of beer falling onto the grass, and how the golden liquid bubbled as it emptied, and the realization that she detested the taste of whatever it was that made her mother so upset.

She tucked the red wine under her shirt and returned to her house, where she poured herself a glass of the Pinot Noir and perseverated over Julien.

Why hadn't she told him to go to hell and called security to escort him off campus?

She picked at a stray cuticle on her thumbnail until her skin bled.

A few hours earlier, Carly Elizabeth Bennett had become the poster child for the polite and spineless; so much so, she had invited her childhood bully . . . no that was way too generous of a word . . . her childhood *monster* to join her in her office for a few minutes of polite catch-up.

And then she devolved into a stuttering, blubbery mess.

At least seeing Victor had made her feel better.

A loud growl from her stomach startled her. Carly worried her stomach pains from the previous night had returned, but then remembered the last thing she'd eaten was a bowl of cereal that morning, and it was now nine p.m.

Carly scoured her refrigerator, well stocked thanks to Rebecca, and picked at a salad from Whole Foods, followed by a bite of a Dove bar from her freezer. When she still wasn't satisfied, Carly pulled from her pantry a bag of pretzels and a container of "Sleepy Time Iced Cookies," with a curled-up sleeping tabby cat on the label. She ate one of the cookies that had a pungent taste, like a mix of strong lavender and licorice, and refilled her wine glass.

The image of Ed Russo—plastic bag tied around his face, and bulging eyes that seemed to stare at her in death pose—flooded back.

Carly gasped anew over the memory of finding the body, and downed the wine before she made a call.

"Carls?" Ava answered.

"He came back. That asshole came storming into my classroom and then he tried to apologize."

"What asshole are we talking about?" Ava asked.

"Julien. He showed up out of the blue with a sob story about how his father died and he had a 'Come to Jesus' moment that made him realize how terrible he was for ruining my life when I was a kid."

"Julien, your stepbrother? I hope you punched him in the face. Tell me you at least slapped him. There's got to be some violence in this story after what he did to you. Please don't tell me you talked to him."

"I did, but only for a few minutes, and I threatened to call campus police if he didn't leave. I went to see Victor after. Major mic drop, I know, but do you know what I realized? Victor is one of the greatest people in the world, excluding you. Wait, I didn't say that right. What I meant to say is that you are the . . ."

Carly tried to continue but her thought pattern short-circuited. The words she meant to say to finish her sentence were now out of reach.

After thirty seconds of dead air, Ava filled the void. "What's going on with you? None of this is even a speck OK. You don't sound right either. I'm coming over," Ava insisted.

"I'm fine. It was a tough day, and I had a couple glasses of wine to help me relax, so if I sound a little sloppy, that's why. I'm exhausted and have an early class in the morning, so let's meet up tomorrow."

"I'm not thrilled about any of this. If you change your mind, I'll be there in a second. But sober up for a minute, Sunshine. Have the cops contacted you again about Russo?"

"No, and it's been three days, so maybe they've locked in on another suspect."

"That's a nice thought but get real and get some sleep. We'll talk in the morning."

Carly ended the call and nearly tripped over the bag of pretzels she'd been inhaling earlier which had spilled across the floor. She'd clean up her mess in the morning.

She leaned on the wall to steady herself as she made an uneven trek toward her bedroom.

What a lightweight. Who gets blitzed after a glass of wine? OK, two and maybe a few extra sips, but still, it's not like she'd guzzled back a bottle of tequila.

Her thoughts turned to a fuzzy jumble again, but Carly made it to her bedroom and stripped off her clothes. Standing naked in front of her full-length mirror, Carly considered the lean slender curves of her body, and giggled over the thought that she was nearly as flat chested as a boy. She pulled on a T-shirt and pair of underwear and stumbled backward into bed.

It was less than a minute after her head hit the pillow that she fell asleep.

A familiar lyric resurrected from some part of her past hummed like an alarm in her head, telling Carly it was going to be a fantastic day, and she better get up right that very second or she'd miss the whole party.

She wondered why she fell asleep on the floor and looked at the clock on the nightstand that glowed a brilliant red. How had she never once noticed how beautiful the clock was? The time was twelve a.m., so it was still the middle of the night, but if she wasted her time sleeping her life away, she'd miss out on experiencing it.

Carly stripped off her T-shirt and panties until she was completely naked and felt freer than she ever had before.

"*Candy, yeah, yeah, yeah,*" she sang. Try as she might, she couldn't remember the exact lyrics. What she could recall in beautiful detail was an image of her mother playing the old song by the guy with the funny name when they lived together in the ranch house.

Bigsby. Pigsby. Pop Sugar. The exact name of the singer was on the tip of her tongue, but the silly ones she came up with instead made her laugh out loud.

A faded copy of the latest issue of *LA Weekly* lay on her dresser and Carly snatched it up. The words on the pages swam as she tried to read them. But she could see the glorious colors of the advertisements. A picture of a DJ spinning against the backdrop of electric blue lights caught her eye. She squinted at the print and saw in large cursive letters, "*Blue is the Color of Cool. Moonshadows: Ranked Top Ten Beach Bar in the World!*"

It was a sign from the universe, it had to be. Carly stumbled to her closet and found what she came for, a black sheer top with the tags still on.

The infectious song kept playing on repeat in her head, and Carly jumped up and down to the beat as she slipped on a pair of jeans and the see-through top and then finished the look with a fiery red matte lipstick.

Her heart felt like it was beating in perfect time to the music, and she grabbed her phone.

She called Rebecca, thinking it was a perfect idea, two young, single girls on the town, but then as she watched her assistant's number come up on the screen, she couldn't remember why she was calling and hung up. She then noticed her latest new contact and hit the call button.

"Victor! I'm Ubering to Moonshadows in Malibu in a minute. So, let me ask you, Mr. Bigtime Hollywood director, are you man or mouse? Join me if you dare."

Not wanting to waste another second, Carly ended the message and ordered an Uber. She then ran outside where she sat down on the curb, her feet beating a fast rhythm while she waited.

Carly reached inside her shirt and cupped her small braless breast underneath the ultra-sheer fabric.

She couldn't remember the last time she got laid. Maybe a year ago? Her potential hookup with Sebastian died on the stinking vine after their terrible date ended with him either ghosting her or disappearing off the grid for reasons still unknown. A fuzzy image popped in her head of a visiting professor from the Sorbonne who was completely naked and sprawled across her bed. It was as though she were studying herself from afar, and Carly was amazed how unabashed she was during intercourse with the near stranger who picked her up at a faculty mixer after she'd downed three vodka martinis to help her relax around the older, tenured teachers.

Carly could see herself, plain as day, without a stitch of clothing, writhing on top of the hairy-chested Frenchman.

She wanted to be that confident girl again.

A pair of headlights cut through the dark as a car turned down her street.

Carly could see the glowing Uber LED light illuminated on the window of the approaching SUV, and she ran into the middle of the street and waved her arms.

The driver side window of the vehicle opened to reveal a middle-aged, balding white male.

"You're going to Moonshadows?" the driver asked. He was staring at her face, but did a quick, discreet sweep of her bare breasts, and then reached for a gold cross medallion that hung on a chain from his neck before he averted his eyes.

"Yes, and as fast as possible," Carly said when the name of the singer she had been trying to remember shone bright in her memory. "Iggy Pop! That's it."

"Excuse me?" the driver asked.

"He sang the song 'Candy.' My mom used to play it when I was a kid. But she's dead now."

"Are you OK, miss?"

"Absolutely. I'm having a great day, and it's just starting," Carly said and got into the backseat.

Moonshadows Bar was a popular Malibu venue perched along the beach that attracted the well-heeled and beautiful locals, tourists wanting to claim their authentic Southern California experience, and other locally deemed non-desirables who hailed from the Valley.

One a.m. and the club was filled to capacity. Carly pushed her way through the crowd and toward a single empty seat at the bar, all the while feeling like a million eyes were upon her, including a table of women about her age who whispered to themselves when she passed.

Jealous crows, searching for scraps on the ground because they weren't glorious enough to fly. She shot them a dirty look, claimed the vacant seat, and motioned the bartender over.

"What would you like?" he asked.

"Stoli, straight up. Hold on, I don't know how I'm going to

pay you. Somebody must've stolen my bag. I had it a minute ago."

"Your bag is on the floor, honey."

Carly turned to see a tall, lanky man with two tattoo sleeves that covered both his arms, from shoulder to wrist, in the seat next to her.

"I like your shirt. How about I buy this round?"

The bartender rolled his eyes at Carly and poured the newly acquainted couple two shots.

"What's your name, honey? I'm Jim. You're a party girl, aren't you?"

Carly put her hands on Jim's shoulders and pushed her hips into his.

"My name is Vivienne," Carly said and laughed as she pictured the prim Vivienne Lady figurine her mother had given her.

Carly grabbed the back of Jim's neck and kissed him aggressively, parting his lips with her tongue and tasting a bitter mash of scotch and nicotine from his now open mouth.

"I was right. You do like to party," Jim said. "You don't live around here, I bet."

Carly shot a glance at the table of women from earlier who all seemed to be judging her with a collective expression of disgust, like she was a freak show crashing their sorority party.

"Why do you say that? You don't think I'm good enough?"

"No, you seem different in a good way is all. Most of the women who come here are fake, pure silicone inside and out."

"What's your name again?" Carly asked.

"I'm Jim. You are a very sexy girl, Vivienne."

"That's right. You're Jim and I'm Vivienne. I like your name. Big Jim. That's what I'm going to call you. Big Jim with big hands." Carly ran her fingers over the spider tattoo that ran across Jim's knuckles. "Do you have other big things too?"

"You know I do."

"Then you better show me. Let's get out of here, too many people are looking at us," Carly said, and this time, gave a friendly wave to the table of women staring at her.

"Do you want to go back to my place?"

"No. Let's take our party outside," Carly said. "Be a good boy and scope out the alleyway for us."

Carly beckoned the bartender over.

"One more round for my friend for the road," Carly said.

"I can't serve you anymore," the bartender said. "You're cut off."

"Screw you then," Carly argued, but her voice got swept away in the din of loud music and the chorus of hundreds of conversations going on around her.

She grabbed her bag and headed to the bathroom while Jim disappeared out the back door to check the alley.

Once inside, a sharp pain sliced through Carly's stomach. She ran inside a stall and when she was done getting sick, Carly lay on the sticky floor and closed her eyes until the spinning stopped and she fell asleep.

Carly's first conscious thought was someone needed to turn down the music.

The next was why her elderly neighbors would be playing rap in the first place, let alone at full decibel.

Her head felt heavy, like it was stuffed with wet cotton. She forced her eyes to focus. She was in a dimly lit public bathroom bathed in a muddy hue of purple.

This was just a crazy dream. It had to be.

A reflection of a trampy woman looked back at her from a mirror above the sink. The woman's hair was loose and wild around her face, and a smear of red lipstick ran down the corner of her mouth. It was the woman's shirt, a black, sheer top worn without a bra that disgusted her the most. Carly stared at the see-through fabric and then did a slow crawl back to the face.

She was the girl in the mirror.

"Oh my God, oh my God, oh my God!" Carly shrieked.

She scanned the room. Her purse lay on the floor next to her. She dove her hand inside and found her wallet, a tube of red lipstick, no car keys, but her cell phone was inside, including a text message from Uber two hours earlier confirming her driver was on the way to her house to take her to Moonshadows bar in Malibu.

Carly wiped away the smear of lipstick on her mouth. Why had she gone to a bar in Malibu, but more important, why couldn't she remember anything between falling asleep at her home to now?

A recent history of her phone activity showed she had placed a call to Rebecca right before she called an Uber. Maybe she called Rebecca and the two had agreed to meet, but she had no memory of their conversation.

She dug away at her cuticle and made a call.

After four rings, Rebecca answered.

"I'm sorry to wake you. I called a few hours ago, but I don't remember anything we may have talked about. I'm beyond humiliated, but I had a few glasses of wine on an empty stomach, and I think it got the better of me. Did we speak?"

"Gosh, no. Hold on, let me check my phone. OK, it looks like you called me, but I didn't answer. My boyfriend was over, so I must not have heard it. Is everything OK? Where are you? It's loud. I can barely hear you. Do you need me to pick you up?"

"No, I couldn't sleep, so I decided to take a walk. I'm outside of a restaurant that's down the street from my house," Carly lied. "I'm sorry I called so late. Please, go back to sleep, and I'll see you in the morning."

Carly's head pounded as she did an inventory of her call history.

She'd called Victor too.

Carly splashed cold water from the sink and decided on an exit plan. She'd call for a car and be done with this strange situation.

"Hey, baby, there you are. You were gone so long, I thought you left. Are you ready for me?"

A tall lanky man in his thirties with a goatee and tattoo inked heavily on both arms had entered the bathroom.

"Ready for what? Who are you?" Carly asked.

"I always wind up with the crazy ones. I scoped out the alley like you said, and it's empty, unless you want to do it here."

The man with the tattoos pulled Carly to him, pushed his

pelvis into hers, and then slid a hand inside the opening in her shirt. His face came closer to hers, and Carly could smell the cigarettes and liquor on his breath. He licked his lips, and right before he tried to kiss her, Carly slapped him as hard as she could across his face.

"Get off me! If you touch me again, I swear, I'll call the police. Who are you?"

The man backed away and gave Carly a wicked grin.

"Yup, you're one of the crazy ones. But remember, honey, you're the one who came onto me first, remember? You didn't have a problem when you were making out with me, so why do you have one now? Hold on. Are you on something? You seemed kind of out of it before. I'm Jim, remember? Big Jim, that's what you called me."

He started toward Carly again, all the while staring at her breasts.

"Leave me alone!" Carly screamed.

Jim continued to close the space between them, until the sound of the bathroom door slamming open stopped him cold.

"One more step, and I'll cut you to gristle and bone."

It was Victor, jaw clenched, eyes feral, and armed with a silver switchblade clutched in a steady hand.

"Hey man, take it easy, OK? I didn't know she was your girl. She's a stupid tease, anyway. There ought to be a law against girls like her. She came in here, dressed all slutty and practically boned me at the bar."

"Not another word out of your low-class, trailer-trash mouth."

Victor smiled, but his eyes stayed rabid, like he hoped Jim would be stupid and accept the dare. He thrust the knife in front of him, blade slicing through air.

Jim retreated backward until he reached the door and then bolted into the hallway.

Embarrassed and ashamed over her appearance, Carly crossed her arms across her chest.

"How did you find me?" she asked.

"I got your message. By the sound of it, I figured you were either loads of fun or in some kind of trouble. When I didn't see you at the bar, I gave the bartender a C-note. He told me you'd gone to the bathroom and trailer-park boy followed."

Victor removed his jacket and placed it around Carly's shoulders.

"I think your look is great, if you do, but you might want to put the coat on, so we don't start a riot when we try to get out of here. Are you OK?"

The events of the evening, or what she could remember of them, crashed around her. Carly fell into Victor's arms.

"I'm not sure what happened. I was at home. I had a glass of wine and fell asleep. That's the last thing I remember before I found myself here with that man. I'm mortified that you saw me like this. Thank you for saving me."

Victor kissed the top of Carly's head and put an arm around her shoulder as he led her out of the bathroom and down the corridor to the bar.

All the patrons seemed to be staring at her.

The table of women from before stopped their conversation and looked at Carly with collective disgust. Carly wanted to explain. She wasn't the girl that they thought she was, but Victor stepped in, like he could read her mind.

"Ignore the tedious lookie-loos. You'll never see them again, and on the bright side of the shiny penny, no one will ever again call you boring."

Victor gave Carly a wink and steered her to the street where he opened the door of a grey Bronco.

Once they were inside, Victor looked at her with a blend of amusement and affection. "All I need is an address. Let's get you home."

Carly didn't remember falling asleep during the ride from Malibu to her bungalow in LA. But there she was, in Victor's arms, as he carried her down the hallway to her bedroom. Victor lowered Carly in bed and covered her with a quilt, before brushing his fingers against her cheek.

"I'm sorry," Carly whispered.

"Get some sleep. I'll see myself out. And don't ever tell me that you're sorry for anything, ever again."

TWENTY-EIGHT
Ava

Ava sat on a pink plastic bench in LA's Grand Central Park. Under normal circumstances, she would've inhaled the extra spicy sandwich she picked up from Howlin' Rays for her late breakfast by now, but instead, her attention was fixed on the man sitting on other side of the table: her ex-husband, Sean, whom she'd known since they were in college at Northridge in the Valley, where Ava studied criminal justice and Sean was a pre-law student.

Her mother had no idea the two had moved into an apartment together as a couple their junior year, and Ava was sure Kyra was going to faint when Ava dropped the bomb during her graduation party that the tall and trim dark-haired boy from Ireland she brought as her date was also her husband.

Their quickie marriage ended when Ava broke the news to Sean that she wanted their union annulled, citing the pragmatic "we're too young" speech. Technically this was true, but the real reason Ava broke up the marriage was when she realized she was turning into her mother, doting on her husband, cooking meals for him every night and tidying up their apartment on a minute-by-minute basis.

Still, she and Sean had remained close friends, and in her line of work, having a tight source in the Los Angeles County Public Defender's Office was a definite advantage, case in point, her current situation with Carly.

Sean scooped up a forkful of Ava's vinegar slaw and then tapped a quick message into his phone.

"Sorry. I was in court right before I got here and I'm playing cleanup. I convinced Neil McNamara to take a plea deal. He'll do three hundred community service hours plus probation, but he beat serving time."

"You mean Big Ginger Watson?"

"The one and only. Big Ginger mentioned you were pretty rough when you brought him in."

"Please, you think I could rough up an MMA fighter?"

"I think you could do anything you put your mind to. Speaking of that, I've got a line on a job that's right up your alley. My office is looking for a new lead investigator. You'd be perfect, and I already told my boss about you. Bail recovery agents are the bottom of the barrel, Ava. You're smart, you intimidate most people half to death without opening your mouth, and you'd kill as an investigator."

"The only thing I'd kill is my boss if I took that job. I work alone, and for the record, I'm great at what I do. Public defenders represent complete scum most of the time, and you know it too. At least with me, I'm bringing in the bad guys to face their due."

"I knew you were going to be a tough sell, but think about it," Sean said and pushed his business card across the table with the name and number of his boss written across the back.

Ava looked at Sean's smooth and strong hands. She wanted to reach across the table and touch them, but the opportunity would be coming soon. The shelf life of Sean's relationships usually lasted four months, which meant her ex invited her to lunch to drop the news he'd broken up with his latest girlfriend. Cue the next scene: Ava and Sean would follow the pattern of what usually happened after his latest heartbreak. Ava would console him for about fifteen minutes and then they'd wind up in bed together for two days until they got it out of their systems. Still, Ava figured one day soon, they'd stop their dance and make it permanent again.

"Remember the girl I was dating?"

She tried to put on a look of understanding friend instead of gloating ex-wife, but Sean's latest relationship was a dud from the start.

"Right, Molly the hairdresser," Ava said.

"No, her name is Morgan and she's a teacher."

Ava threw up her hands, as if she'd forgotten. Of course, she remembered Morgan, the kindergarten teacher. Sean showed Ava a picture of Morgan after he and the teacher started dating. Morgan had a dewy complexion, a dark bob, and she looked innocent and borderline virginal in her cardigan sweater set.

"Sure, I remember her."

"We're going to move in together. I wanted to tell you first."

Ava was sure she was smiling. Her mouth contorted into some ridiculous happy grin, but she pictured herself grabbing the plastic fork out of the coleslaw and stabbing it into Sean's neck.

"That was quick, I mean four months, Sean. How can you know anyone after dating them for four months?"

"I knew you were going to tell me it's too soon, but honestly; I've never been happier. You know when you're with someone and they totally get you?"

Ava wished she had a cigarette, even though five years ago, she'd given up the habit cold turkey. "You're sounding like a Hallmark card, and that's a major disappointment coming from you. Does Morgan know you were married before? I'm pretty sure Snow White wouldn't approve if she knew her boyfriend was a retread."

"Be nice, Patel."

Her cell phone chimed on the table. It was in incoming text from Carly, confirming their meet-up spot.

"What intel do you have on the Ed Russo case?" Ava asked.

"A buddy of mine in Vice said they've got their sights locked on a suspect who works at the school. They're building a case against your friend, so unless Carly can come up with an airtight alibi, things aren't looking good for her."

"I need a favor. Find out everything you can about a man named Julien White and get back to me ASAP. I'm not screwing around. This is mission critical. I'd do it myself, but I don't have time."

"Just so I know what I'm dealing with here, who is Julien White?"

"Julien White is Carly's stepbrother and the devil in disguise. I don't believe for a minute he showed up by chance after fifteen years of radio silence to check on her health and welfare. Whatever his intention is, I'll bet all my money it isn't good."

TWENTY-NINE
Carly

Carly left a message with Victor, hoping they could get together so she could thank him with a clear head for saving the day. Maybe she'd even tell him about the situation with Ed Russo and how the police were gunning for her as the lead suspect into his death.

Scratch that. If Victor didn't think any less of her after finding her at Moonshadows, barely dressed and in the company of a scraggly loser who wanted to have sex with her in the women's bathroom, what would Victor think if he discovered another sordid tidbit from her life?

She thumbed through the books she'd checked out from the college library, all self-help and deep-dive philosophical tomes to help her figure out whether she had some deep, dark thing slithering around her subconscious.

Three hard knocks sounded on the other side of her office door. She opened it and was face-to-face with LAPD officers Zachary Smith and Lila Rodriguez.

"Miss Bennett, you're a difficult woman to find. You've moved offices," Smith said. "Can we speak to you?"

"This is my place of business and showing up here unannounced is inappropriate at best."

"Those are some interesting books you've got on your desk," Smith said. He brushed past Carly, entered her office, and read the book titles aloud. "*The Power of Your Subconscious Mind*, *Incognito: The Secret Lives of the Brain*, and Freud's *The Unconscious*. I think I see a theme here."

"The b–b–books are research for a creative writing assignment for one of my classes," Carly lied, and then bit her tongue to keep herself from stuttering again.

Rodriguez picked up the Freud paperback and studied the

back cover. "I read this during college. I was a psych major at Long Beach, until I switched to law enforcement. Knowing what makes people tick is a huge resource when you're working the job."

"What does the professor's book selection tell us about her?" Smith asked his partner.

"Freud believed unacceptable thoughts, memories, and motives are repressed in the unconscious mind. Under this line of thinking, Miss Bennett's anger at her mother for sending her away from her family home could have been repressed in her unconscious, and ultimately influenced her behavior, even though the professor wasn't aware of it," Rodriguez said. "Maybe Carly had a previous beef with Russo. Whatever unresolved childhood trauma that was lurking underneath could've triggered her."

"If any of my students came up with this storyline, I'd tell them they had a weak plot," Carly said, her line delivered with precision and grit this time.

Her tough-girl shell be damned. Carly's heart was pumping so hard, she worried the officers would be able to hear it in the tight confines of the room.

She moved to the other side of her desk to buy herself some space from the officers but remained standing.

"Have you located your friend Sebastian to back up your whereabouts at the time Mr. Russo was murdered?" Rodriguez asked.

"That's the thing. I only knew Sebastian in passing. We met at the library, got along well enough, and decided to meet at Nobu for dinner."

"The restaurant's staff confirmed that you were there alone the entire time," Smith said.

"He was late, and I thought he stood me up, but I saw Sebastian in the parking lot, and we went to the beach. I tried to call him, but his number is out of service. Haven't we covered this already?"

"The day Mr. Russo was killed, you were on campus and then paid a visit to your friend, a Miss Ava Patel, in Chinatown. Where did you go between there and Nobu?" Smith asked.

"I planned to get to the restaurant early, but then I decided to make a quick pitstop at home to change before my date."

"Was anyone with you at your home?" Rodriguez asked.

"I live alone," Carly answered.

"At the time of your mother's death, you were in San Francisco at a boarding school, Chatham I believe," Rodriguez continued.

"That's right. My mother and I were very close. I was devastated over her death."

"Instead of continuing to dance around, it would be a lot easier if you come clean about your involvement in the murders of Mr. Russo and your mom," Smith said.

Rookie cop posturing, Carly thought.

"I had nothing to do with either murder! Your accusation that I would kill my own mother is insane. I want you to leave my office right this minute."

"Your call," Smith said.

Carly threw open the office door. The red-headed female student Carly couldn't place from the other day, waited on the other side.

"I'm sorry, Miss Bennett. I can come back later. I was hoping I could speak to you. I don't know if you remember me. I'm Amelia Peterson, remember?" the student asked. "I took a writing class of yours a few years ago."

"Thanks for stopping by, but this isn't a good time," Carly answered.

"Don't go on account of us. We were just leaving," Smith told the girl, and then turned his attention to Carly. "We'll be seeing you soon."

Now alone and feeling like the walls were closing in, Carly grabbed her briefcase and did a fast walk to her car. She wiped a trickle of sweat from her forehead, and took in her haggard reflection in the rearview mirror.

The only way out of the current mess would be to find out the truth.

Carly pulled up the funeral service information for Russo from the USC student newspaper story that was posted online. She then reached in her bag for Julien's business card. Before she added his contact information to her phone, Carly memorized her stepbrother's number by heart.

THIRTY
Ava

Following her lunch with Sean, Ava hooked her GMC Sierra truck off the 110 exit toward Carly's school and tried to make out the treasure-map-like directions her best friend gave her for their meet-up spot: under the largest tree next to the English building on the campus quad.

As she pulled into a visitor's parking space, her cell phone buzzed on the truck's console.

It was Sean.

"Tell me what you got," Ava answered.

"If you're trying to nail this guy, I don't have a smoking gun, but here's what I know. Julien White got his undergrad degree from Berkeley and then went to Brown where he earned his masters and doctorate in psychiatry. From what I can tell, he's not hurting for money. He bought a house in Silver Lake three years ago for two million, and he also owns a home in Aspen. He sees patients at a high-rise in the city and is affiliated with Cedars-Sinai."

"Thanks for digging this up, but I'm looking for something messy. Any arrests or time served?"

"No, not even a parking ticket. But there's one thing you might want to look into. When Julien was a senior at Berkeley, the college settled a lawsuit that was filed by a psychology professor against the school and your boy."

"What was the grievance?" Ava pressed.

"That's the thing. The case was settled, so it's sealed. I have the name of the former Berkeley professor, Sheila Hardy. I did a quick search, and I think she may be teaching psychology at a community college."

"What's the school?"

"Riverside City College."

"I got a whole lot of nowhere trying to find Sebastian Foster, which is clearly an alias. I'm hoping you got better intel on the Karmann Ghia," Ava said.

"Carly said the plates were Nevada and the make was a seventy-four?"

"Bingo twofold."

"Seventy-four was the last year the car was produced. Karmann Ghias had lost their popularity by then, so the manufacturers put a cap on the number of cars that came out of the factory."

"Less needles in a haystack for us to find, no?" Ava asked.

"The only seventy-four Karmann Ghia currently registered in the state of Nevada belongs to a Mr. Garrett Abbott."

"Perfect. Sebastian Foster is Garrett Abbott. I could kiss you right now."

"Don't get ahead of yourself, and remember, I'm spoken for these days. Unless Carly's date is aged seventy-eight and died last year from a heart attack while golfing, it's safe to say these two men are not one and the same. I found a number for Garrett's wife, Yvonne Abbott, and left a message. If I hear more, I'll ring you up. I'm due back in court, so before you ask me for another favor, I've got to go."

After Sean hung up, Ava focused on why Julien had surfaced after being dormant for the past fifteen years. In her line of work, Ava learned people didn't change, and the bad ones got worse with time, which meant one thing: The reemergence of Carly's stepbrother coinciding with Russo's murder needed probing.

She pulled out a small notebook she kept in her duffel bag on the passenger seat and wrote down Sheila Hardy's name and wondered why a professor at Berkeley would've downgraded to a community college gig in Riverside, a city an hour east of LA. She also wrote down the name of Victor White. Carly had always spoken fondly about that stepbrother, but still, one couldn't be too cautious when your best friend is accused of murder.

The first throbs of a headache started up, and Ava popped the glove compartment, extracted a bottle of aspirin, and crushed three white pills under her tongue.

As she cut through campus, Ava could feel the stares of the young co-eds and a few professors who looked at her like she was a curious and dangerous animal at the zoo. Ava's hair was purposely messy and spiked to one side, and she wore a pair of black aviator sunglasses, a leather jacket over her snug-fitting T-shirt with her company's "Ava's Bail Recovery" logo on the front, red bicycle shorts and a pair of scarlet Dr. Martens boots.

Ava reached the quad and the English building, where she spotted Carly's assistant, who was spreading a blanket underneath a large magnolia tree.

Rebecca, who was barefoot and wore a long loose hippy skirt, was busy pulling out food containers from a shopping bag.

"Where's Carly?" Ava asked.

"Oh, I didn't know you were coming," Rebecca said. She was smiling at Ava, but her eyes looked wide with surprise and a good dose of fear. "I'm not sure I brought enough food for everyone, but you can share mine."

Rebecca sat cross-legged on the blanket and patted the space beside her for Ava to sit. Not her style. Ava leaned against the tree instead.

"This is perfect. I was hoping we'd get a chance to get to know each other better. I'm way intrigued by your culture. Where you're from is amazing," Rebecca said.

"I wouldn't exactly call the Valley amazing. Have you been there?"

"Oh, you're joking! I get it now. Carly told me you were funny. I was talking about India, of course. I took a trip there the summer after I got my undergrad degree. India is magical. I did yoga and meditated on the banks of the Ganges River with a spiritual guide every morning. Are you Buddhist or Hindu?"

"Neither." Ava looked through her aviator dark glasses at her phone and willed someone to call her.

"I didn't mean to insult you. India is the birthplace of so many fascinating religions. You're not Buddhist or Hindu, so maybe you're a Muslim or Christian, or possibly Sikh?"

"I'm an atheist and I haven't been to India since I was two. If you want to know where you can get good sushi in the Valley, I can help you out, but if you're looking for some kind of connection about a place I don't know, you're going to be disappointed."

A blossom of red shot up Rebecca's neck. "I'm sorry, but I'm trying here. You don't like me, do you?"

Rebecca's redness made its ascent up her chin. Before Carly's assistant fell into a puddle of tears, Ava considered what Carly would do in the situation. Her friend would hug Rebecca and say nice things to make her feel better.

Ava moved from her perch and sat across from Rebecca on the blanket. Hugging was out of the question. This was the biggest gesture she could handle at the moment.

"Sorry if I seemed like a jerk before. It's nothing to do with you, I'm not having a good day," Ava said.

Rebecca brightened and mustered a smile for Ava.

"That's nice of you to open up to me. I probably sounded like a big baby before," Rebecca said. "I heard you and Carly have been friends since you were at boarding school together. What was Carly like when she was younger?"

"Carly? She was quiet and spent most of her time in the school library."

"I bet she was pretty then too. Not me though. I was a chubby kid with frizzy hair, but my mom insisted I perm it like all the other girls. I spent my middle school years looking like a Chia pet gone wild."

Ava gave Rebecca a slight nod. Her Chia pet line wasn't half-bad.

"Is that beer or something stronger?" Ava asked, and pointed to a large mason jar with brown liquid inside.

"It's iced tea for Carly. She called me last night and said she was out for a walk, but I knew something was wrong because who goes for a walk at one a.m.? I think she's suffering from post-traumatic stress disorder after finding the janitor in her office. If that wasn't enough, I saw Carly this morning, and she told me a relative showed up out of the blue. I got the feeling it wasn't a happy reunion. Do you know who the relative is?"

"That's Carly's story to tell."

Rebecca looked crushed over the remark. Carly's assistant was a fragile girl. Rebecca seemed to want Ava to like her, and it wasn't as if Ava didn't, so she tried again.

"The tat on your arm is cool. '*I am, I am, I am.*' What does it mean?" Ava asked.

"It's a line from Sylvia Plath's 'The Bell Jar,'" Rebecca answered and perked up again. "It's the first book Carly assigned when I was in her English lit class my freshman year. Carly's lectures and Sylvia Plath's genius inspired me so much, I went straight to the tattoo parlor after I finished the novel. It was my first tattoo, and I'm close to being a full-fledged tattoo addict now. How many do you have?"

"There's no ink on me. I hate needles."

Ava was relieved to get an incoming text from Carly, and figured her friend was letting her know she was minutes away. Instead, Carly's message said she was caught up with something unexpected and couldn't get away.

"Carly's out, so I am too," Ava said.

"I just got the message from Carly as well. Why don't you stay, and we can have lunch together?"

"Thanks for the offer, but I got intel on a bail jumper I've been trying to pick up for weeks."

Ave beat a fast path back to the parking lot, and her headache broke by the time she reached her truck. She dug out her notebook and the name of the teacher who sued Julien and dialed the number for the Liberal Arts department at Riverside City College. When the receptionist answered, Ava recited the story she made up on the walk to her truck.

"My name is Mrs. Brenda Savich," Ava said in a flat Midwestern accent. "I think an old friend of mine is teaching at your school, and since I'm in California on vacation with the grandkids, I'm hoping my friend might be teaching a class today. We're driving through your area from Yosemite, and I thought I'd try and catch her if she's still on campus. You'd be a doll if you could help me."

"What's the name of the professor?"

"Sheila Hardy. I'm dating myself, but we taught at Berkeley

in 2012," Ava said, basing the date on a quick calculation on when she thought Julien would've attended his undergraduate studies at the college.

"Hold on, let me check . . . yes, our Sheila Hardy was a professor at Berkeley at the same time. I'm pulling up her schedule now. You're in luck. She's teaching today, and her last class starts at five."

Ava headed out of the city and looked back at the smog hovering like a dirty smudge over the LA skyline. She punched the gas and asked for a blessing from the universe so she could save her friend.

THIRTY-ONE
Carly

Carly approached Eat Drink Americano on Third Street in Downtown LA and waved back at Victor, who was sitting at an outside table for two. He rose to greet her and gave her a kiss on both cheeks.

"That's very continental of you," Carly said.

"It's always a good day when I get to see you, so I ordered the most festive-sounding cocktail on the menu." Victor took a sip of a tangerine-rose-colored drink and raised his glass in Carly's direction. "It's called a Good Humor, which is supposed to be a mix of vodka, tamarind and ginger, plus some fake-sounding thing called 'atomized Montenegro.'"

"Thanks for meeting me. If a human could die of embarrassment, I'd be six feet under and dropping," Carly said. "I didn't think I had too much to drink last night, but I guess I was wrong."

"Like I told you before, no more sorries, because otherwise, a person sounds pathetic, and you, my dear, are not even close. Plus, I got to feel a little less crappy about myself for sitting on my hands when you were getting shafted by Julien back in the day. And I won't lie, I think I grew a couple new hairs on my chest after almost throwing down with Mr. Tattooed Love Boy. Honestly, I was glad I got there when I did, and nothing happened to you. Now, let this be the moment we swear on something holy that we will never mention the Moonshadows' event, unless in five years, it's far enough in the rearview mirror that you want to revisit it for a chuckle. What do you hold so dear that you will swear on this sacred promise between us?"

Victor's eyes were bright and playful, and Carly didn't mind the thought of being in on their private joke.

"It's a deal. I swear on . . ." Carly started, but fumbled for the perfect response. "This is harder than I thought it would be."

"Don't overthink it. All you have to do is spout off the first thing that pops into your head because that first thought will be the truth."

Carly looked toward the rhythm of traffic on the street, hundreds of lives moving toward their destinations, and there she was, an inconsequential blot in their periphery, but the person sitting across the table from her wanted to draw her into a circle that was all their own.

Without thinking, she answered. "I hold my mother's memory most dear."

Victor closed his eyes, and Carly was surprised when she saw her stepbrother shiver.

"That was honest, and thanks for being real with me. It's my turn now, so let me see if I can be as gutsy as you."

Victor looked to the sky, rocked in his chair for a moment, good old Vic, never one to stay still, and looked back at Carly with intensity. "I hold most dear the sweet memory of little Carly Bennett, the shy twelve-year-old who felt out of place among the swine and their riches, but who, even at a tender age, was more golden than they could ever dream."

"That's one of the nicest things anyone has ever said about me," Carly answered.

"I meant every word of it, although on replay, I'm guessing it might've come across a little creepy, but I swear, I'm not a creep. My childhood was spent with a bunch of rich creeps, blood relatives included, and now I work with different kinds of creeps in Hollywood, but I like their playground too much to quit them."

"You told me that you'd share the story about what happened between you and Julien. Sorry to drag up old muck, but I'm still on the fence about connecting with him, and I'd like to get a clearer picture of what he's like now," Carly asked.

Victor sat back in his chair and fiddled with his cocktail straw. Avoidance.

"I did promise you that, didn't I? Three years ago, Chris

was getting worse, and Julien showed up at Paramount like the Grim Reaper to tell me. Jules and I still spoke, maybe a couple times a year at best, but after what he pulled on you, I never trusted him again. He couldn't convince me to see Chris, and I'm still OK with my decision. But I did agree to have dinner with Julien. There's something about Julien's charm that pulls you in. You feel like you've been invited to the best, most exclusive party in the world with the very best party favors, but once the champagne and coke buzz is gone, all you're left with is a terrific hangover, and you realize the bright and shiny set you thought you were on is a junkyard."

"What happened at dinner?" Carly asked.

"I didn't want to be alone with Julien, so I brought a date. Her name was Franny, and we were somewhat serious. Jules was his usual smooth self during dinner. When I drove Franny home, she was quiet. Then she stopped returning my calls. I was hurt and figured I'd been ghosted, until Franny showed up on my set, red-eyed and looking like she hadn't slept in days. I took her to an empty conference room where she confessed that she'd hooked up with Julien the night after our dinner. I thought she'd apologize, but she wanted intel on why Julien stopped responding to her after their single night of passion."

"Julien slept with your girlfriend? That might be one of the most disgusting things I've ever heard," Carly said. "Did you confront him?"

"I thought about it. I thought about beating him up too, but in the end, I didn't do either. I knew the best way to get back at Julien was to ignore him, like what he did hadn't gutted me. It wasn't so much about Franny, but more that my own brother would betray me like that. Do you know why he did it?"

"I'd say power or humiliation."

"Julien did it because he could. My brother was always a B student with A-plus looks and a very keen ability to manipulate. I was smarter, but looks trump brains in this world, no matter what people tell you. Now top that story."

Victor moved forward in his seat and smiled. The playful Victor was back.

"I've been under a lot of stress lately, and I think it might be getting to me," Carly said. "A janitor at my school was killed, and his body was found in my office. My name was written on the floor next to his body, so of course, the police are looking at me as a suspect."

"I've got to hand it to you, only you could beat my story. But I've watched enough cop movies to know, when they lock in on a suspect, they get tunnel vision on anyone else, even the real killer. Did you know this janitor person? I don't read the news, so this is news to me."

"We were acquaintances. Ed Russo was a nice person, except for the end. He knew a secret of mine that I regretted. The last time I saw him, I thought he was trying to leverage what he had on me to get something in return."

"That's motive in spades, hearts, clubs, and diamonds. And then with Julien rearing his ugly head, that's a perfect storm of stress. Do you need any help? I could hire a PI for you. Give me the word and it's done."

"My best friend, the one I told you about from school, she's in law enforcement. She's digging in to find out who killed Ed."

"Do you trust her to get the job done?" Victor asked.

"If anyone is going to have my back and find out what happened to Ed, it's Ava Patel."

THIRTY-TWO
Ava

Ava slunk down in the driver seat of her truck and pulled an outfit from her bag of tricks—aka a weathered camo duffle—that she kept in tow for her job when she needed to pick up a bail jumper. Although Sheila Hardy wasn't running from the law, Ava wanted to blend into the current scene and appear non-threatening, which she knew from experience would give her a better chance of gaining Hardy's trust.

Ava changed into a nothing-beige sweater, a mid-calf-length skirt, and as a final touch, donned a pair of glasses and then a pageboy hat to cover her spiked hair, the entire ensemble making her look drab and unassuming, like a cross between a mousy librarian and an insipid insurance salesman. With her new look, she could melt into the concrete, and no one would even notice.

The common area of the building where Sheila was teaching her last class of the day, "Introduction to Psychology," was nearly empty. Ava pulled out the only book she owned, a dog-eared true-crime novel, but kept a discreet eye on the classroom since she assumed Sheila would leave immediately after her lecture was over. Ava wasn't a psychologist or a professor on the subject, but in her line of work, understanding people was critical, and Ava would bet her soul the former Berkeley professor considered her current job a soulless endeavor needed to pay the bills.

Five minutes later, a dozen or so students spilled out of the classroom, followed by a very tall and thin woman in her fifties who Ava recognized from her earlier Internet search as Sheila Hardy. The professor had bottle-dyed red hair that fell to her shoulders and her posture was slightly stooped, like Sheila

Hardy was trying to compensate for her excessive height or someone knocked the legs out of her confidence years prior and she was never able to recover.

Ava waited until the teacher was alone and then approached her with a smile.

"Sheila Hardy?"

"Yes, that would be me," the professor answered. Her response was polite yet clipped, and Ava thought Hardy was trying to place her as a student from one of her classes.

"I'm Ava Patel. We've never met, but we have a mutual acquaintance in common."

"Who might that be, dear?"

"Julien White."

Sheila blanched long enough for Ava to notice, but then the professor regained her footing.

"The name doesn't ring a bill. I've had so many students through the years, it's hard to remember them all."

"You obviously remember Julien. I never said he was one of your students."

"You're wrong about that. I'm afraid I can't help you."

Sheila brushed by Ava and walked briskly through the common area and toward the exit.

"Hold on, I'm not here to jam you up, but I know Julien did something to you at Berkeley," Ava said.

The professor, who had sprinted to the exit, was now in the parking lot and kept her back to Ava as she approached a white Prius.

"I bet you hate him as much as I do," Ava said.

Sheila stopped and turned to face Ava.

"If you're his estranged wife, I feel sorry for you, but I'm not interested in getting involved in a domestic dispute, especially when it involves Mr. White."

"It's nothing like that. I've never met Julien, but he's the stepbrother of my best friend Carly, and he royally screwed her. Julien framed Carly and got her sent away from her mother when she was a kid. Now he's resurfaced after fifteen years and claims he wants to be part of her life. I'm trying to protect her. There's also been a recent crime where my friend works, and the cops are trying to pin her for it. I'm looking into whether Julien might be involved."

"I'm sorry for your friend, but I can't talk to you. I'm under legal obligation."

"I know about the lawsuit you filed against the school and Julien. I don't know the details, but I'm guessing Julien did something horrific to you, like he did to Carly. The people involved in the case are likely retired or have forgotten about it. But I'm guessing you never did."

"No, I remember everything that happened," Sheila answered in a quiet voice.

"Is there somewhere we could talk? You have my word what you tell me will be confidential."

"I don't know you from Adam. How do I know I can trust you?"

"I don't lie or go back on my promises."

Sheila held Ava's stare but then closed her eyes, as if she were looking back at the memory of Julien White and made her decision.

"Fine, but if you ever tell a soul we spoke, I'll deny it to the grave. There's a bar about five miles from campus. You can follow me. If I'm going to talk about Julien, I'll need a drink."

The South Side Saloon was a small, badly lit bar with the requisite pool table and jukebox and a sole, bedraggled-looking patron with a drooping mustache and a pock-marked face with three empty bottles of Budweiser sitting in front of him.

Sheila claimed a table in the back and beckoned the bartender over. "I'll take two shots of tequila with a Corona chaser. Make it Jose Cuervo if you have it."

"I'll take a Corona," Ava said, and waited until the bartender left to continue her inquiry. "Just so we're clear, whatever you tell me is for background and my ears only. I want to know what I'm dealing with."

Sheila raised her index finger, indicating she needed a moment, and then cocked her head in the direction of the bartender who was approaching their table with the drinks.

"One second," Sheila said. She picked up the first shot glass of tequila the bartender put in front of her and then downed it in one fast drink. "What you're dealing with is a monster. Julien White is the most dangerous kind because he'll fool you with his charm. He was a bright, charismatic, beautiful young man."

Bring it on, Ava thought.

"He's a sociopath," she said.

"No, Julien is a psychopath, although there are some similarities between the two."

Ava hated the taste of liquor but put the bottle to her lips and pretended to take a drink in an effort to make Sheila comfortable and not feel judged as a woman drinking alone.

"Psychopaths are empty vessels but good actors. They can't feel anything, but they mimic what they see," Ava said.

"Technically, you're correct. Both psychopaths and sociopaths are antisocial personality disorders. But psychopaths can't form emotional attachments, and they're aggressive predators. They use others to amuse themselves and to get what they want. Think a cold-blooded snake on the inside who can turn on the charm for their own benefit."

"I already know Julien is manipulative."

"Exactly, and that helps him gain people's trust. But it's all an act. Julien, like other psychopaths, are like parrots, as you so deftly described. They learn how to mimic emotions, despite the fact they're unable to feel them. One of the greatest skills a person like Julien possesses is the ability to find weaknesses in others and exploit them. You said Julien popped back unexpectedly in her life. Did he give your friend a sob story?"

"He said his father died recently, and that made him have a 'Come to Jesus' moment."

"Psychopaths are generally very good at lying to cover their tracks, and this includes making up stories about being a victim to gain sympathy from the people they're trying to manipulate. The victims likely won't even know they're being played, like I was. You're probably thinking this already, so I'll say it. With my background, I should've been able to read my student's behavior. If you can believe it, I was once on track to be head of the Psychology department at Berkeley, but Julien ruined all that for me. But truth be told, I allowed myself to be a pawn in his game, so I'm the one who is solely responsible for ruining my life."

"What did Julien do to you?"

Ava leaned across the table, close enough to seem caring and gain trust but far enough away as not to make Sheila feel cornered.

"He convinced me I was having a breakdown. I wasn't a weak person when I met him, Ms. Patel."

"Of course, you weren't. And please, call me Ava."

Ava gave Sheila a warm smile. She needed Julien's former teacher to trust her.

"Julien made you think you were losing your mind?"

"That's exactly what he did. When Julien was my student, he was very popular. It was his junior year when the incident occurred. Julien was one of the stars on the school's lacrosse team. I taught Julien as a freshman, and his classwork focus seemed much better then. But when he took another one of my courses a few years later, I got the impression he was spending more time worrying about sports and his other extracurricular activities than his studies. His grades started to slip in my class, so I gave him a warning. For midterms, my students were required to turn in a research paper of their choice. But on the day that it was due, Julien showed up empty-handed. After class, Julien was distraught and told me he had been up all night at the library working on his paper and finished most of it, but he said he must've fallen asleep. He was apologetic and profuse in his compliments, even saying that I was his favorite teacher. But rules are rules. I gave him an F. That's when the trouble started."

"He wanted payback for the bad grade."

"Of course, but I didn't realize it at the time. After I failed him on the midterm, Julien showed up at my office one afternoon and told me he lied about falling asleep in the library. He said the reason he didn't turn in the assignment was because the subject matter he chose was too painful. Julien was close to tears when he explained how hard he worked, but halfway through writing the paper, he was too overwhelmed to continue."

Ava kept eye contact, nodding as if she understood.

But this woman was a first-class sucker.

"What was he writing about?" Ava asked.

"The emotional effects on children with a parent who dies by suicide, and if the child will one day be more likely to kill themselves as a result. I'll never forget Julien's face when he told me how he witnessed his mother's suicide. He was sobbing, to the point I held his hand and tried to calm him down. The only thing that seemed to make him feel better was when I promised I'd help him, and we could work on the paper together. It's funny what the ego does to block you from the truth."

"You helped him with the assignment?"

"I didn't write it for him, but I let Julien bounce ideas off me. We met either in my office or at a diner off campus for a month. That was the deadline I gave him to turn in the assignment. He and I became close."

"How close?" Ava asked.

In her line of work, Ava had to be a chameleon and play the game to get her man or woman, depending on the mark. Her strategy to squeeze every ounce of information from Sheila Hardy was to dance as close to the edge of drilling her without appearing to pass judgment.

"Sorry if I'm getting too personal. I can tell that you're a lovely person who was done a terrible injustice by a slimeball. I promise, I'm just trying to get a clear picture of Julien."

"I understand. You seem to be an insightful woman, Ms. Patel, so I'm guessing you know the next twist. One night, Julien showed up at my house. He'd never been there before, and I wasn't in the habit of inviting students over. I told Julien we could talk in the morning, but he insisted I was the only person he trusted. I was worried about his mental state, so I let him in. We sat on my couch, and Julien told me about his mother's death. Julien was so upset, I reached for his hand. I didn't mean for it to happen. I was only trying to comfort a grieving student, but then Julien kissed me."

Ava kept her expression neutral, but she worried her trip to Riverside was going to turn into a total waste if Sheila's version of events were tainted or downright lies as retribution for being spurned.

"The two of you had an affair," Ava said in a neutral tone.

"Yes, it sounds tawdry when you say it though. As shameful as it is to admit, my affair with Julien was the most memorable time of my life. You think I'm weak, don't you?"

"I think people make mistakes and their judgment can get skewed for a variety of reasons."

Sheila downed the dregs of her drink and beckoned the bartender over.

"Thanks for humoring me. The day before Julien was supposed to present his midterm paper to the class, he was never more attentive. We were in bed together after we made love. That's when Julien told me he needed to get an A in my class to boost his GPA enough so he wouldn't fail out of school. I remember feeling like the adult then. I told Julien I'd be happy to give him the grade, but only if he earned it. Julien was profuse with compliments and said I was the strongest person he'd ever met. Then Julien told me he loved me for the first time. We had sex again, and when we were done, Julien suggested I should give him the A without him having to write the paper since we'd already discussed his project at length."

"He was using you," Ava said.

How could a woman with a PhD be so gullible?

"Yes, and I should've known. I thought I was teaching him an important lesson. I told Julien I looked forward to his presentation the following day."

The professor looked vacantly at the bar, as if the memory was replaying in front of her, and told Ava the story.

Sheila stood by the white board in front of the classroom preparing for her "Brain, Mind, Behavior" course and watched her students enter. She knew she'd feel a guilty thrill when Julien walked in, but this time, she was also proud of her beau. After all, he had worked so hard over the last month to overcome the pain of his mother's suicide, and with that, came a personal sense of accomplishment for Sheila, since Julien told her none of the other counselors that he'd seen through the years had been able to help him heal from the terrible incident that was blocking his path forward.

Julien was going to nail his presentation. She was sure of it.

Sheila wrote down three words on the board, "Past, Pain, Present" when she caught a glimpse of Julien's shiny black hair and his lean build out of the corner of her eye. Technically she knew she shouldn't be screwing her student. That's how others would coin what was going on between the college junior and his professor. But Julien was different, a visually stunning, smart young man who acted much older than his twenty-one years. After he graduated, they would be free to carry on their relationship in public.

The college had strict policies forbidding faculty from dating undergraduates, but Sheila knew what she had with Julien was different. In all her forty-two years, she'd never felt more alive.

"Everyone, take a seat. I know you're all waiting on pins and needles to hear my lecture today on 'The Developing Brain,' but before I get to that, we're going to hear from a classmate, Julien White. Julien's paper is titled, 'Suicide, Mental Illness, and Its Effect on Children Left Behind.'"

Sheila narrowed her focus to Julien, who was sitting in front of her in the middle row of the classroom. She tried to give him an encouraging look without being too obvious of her affection.

"Are you ready, Julien?"

An awkward silence hung in the air as Julien looked at her blankly. Julien panned the room like he was searching for a prompt from the other students to clue him in on whatever the middle-aged professor was talking about.

It was his nerves getting the best of him.

Sheila tried again.

"I realize it's not always easy to share what may be a difficult topic, but, Julien, please be assured you're in a safe place. Can you please join me in front of the class?"

Sheila thought she heard a snicker, but decided it was one of her competitive students trying to intimidate Julien before he started.

"I know I'm looking forward to hearing more about Julien's work. Can you join me in front of the class, please?"

That's when the floor seemed to fall away beneath her.

Something was wrong. There was Julien . . . her Julien . . . still looking at her with a confused expression, as if he had no idea what she was talking about.

Then came the words that would haunt her forever.

"I'm sorry, Miss Hardy, but you're mistaken," Julien said in a clipped tone.

The laughter then started in earnest.

Sheila felt hot and clammy, but she had to continue her lecture. Julien had to be scared, but why was his voice so cold, and why were some of her students looking at her like she was the punch line of a joke?

Sheila stumbled through the next forty-five minutes of class. In a few instances, she was sure her voice was shaking.

She somehow made it to the end of the class and was never more anxious to talk to Julien. She wouldn't even be mad for the odd way he'd acted.

Sheila dismissed the class and was relieved to see Julien was hanging back to talk to her. But when he approached, another student, Brittany Smith, a lovely looking, voluptuous blonde, was stuck to his side. The two approached her desk together.

"Julien, can I talk to you for a minute?" Sheila asked.

Julien's companion latched her arm around his. "Julien told me what you did. Everyone knows. You need to leave him alone."

"I don't know what you're talking about," Sheila said in a halting voice. "Julien, could you explain yourself?"

"I'm sorry, Miss Hardy. I think you're a good teacher, but you need some help. I didn't want to get you in trouble, but I can't be harassed like this any longer. You need to leave me alone."

Julien looked past her then to the hallway, where the dean of the School of Psychology was waiting.

Sheila's eyes misted and she continued.

"I'm sorry that happened to you," Ava said.

Ava was not a hugger. Not a pat on the back, "let me hold your hand to make it better" type of girl. Hugs or any type of unwanted intimacy from anyone outside of her tight inner circle made Ava want to slug the offender.

But duty called.

Ava reached across the table and gave Sheila's hand a light squeeze.

"What happened next?" Ava asked.

"The dean escorted me to my office and told me I was suspended of my duties until an investigation was complete. I told him his accusations were wrong, but then the dean handed me two notes he claimed I'd written. I'd never seen the letters before, but the writing looked exactly like my own."

Julien had a pattern.

"What did the notes say?" she asked.

"They were confessions of my undying love for Julien and threats that I'd kill myself and Julien if he didn't reciprocate my feelings."

"Julien has a knack for forgery and gaslighting people. He pulled a similar stunt on my friend, minus the seduction, but he made her believe something that wasn't true. I'm guessing your story doesn't end there."

"I wish it did. I got a visit from the campus police at my house a few days after the incident with the dean. The campus police accused me of stalking Julien. They showed me e-mails from my own account that I allegedly sent to Julien. In hindsight, I left him alone in my office a few times. He must've sent the e-mails to himself from my account when I wasn't there. The e-mails were as bad as the letters. They said I'd fail Julien if he didn't return my advances. I swore to the officers that it was a mistake, that my e-mail account must have been hacked, but I was put on a mandatory leave until the college could finish the investigation."

Sheila guzzled back the rest of her beer.

"I spent the next two weeks holed up in my apartment, believing I was losing my mind. When the two weeks were up, I got a call that the dean wanted to meet me. I remember walking through campus and the students were staring at me like I was a pariah. I've never been married or had children. The one thing that ever gave me any sense of self-worth was my profession. But I'd become a laughingstock. When the dean fired me, I had nothing left."

"You filed a lawsuit, so you must've found out Julien played you."

"After I got fired, I drove around aimlessly for hours. At one point, I stopped at a diner where I could've sworn Julien and I went when I was helping him with his paper. I was sure I was delusional, but I went inside. That's when everything changed. A waitress asked if my son would be joining me. I was confused, but she said she was referring to the good-looking, dark-haired man who I usually dined with. From there, I built a case. It was flimsy, and more of a 'he said, she said,' argument, since Julien later claimed he met me at the diner once to tell me to leave him alone. But it was better than nothing."

"What were the terms of the settlement?" Ava asked.

"I didn't get a dime. But the wrongful termination was lifted, which was crucial to me.

"The condition of the settlement included my employment with Berkeley would remain terminated, but it would be based on a mutual decision if anyone asked. The party line was that I wasn't forced out. As for Julien, he came out smelling like a rose. The board wiped his slate clean, and his failing grades for all his classes during the semester were waived since Julien said he couldn't concentrate because I was sexually harassing him. My career as a respected academic was over. That's why I wound up here."

Ava put two twenty-dollar bills on the table to cover the bill and stood to leave.

She had one last question to ask.

"Do you think a person like Julien could change?" Ava asked.

"If I'm talking objectively here, I suppose it's possible with the proper treatment and counseling. But I believe Julien was warming up with me, and he's likely perfected his techniques through the years. As for your friend, she could be in a world of trouble."

THIRTY-THREE

Ava

The celebration-of-life service for Ed Russo was being held in the backyard of his ex-wife's mid-century modern in Encino. Ava parked her truck a block away, slipped on a pair of nude pantyhose and a conservative black dress she'd stuffed in her duffel bag for the occasion.

Her Americanized side thought she was an idiot to change, since her earlier outfit from her meet-and-greet with Sheila Hardy would've been appropriate for the occasion. But her mother had always insisted that funerals were a sacred time to remember the dead, and as such, dressing in a respectable fashion was necessary, despite that she was at the service solely to do some hard digging into Russo's case.

Ava signed a fake name in the guestbook when she entered the house and made her way to the backyard that was set up with about fifty foldable chairs in a semicircle, with a large table in the center that held a giant bouquet of lilacs and white roses, a framed picture of Ed Russo, and what was left of the man in a gold-plated urn.

A tall, fidgety blonde wearing a black dress and a matching hat caught her eye. Ava took a seat next to the woman and then did a discreet sweep of the crowd.

"What are you doing here?" Ava whispered to Carly.

"I came to pay my respects and to try to figure out what happened to Ed. Are you wearing pantyhose?" Carly asked.

"You shouldn't be here. Don't make it obvious, but your friends from the LAPD are positioned at eleven o'clock."

Carly jerked her head in the direction of officers Smith and Rodriguez, then grabbed Ava's hand.

"I think I'm going to have an asthma attack."

"No, you won't. Just be cool. And don't say anything about Russo if its open mike night after the service."

A pastor from the Unitarian church began his sermon about how the Father's house had many rooms, and Ava nodded, as if she were listening. She took another subtle pan of the crowd and noticed the male LAPD officer was still fixated on Carly, who was now crying quietly and dabbing her eyes with a Kleenex. Ava locked eyes with the male officer and gave him a hard stare until he looked away.

After the sermon was over, a forty-something woman with a dark bob took to the podium and addressed the crowd with a throaty voice.

"Thank you all for coming. If we haven't met yet, I'm Heather Russo, Ed's wife. On paper, I'm Ed's ex-wife, but after having been married to him for fifteen years, and still loving him despite our divorce, I feel like he's my partner, even in death. I met Ed when we both were at a little A.M. radio station where we worked constantly but were paid terribly. Still, it was the best job of my life because that's where I met Ed. It was impossible not to fall in love with the man with the big voice and even bigger heart."

"I have to get out of here," Carly whispered.

"Just breathe and don't make a scene. You'll get through this."

Heather Russo continued. "Over the last few days, I've been thinking about what Ed would want me to say about him, but it finally came to me. I could hear Ed's voice in my head, plain as day, responding to my question with one of his own, 'How would *you* like to be remembered?' So let me share Ed's greatest passion. He loved his sports broadcasting career, but I know he'd want to be remembered for how hard he fought for his sobriety, and the helping hand he always offered others struggling with addiction. Ed often told me, even those who are in the deepest throes of their disease aren't a lost cause."

A high-pitched wheeze came from Carly, like a steaming hot teakettle that was boiling over on the stove. Before Ava could try and calm her down, Carly shot up from her seat and sprinted toward the house.

The entire crowd of mourners seemed to move their heads as one in her direction, but Ava kept calm and followed her friend's path until she found Carly sitting on the curb in front of the house, clutching her inhaler.

"I guess you forgot the part where I said not to make a scene."

"I barely avoided a fire-alarm asthma attack just now. Plus, I couldn't stand to be at the service for one more minute. The cops came to my office today. They're digging in on their theory that I killed Ed and my mother."

"We both know that's ridiculous."

"Any word on Sebastian Foster? Without him, I've got no alibi."

"I'm working on it. As far as your mom goes, you've got an airtight alibi since you were at Chatham when she died."

Carly turned away from Ava, took a hit from her inhaler, and fixed her gaze to the pavement.

"I'm going to ask you a question, and I need you to be completely honest with me," Carly said.

Ava looked at her childhood friend and could picture Carly as a gangly twelve-year-old girl who seemed like she wanted to disappear inside herself as the two misfits found solace in each other and took in the wonder of the night sky from the roof of their dormitory.

"You know I'd never lie to you."

"Do you think I'm capable of killing a person?" Carly asked.

"Of course not."

When Carly began to cry, Ava pressed close to her on the curb and secured her arm around her friend's shoulder.

"I know who you are. I always have, even when you royally screwed up. But I want you to go home now and promise that you'll let me handle Russo's case. If you feel the urge to look into your mother's death, I can't stop you, but be careful and stay away from your stepbrother. And make that plural."

"About that, I saw Victor."

Ava did a slow and impatient headshake. "Leave the past alone, Sunshine. Things that were rotten yesterday don't improve tomorrow. Bad people only get worse with time."

"Victor didn't have anything to do with what happened to me. He got burned by Julien too."

"Maybe so, but I wouldn't trust anyone with the last name of White right now, especially Julien. He was the devil when you were a kid, and I believe he's only perfected his game. I paid a visit to Julien's former Berkeley professor. She claimed Julien seduced her, and once he got her under his spell, he tried to convince her to change his failing grade. Then he gaslit the poor woman and convinced her she was crazy. Does that sound familiar?"

"I won't reach out to Julien," Carly said. "I'm sorry I was so gloomy before. It's all the stress that's turning me into an idiot."

Ava listened to what she knew were more false assurances and waited until Carly's car was out of view until she resumed her digging.

You could usually unearth some good scoop at funerals.

Inside the second-floor office of the house, Ava started toward a stack of bills atop a rolltop desk when a heart-wrenching sob came from inside the closet.

Ava rapped twice on the wall, and then opened the closet door to find Heather Russo huddled in the corner amid a pile of shoes with a nearly empty bottle of wine in her hand.

"Can I help you?" Heather asked, and tried to hide the wine bottle behind her back.

"I was looking for the bathroom. Are you OK?"

"Please don't tell anyone about this," Heather said. "This is supposed to be a dry service, and half the people here knew Ed through his AA meetings."

"I won't say a word. This must be a horrendous day for you."

Heather exited the closet, still clutching the bottle of wine as if she were on a sinking ship and it was the last life preserver on the boat. "I should be pissed at Ed. He lost himself to alcohol and all our money in the process, but right now, I miss him so much, I feel like I could explode. I can't believe someone killed him."

"Do you know anyone who'd want to hurt your ex-husband?"

"Not that I can think of. Ed borrowed money a few years ago when he was trying to get us out of debt, but he paid it back after he landed the janitor job."

"Maybe he was seeing someone, and the relationship soured?"

"When he first started at USC, Ed got involved with a girl at the college. We were separated at the time, but at that point, any intimacy between us was barely something I could remember. I was happy for him."

"Did Ed mention the girl's name?"

"He might've told me, but I don't remember," Heather said. "I do know it all went to hell. I think things got hot and heavy with the woman, but he broke it off because she was a lot younger, and it sounded like she was a jealous mess. Ed didn't want the drama, since he worried it might affect his sobriety, so he broke things off with her."

"If you remember the person's name, or anything else, please give me a call."

"I talked to the other officers before the service, and the male one, Smith, told me he was the point of contact with the LAPD."

Ava did a careful bob and weave with her answer.

"I'm not a cop, but I work in law enforcement, and I'm looking into what happened to your ex-husband," Ava said and handed Heather her card.

"There's one more thing. The night that Ed died, he called me from the parking lot at USC. He felt bad about hurting a woman at school. Apparently, he knew she'd been drinking on the job, and he told her to go home so she wouldn't get fired. Ed, being Ed, asked her out, but when she declined, he let his ego get the better of him. Ed insinuated that he was going to tell her boss about her screwup. He went to the school to apologize to her. I guess he brought her flowers and a note and was going to leave them on her desk. That's the last time Ed and I ever spoke."

"This woman, is she the same person your ex-husband was dating?"

"I don't know. I did get the impression the woman he dated had some heavy baggage. She sounded like one of those people who on the surface seem like they have a perfect life, but deep down, they're monsters. People like that, no one can help them, but if you try, they'll prey on your kindness and take you down with them."

"Did you tell the LAPD officers about the woman?" Ava asked, and prayed the answer was no.

"You bet I did. If she's involved in Ed's murder, I want to make sure she pays for what happened to him."

Heather took a long drink from the bottle as if to punctuate her point.

"The cops didn't mention this woman's name, maybe in passing?" Ava asked.

"No, believe me, I asked, but they're keeping the investigation under wraps. That's what they told me," Heather answered.

Ava thanked Heather Russo, felt a throb of a fresh headache beat at her temples, and headed to the street.

THIRTY-FOUR
Julien

Julien watched his lover's back rise and fall slowly with each breath. He slipped out of bed, got dressed and went to the kitchen where his briefcase still lay on the floor.

Inside, he pulled out the box he'd promised his lover and left it on the counter, all the while thinking about his attorney, which prompted another slow boil of frustration over what his prick lawyer didn't do for him.

It's not like he could fire Lawrence. His lawyer was too invested in Julien's affairs. Still, Julien was troubled by his personal failure to convince Lawrence to assist him in a matter the lawyer kept insisting was out of his purview.

Since he was a child, Julien was keenly aware he possessed the unique ability to convince anyone of anything. He'd learned from the best. Yet attorney–client privilege apparently was the one impenetrable barrier he wasn't yet able to bend to his will.

A thirsty-looking ficus plant by the sink caught his attention. Julien turned on the cold-water tap, picked up a glass lying upside down on the dish rack and filled it with water. He took his time watering the plant, picked off a few dead leaves when he'd finished, and took a hasty step back when he noticed a fat, black spider dangling from the lip of the pot.

How Julien detested bugs.

Insects were tiny, prehistoric-looking bloodsuckers that made his skin itch by sight alone.

Julien grasped a sticky strand of the spider's web between two fingers and pulled until it broke. He then studied the spider as it skittered across the counter in hopes of finding a hiding place. Julien waited until the bug had almost reached the spice rack and then smashed it with the base of the planter, all the while wondering how a species of insects could survive as long as it did by hiding in plain sight. He whisked the bug into the sink and watched the dead bug disappear down the drain.

He closed the front door behind him and headed to his BMW, which was parked a block down from his lover's place. He reached for his phone that showed no new calls. That was a surprise. Carly should've contacted him by now.

From a clinical standpoint, Julien considered the range of emotions his stepsister likely felt: Shock, anger, hurt, self-blame, denial and redemption, knowing that her mother never stopped loving her and planned to bring her home, coupled with his sudden reemergence, not to mention the fact it seemed like she knew the man who died at USC.

He put the BMW in drive and was halfway down the block when his cell phone rang.

"It's Carly. I haven't changed my mind about you, and I'm not forgiving you either. But I want to know more about my mom before she died. You're the only person who still has that information. If we meet, will you be honest with me for once?"

"Of course. I promise, I'll tell you everything I know."

THIRTY-FIVE
Carly

Carly parked in a lot by the merry-go-round at Griffith Park, a massive landmark in the city that included its eponymous observatory, the Los Angeles Zoo, museums, and hiking trails that offered some of the best views of the Eastern Santa Monica Mountain Range in all of LA. Carly was comfortable enough with the meet-up spot that Julien had suggested, since she had frequented the park's trails many times, and it was one of the busiest hiking spots in Los Angeles.

In other words, the location posed a low risk of her having to spend much, if any, alone time with Julien.

She reached into her glove compartment for a pocketknife that she placed in the front pocket of her shorts. She needed to be prepared if Julien tried to pull anything.

Carly pulled out her Hydro Flask and took a drink of the special iced tea Rebecca had prepared for her. The cold marigold and silver needle tea tasted sweet and much improved over the hot version Rebecca had given her the night of Russo's murder.

She took a long exhale from her inhaler, grabbed onto what was left of her courage, and set off to find her stepbrother at the carousel.

It was middle-of-the-week during a school day, and the carousel area was sparsely populated, except for a few tourist-looking families at the ticket booth.

Julien was nowhere to be found.

Carly picked at her thumbnail until it bled and checked her phone. Julien was ten minutes late and might stand her up in some kind of twisted power play. She imagined him looking at her through binoculars from some remote location and having a good old laugh over how he'd duped her.

Game, set, match. Julien wins again!

She was being a scared baby. Julien was running late, that was all. Carly returned to the parking lot to see if he had arrived. Julien wasn't there either, but a red Hummer was parked in the spot next to hers. A large man with calves big enough to be a professional rugby player stood next to the Hummer. He was talking on his phone and throwing a ball to a black-and-white dog. The animal noticed Carly, lost interest in the game of catch and bounded over to her with its tail wagging.

"Buddy, not everyone wants to play with you, get back here," the man from the Hummer called out.

"I don't mind, I like animals," Carly said as the man approached. "Your dog's name is Buddy?"

"His official name is Jasper, but that never stuck, so I went with Buddy instead. I had no choice. He won't answer to anything else."

"Most dogs have a mind of their own. You have to respect their independent spirit," Carly said. She leaned down and petted the patch of white on the dog's neck, and Buddy reciprocated by giving her a big, sloppy lick on her cheek.

"Really, Buddy? Geez, I'm sorry about that. Buddy has a habit of running up to pretty women. Since you and my dog are on a first-name basis, I should introduce myself. I'm Bradley. And Buddy here, he should know better. He's a Border collie, and Border collies are as stubborn as they come."

"Your dog isn't a purebred, is he?"

Julien was walking toward them from the other end of the lot with a laser focus on Bradley.

"No. Guilty as charged. But mixed breeds usually live longer," Bradley said.

"I believe what you're *trying* to say is that mutts have a lower incidence of genetic disease compared to purebreds. It's been proven in numerous studies," Julien said.

He pointed at the Hummer.

"Is that yours?" Julien asked. "That's a sweet ride."

"Yup, the beast is all mine, but the Hummer is a gas guzzler," Bradley said.

"A color like that has to be custom."

"Right again. It's cherry red with a metallic glaze. There's no other Hummer on the road like this baby."

Carly tuned out the two men's car talk discussion when a memory surfaced. She was living with the Whites, and one of the doctors from Christopher's practice, Phillip Edwards, came to the house. Carly sat on the front step and witnessed Julien and one of his friends dress down a yellow Corvette the doctor parked in the driveway. Julien called the car a "giant testosterone-fueled phallic symbol," and Edwards a "phony," who was trying to make up for inadequacies in his manhood by driving such a ridiculous vehicle.

Maybe Julien had changed his mind about fast, shiny cars, but then her stepbrother dropped the sickle.

"You bought the Hummer because you thought it could help you get more pussy, right?"

"What's your problem, dude? You shouldn't use that kind of language in front of a lady."

"I'll get to that in a minute. But we need to talk about your predictable behavior first. *Cherry red?* Could you possibly be more textbook macho jerk, Bradley? Or I'm guessing you usually go by Brad or plain 'Bro' when you're not trying to impress to get in a woman's pants. You're terribly basic, aren't you?"

"What are you talking about? You don't know anything about me, man."

Bradley looked like he was ready to punch Julien, but Julien seemed completely unfazed. He sighed like he was humoring a child and motioned to Carly to move away from Bradley and closer to his side.

"Oh, Bradley, Brad, Bro, that's where you're wrong. I think the reason you speak so disrespectfully to women is because you had a toxic relationship with your mother. And your dad was out of the picture. Am I right?"

"You have no idea what you're talking about," Bradley said, but the edge deflated from his voice.

"If you can't acknowledge the reason for your behavior, that's understandable coming from a simple person such as yourself, but you owe Carly an apology."

"What are you talking about, man? I just met her."

"True, but I parked two spots down from you, and I heard you talking on the phone to a person I'm guessing is your buddy. What did you say you wanted to do to my sister again?"

Bradley raised his hands at his sides in a surrender gesture.

"She's your sister? Look, I didn't mean anything by it. It was just guys talking. You know how it is."

"No, I don't. Now say you're sorry."

"I'm out of here, I'll leave you two alone, OK?" Bradley answered, like he was asking for Julien's permission.

"No. You need to say you're sorry first," Julien insisted. His voice sounded like the glint of steel from a fresh razor in the pack.

"I'm sorry. I was a jerk for saying that about you, Carly. I'm going to leave now."

"Excellent choice. Have a nice day, Bradley."

Bradley snapped a leash on his dog, and the two jogged in the direction of the cherry red Hummer with the metallic glaze.

"Why did you do that?" Carly asked. She covered a hand over her mouth to hide her smile.

"The guy was a sleaze, and I was defending your honor. Chalk it up to my long to-do list of trying to make amends. Let's forget about the jerk and get on with our hike before it gets too hot. I'd suggest we take Fern Canyon Trail. It's a few-mile loop, but the trail offers a perfect view of the Saint Gabrielle Mountains."

Carly agreed. She expected to fall behind Julien, but he stayed next to her and the two walked in tandem up the path.

"I'm sorry about Christopher. When did he die?" Carly asked.

"A few months ago. He had lung cancer. For a man like him with all the money in the world, and all his connections in the medical community, even that couldn't save him. He tried conventional treatment first, but when that didn't work, Christopher went to Switzerland for experimental therapy. When he left the US, he was skin and bones. He was supposed to be on his deathbed, but when I flew to Switzerland to see him, my father looked like his old self. I was hopeful, but by the time he returned to the States, he went downhill. Victor and I had a falling out, like I told you, but I reached out to him to see Dad. Victor refused."

Carly weighed telling Julien about her meetings with Victor, but something primal told her not to reveal that card yet.

"Christopher kept getting worse," Julien continued. "My father's lawyer called and told me to come home. I was in New York and took the red eye to LAX, but Christopher died before my plane landed. At least we had some time together before he died. You didn't get that with your mother, and I was the cause of it. I don't expect you to have had a change of heart, but do you feel any differently about me now?"

"I think you talk a good game, but I don't trust you. You have a habit of being present during the worst moments of my life."

"I'll keep taking the arrows because I deserve it. Despite what you said before, a killing in a person's workplace can cause lingering trauma. If you'd like any advice, I'll transform into Dr. Julien. My patients pay two hundred dollars an hour for my session, but for you, dear sister, you get my undivided attention free of charge."

Carly ignored the offer and bristled over Julien's term of endearment.

The two walked in silence until they cleared the challenging part of the route's steady incline and reached the summit's peak and its view of Griffith Observatory below.

"LA's an empty city. It's stale and expansive with too much concrete and a sterility of anything original," Julien said. "Most of the people who live here are desperate to be perfect. My mother used to tell me Los Angeles had no soul. I grew to discover she was right. You were always an original, though, a hidden gem compared to the obnoxious rich kids at my school. You weren't like any of us, and that made me hate you. I'm sorry for that."

"You apologize a lot. But it doesn't mean that I believe you."

Carly moved away from Julien and to a bench at the lookout point.

"Go on, ask me anything you want. I swear, I'll tell you the truth," Julien said.

"When I met you, you were decent enough, but when my mom and I moved in, you became distant."

"I was jealous. You were only a kid, but you had everyone's attention because you were special. I made a plan to gain your trust. I figured my betrayal would be more devastating if you liked me."

"Was Victor suspicious?" Carly asked.

"Vic? He was a smart kid, a genius really. Not trying to be boastful, but I'm smart. Vic though, he's smarter than I'll ever be. But when he was a kid, Vic looked up to me way too much to see the truth. He caught onto my game later."

"You said that my mom was going to bring me home. Why did she wait?"

"Em wanted to surprise you. She was scheduled to fly to San Francisco the morning after she was murdered. She was upset you were having a hard time adjusting, and the situation at our house had become untenable. Em and Christopher were fighting all the time. I blame Christopher for most of it."

"I don't understand," Carly said.

"It was my father's idea to ship you off to boarding school, and in the end, I think Emily resented him for it. Granted, I planted the seed, but Christopher took the bait. He loved your mom and could see how upset Em was when she thought you were acting out with your stomach issues and then the incident with your English teacher. Christopher wanted to protect his wife and convinced her Chatham would fix everything. When it didn't turn out that way, Em blamed Christopher."

"I was the cause of their marriage problems?"

"You were partially to blame. Let me rephrase that, I was partially to blame, but not for all of it. About a month after you went away, my father was sure Em was having an affair."

"My mom wouldn't cheat."

"That's what I told my father, but you have to understand. Christopher was a very jealous man. My mother cheated on him, and he wasn't the same after that. He probably assumed Em did the same thing. It seemed like they were headed for a divorce, but then Emily died. To this day, I believe you and your mother would've been better off if you'd never met us."

"Amen to that. I want to know about my mother's death."

"It still haunts me. I was probably one of the last people Emily talked to before she was killed."

"You were at the h–h–house?" Carly said.

She'd kept her cool so well up until this point. Julien would surely call out her ridiculous stutter and make her feel small.

But he continued, like nothing happened.

"No, I was in San Diego for a senior class trip. Vic had all but moved in with his friend Bodie's family. After you left, and Vic wasn't around, your mom and I got closer, and I trusted her more than my dad, especially if I had a problem. My father wasn't a good man, but I'm guessing you didn't know that."

"I liked Christopher at first, but he changed after you lied about me."

"I'm sure he was decent enough when you first arrived. My father was all about appearances. His patients loved him, and so did everyone else at his practice. But behind closed doors, he could be a monster."

Carly picked at her bloody cuticle and slid her hand underneath her leg so Julien wouldn't notice.

"Christopher used to beat me with a belt as punishment when he thought I was acting up."

"If that's true, I'm sorry, but Christopher never struck me as a violent man."

"Everyone has a secret they want to keep. My father was smart and never hit me when you and Em lived with us," Julien said.

"Did Christopher hit Victor?"

Julien raised one eyebrow and studied Carly.

"Why all the questions about Victor? Are you two in touch these days?"

"I haven't seen Victor since I was sent away," Carly lied. "I was just curious."

"Fair enough. Christopher never hit Vic, and I don't think Vic even knew about what was happening to me. In a way, I was glad to take the beatings to spare him. The most awful beating my dad ever gave me was a few months after my mother died. Christopher took me to a fundraiser for the UCLA

Pediatric department where he was an attending physician. Christopher was being honored since he donated two million dollars to the wing, and he insisted I introduce him at the event. When I got on stage to make the presentation, I was nervous and started with a joke. I didn't plan it, but it came out of my mouth, and everyone started laughing, so I thought my dad would be proud of me that I was doing a good job. But I was wrong."

"What was the joke?" Carly asked.

"I said my dad didn't need to be a doctor since he was wealthier than everyone in the room put together. Christopher smiled, so I figured he thought it was funny. But when we got in the car, he was silent, and I knew I'd made a mistake. We got home, and I did my usual routine. I went to my closet and picked out a belt for Christopher to whip me. My dad never hit my mom, but after she died, something changed in him, and he took it out on me. After he remarried, I'd never seen my dad happier. I don't know where my father's violent tendencies came from, but I was relieved when they stopped, and I believed Emily was the cause for it. But after you left, the fighting started up between your mom and Christopher, and I started to worry about Em's safety."

Julien sat down on the other side of the bench next to Carly. She stiffened and shifted her body away.

"Are you saying Christopher hit my mother?" Carly asked.

"I only saw it once. Like I said, my father was a jealous man. I got home early from a lacrosse meet, and I heard them arguing up in their bedroom. Vic, of course, wasn't home. Emily was screaming, and I ran upstairs. My dad was there, and so was his best friend, Phillip. He used to come by the house with his big yellow convertible."

"I remember the car."

"My dad had Phillip pinned against the wall and Christopher kept screaming, '*I'm going to kill you.*' I knew something bad was about to happen, so I grabbed my father and pulled him off his friend. Phillip kept saying he wanted to explain, but my dad wouldn't have any of it. I got Phillip out of the house, because I was afraid if he stayed around, my father would kill him. When I went back inside, Christopher and Emily were on the deck. That's when I saw Christopher's hand go up, like he was about to strike Emily. I don't remember what I said, but the two of us went at it. At one point, he pushed me into the pool. When I got out, Emily was sobbing, and my dad was gone. I asked Em what happened, but she wouldn't tell me. I figured it out though. I believe my dad caught your mom and Phillip in bed together. I'm sorry to tell you that."

Carly wanted to scream into the canyon below, but she stayed silent.

"I sat with Emily on the deck until she stopped crying. We talked for a while, and she told me she was going to bring you home. Em also said her marriage was probably over."

"You said Christopher found my mother's body?" Carly asked.

"He found Em in their bed after he got home from work. I see what you're getting at. You were always a smart girl. My father was far from a perfect man, but I don't think he was a killer."

"Who do you think murdered my mother?"

Julien reached for Carly's arm, but she pulled away and moved to the farthest recess of the bench.

"Please don't touch me."

Julien nodded, as if he understood.

"I'm sorry. I was only trying to comfort you," Julien answered. "As to your question, the police theorized the people who broke in killed her. But the way Em died, it seemed more personal to me. From a psychological perspective, your mother was smothered to death with a pillow. Whoever killed her, in my opinion, was someone who was very close to her. They loved your mother very much, but were equally incensed and couldn't control their rage. In the end, the killer couldn't bear to see Em's face when they took her life. My father said when he found Em, the bedcovers were pulled up to her chest, like the killer tucked her in before they left. That doesn't sound like the behavior of a robber to me."

"Do you still live at the house? I'd like to go back there," Carly asked.

"I inherited the family home after Christopher died, but I couldn't wait to get rid of it. There were too many bad memories there, so I sold it right after my dad's funeral. Speaking from a clinical perspective, I don't recommend you going there. It could be detrimental to your well-being. Please know that I'm here for you. I know I have a lot of work ahead to make you trust me again. But no matter what, we're still family."

Carly rose and faced her stepbrother.

"I don't consider you family."

"I realize why you would feel that way, but I hope you have people in your life you can lean on. Are you in a relationship?"

"Not currently, but I have a good friend."

"A good friend can be much more valuable than a romantic partner. What's this person's name?"

"Ava. She and I have been friends since Chatham."

Just saying Ava's name made Carly feel more powerful.

"Is she an educator too?" Julien asked.

"Ava? God no. She has a bail bonds business in the city. Ava isn't someone you'd want to cross."

"Is that so? I'd like to meet your friend sometime. She sounds colorful," Julien said.

The intonation in Julien's voice didn't come off as an insult when he said the last word. But if her stepbrother possessed the same soul as he did as a young man, his word choice was done with purposeful intent.

"Ava thinks you're trouble. She looked up a professor you had at Berkeley. The teacher claimed you seduced her and made her think she was losing her mind when she wouldn't change your grade."

Julien smirked.

"Your friend is checking up on me? That's a lark. This Ava person needs to vet her sources. The professor in question was the problem in the mix. She stalked me for an entire semester. I had coffee with her once to discuss a paper for her class, and that was a huge mistake. She took that as a sign that I wanted to pursue a sexual relationship with her, which was nothing further from the truth, and then she concocted a fantasy where we were a couple. She gutted my junior year, and I needed to cut and run. I transferred to Brown. I hope you have an open mind and realize there are two sides to every story."

Something dark seemed to flicker across Julien's eyes, but then it was gone.

"I'm sorry if I sounded angry," Julien said. "I want more than anything for you to forgive me, and the situation is difficult enough without these false accusations being resurrected by a very sad and delusional person. Our conversation has been so heavy since we got here. Let's go back to the park and get something to eat. The food here is the pits, but it's part of the kitsch. My mother used to take me on the carousel when I was a kid. I always hated riding the thing, but I do love nostalgia."

A ride on the carousel didn't sound so terrible.

Carly followed Julien until they returned to the main park area; she waited by the merry-go-round for her stepbrother who headed to the concession stand.

The tinny sound of the "Carousel Waltz" hummed from the overhead speakers. Carly smiled while she watched the colorful horses bob up and down. She recalled the summer before she met the Whites and her final trip to the county fair with her mother. The merry-go-round had always been her favorite but, being twelve at the time, she declined her mother's repeated invitations to ride the carousel, because a sixth grader was too old for a "baby ride." After they left the fair, Carly regretted it.

"You look enchanted watching the carousel go around. You must go on the ride before we leave. I won't take no for an answer," Julien insisted.

He held a box of popcorn from the concession stand.

Before Carly could argue about how ridiculous she'd look, her stepbrother was already at the ticket booth and returned with a curling roll of tickets, more than enough for the ride.

"This is silly. I'm too old to ride a carousel."

"What's silly is if you don't do something that you obviously want to do," Julien answered, and turned his attention to the older male attendant. "Make sure she gets the prettiest pony on the lot."

"I'll be the only adult on the ride. If you're going to make me do this, then you have to join me."

"All the spinning will make me sick. I do much better in the world if everything stays still."

The "Carousel Waltz" began to play again, and Carly found a seat on a cream-colored pony with a gold star on its saddle. When the merry-go-round began to spin, Carly looked out to the crowd.

Julien waved at her from a bench. As he ate the popcorn, a ridiculous thought popped into her head, like she was the entertainment and Julien was enjoying the show.

After a minute, Carly relaxed. Ahead of her, a little girl clutched onto the painted mane of her pony while her mother tried to comfort her.

"I'll tell you a secret. The horses are magical and won't hurt you, sweetheart," Carly called out to the girl.

The music played louder as the ride began to spin.

As the crowd whirred by, everything became far too bright, and the ride seemed to spin faster and faster.

Now certain she was going to faint, Carly grabbed onto her horse's neck and slumped over.

"Stop the ride!" Julien yelled. "I said, stop the damn ride!"

The circular platform slowed to a halt. Right before it stopped Julien rushed onto the ride. He lifted Carly off the horse, and with a steady arm around her waist, guided her to a nearby bench, where he put a hand on her forehead and an index finger on her inner wrist.

"You're clammy and pale, and your heart is racing a mile a minute. I'm taking you to the hospital," Julien insisted.

"That's not necessary. I got d–d–dizzy on the ride," Carly stuttered, too sick to care how she sounded this time. "It was hot on the trail, and I don't think I ate anything today. I feel much better now, except for my pride. How foolish did I look?"

"You didn't look foolish at all. There were only a handful of people on the carousel, and if it makes you feel any better, I don't think you'll see any of them again."

Carly accepted the bottle of water Julien handed her. Without thinking, she laid her head on his shoulder.

THIRTY-SIX
Carly

The last time Carly had taken the route to the Whites' estate had been in a cab fifteen years earlier, after she ran away from Chatham.

Carly took a puff from her inhaler that was on the dash and tried to clear her mind. But her brain felt like it was tied in a knot. She could picture her tongue, languid and unable to articulate the words in her head. She'd never stuttered once before she moved in with the Whites, and had even thought about joining the middle school debate team before her life was upended. But Julien had stolen her promise. And her voice too.

She had to remember that.

"The girl wore her hair in two braids, tied with two b–b–blue bows."

So much for her practice phrase. She had to get herself together.

The ocean disappeared when Carly took the turn toward the Whites' estate.

Her Jeep climbed the final leg of the hill until the beautiful house where she once lived presented itself in the distance.

The home was perched at the top of the steep road, allowing for unobstructed, sweeping views of the Santa Monica Mountains and the Pacific Ocean below.

Emily had once told her that Christopher had it custom-built as a replica of a grand French country estate, with a few generous extras including an acre-sized topiary maze and in-ground fountains, designed to look like replicas from the Palace of Versailles, laid out at each compass point of the property.

The estate seemed to taunt her anew, as if she were a poor

orphaned waif in a Dickens novel, with her mall-bought clothes and three-year-old car.

A quarter-mile before the gate, Carly pulled her vehicle onto the shoulder and coasted to a stop behind a grove of trees. No one would see her there. No one had noticed when she'd hidden at the exact same spot fifteen years earlier.

The plan, at the time, had been to try and convince her mom to let her come home.

The lost hours from the night she ran away from Chatham nagged at her from the sidelines, like a Greek chorus, reminding her that she might've witnessed her mother's murder but did nothing to stop it.

She laid her head against the steering wheel and willed herself to remember what happened.

THIRTY-SEVEN
Carly

March 2010, Greyhound Bus Station, Los Angeles

Carly clutched the straps of her backpack and narrowed her eyes, trying to look tough. She glanced at the clock atop LA's Seventh Street Greyhound Bus station and saw she still had forty-five minutes until her connecting bus to Malibu would leave. She pulled out her copy of *Little Women*, and decided she'd read to kill the time, when the blinking convenience store sign across the street caught her eye.

The plan that she kept rehearsing in her head on the eight-hour bus drive from San Francisco seemed simple enough. She'd hide in the bushes of the house until she was sure her mother was alone, and then she'd confront Emily. Carly would be angry at first, because she was. How could her mother turn so cold and ship her off, like she didn't love her daughter anymore? When Emily expressed remorse over what she'd done, Carly would let the dam break, run into her mother's arms and confess to how much she missed her. And wouldn't Emily please let her come home, where Carly would be a good girl this time.

But now that Malibu was only a forty-five-minute bus ride away, the simple plan sounded downright terrifying.

Her stomach growled, and Carly reached for the twenty-dollar bill in her skirt pocket.

A convenience store sign, EZ Eats, blinked across the street.

Carly exited the bus and ran across four lanes of traffic.

A car horn blasted behind her as she reached the curb.

The convenience store was located in a strip mall next to a Chinese restaurant.

The bell chimed when Carly entered the store. The cashier, a skinny male wearing a Green Day T-shirt, barely looked up from his magazine when Carly passed.

Carly purchased some chips, a soda, and a candy bar, comfort food to feed her belly and maybe even soothe her rattled nerves.

She left the store and headed toward the bus stop.

"Do you need a ride?"

Carly turned.

A heavy-set man in his thirties was standing next to the Chinese restaurant with a large takeout bag in one hand.

"I've got a ride. I'm taking the bus to Malibu," Carly replied in a small voice to the stranger.

"Then this is your lucky day. Malibu is where I'm going. I'm a contractor and have a job there. I was just grabbing some lunch for my crew," the man said.

Carly did a quick once-over of the stranger. He was clean cut and wore a polo shirt with the insignia "Grammercy Construction" emblazoned on the lapel.

Her mom always warned her never to take a ride from strangers.

"That's OK. Thank you for the offer though," Carly responded.

The man pointed to a workmen's truck at the far end of the empty lot which had the same logo as the one on his shirt.

He smiled, showing off a set of perfect white teeth.

"I'm Steve, and my niece is about your age. My sister would give me the business if I let my niece take the Greyhound bus by herself. Plus, it's going to take you twice as long to get to Malibu that way. I'm a nice guy, I swear," Steve convinced.

His tone was friendly and unthreatening. He didn't look like a weirdo. Not one bit.

The bus idled across the street, going nowhere for the next twenty minutes. Carly replayed every stranger-danger conversation she'd ever heard, but after going truant from school and taking a bus ride alone across the state, her new situation felt thrilling.

"I'll take a ride, as long as it wouldn't be too much trouble," Carly said, confident this time.

Steve shook his head, still with the big smile and giving off harmless-uncle vibes.

"No trouble at all. What's your name?" he asked.

"Brittany," Carly lied.

She followed Steve to his truck, but second-guessed her decision when he opened the passenger side door. The car was messy and smelled like fast food. The floor was littered with crumpled McDonald's bags, and a screwdriver sat on the console between the front seats.

"Sorry for the mess. I gave a ride to some of my workers this morning and didn't get the chance to clean up. I've got a great crew of workers, but they're big slobs. One of the guys must've left that in the car," Steve said, and gave a nod in the direction of the screwdriver.

Steve snatched up the trash and tossed it on the ground, outside the truck.

"Not to rush you, but if you want a ride, I need to be in Malibu in fifteen to feed my guys before we get back to work," Steve said.

A small, sane voice inside told her to return to the bus station, but Carly ignored it. She didn't want to be a scared little girl anymore.

Carly slid into the passenger seat but made sure her body was close to the door in case she needed to make a fast exit.

When Steve got inside, he snapped the locks in place.

Carly's eyes darted toward the ignition. Why wasn't the man starting the car?

"I like your style, Brittany. That's a real pretty skirt you're wearing."

"Thanks," Carly answered.

Her heart raced as she looked at the screwdriver, sitting between them.

"How old are you? You're real pretty. I bet your legs could go all the way up to heaven."

The stranger cupped his hand around Carly's leg, above her knee, and gave it a squeeze.

"Hey, don't do that!" Carly yelled.

"Come on, honey. I'm doing you a favor, and now you're going to do me one."

"I'd like you to get your hand off me. P–p–p–please," Carly stuttered.

"I like how you say, 'please,'" Steve said, and slid his hand further up Carly's leg.

Carly froze as the man's hand continued to ascend.

"I said I want to go home!"

Without thinking, Carly grabbed the screwdriver on the car's console, gripped it between her fingers and plunged it toward the man's face.

"Jesus, oh Jesus!" Steve cried.

It wasn't until she got out of the car that Carly saw what she'd done.

The screwdriver jutted out of the man's right eye. It was stuck there, unmoving, even as Steve thrashed around in the front seat.

"Help me," Steve begged.

Carly snatched up her backpack and ran as fast as she could back to the bus station.

Once inside the terminal, Carly rushed to the bathroom and splashed cold water from the sink onto her face.

Her heart was beating in an unnatural rhythm, and she wondered if she should turn herself in to the authorities. It wasn't like she meant to kill the stranger, if she actually had. Carly was only trying to protect herself, and wouldn't the police understand, considering what the bad man tried to do to her?

But if she confessed, and her mother found out, there was no way Emily would ever love her again.

All Carly knew for sure was she had to go home.

Keeping her head down, Carly pushed past the rows of vending machines and went outside, where her bus was now boarding.

Carly took a quick look across the street toward the convenience store, but beside a few cars parked in the strip mall lot, it was empty. She tried to look calm when she handed her ticket to the driver, and then nearly sprinted down the aisle before finding a seat in the back of the bus.

She kept her eyes glued on the convenience store and willed the bus driver to stop gabbing to every passenger and get inside the damn vehicle so she could escape before it was too late.

Carly stuffed the ticket stub into her pocket when she saw a speck of blood on her skirt. Her eyes darted to an older woman sitting in the seat across from her, but the lady was engrossed in a crossword puzzle book and hadn't caught on that the twelve year old in the adjacent seat was very likely a killer.

"This is Greyhound bus number forty-two with stops in Santa Monica, Malibu, Oxnard, and Ventura," the bus driver's voice droned over the PA system. "Please take your seat since we'll be leaving in a few minutes."

She wanted to scream for the driver to leave already. Instead, she took an extra shirt from her backpack and used it to try and scrub the blood spatter off her skirt, but the stain wouldn't come out, no matter how hard she rubbed.

Carly pressed her face against the window so no one would see her cry.

She cried even harder, out of relief this time, when the bus doors closed, and the vehicle pulled out of the station.

A siren blasted its warning, and Carly nearly jumped from her seat when two police cruisers, followed by an ambulance, tore into the convenience store parking lot.

Carly kept her eyes on the scene and was sure the police would come running across the street with guns drawn, but the bus pulled onto the main road and headed to Malibu.

Carly told the cabdriver to drop her off at the base of the mountain road that led to the house.

"Are you sure? It doesn't look like there's much of anything around here," the driver asked.

"My friend's house is right around the corner. You can't see it from here."

After paying the fare, Carly darted behind a grove of sugar

pines and waited until she heard the car drive away. She then climbed up the hill, doing her best to stay hidden in the shadows.

It was dark by the time she reached the gate of the estate. Still, she didn't want anybody to see her, so she found a hiding place behind some eucalyptus trees that would give her a direct view of the house but would still offer cover.

Carly tried to block out the images of the screwdriver submerged in Steve's eye, but they kept replaying in her head.

She slid to the ground and hugged her knees against her chest. Carly allowed herself to cry for exactly ten minutes, and then focused on what she needed to do. She was so close now, and she missed her mother so, so much. Everything would be better with her mom by her side.

Carly wiped her wet cheeks with the back of her sleeve and studied the house. Emily's car was the only one in the driveway. Her stepfather was likely working a late shift at the hospital, and Julien and Victor would be out on the town with friends.

A light switched on in her mother's upstairs bedroom.

Inside her backpack, Carly pulled out a small Ziploc baggie.

Emily's shadow passed by the curtain, and Carly's heart ached anew.

But she couldn't face her mom without some help.

She reached inside the baggie, where her index finger and thumb rubbed against either side of the little white pills that the nurse at Chatham had given to her and the other "difficult" girls to "help calm their anxiety." Carly had never taken one before. She'd pretended to, always the obedient one, but had squirreled them away in her pocket. She'd seen her roommates buy and sell the pills to other Chatham students. Carly had saved hers in case she ever needed collateral to help her survive the place.

Carly held her nose, placed the pills on her tongue, and swallowed.

THIRTY-EIGHT

Carly, Present Day

Carly exited her car and ran along the tree line until she reached the gate, but darted into the shadows when a woman exited a white Mercedes parked in the driveway.

The female, likely the lady of the house, appeared to be in her early forties, with dark hair that fell to her shoulders. She was well dressed in linen pants and a turquoise silk blouse, and probably enjoyed a life filled with cotillion lessons as a child, a proper budding lady's education at Wellesley and a summer after graduation spent in the south of France where she met her older and adoring husband.

She pictured the female sleeping in her mother's old room and tucking in her own little blonde-haired girl at night.

"Is someone there?" the dark-haired woman said and looked in Carly's direction.

The automatic gate opened slowly, and Carly raced back to her car.

She hit the gas and didn't slow down until she reached the highway.

THIRTY-NINE
Rebecca

Rebecca struggled to balance the three grocery bags with food from the organic grocery store on the corner and a few items from David's online store, and opened the door to Carly's bungalow. Her boss wasn't taking care of herself. Carly's discovery of Ed Russo's body had to be the reason behind her emotional tailspin.

She couldn't make Carly stop worrying, but Rebecca could at least do her best to get her boss to eat. She set the grocery bags on the kitchen counter and opened the fridge.

"This is bad," Rebecca said when she saw most of the groceries that she'd stocked the previous week were untouched.

Rebecca sprang into action. She tossed the old groceries and restocked the refrigerator and pantry and made a fresh batch of iced tea. Next, she put some soothing lavender in a vase and set it on the kitchen table and lit a tranquility candle to clear out the bad energy that seemed to be lurking in every corner of the place.

Rebecca knew all too well stress could literally kill a person. Her father, Bruce, had died when he was only forty-seven, collapsing on the front porch from a fatal heart attack after he'd returned from a job he absolutely loathed as an ad salesman for a local radio station. Her mother would later say his heavy commute into Cleveland each day left her a widow; that, and the tumbler of scotch and triple scoop of rocky road he consumed each night before bed. After dinner, Rebecca would sit at the foot of his recliner on the den's rust-colored shag carpet and play dominos while her dad indulged in his treats.

"Find a job that you love to do, Becky. Promise me that," her dad would say.

She'd done just that, and it was all because of Carly.

Rebecca washed an empty wine glass in the sink and then went to Carly's study to drop off papers her boss had left at school and needed to grade before morning. It wasn't like her mentor to be so forgetful.

She noticed Carly's tortoiseshell reading glasses by the computer. Rebecca secretly guessed the lenses weren't prescription, and Carly wore them to appear more studious, since she was a relatively young professor and likely wanted to downplay her looks to ward off attention.

Rebecca loved her boss's humbleness and fantasized what it would be like to be Carly for a day.

She looked over her shoulder before trying on the glasses. She stole into Carly's bedroom and took a pan of her reflection in the dresser mirror. Rebecca sighed as she took in her straight, mousy-brown hair and round face that completely lacked cheekbones. She was hoping the glasses would make her look more sophisticated, but instead, Rebecca thought she looked like a bug-eyed owl. She was such a complete and utter frump. Why did everything about her have to be so ordinary?

Carly's honey-colored barrette caught her eye.

Lifting her hair, she clasped the clip in place and gave her reflection another look.

The combination of the glasses and her messy up-do might actually be OK. Her phone buzzed in the back pocket of her jeans. Rebecca fished it out and saw a FaceTime request from David.

"Wow, I'm looking for my girlfriend, have you seen her?" David asked and touched the tip of his tongue to his upper lip.

"You're not supposed to see me like this. I'm sure I look ridiculous."

"Are you kidding? You look gorgeous. Where are you?"

"I'm at my boss's house," Rebecca answered, giggling. "I picked up some St. John's Wort and chamomile supplements like you suggested, but I don't think Carly is going to take them."

"Some people are resistant to homeopathic remedies, but at

least you tried," David answered. "I finished work. I can meet you at your place in an hour."

"I wish I could, but I should stay until Carly gets home. She could use a friendly face. Carly's been under a lot of stress lately."

"Your friend is an adult, and I'm guessing she's lived this long to manage without you holding her hand. Are you sure you can't meet me?" David asked.

"I'm sorry, your offer is tempting, but I should be a good friend."

Rebecca glanced back at the mirror. She twirled a lock of hair, admiring her reflection.

"If you're going to stand me up, you have to do something for me in return. Are you sure you're alone?"

"I called Carly on the drive over, and she said she wouldn't be home for at least an hour."

"Your new look is driving me crazy. Move the phone away so I can take you all in. Can you do that for me?"

"No, that's silly," Rebecca said. She remembered the popular girls in high school who constantly posted half-naked pictures of themselves on social media without a single care.

"You have no idea how gorgeous you are. I need to see all of you or I'm going to drive to your boss's house right now and take you there."

Rebecca propped the phone against Carly's dresser and swayed her hips back and forth in front of the screen. "I look ridiculous, don't I?"

"Don't you dare say that about yourself. You look sexy as hell. Now take off your clothes but leave the glasses on and your hair like it is."

"I can't! What if Carly gets home early?"

"She won't; you said she wouldn't be back for an hour. If you're uncomfortable taking off your clothes, then unbutton your jeans and slip your hand inside."

Rebecca considered David's provocative request. Phone sex was nothing she'd ever done, and she couldn't necessarily rule it out since her new boyfriend seemed to have a wild side. Rebecca pictured Carly walking in to find her pleasuring herself and decided she couldn't take the risk.

"Sorry to be a prude, but I can't. I'll make it up to you later, I promise."

"I pushed too far. I'm not usually like this, but I've been dying to see you all day, and when I saw you with that new look, I went overboard. Will you forgive me?" David asked.

"Of course. I'll call you when I leave."

She ended the call and took another view at herself in the mirror. She did look attractive. A wonderful sense of lightness came over her, as if she were no longer shackled to Becky Hupfeld and her former drab self. Rebecca threw her hands above her head and twirled around in three giant happy circles.

"Whee!" Rebecca cried, but stopped cold when she sensed someone was watching her.

"What are you doing?"

The British accent sounded cold and judging.

"My gosh, you scared me! I didn't hear you come in," Rebecca said.

A bulge of a gun poked out from underneath Ava's bail bonds recovery T-shirt.

"The front door was open, and Carly's car wasn't in the driveway, so I thought someone broke in. How did you get in here?" Ava demanded.

"Carly gave me a key. I dropped off groceries and some papers she needed to grade."

Ava's eyes felt like heat-seeking missiles as Carly's best friend stared at the glasses and then Carly's barrette that was still in Rebecca's hair.

"Those are Carly's."

"I've been thinking about getting a pair of glasses. I saw Carly's, and I was curious how they'd look on me. Then I saw the hairclip. I was trying a new look. I wasn't planning to steal them, I swear," Rebecca said, and snatched off both items and placed them on the dresser.

Rebecca's entire body felt like it was burning red with humiliation. Her only saving grace was that she didn't take off her clothes when David asked.

She wouldn't have been able to survive if Ava had caught her completely naked and twirling around in Carly's bedroom.

"I was just leaving. Please don't tell Carly what I did. I beg of you. It was innocent, I swear. It would kill me if she thought less of me in any way. I look up to her, you know."

Ava took off her aviator sunglasses and gave Rebecca a barely distinguishable nod.

"Don't sweat it, kid. But don't do it again."

Ava wiped Carly's glasses and barrette clean with the bottom of her T-shirt. She wanted to tip Carly off that her assistant was a bit cuckoo. She had made Rebecca a promise, though, and Ava wouldn't go back on it, unless she thought it was critical for Carly to know. Rebecca seemed harmless enough, but Ava decided she'd keep an eye on her.

A car's engine sounded from the road, and Carly's car pulled into the driveway.

"I wasn't expecting you." Carly's eyes darted anywhere but in Ava's direction.

"What gives? You seem squirrelly," Ava asked.

"My stomach is upset, and I felt dizzy earlier, but I think it's just stress."

"What aren't you telling me?"

"You're going to be angry, but I saw Julien today. We hiked at Griffith Park."

"Are you out of your mind?" Ava asked.

"You told me to back off Russo's case, and I did, but I'm not going to stop looking into what happened to my mother, and Julien is my only connection to the past because Victor had moved out of the house by then. When I saw Julien today, he shared some new details about my mom's life before she died."

"I hope you had your bullshit meter on high alert. What lies did he spew this time?" Ava asked.

"Julien claimed my mother may have been having an affair. How do I get my hands on a police report about a murder? I need to get ahead of this before the police pin my mother's murder on me too. And I need a different source than George Halloran from the LAPD. He thinks I killed my mom. And Ed too."

"So I've heard."

Ava placed a call to a sheriff deputy contact who worked at the Temple Street Station in the city. Five minutes later, she had a name.

"My buddy confirmed that Halloran is a first-rate prick, but not his former partner who also worked your mom's murder. His name is Dylan O'Rourke. My friend said O'Rourke is an upstanding guy, so at least you have that in your favor. O'Rourke is still at the Malibu sheriff substation and close to retirement. I'll meet with him first thing tomorrow."

"I need to do this on my own."

"Your call but let me give you a tip. Cover your ass, and remember, sometimes you have to lie to get people to tell you the truth."

FORTY
Ava

Ava tucked into the alleyway across from the Japanese American Cultural and Community Center in LA's Little Tokyo neighborhood and considered the meeting she had with Carly. She thought her friend was wise to try and get ahead of the curve with the police, but she also realized Carly could be putting a brighter spotlight on herself by asking to meet with O'Rourke.

It was after ten p.m. Ava pulled out her phone from the pocket of her leather jacket, and through the darkness, focused on a third-story apartment across the street. Based on a source's tip, she believed inside the studio apartment was her mark, Jared Sato, a twenty-five-year-old actor who'd been slapped with a felony assault charge for attacking his girlfriend at a suite in the Chateau Marmont. His fall from Hollywood's B-plus list made headlines for a few days, and then his case had a second coming with the media when he posted bail but was a no-show for his court date.

Her phone buzzed. Ava answered when Martie Blazer's name appeared on the screen.

"I need you to move," the bail bondsman said. "I got an anonymous tip from one of Jared's buddies that he's been hiding out in Redondo Beach."

"Come on, Martie, anonymous tips are for chumps."

"The caller sounded legit and scared out of his mind. He wants to talk to you first before he takes you to Jared. The guy is waiting for you in the parking garage on San Pedro. It's only a block away, so I told him you'd be there in five."

"You're making a mistake. I've good intel that Sato is at his uncle's place. I'm across the street and about to move in."

"Make up your mind, Patel. I need you to meet the guy on

the fourth floor of the parking garage now. If you don't want to do it, I'll call someone else to finish the job, and I'll give them the ten grand instead."

Ava looked up at the still dark apartment.

"I'll be at the parking garage in five minutes. What do you know about the caller?"

"He's a male and driving a white Honda Accord. Take the elevator to the fourth floor. When he sees you, Sato's buddy will flash his lights."

Ava entered the parking garage through a rear door and took the stairs up to the fifth level.

Growing up in a traditional Indian family, Ava's mother often told her to trust her third eye, which represented the sixth chakra and provided a person with direction, wisdom and clarity.

Ava always hated that Hindu shit. But at that moment, her intuition was telling her something about the current situation didn't feel right.

Still, she'd taken the job and planned to finish it.

Ava felt for her gun holstered underneath her jacket and followed the descending set of yellow arrows on the cement floor until she reached the bend that connected to the fourth level.

She hid behind a pillar, took a quick look at the scene, and snapped a picture with her phone. Ava then squatted down and looked at the image. The fourth-floor parking level was halfway full, which gave her a decent view of the vehicles, but didn't provide her as much cover as she would've preferred. Added to the fact, at least six of the parked cars were white sedans.

Ava bolted up when she heard the clipped sound of someone walking in her direction.

"Well played, Miss Patel. I suspected you were smart, but I was still giving it a fifty-fifty chance that you would follow directions and exit the elevator as you were told. I know you're here, so please, don't be rude and make yourself visible."

Ava pulled her gun and swung out from her position.

Walking in her direction was a handsome, dark-haired man,

a few years older than her and dressed in a well-made suit. The male continued to approach, his gait confident, his hands held wide at his sides.

"Stay where you are," Ava commanded, and trained her weapon at the man's chest.

"Violence should only be a default if you can't control the situation with your intelligence. Please, let me introduce myself."

"I know who you are. You're Carly's stepbrother, the one who screwed her over."

"Yes, I'm Julien White. Nicely done, Miss Patel, or may I call you Ava?"

"I don't want my name to come out of your mouth, period, and if you take another step, I'll shoot."

Julien stopped his pursuit and gave Ava an amused smile. "You've disappointed me. Parking lots always have security cameras so they can record crimes like theft or vandalism, or even assault, if you can imagine something so awful. I'd venture to say it's a given that we're being recorded this very second, and here I am, an unarmed individual walking to my vehicle only to have someone pull a gun on me. I don't believe that will bode well for you, Miss Patel."

"If you call me 'Miss Patel' one more time, I will shoot you. You've gone to all the trouble to bring me here, so what do you want?"

"I'm trying to reconnect with my stepsister, but I understand you've been digging around and spoke to a former teacher of mine."

"I have no idea what you're talking about."

"Please drop the charade, Miss Patel. You don't like me saying your last name because you're ashamed of your heritage, correct? Your physical appearance and your current choice of employment are an easy tell of what you hate about yourself. You replace a sari with a leather jacket, and instead of being an obedient wife, you make a living by bringing in felons. You befriended Carly because she was the blonde-haired, blue-eyed girl you always wished you could be. Deep down, you don't like Ava Patel much, do you?"

"You don't know anything about me. But I know who you are, and I know what you did to Carly when she was a kid, and now you're trying to weasel your way back into her life with made-up stories about her mom. I promise, I'll finish you if you try to hurt her again."

"Your threats of violence are too much. I like what I know about you, I do. Most people are dreary and ordinary. But if you continue to spread false rumors or try to put a wedge between my stepsister and me, you'll regret it."

"You don't scare me."

"That will be your downfall, I'm afraid."

"The only thing that makes me afraid is that you probably cost me ten grand. If that's the case, then you're going to be the one who's in trouble."

Ava didn't move, gun still pointed at Julien's chest with precision.

"You put on such a tough act, but I can see that it is merely a protective mechanism, so people won't see your inadequacies. I'm giving you the courtesy of a warning since you're obviously important to Carly."

"Did you kill Ed Russo?"

Julien waited to respond, and Ava thought she could see him work the name through his memory.

"You mean the janitor where Carly works? Now you're truly grasping at straws. Don't forget what I said, Miss Patel."

A flash of headlights flicked across the cement walls as a vehicle drove down the semicircle loop to the fourth floor. Ava holstered her gun and did a quick pivot behind the pillar so she would be out of sight.

When the car passed, Ava came out from her cover.

Julien was gone.

FORTY-ONE
Carly

Carly waited in her car outside the Malibu Lost Hills Sheriff Station in Agoura Hills, an upscale town about an hour north of Los Angeles, and watched the minutes tick by until it was eight thirty a.m.

As soon as the station opened to the public, Carly asked for Dylan O'Rourke at the reception desk. She gave the female behind the glass partition a fake name and a line about how she had critical information about Emily White's cold case.

After a few minutes, the glass door to the inner precinct buzzed opened and a man in his mid-fifties appeared. The male had a solid build, thick salt-and-pepper hair and a goatee that almost hid a patchwork of acne scars that otherwise marred a handsome face.

"You said you had some information about Emily White's case?" the man asked in a raspy baritone.

"That's right. I'm her daughter, Carly Bennett."

The detective paused for a beat, and then resumed his stoic game face. "Detective Dylan O'Rourke. Let's go where we can talk in private."

The detective led the way to his office and shut the door after Carly entered. He beckoned her to sit, took off his blue suit jacket and then sat across from her at his desk. "You'll understand why I find your sudden interest in your mom's case to be unusual, since Mrs. White died fifteen years ago, and you're only reaching out to me now."

"My mom and I were estranged at the time of her death, but not by any choice of mine. She sent me away to a school in the Bay Area, but regardless, I was wrecked when she died. No matter what happened between us, my mom was everything to me."

"I imagine that must've been a huge betrayal. Your mom remarries, creates a new life for herself, and ships you off to a boarding school. I remember my partner drove up to San Francisco to interview you. The headmistress of the school confirmed you were on campus the day Mrs. White was killed."

"That's right," Carly lied.

O'Rourke put on a pair of reading glasses and leafed through a large file on his desk.

Her mom's murder book.

"My partner said that you had a hard time fitting in at school. I spoke with the district where you attended part of eighth grade at Malibu Middle School. You got suspended for sending threatening letters to a teacher."

"That wasn't t–true. Somebody set me up," Carly protested.

O'Rourke looked up from her mother's file.

"You've got a stutter. No judgment from me. My kid had one too. It used to come out at the worst possible times, but mostly when he was nervous. Are you nervous about something, Miss Bennett?"

"Of course, I am. Who wouldn't be nervous in my position?"

The detective started to thumb through the file again.

"We've got all our files digitized these days, but we still keep hard copies. I prefer holding something in my hands. I'm old school that way," he said.

"I'm guessing some parts of my mom's case are public record. If you have questions, I'll answer them, but only if you share what you can in return."

O'Rourke raised an eyebrow. "Sure, I'll play along. Who goes first?"

"It's your place of business, so by all means," Carly said.

"OK. Where were you really on the day your mother was killed?" he asked.

"You're making this easy. I was at school," Carly said, which wasn't a complete lie since she had woken up that morning at Chatham. "Now it's my turn. The original theory about my mother's death was that she was a victim of a robbery?"

"That's correct. There'd been a rash of break-ins in Malibu around the time of Mrs. White's murder. We picked up security surveillance from two houses that were hit, and it showed the robberies were a tag-team job. Two people dressed in black. A quick in-and-out hit. There were never any arrests. The running line at the time was the same two people broke into your mom's place and thought the house was empty, like the other homes they hit. But they panicked when they saw a potential witness and killed her."

Carly stared at the murder book and thought about the pictures of her mother's body from the crime scene that were inside.

"Was Christopher a suspect?" she asked.

"We locked in on Mr. White at first, but he had an airtight alibi. My partner and I went to the house that night. Christopher called 911. Granted, everyone acts different when they find a loved one murdered, but Christopher was too calm, and his answers seemed rehearsed. Your stepfather said he was doing rounds at UCLA hospital earlier that night. I checked with the head of surgery, and he confirmed your stepfather left work a little before midnight. The coroner placed your mother's death about the same time. Did you know a man named Phillip Edwards?"

"He practiced at my stepdad's medical office. Mr. Edwards used to come by the house, and he had a yellow convertible. What's the name of the doctor who vouched for my stepdad?" Carly asked.

"Jacob Foli. He died of a heart attack a few years ago. You have two stepbrothers, Julien and Victor White. What was their relationship like with your mother?"

"Civil, I guess. Victor was always kind to me when I was a kid, but Julien was closer to my mom than he was."

"We questioned your parents' housekeeper, Doris Romero. She recalled an instance when she saw your stepfather fighting with Mr. Edwards. Your stepbrother Julien was there too, and the housekeeper said she saw Julien pull the two men apart. We spoke to Edwards, and he said the fight was a misunderstanding. When we questioned Julien, he backed up the housekeeper's claim, and said Christopher and your mother were having some problems in their marriage."

Carly weighed whether she should tell the detective about the rumored affair. She rolled the dice, hoping he'd give her something of interest in return.

"I saw Julien yesterday. He thought my mom was having an affair with Mr. Edwards. Julien's alibi checked out?" Carly asked.

"We vetted his story. He was on a school trip in San Diego. Dozens of people saw him that night. We checked Victor's too, and it was clean. Victor was at a friend's house where he'd pretty much moved into by that point. The parents vouched for him."

The detective volleyed his next question in their back-and-forth game. "Did your mother ever mention anything to you about Julien's psychiatrist, Dr. Brian Whittaker?"

"I know Julien saw therapists, but I don't remember their names."

"Your mom was a beautiful woman who was married to a wealthy Malibu doctor. The media ate it up. Whittaker called me after he saw the coverage. He was concerned about Julien and wanted to reach out to the boy. But Whittaker said he was cut off from the family after Christopher threatened him."

"It sounds like you don't necessarily buy the robbery theory, or the fact that I'm a suspect in my mother's case."

"Don't get too excited, Ms. Bennett. Everyone's a suspect until I know for sure they have an airtight alibi. On paper, you seem like a nice enough woman, but almost everyone has secrets they'd risk anything to keep."

FORTY-TWO
Carly

Carly rode the elevator up to Phillip Edwards's Santa Monica practice and took in his headshot from his practice's website on her phone. Fifteen years later, he somehow looked unchanged from when he'd driven to the house in his yellow convertible to play tennis with Christopher and then knock back a few martinis on the deck.

Edwards was somewhere in his early sixties and still handsome, with thick blond hair, blue eyes and a prominent cleft in a strong chin. She hated the thought, but Carly couldn't dismiss the possibility her mother had been attracted to him.

The elevator chimed its arrival on Edwards's floor and, as Carly exited, she answered her ringing phone.

"Where are you?" Rebecca asked. "There's a line of students outside your office. I told them you got hung up in traffic, but that was twenty minutes ago."

"My office hours aren't until three," Carly said. She checked her watch. It wasn't even noon yet. She had plenty of time to talk to Edwards and then drive back to USC.

"This is all my fault. I rearranged your schedule this week so you could get out early. I know how much stress you've been under lately, and I was trying to help. I posted the revised office hours on your door this morning, so some of your students must've seen it. I gave you the schedule yesterday, but I should've pointed out the changes I made. Please don't be mad at me."

"No, it's fine. Tell the students to stop by my office later."

"I made the mistake, so let me fix it. I'm here already. Why don't I fill in for you?"

"That's a perfect plan, Rebecca, thank you. If any student has issues that can't wait until I'm back on campus, they can call me."

"I'll try not to screw anything up again. Thank you for believing in me."

Carly ended the call and passed by a very pregnant woman who was leaving Phillip Edwards's office. Inside, the waiting room was empty except for a middle-aged receptionist in dark blue scrubs who was tucking into a microwaved frozen meal.

Carly rapped her fist on the glass partition between them.

"Excuse me, I'm here to see Dr. Edwards."

"The office is closed for lunch. We open in an hour," the receptionist said.

"I'm not here for an appointment. Phillip is an old family friend. I'm in town for today only, and I know Uncle Phillip would be disappointed if he didn't get a chance to see me," Carly said. "Is there any chance you can give me his cell phone number?"

"I can't do that, but if you're a family friend, you may be able to catch him at the Riviera Country Club downtown."

Carly wasn't a golfer, but she was familiar with the Riviera by reputation. It was located in the posh Pacific Palisades and catered to the Hollywood set, PGA pros and the well-heeled LA set.

She idled her car in front of the building, removed a stack of student papers from a manila folder and wrote Phillip Edwards's name and the word "confidential" across it.

After she valeted her car, she approached a silver-haired man in a suit who oozed self-importance.

Carly fished her glasses from her bag to give herself a more professional look and started with a compliment.

"I can tell you're in charge," Carly said. "It's imperative I speak with Dr. Phillip Edwards. I'm his assistant. I've been trying to reach him, but his phone must be turned off. We encountered an emergency, and it's critical I speak to Dr. Edwards."

"I'm Klaus Koeller, the general manager." As he shook her hand, he glanced at the doctored manila folder Carly was clutching to her chest.

"I'm sorry, but our club is members only. Any guests need

to be approved first and accompanied at all times with our member."

"If I don't deliver this to Dr. Edwards immediately, he'll be very upset. I need your strictest confidentiality, Mr. Koeller."

"If this does pertain to Dr. Edwards, we're very careful about sharing information about our guests."

Carly moved closer and spoke above a whisper when she responded.

"Dr. Edwards is currently involved in a research investigation at UCLA's medical lab. We received some highly disturbing results from one of the study's participants. He had an adverse reaction to a drug Dr. Edwards administered to him this morning. The patient is in critical condition and may die. If you could tell me where I can find Dr. Edwards, I'll brief him on the situation and be on my way."

"One moment," Koeller said, and walked in a clipped pace to the front desk, where he picked up the phone and then returned in less than a minute.

"The doctor just finished on the golf course. Dr. Edwards is at the restaurant now. I've alerted the maître d'. He's expecting you."

Carly followed the maître d' to Edwards's table overlooking the green.

Her stepfather's old friend was accompanied by another man with a buzz cut who was drinking a beer.

"Mr. Edwards, I doubt you remember me, but I'm sure you remember my mother," Carly interrupted.

"I'm sorry, I don't think we've met. Who's your mother?" Edwards gave Carly a politician's smile.

"My mother was Emily Bennett."

Fifteen years might have passed, but Carly could tell from the doctor's surprised expression that he remembered her mother.

"Of course, I remember her. Emily was a lovely woman, and I'm sorry about what happened to her. If you give me your number, I'll have my assistant call you to set up a meeting."

"No, my mother is dead, and we're not going to figure out

a time that works for you. I know you were sleeping with my mom before she was killed."

"Miss Bennett, let's go outside where we can talk."

Edwards led Carly to a shaded bench that overlooked the eighteenth hole.

"How do I know you're Emily's daughter?" he demanded.

"You used to drive a yellow convertible when you came over to the house."

"I still drive one. Anyone could've known that. I need to see some ID."

Carly felt annoyed over the request but pulled out her driver's license from her wallet and handed it to Edwards.

"Yes, you're Emily's daughter. I'm sorry if I seemed abrupt. After your mother was killed, I was questioned multiple times by the authorities. The story was all over the news, and it was a nightmare. I don't think Emily's case was ever solved, and I was worried you might be working for someone who was digging around about her murder again."

"I know you and Christopher got in a fight at the house right before my mother died."

Edwards looked away.

"I don't know what you're talking about," he said.

"I've got multiple sources, including my stepbrother and the police."

"It was so long ago. Christopher and I were good friends, and good friends sometimes disagree."

"I'm sure you remember the incident. Christopher had you pinned against a wall and was threatening to kill you. My stepbrother Julien had to break it up. It doesn't take a genius to figure out what was going on. Did you kill my mother because she ended your relationship?"

"Of course not. I never hurt your mother, and the two of us weren't having an affair. Chris came home early and found Emily and me in her bedroom. She was bent over the desk with her pants down, and I was behind her."

"You can ease off the graphic details about your sex life with my mother."

"No, it wasn't like that. Emily was my patient. I was treating her for something, and she called me that morning and needed my help. That's why I was at the house. Chris and I both worked at the same practice, and Emily preferred her husband didn't know."

"Was my mother sick?" Carly asked.

"I can't talk about specifics."

"Any doctor–patient confidentiality ended when my mom was murdered. I'm not trying to cause you any issues. I want to find out what happened."

"Emily was trying to get pregnant. I started her on IVF treatments. I always told my patients, having a baby wouldn't fix any problems in their marriage. Still, I had an insider view into Emily and Chris's life, and Emily thought a baby was going to make things better between them. I couldn't tell her no. The day of the huge blowup with Christopher, Emily was having problems self-administering the shots. The IVF process was a lot more challenging back then. Emily called me in tears, and I promised I'd come by the house after work."

At least her mother wasn't having an affair.

"Christopher didn't know about the IVF treatments?"

"Emily begged me not to tell Chris, so I didn't. Chris was supposed to be at work. I'll never forget the look on his face when he thought I was having sex with his wife."

"Why didn't you tell him the truth?"

"I tried, but Chris went into a rage. He threw me against the wall, and I was sure he was going to kill me. That's when Julien showed up and broke up the fight. Chris was still furious and said he knew Emily was having an affair, but he didn't know with who until he found us together. Julien walked me out. I left while I could. Chris called me later and apologized after Emily set him straight. Our friendship wasn't the same for a long time after that."

"The police said Christopher had an alibi for my mother's murder that checked out."

"Chris told me he was working at the hospital that night. The doc in charge was Jacob Foli. He vouched for your stepfather's whereabouts. Jacob and Chris were friendly, but Jacob was more of a kiss-ass to Chris, even though Jacob was higher up in the food chain at the hospital. Your stepdad was richer than God, but you already know that. That's why I think Jacob always deferred to Chris."

"I know Christopher was well-off," Carly said.

"Well-off is an understatement. Chris was probably a millionaire a million times over. It was family money. He didn't brag about it though. The only reason I knew was because Chris told me once after a few too many cocktails on his deck one night. He said it's nearly impossible to know who your real friends are when you have that kind of money, because everyone is on the take."

"I'm hoping to talk to people who knew Christopher and my mother. The doctor you mentioned, Jacob Foli, who worked with Christopher—he passed away, I believe."

"Jacob died ten years ago. He opened a restaurant in LA that folded. Jacob always wanted to be a big shot, but it didn't work out."

"Did my mother ever mention anyone who might've been causing her problems?"

"Not Emily, but right before our blowup, Christopher mentioned he'd fired some psychiatrist who was treating Julien. I got the impression that the shrink did something bad. It's a shame what happened to Emily. Chris too."

"I should've talked to Christopher when I had the chance."

Edwards looked confused.

"I understand why you'd want to know what happened to your mother. But sometimes, it's best for everyone to let the past go."

"What do you mean by that?" Carly asked. She rose from the bench, crossed her arms, and tried not to appear intimidated by his remark.

"If you dig around, trying to turn up ghosts, innocent people can get hurt in the process."

"Is that a threat?" Carly asked.

"No, but a warning of what could come. I'm sorry about what happened to Emily. You seem to have done well, despite your earlier circumstance. My advice is to move on. Good luck, Miss Bennett."

Back inside her car, Carly looked up the number for Julien's former psychiatrist, Brian Whittaker, a name on repeat that Julien, O'Halloran and now Edwards had raised.

She called Dr. Whittaker on the drive back to the city.

When the receptionist answered, Carly played it straight this time.

"My name is Carly Bennett. My stepbrother, Julien White, was a former patient of Dr. Whittaker's. It's urgent that I speak to him."

"The doctor is with a patient currently. I can take your name and number."

"It's an emergency. I need to speak to him immediately," Carly pressed.

"What's your name?"

"Carly. Carly Bennett."

A minute later, a male voice came on the line.

"This is Dr. Whittaker. Has something happened to Julien?" he asked.

"I'd prefer to talk to you in person since it's a private matter."

"I'm booked with patients until this evening. I can meet you at my office tomorrow morning at nine. Please understand, there are some things I can't share about Julien since he was my patient. But even after all these years, I've never forgotten him. Julien was a very bright and equally troubled young man."

Carly ended the call with Julien's former psychiatrist, ready to return to campus, when a new text message came in from Julien.

Can you stop by my office tonight? It's urgent. I found some personal items that belonged to your mom.

FORTY-THREE
Rebecca

Rebecca pushed her new eyeglasses up the bridge of her nose and hoped the next in line of Carly's students would for once give a hoot about writing. She leaned back in her boss's chair and considered the last undergrad she saw, a surfer-looking sophomore from San Diego who complained about the "C" Carly had given him.

After Rebecca did a quick scan of his assignment, she knew her boss had been merciful with the grade on the quick-dash essay that was pure "I don't care" material, complete with the ending, *Brandon woke up and realized it was all a dream*.

She settled in at Carly's desk and readied herself for the next student.

"Come in." Rebecca liked how sophisticated her voice sounded.

A tiny, dark-haired girl, with a pixie cut and skin so pale it would make a ghost envious, crept inside and kept her eyes on the floor.

"You're not Miss Bennett," the girl said.

"No, I'm her assistant. Carly was swamped, so I'm helping out today. I'm a graduate student, well, an almost graduated graduate student, but I've been in your shoes. Let me guess. You've written something you absolutely love, and you can't wait to share it, but you reread it, and now you think it's complete trash. Am I right?"

The young woman looked at Rebecca with relief and nearly collapsed in the chair across from her.

"That's exactly how I feel. I keep second-guessing myself."

Rebecca adjusted her glasses and read the young woman's story about a shy and bullied little boy who sneaks out of his bedroom at night to look at the moon in hopes of one day lassoing it so he can use the power of the universe to make him strong. The story was a bit overwritten in places, but for the most part, the narrative rang with emotional authenticity, and Rebecca even teared up at the end.

She looked at the name on the paper. Violet.

"You have a great deal of talent, Violet. My only piece of advice is, don't try and make every sentence a masterpiece. Nicely done."

"You think so? I can't tell you how much that means to me. Will you be filling in for Professor Bennett again?"

"I'm not sure."

"You should take over her office hours. Professor Bennett is great, but it's nice when a teacher gets you."

A lovely warmth pulsed through her over the compliment, to the point where Rebecca had to keep herself from hugging the student. Instead, using her newly acquired professional composure, she escorted the girl to the door.

On the other side was a man with a bouquet of flowers so big, it blocked his face.

"The flowers are beautiful. Carly will love them," Rebecca said.

"They're for you, silly."

David's head popped up from the other side of the massive flower arrangement, and he gave Rebecca a quick kiss on the cheek. "It's your first day as a teacher counseling the future writers of America. I wanted you to have something special."

"You're so lucky, Miss Hunter," Violet said.

"Please, call me Rebecca. Miss Hunter makes me sound old."

Violet smiled at Rebecca and then gave David a shy, admiring glance before she hurried down the hall.

The scent of roses and lilacs from the bouquet reminded Rebecca of spring's hoped-for arrival after a long Ohio winter. She wondered if Violet thought Rebecca had an enviable life. Rebecca flashed to the long line of losers she'd dated since she arrived at USC, but with her new man, the dreary days of Baby Fat Queen Becky Hupfeld were far behind her.

"You didn't have to do that, but I love that you did. I feel like Miss America. But for the record, I'm not a teacher, I'm a stand-in today."

"Your boss should pay you more. What's her excuse this time?"

David took Rebecca's hand, pulled her into Carly's office and shut the door.

"I changed Carly's office hours. I mentioned it to her yesterday, but it must've slipped her mind. I didn't want her to feel bad about it, so I told her it was my fault. I'm worried about her. Ever since that janitor died, it's like she's become someone else. Oh gosh, I probably shouldn't have said that."

"Is this the office where your boss found the janitor?" David asked.

"No, Carly was so traumatized, she asked the dean to move to a new one."

"She sounds unstable. You should take over for her until she can get herself together. Wait, but you're already doing her job," David said and rolled his eyes.

"No, I'm only helping out today. But I enjoyed talking with the students, and I think I might've helped the girl who was just here. Do you think I'd be a good professor?"

"You're damn right you'd be a good professor. You've been spending too much time worrying about your boss. If you've got concerns about her, maybe you should tell someone. If she needs help, it would be for her own good."

Rebecca let David's critique sink in.

"I don't want anyone to take advantage of you," he said. "So, Professor, when are your office hours over?"

"They ended five minutes ago."

"Hmmm. You mentioned Carly wouldn't be back until three. That gives us two whole hours in a locked room."

David set the flowers on the desk and picked up a framed picture of Carly and Ava. "I'm guessing one of these women is her. Is your boss gay?"

"No, that's her best friend. Carly is the blonde. She's pretty, I know," Rebecca answered, certain her boyfriend was comparing her to Carly at that very moment.

David would now recognize that she was plain and ordinary, through and through. No one held a candle to Carly.

"Meh, not my type. She looks like one of those fake, high-maintenance women who always want to be the center of attention. I avoid those women like the plague. Now come here."

David took her in his arms and pushed her against the wall. Rebecca gasped in surprise when he reached inside her skirt and pulled off her underwear.

"I can't," she panted. "Not here. We could get in trouble."

"Be quiet. You can do that, right?" David whispered.

She closed her eyes and pictured the words, "*I am, I am, I am*," as David slipped inside her.

FORTY-FOUR
Carly

Julien's practice was in a high-rise on Maple Street downtown. It was nearly seven p.m., and the office building appeared to be completely empty. Carly took the elevator to Suite 17A. A sign with the words "Julien White, PhD," was posted on the door which was ajar.

She had tentative plans to meet Ava for dinner in Koreatown and didn't want to cancel, but if Julien had items that belonged to her mother prior to her death, she had no choice but to see her stepbrother again.

Carly rapped her knuckles against the door.

When no one answered, she entered the reception area.

The lighting was dim, and she jumped when the dark edges of a figure appeared from the inner office. She exhaled. It was Julien.

"Please, come in. I'm sorry to ask you to come by this late, but I had several emergency appointments. I finished seeing my last patient a few minutes ago."

"You found some items that belonged to my mother."

"I was going through some of my father's things this morning. I found a letter. The envelope is addressed to you at the school, and Em's name is on the return address. I think your mom wrote the letter but never sent it. There's also a necklace of hers. I put the letter and necklace in my briefcase this morning because I knew you'd want them right away."

Julien led Carly inside his office, which had a desk on one side of the room and a sofa and chair on the other. There were no diplomas on the wall or photographs. The room was a cold, impersonal slate.

"I keep my office purposely bland," Julien said, as if he had read her mind. "I like my patients to concentrate on themselves rather than a bunch of useless decorations."

Julien pulled a manila envelope from his briefcase. "This is it." He handed it to Carly.

She snatched the note and imagined her mother sitting alone at her bedroom desk, trying to come up with the perfect words for her little girl.

"There's no stamp on the envelope," Julien said. "I was thinking Em planned to mail it to you, but maybe she changed her mind and decided she'd give it to you in person. You can open the letter now if you want."

Carly wanted to rip open the envelope. But not here.

"I'll read it later when I'm alone."

"Of course, you want privacy for such an intimate moment. It's funny. Seeing the letter from Em brought back memories. Christopher used to drag me downtown to meet with his lawyer. The guy is a stuffy old shirt. I never liked him, but I use him sometimes because he's a real killer when you need one. I remember a detective had been drilling Christopher all afternoon. This was after Em died. After the cop left, Christopher and I drove downtown to talk to Lawrence, the lawyer. He and Christopher hatched up a crazy theory about who killed your mom."

"Who did they say it was?" Carly asked.

"You."

Carly gripped the side of Julien's desk to steady herself.

"I don't mean to upset you. The whole idea that you would kill your mother is absurd."

"Why did they think it was m–m–me?" Carly stuttered.

"Who knows if they even believed it. Lawrence was likely trying to look out for Christopher if you decided to sue him. I protected you though. Granted, I was an ass to you before, but I shut down their bogus theory. If my dad was any kind of decent human, he would've told his lawyer to screw off."

Carly moved to the window and looked at the LA night skyline sparkling like diamonds on black silk.

The latest reveal cut to the bone. Christopher had let her

down, but Carly had no idea he'd tried to pin her for her mother's murder.

"Now I've upset you. At the very least, let me give you something to make you feel better."

From his briefcase, Julien pulled out a small jewelry box, which he opened. Inside was a ruby pendant that hung on a delicate gold chain.

The tears came in an instant. Carly didn't try to stop them. Her mother had admired the necklace when the two of them visited the gift store at Hearst Castle in the small California beach town of San Simeon right before the Whites came into their lives.

"Em would want you to wear it." Julien removed the necklace from the box and positioned himself behind her. "It will look beautiful on you."

Carly felt Julien's breath warm on her neck when he clasped the necklace in place.

She wrapped her fingers around the ruby pendant but winced when a sharp pain shot across her abdomen.

"Are you all right?" Julien asked.

"I'm fine, just embarrassed. My stomach has been acting up. I've been so busy, I think I forgot to eat."

"You almost fainted at the park too. How long have you been feeling like this?"

"I guess for about a week now."

"That makes perfect sense. Traumatic memories, when they awaken, can manifest into physical symptoms."

"What are you saying?"

"Whether you recognize it or not, seeing me again reminded you of the stomachaches you used to get when you were a child. Some stressful experiences lay dormant. Those memories hide like shadows in the body. When these memories 'wake up' it can lead to post-traumatic stress, which can manifest in different ways. Like your stutter. Not to embarrass you, but you didn't have the stutter when I first met you. In my opinion, childhood stress, loss and humiliation were the catalyst for your stutter, and it appears your stutter manifests under times of stress."

"You're saying that all my symptoms are self-induced?" Carly said.

"Except your asthma, which I believe is a genuine affliction. Your case is textbook. I reappear in your life, and your stomach pains do too. I don't think anything is wrong with you. But if you're not feeling well, I can take you to the emergency room. Give me the word."

"I'm OK, I promise."

"I'll give you a ride home then. Let me get you some water first," Julien said.

Julien headed to the small refrigerator when a male voice called out from the hallway, "Is anyone here?"

"It's the cleaning crew," Julien said to Carly. "They're early. You mentioned you haven't been eating well. I'll cancel my plans and take you to dinner."

"I'm going home. It's been a long day."

"There's nothing wrong with you. I'm sure of it," Julien said. He took his stepsister's hand and patted it. "I want you to say it now. Go on. Repeat after me. 'There's nothing wrong with me.'"

Julien's hand was cool and dry. He wouldn't let go until she did what he asked.

"There's nothing wrong with me," she repeated.

"Good, now stop worrying so much and call me if you need to talk. I realize there's a lot you're working through."

Julien escorted Carly to the elevator. When the door closed, when she was alone, Carly slid to the floor. Maybe everything Julien said was true. She was a self-saboteur.

Carly rose as the numbers of the elevator descended, and the elevator leveled at the lobby.

She held tight to the manila envelope with her mother's letter as she exited and headed to the street.

The night air seemed to wake her from Julien's cocoon.

She couldn't let herself believe the hype.

FORTY-FIVE
Ava

Ava knew from experience that devils never changed.

She tightened her camera's focus on the entrance of Mixtape, a hipster bar and restaurant in downtown LA. After Carly's vague text about having to cancel their dinner plans at the last minute, Ava tailed her friend from USC to Julien's practice, where Carly stayed for twenty minutes and then left alone carrying a manila envelope. Ava then followed Julien across town to the bar, where she'd been camped out at a parking space across the street for the past hour with her binoculars in hand, in addition to a bottle of apple juice for sustenance.

She was determined to figure out Julien's endgame before her friend got hurt, or worse, and she couldn't shake her gut feeling that his sudden arrival coinciding with Russo's death couldn't be random.

"There's my boy," Ava said, and snapped a few close-ups of Julien and another man exiting the club. The two stopped at the valet stand and stood close while they spoke.

Ava pegged the man with Julien as somewhere in his late twenties. He was blond, good-looking and wore a suit, like Julien. Two beautiful, elitist boys who thought they were better than everyone else.

People like that made her want to spit.

Ava had encountered plenty of their privileged class during her stint at Chatham, where the rich boys would show up on the weekend with their braggadocio and swagger and whisk their Chatham dates away in their Beemers and Bentleys.

The rich boys never pretended Ava was their type. Her skin was the wrong color, and her Mohawk was perverse and unacceptable.

She hoped her sheer presence and aloofness rattled them to the depths of their shallow core.

Chatham had become her prison sentence after a set of jackass rich boys got her sent there in the first place.

On her thirteenth birthday, her mother dropped off Ava and her little brother, Narun, at a newly opened movie theater in the upscale neighboring community of Westlake Village. Ava held Narun's hand while they stood in line for their tickets, her little brother squirming and begging for a box of Haribo Goldbears, when she noticed two teenage boys park their Mercedes convertible in a handicap spot.

"I don't think they're supposed to do that," Narun said.

"Mind your business," Ava answered. "The seats at this theater recline all the way back, and you can press a button and a waitress will come over and take your order. Don't tell Mama, but you can get as much candy as you want."

Ava held Narun's hand but kept an eye on the teenagers, who were now a few paces away and assessing the ticket line that snaked down the block.

Thinking they'd found the weakest link, the boys worked their way into a spot directly in front of Ava and her brother.

"Hey, you can't butt in line," Narun said.

Ava pushed her little brother behind her when one of the boys turned to address them.

"Hey, little brown curry, how about you shut your mouth?"

Ava remembered the fury she felt, but she didn't recall lunging at the older boy or throwing him to the ground. It was all in the police report; that and how she refused to stop hitting the seventeen-year-old prep-school student, even when the manager of the movie theater warned the authorities were on the way.

After that, her mother insisted Ava needed to go to a "finishing school," an American dream for a girl like her that would smooth off all her rough edges. When Ava got a scholarship to Chatham, which Ava was sure had all to do with the school wanting to check off a politically correct ethnicity box and not her so-so grades, she was sent away to become a proper lady. But mostly to avoid juvenile hall.

Ava took a picture of the preppy blond as he jogged across the street to a white Range Rover. She followed with a shot of his license plate. The blond popped open the trunk, retrieved an envelope and leaned against his vehicle.

On the other side of the street, Julien climbed into his BMW and pulled up next to the other man, who got into the passenger seat.

"Where are we going, boys?" Ava asked. She dropped the camera and hammered the gas, settling in two spaces behind the BMW that was crisscrossing fast through the city until it pulled onto the 101.

She hung back, keeping pace with the Beemer. Then Julien abruptly pulled across four lanes of traffic and veered off the exit ramp for Silver Lake Boulevard.

Julien was going back to his place, Ava realized, which posed a potential problem. She'd worked the neighborhood before and, thanks to Sean's intel, Ava knew where Julien lived.

If she were going to get anything decent from this tail, she'd need to get to the destination first.

Ava executed an expert bob and weave through the lanes and reached the exit in time to see the BMW turn right at the lake. As soon as Julien's car disappeared around the corner, Ava cut to the left in the opposite direction and floored it. Her speedometer reached ninety as she hugged the curve of West Silver Lake Drive that would take her close to Julien's house.

Half a mile later, she pulled her car to a hurried stop on a street parallel to Julien's and calculated which house would back up to his. She then climbed over the fence of a vacant mid-century modern with a "For Sale" sign on the lawn.

Hopefully, there wasn't a Rottweiler waiting to eat her in the backyard.

She pulled a baseball cap low on her head and leapt over the property's fence, but when she got to the rear yard, she had a problem.

There was no dog, but being a short woman on a stakeout didn't always have its perks, especially when there was a high wooden fence that beat her vertically by a good six inches and was coming between her and a clear line of sight to

Julien's place. But there was always a workaround if you were a smart girl.

Ava clipped her camera to her hip and headed to a giant magnolia tree on the edge of the property. She shimmied up the trunk, found a sturdy branch and lay down flat on her belly. Once she got in position, Ava pointed her Canon EOS DSLR camera with its super zoom lens at the back of Julien's million-dollar home, and held it tight. She couldn't afford to miss the shot or drop the camera. At almost seven grand, the camera had cost her more than two months' equivalent of rent for her downtown LA studio apartment.

Rent was obscene in SoCal.

A photojournalist buddy who shot Rams games for the *LA Times* had recommended the camera for its quality and ability to take closeups from a distance. For stakeouts like this, the camera had more than made up for the hefty investment.

She was hoping for good luck, and fortune granted her wish. The lights of Julien's place came on. The shades were open, giving her a direct line of sight into the living room.

Julien and his preppy companion came into view like they were standing right in front of her.

"Gotcha," Ava said.

Julien went to a bar and the other man followed. Julien poured two tumblers of scotch. He handed a drink to the other man, who still had the envelope that he'd retrieved from the trunk of his Range Rover. The envelope was tucked under his arm.

Julien gave his visitor a million-watt smile and extended his hand with his palm up, as if he wanted something.

The preppy in the suit handed Carly's stepbrother the envelope and leaned against the bar while Julien tore open the envelope.

Ava kept snapping pictures, still not sure what was unfolding. She focused in on Julien's face.

His expression changed. Julien was still smiling, but there was now something dark and menacing there, a flickering image of his true self when his mask slipped.

Ava wasn't scared of scumbags. But this was next level.

Julien took several sheets of white paper from the envelope, studied them and then hooked his index finger at the blond, beckoning the other man to come even closer.

Here comes the payoff.

But Ava was surprised at what came next.

Julien pulled the other man's body into his own and his smile seemed to fill up the camera frame.

Ava captured his Cheshire cat grin right before Julien slid one hand inside the man's waistband and then gave his visitor a deep, sensual kiss.

When the lights went out twenty minutes later, she jogged back to her car and considered what she'd witnessed. Her gut told her that whatever had transpired in Julien's house was not driven by a matter of the heart.

So, Julien liked boys. Big deal. Love is love, or more likely lust in this case. But what was in the envelope that got Julien so excited?

Ava circled her car past Julien's house. An Uber was now in the driveway. Doing a cheap bit of psychology, Ava decided Julien didn't like the other man enough to drive him home, which meant Julien was using the other man to get something he needed.

It was late, close to midnight, but she called someone who'd help.

"I need a favor," Ava said.

"Of course, you do," Sean answered.

"Do you still have cops who can get you info on the fly?"

Sean yawned in the background. "You're serious?"

"Deadly."

"Is this about the Russo case?"

"It's a definite possibility. I need you to run a license plate for me, and I need it done now."

Ava waited in silence and wondered if Sean had hung up.

"What's the info on the plate?" he asked.

"That's why you'll always have my undying love. Hold on, I'm sending it to you," Ava said, and texted him the picture of the license plate from the Range Rover that belonged to the preppy.

FORTY-SIX
Carly

Carly placed her mother's letter on her kitchen table and compared it to the note Julien penned that had torpedoed her life fifteen years earlier, which she'd saved as some sort of hideous milestone in her life, or more so, as a reminder to stay strong.

The handwriting in both was different, but that didn't exclude the possibility her stepbrother was still a very good forger.

Her teakettle whistled on the stove. Carly dropped the flowered tea leaves Rebecca had given her into a cup of boiling water. She took a sip but decided the tea wouldn't do the trick.

She poured herself a glass of wine, clasped the ruby pendant that still hung around her neck, and sobbed when she reread her mother's note.

My Carly,

Please know I only wanted the best for you.

I hope you'll forgive me one day.

I can't wait for you to come home, and we'll work through whatever issues you have together.

I love you more than you'll ever know.

Mom

Their reunion had been so close.

Carly wiped her eyes with the back of her hand and finished off the wine in a series of quick swallows.

Her stomach made a strange gurgling sound.

She was hungry, that's all.

Carly combed through her pantry and pulled out the box

of Sleepy Time Iced Cookies. She ate one and then some leftover salad in the fridge. Not a great dinner, not even a good one, but at least she'd have something in her system.

Plus, she was so, so tired.

Right before she fell asleep, Carly was certain she could smell her mother's perfume in the room.

"Wake up."

Her mother's voice was in her ear.

"I need you to tell me something."

Carly tried to wake up, but she was so, so tired.

"Why did you kill me?"

Carly shot up as a shadow passed her doorway.

She stumbled out of bed and slid a hand against the hallway for support until she reached her kitchen, where she grabbed her keys and bag.

The cool spritz from her lawn sprinklers doused her bare feet. Carly slipped on the wet grass, but righted herself and ran to her car.

It took two tries, but Carly fit the key in the ignition and latched her seatbelt in place.

She looked at the night sky and blinked heavily when the stars overhead seemed to transform into a flock of birds that came together as one and then scattered until they flew out of sight.

Carly put her car in drive.

It was the airbag that woke her up.

Carly looked around with a start, trying to get her bearings. She was strapped in the driver seat with the airbag deployed against her chest.

How did she get here?

She untangled herself from the seat. A cool breeze blew against her bare legs when she exited the vehicle.

This wasn't like her, not one bit.

Carly spun around, searching for any clues to help her understand what had happened.

She was dressed only in a long T-shirt and a pair of white

cotton panties, and her car's hood was crumpled like an accordion against the trunk of a large tree on the sidewalk of a residential street.

A bus with Highland Park posted on its marquee approached. A few looky-loo passengers pressed their faces close to the window and stared at Carly's bare legs as the bus passed.

Horrified, Carly ran to her car. Her purse and phone were scattered on the floor of the passenger seat.

A strange prickly sensation stung her right ankle. Her feet were bare and filthy, and she had a large, bloody gash on her ankle.

She grabbed her phone and dialed Ava's number. When the call went straight to voicemail, she tried Rebecca, who answered.

"Carly? Is everything all right? I don't mind the late-night calls, but it's after midnight."

"It's an emergency. I had an accident."

"What happened?"

"I'm not sure. I'm somewhere in Highland Park. Hold on," Carly said. She pressed the map icon on her phone. "I'm on Range View Avenue at the corner of Nolden. Could you pick me up?"

"I'm a few minutes out. Are the police there?" Rebecca asked.

"Not yet. I need you to bring me some clothes."

"I'm leaving now."

From the backseat of her car, Carly pulled on a pair of sweatpants and shirt from Rebecca. She gave up on trying to pry on a pair of sandals two sizes too small when flashing lights from a police cruiser illuminated the rear window.

Carly grabbed a breath mint from her bag as a flashlight shone in the window.

"I need you to come out of the vehicle," a male voice said.

Carly popped the mint in her mouth and exited the car, where a middle-aged LAPD cop with a paunch and a dark mustache stood.

"I'm Officer Randy Stone. I need to see your license. Is this your vehicle?"

"Yes, it is," Carly said, and fumbled through her bag until she found her license and handed it to the officer.

"Have you been drinking, miss?" the officer asked. The officer pointed his flashlight at Carly and her filthy bare feet.

"I had a glass of wine, but that was hours ago," Carly said.

"I'm going to need you to do a breathalyzer."

Rebecca approached from the rear of her VW Bug with a blanket in hand.

"I was driving the car," Rebecca said. "Carly was at my house, and we had dinner. She had a few glasses of wine, and I offered to drive her home. A dog ran right in front of the car, and when I swerved to miss it, I lost control and hit the tree. I'm glad no one got hurt."

"What happened to your shoes, Miss . . . Bennett?" the officer said as he paused to search for her name on the license.

"I'm not sure," Carly said.

"Carly wasn't feeling well after dinner," Rebecca continued. "She got sick in the bathroom and didn't make it to the toilet. She puked on her shoes. I tried to clean them up and left them on my deck. You're feeling better now, right Carly?"

The officer looked back at Carly for her version of events. Rebecca nodded and gave Carly a wink, cuing her to play along.

"I am, thank you," Carly said.

"Why are your feet dirty, Miss Bennett?" Officer Stone asked.

"When we were walking to her car, my sprinklers were on and she stepped in a puddle," Rebecca said.

"If you were driving the car, whose car is that?" the officer asked.

"My boyfriend was at my house. I called him after the accident. He drove over here, dropped off my car and got a ride back to my place. You just missed him," Rebecca lied.

"It seems like you're the only one with the answers," the officer said to Rebecca. "So I'm clear, you drove your friend home instead of calling her a ride?"

"That's right. Carly wasn't feeling well. I wanted to be sure she was OK."

"It's a felony to lie and take the blame for an accident if

someone else was behind the wheel and driving under the influence."

"I don't lie, and I don't appreciate being accused of something like that," Rebecca snapped.

Officer Stone looked between the two women and then handed Carly her license.

"Make sure your friend doesn't get behind the wheel," the officer said to Rebecca and then returned to his car.

When the officer left, Carly threw her arms around Rebecca and gave her a hug.

"You were brilliant. I don't know what I would've done without you coming to my rescue," Carly said.

"You don't remember what happened?" Rebecca asked.

"I remember going to bed, but nothing after that."

"I don't know what's going on, "Rebecca answered. "But you're starting to scare me."

FORTY-SEVEN

Ava

Ava carried her clipboard under one arm of her navy-blue blazer, bypassed the main office of USC's Facilities and Maintenance department and walked with purpose toward two men dressed in dark pants and grey uniform shirts.

It was seven forty-five a.m., and Ava figured the old guard in the Custodial department was planning to milk every second of their freedom before they had to clock in for their shift.

She moved in for the kill while she still had a window.

"Excuse me. I'm hoping one of you can help me out. Did either of you know Ed Russo?" Ava asked in the best neutral Americanized accent she could muster.

"Maybe, depending on who you are," the heavier of the two men said.

The custodian had a thick shock of white hair and was wearing a nametag that read, *James Greco*.

"I'm the last line of defense before Ed Russo's family gets the money that's owed to them," Ava said, and closed the space between herself and the two men. "I'm an insurance investigator, and between you and me, your HR people are giving me the run-around. The lady I spoke to . . ."

"Deb Hyland," Greco said.

"That's right," Ava said and shook her head. Annoyed. "Deb Hyland was tight as a sewed-up zipper and wouldn't tell me anything about the circumstances around Mr. Russo's death. She kept citing personnel issues and palmed me off to the university's lawyers. What I'm guessing is that USC is circling its wagons since they're afraid Mr. Russo's family is going to pin them in a wrongful death lawsuit since he was murdered on campus. Your name is James?"

"You can call me Jimmy."

"All I'm trying to do, Jimmy, is tie up a few loose ends for my supervisor so we can close this investigation and get Mr. Russo's family his life insurance money. Can you help me?"

"I've got a few minutes. Follow me."

Ava trailed the custodian to the back of the building, where he pulled out a pack of Marlboro cigarettes.

"You mind if I smoke? I'm trying to quit, but my mind hasn't gotten there yet," he said.

"Feel free. I need to verify that Mr. Russo wasn't exhibiting any signs of depression prior to his death."

"Ed? He was as upbeat as they come. But word on the street is that Ed was found with a plastic baggie around his head. That sounds like a pretty freaky way to kill yourself."

"I don't make the rules about these things. I have to dot the i's and cross the t's on the list of questions my boss gives me. I'm a cog in the wheel, but if I get the questions answered, there's a better shot that Ed's family will get their money."

Ava scribbled away on her clipboard like she was taking detailed notes.

"I hear you there. I'll tell you what I know about Ed. He was a pretty good guy. He could talk your ear off about sports, and he was definitely a showboat, but he was OK otherwise. He never went out with us for drinks on Friday because he swore off booze, so I didn't get to know him that well. People are different when they're not at work, but Ed seemed like a decent enough guy. He was a lady's man for sure, I can tell you that."

Jim pursed his lips and nodded, like he was telling Ava a juicy one.

"Was he in a relationship that went south and maybe things got ugly?" she asked.

"I wouldn't know about that. But I can tell you that Ed dipped his toe in the USC lady pool more than once."

Ava refrained from wanting to sucker punch Jim for saying something so lame.

"Was he seeing someone who worked here?"

"Maybe, but the girls I saw him with looked younger."

"Do you know their names?" Ava pressed.

"I wasn't formally introduced to any of them, but I got to know one of them pretty good."

"What do you mean by that?"

"I don't want to speak ill of the dead, but one time I was working a late shift, and I heard a big commotion in the janitor's closet. I opened the door, and there was Ed, going at it with a female. Ed was on the short side, but he was built like a brickhouse and talked a good game. I guess women like that sort of thing."

"When did this happen?"

Jim sucked his teeth and took a drag of his cigarette.

"Probably a couple of years ago, but I'm not sure on the exact dates. I do remember Ed had only worked at the school maybe six months. He was embarrassed when I found him. Later he told me he'd gotten caught up in the moment, and it was the chick's idea. I guess she had a crazy libido or something."

"Did Ed tell you who the girl was? Or maybe you remember what she looked like. Was she a blonde?"

"No, that girl had dark hair, down to her waist. She looked like one of those bohemian chicks. And she had a lot of tats. It wasn't like I was trying to look at her in the closet with Ed, but she was buck naked at the time. I remember she had a tattoo of an elephant on her wrist. "I remember it, because I took my grandkids to the zoo the weekend before, and the youngest made me sit out in the blazing heat for an hour so he could see the elephants. You think that girl killed Ed?"

"I'm not sure, but you were a big help."

By the time she reached her truck, Ava was pumped with adrenaline, like she had scored four out of five correct lottery numbers and was waiting for the last one to be called in her favor.

It wasn't a slam dunk that Rebecca had killed Russo, but Carly's assistant had conveniently left out the fact she'd slept with him.

And then there was Julien, whose sudden reemergence into Carly's life still stunk to her like three-day-old fish rotting in the desert.

Ava placed a call to Sean. It was time to tighten the noose.

FORTY-EIGHT
Carly

Carly hugged the sides of her toilet and heaved. After Rebecca had brought her home the previous night, she'd gone straight to bed and had woken up with a fierce headache and wicked stomach cramps.

She splashed cold water on her face and willed herself to move. It was already eight a.m., and she had an appointment with Dr. Brian Whittaker in an hour. No matter how awful she felt, she had to get herself together.

Carly dabbed blush on her cheeks to hide her wan complexion and took four aspirins.

The light of her bathroom seemed to dim and then get very bright as the next wave of nausea hit. She counted to twenty; when she was done, the terrible feeling had passed.

One hour and an Uber ride later, Carly was in Santa Monica.

Dr. Whittaker's office was a located in a rear bungalow of a large private home a block away from the beach in Santa Monica.

Carly rang the bell, and when an intercom buzzed, she introduced herself.

The door opened to reveal a tall, lanky man in his late forties, with a runner's build and sandy-brown hair.

The psychiatrist shook Carly's hand with a firm grip and led her inside his office, where he motioned her to take a seat across from his desk. On the wall behind it were framed diplomas that showed off his impressive pedigree: an undergraduate degree from Brown, a Master's at Harvard and a PhD earned at Princeton.

"You said over the phone you wanted to talk about Julien," Dr. Whittaker said. "Is he in some kind of trouble?"

"I wasn't trying to be deceptive earlier, but I didn't think you'd meet me if I told you the truth. I'm looking into my mother's death."

"I see," Dr. Whittaker said. He leaned back in his chair and shot a look at the clock on the wall. Her pivot from Julien seemed to make the doctor's interest wane, so she redirected her course.

"Julien is a big reason I'm looking into my mother's murder. I'd like to know more about my stepbrother, and I'm hoping you can help me."

"Do you have a relationship with Julien now?" Whittaker asked.

"I wouldn't call it a relationship. Julien showed up out of the blue last week. I haven't seen him since I was a kid. Do you know what Julien did to me?"

"I can't get into specifics, but Julien seemed very remorseful for his actions," Dr. Whittaker said, and leaned in closer to Carly again. "How is Julien?"

"He's a psychiatrist, like you. I'm guessing the two of you aren't in touch."

"I haven't spoken to Julien in years. His father forbade it."

Carly tried not to show her excitement. This was the story she was hoping he'd tell.

"What happened between you and my stepfather?" she asked.

"I was with a patient at the time. Mr. White barged into my office. He was irate, to the point I was going to call the police. He pushed me against a wall and said he knew what I tried to do to Julien, and that I was a sick pervert for wanting to seduce his son. He claimed I told Julien I was in love with him. None of it was true. I never once touched Julien inappropriately, let alone any other child. I tried to explain this to Mr. White, but he wouldn't have it. He said if I bothered Julien again, he'd have me arrested."

"Why did Christopher think you'd tried to seduce Julien?"

"Julien was upset once during a session. I put my arm around him, but that was the only time I touched the boy. I believe Julien misinterpreted my intentions or made up the encounter to get me in trouble so he wouldn't have to continue treatment.

It was obvious from day one that Julien hated his sessions with me. The only exception was our last meeting when Julien had a breakthrough."

"What was your diagnosis of my stepbrother?" Carly asked.

"He was a bright kid, but he had some issues that could've been inherited from his mother. In my opinion, Julien was an acute psychopath with a borderline personality disorder."

Whittaker's professional assessment felt like vindication. On the surface Julien was like a perfect shiny apple, but inside he was rotten and squirming with maggots.

"Did you know my mother?" Carly asked.

"I did, but not well. She was always friendly when she picked up Julien after a session, but we never spoke at length."

"Do you remember the last time you saw my mother?"

"No, but I did speak to her the night she was killed. Julien called me that morning. He said that he wanted to reach out to me earlier but was afraid his father would find out. Julien sounded remorseful, since he told Christopher I put my arm around him during a session. Mr. White took it that I was coming on to his son. Julien sobbed and begged me to forgive him."

"Why did you call my mother?"

"I was hoping I could reason with her. Julien needed help. Trying to convince Christopher was a dead end. I was concerned Julien was suicidal. I tried to explain that it was imperative for Julien to continue treatment, but your mother warned me not to bother the family again. I had no choice but to let it go. It was a shame because Julien was making progress. During our last session, Julien called you at school to make amends.

"I don't know what you're talking about."

"Julien called you from my phone. I remember. On days when Julien was upset or refused to talk, I'd move our session from my office to a bench that overlooked the ocean. I hoped the change of scene would help him open up."

Carly tried to make sense of Whittaker's story. The only answer was that Julien had outwitted him.

"Julien never called me when I was at school," Carly said.

"That can't be. We were sitting on the bench. Julien moved

away to make the call, and I allowed it so he could have some privacy."

Whittaker shook his head and looked wistful, as though he now understood but was disappointed in himself or the outcome.

"Julien must've lost his nerve then but still told me he went through with it so he wouldn't look weak. It was always important for Julien to be the one in control. I hope he was able to right his course."

Carly thanked Dr. Whittaker and called for a car since hers was still at the mechanic after her accident.

Carly glanced quickly at her phone. She had a ten thirty class, and her time with Dr. Whittaker had gone on longer than expected. It would be cutting it close, but she should be able to arrive on campus just in time.

FORTY-NINE
Carly

"You need to take the next exit," Carly told the Uber driver.

"Sorry, miss, but we're not going anywhere until the accident clears ahead."

Carly sat in the backseat of a red Prius. She and her twenty-something male Uber driver had been stuck, unmoving, on the I-10 route from Santa Monica to USC for the past ten minutes. Even when they did reach the exit, it would take them another fifteen minutes to drive to campus.

Carly tried Rebecca's phone again.

"Hey, ho! It's Rebecca. You know what to do after the beep and have a very positive day!"

"Rebecca, I hope you got my last message. I'm stuck in traffic, and I need you to cancel my ten thirty class. Tell the students to come by my office in about an hour if they have any questions. You're a lifesaver."

Carly hung up and looked out at the eight lanes of grid-locked traffic that surrounded her in every direction. "I have to get to school. I'm a teacher and I'll be late for class," Carly pleaded.

"I understand, everyone is in a hurry to get somewhere, but this is LA. You've got to be totally Zen when you're driving, otherwise, the stress will kill you," the driver said.

"You have no idea what kind of stress I'm under," Carly sniped.

She didn't like being rude, but a lecture when she was about to miss her first class of the morning wasn't going to fly.

The inside of the Prius suddenly felt like an oven on broil. "Can you open the window? I need some air."

"I can turn on the AC."

The driver's voice sounded far away, like someone was talking while she was underwater.

Carly placed her palm against her now slick forehead.

"Please, open the window!" Carly shouted.

"You're not going to get sick in my car, are you?" the driver asked.

"That's the least of my worries. Get me to campus, ASAP."

Thirty minutes later, Carly fast-walked through the English building and to the lecture hall out of due diligence. She had missed the start of her freshman "Introduction to Creative Writing" class, and she was sure most of her students had been thrilled when they discovered their professor was a no-show, which meant they were free to go.

Carly was already drafting a mental apology e-mail to her students when she walked into the lecture hall.

"For homework, you can pick any Avenger character, but here's the twist: I want you to transform the character into the protagonist of a classic play or a novel. Think Black Widow as Jane Eyre, Thor as the Great Gatsby or the Hulk as Stanley Kowalski. Your assignment is to write up jacket copy for your plot. Give me your best elevator pitch, but the most important thing is to have fun and go full throttle with your imagination."

Carly stared at the person standing in front of the room, teaching her class. The woman was polished and well dressed in a white tuxedo shirt, a black pencil skirt and pair of high heels. She wore a pair of tortoiseshell-frame square glasses, and her dark hair was swept smartly off her face with a barrette.

A petite girl in the front row raised her hand.

"Yes, Violet," the teacher said.

"Your homework assignment is brilliant, Rebecca!"

"Rebecca, what are you doing here?" Carly said, barely recognizing the well-put-together young woman teaching her class.

"Oh, Miss Bennett, there you are. I was wrapping up," Rebecca said. "Everyone, I need a minute. Please start working on your assignment until I get back."

"Thank you for filling in, but I'll take it from here," Carly said.

"Can I have a word in private, Miss Bennett?" Rebecca whispered. She walked up the aisle and past her mentor in a confident gait.

When they reached the hallway, Rebecca turned toward her wearing a pair of glasses that looked like a dead ringer for her own.

"I told you to cancel class," Carly said. "I called you and left messages when you didn't answer."

Rebecca smoothed a line in her skirt. The new Rebecca, neat as a pin and unruffled by Carly's judgment.

"I must've missed them. You weren't here again, so I figured I needed to fill in for you."

"Thank you, but that wasn't necessary. I know you were trying to do a nice thing, but I'd prefer you run anything by me before you take over my classroom without permission. It's not that I don't believe in you, but the department has certain rules, and I'd prefer neither of us gets in trouble."

"I was trying to help!" Rebecca protested.

"I know, and I'm not mad at you," Carly said. "You look different."

"I feel different. You think I look stupid, don't you?"

Carly was surprised at Rebecca's sharp tone.

"No of course not. I think you look wonderful, but I love how the old Rebecca looked too."

"The dean wants to see you."

"Scanlon?"

"Yes, the dean. He said it was urgent," Rebecca said, giving a hint of a smug smile.

Carly stared harder at Rebecca. She must be mistaken. Rebecca would never do that to her.

"Did he say what it's about?"

"No, only that if I saw you, I was supposed to relay the message to go to his office right away. You should go. I can finish the class."

"I've got it covered. Is anything wrong?"

"Of course not," Rebecca said.

Rebecca turned from her mentor, her black high heels tapping out a brusque rhythm on the cement floor as she retreated down the hallway as though she was the one in charge.

Carly returned to the classroom, but was distracted for the entirety of the last fifteen minutes. She wondered why the dean would want to see her, not to mention why Rebecca was acting so oddly.

When class was over, she made a straight line to the dean's office.

Carly was ushered inside and took a seat while she waited for Scanlon to finish a phone call. She distracted herself by looking out the window, and willed the powers that be to help her not melt into a stuttering mess in front of her boss this time.

"Yes, I know English majors are down in the undergraduate level by ten percent. No, I don't see why that's a problem, Harry," Scanlon said.

He noticed Carly, gave her a small wave and then went back to his conversation.

"Do I have any ideas? Sure, here's a thought. Maybe you shouldn't make it so bloody hard for kids to get into this school in the first place . . . No, it seems to me that it's your problem to fix, not mine. I take one for the team every time I secure donations for the school, and I do a damn good job of it, despite the fact that it's not in my job description to scurry around, asking for cash. In the last year alone, I've been responsible for netting over two million dollars for the English department. Maybe you should think about considering a promotion for me, instead of ringing me up to give me the business about declining enrollment."

Scanlon grumbled out a few more complaints and ended the call.

"My assistant said you wanted to see me, but if this isn't a good time, I can come back," Carly said.

Scanlon crossed his arms across his chest and looked as though he just ate something far beyond its expiration date when he stared back at Carly.

"You've done some good work at the school, Miss Bennett. But that's the only nice thing that you will hear about yourself in this room. It's come to my attention that you're having personal difficulties that are causing issues with your work at the college. Do you know that your actions are a direct reflection on me and the department? I don't take too kindly to being embarrassed by one of my teachers."

"I don't understand."

"No need to be coy. I think you know exactly what I'm talking about. There's been a complaint lodged against you."

"A complaint, by who, a student?"

"I'm not at liberty to say, but I was appalled when I heard it. Your behavior as of late has been increasingly erratic, and I now believe you may be a risk to our department's reputation."

Scanlon leaned back in his chair, laced his fingers together and rested them on his ample stomach, as if trying to put some distance between himself and his troubled employee.

"I understand you were involved in an incident recently where police were called to the scene."

"It was a m–m–misunderstanding," Carly stammered.

"That stutter of yours that I've heard as of recent is troubling. We can't have our teachers stumbling through a lecture."

"I've never stuttered in class," Carly said. "And the incident with the police was a fluke."

"That's not how the person who filed the report saw it. The complaint claims you were in an accident last night, and the officer at the scene believed you'd been drinking. Not only that, but you were barely dressed and exhibiting bizarre behavior. We verified this account with the police. Our faculty needs to uphold the very highest of standards for our students, our donors, and the community. Until a thorough investigation has been conducted by the school, you are, as of this moment, suspended and not allowed to set foot on campus. Do you understand, Miss Bennett?"

Carly felt like she had a pound of dry sand caught in her throat as she fought to speak.

"Now take what you need from your office and then I'll need you to leave. Please make this as seamless as possible. I'd hate to have to call campus security. It's a shame, as I believed you once held great promise, but I'm afraid I was mistaken. If you plan to file a lawsuit against the school over this, please note that you'll face a very difficult battle."

Carly balled her hands into fists, and for the first time in a very long time, Carly found her voice.

It came out strong and clear.

"I'm the one who was mistaken. I should've told you weeks ago that you were a greedy windbag when you kissed up to that donor and expunged the record of my former student who plagiarized. When I started here as a professor, I was in awe of you, but now I see that I was naive," Carly said. "And for the record, I don't plan on filing a lawsuit against the school for this bullshit suspension. But I do plan on filing an ethical complaint against you for putting money ahead of morals."

"Miss Bennet . . ." Scanlon said.

But Carly was already out the door.

Fairly certain she was now out of a job but feeling downright fizzy for finally getting the guts to dress down Scanlon, Carly entered her office with her head held high.

Her moment of triumph took a backseat when she saw Rebecca, sitting in *her* chair and looking all too comfortable at *her* desk. Violet, with notebook in hand, was seated across from her and writing down Rebecca's every word, a familiar tableau except for Carly playing the role of the promising young teacher and Rebecca the adoring student.

And then it all came together. Of course, it was Rebecca who filed the complaint. No one else knew about the car accident, and it was Rebecca who she'd called from the Malibu bar.

Carly pushed her way inside to reclaim what was hers.

"Rebecca, I need to talk to you."

"Oh, Carly, I was talking with Violet about the assignment. We'll be done in a minute."

"This is my office, and your conversation has ended. Violet, I need you to leave. If you have questions, you can contact me directly."

"But I thought you were—" Rebecca started to say, but Carly cut her off before she could finish. If Carly had one shred of dignity left, she didn't want Violet or any other student to catch on that she'd been suspended.

"Whatever you thought was wrong. I need my office."

Violet gave Rebecca a confused look, but then left quickly and Carly shut the door behind her.

"Get out of my chair," Carly said.

"Why are you being so mean? You weren't here, and Violet came by with a question. I was trying to help."

"Unfortunately for me, I used to believe that. What did you tell Dean Scanlon?"

A blotch of red blossomed up Rebecca's neck and she scratched at it nervously.

"I was worried about you. I didn't know what else to do."

"If you were worried, you should've come to me directly and not told the dean of the English department that I'm having a nervous breakdown."

"That's not what I said. I tried to help you, but whatever I did was never good enough. You never once listened or took me seriously. I thought if I told Scanlon, you'd pay attention."

"You told Scanlon about my accident and said I was acting erratically," Carly accused. "You poisoned me to my boss after I gave you a chance and helped you financially when your boyfriend left. I trusted you, Rebecca. I thought we were friends."

"The way you were acting scared me. Your students need you, and I need you too, but you let me down. You're supposed to be perfect."

Carly threw her hands up over the absurdity of the situation.

"If you think I'm perfect, God help you and the rest of the planet," Carly said. "I want you to leave right now, and I don't want you in my classroom ever again."

"You can't do that! I'm a good teacher. You should've seen me with the students, they loved me, and we had a special connection because I used to be in their shoes. But you never gave me a chance to teach, not once. All I did was manage your schedule and pick up your dry cleaning, like I was your slave."

"Go home, Rebecca. I don't know what your grand plan is,

but I can only guess. I'll call Bert and tell him that you set me up for your personal gain."

"You're the one who screwed up, not me. Everything I did was for your own good. You couldn't even get to class on time anymore. I was trying to help the students because you became a mess after Ed Russo died. You've got problems, Carly, but I didn't realize it until now."

"You're fired, Rebecca."

Rebecca's mouth dropped open in surprise.

The two women stood facing each other in silence for a moment, until Rebecca raised her arm and slapped Carly hard across the face.

Rebecca clapped her hands over her mouth and took a quick step back when it seemed that the gravity of her action took hold.

"I'm so sorry! I don't know what came over me. You have to forgive me," Rebecca pleaded.

"Get out. I don't ever want to see you again."

Rebecca raced out of the office, and Carly watched her former assistant rip off her high heels and then sprint down the corridor until she was out of sight.

Now alone, Carly packed the remains of three years spent at the college into a single cardboard box. Then she officially left the English building as another part of her life slipped away.

After she loaded the box in the trunk of her rental car, Carly realized she'd placed her phone on silence mode and that she'd missed five calls from Ava.

When Carly called her back, Ava answered on the first ring.

"Christ, Bennett, where are you?"

"I'm leaving school. I was supposed to teach another class this afternoon, but something happened."

"Get out of there now. I just got off the phone with Sean. He got a tip that the officers working Russo's case got a warrant for your arrest about an hour ago. They're on the way to campus to pick you up. Whatever you do, don't go home, and stay in contact with me. I may know a way to get you out of this."

FIFTY
Ava

Ava parked her truck down the street from Rebecca's duplex and waited for her to come out. Stakeouts could be a major yawn, unless you utilized your time well, and in the case of saving Carly, every click of the minute hand on the clock counted.

She scanned the pages of her notebook where she'd squirreled away details about the case, pausing on the name Yvonne Abbott, the widow of Garrett Abbott, and the possible owner of the Karmann Ghia that Sebastian Foster, aka the phony who'd accompanied Carly to Zuma Beach, had claimed to be his. Ava googled her name.

"Bingo," Ava said.

Yvonne Abbott, a maroon-haired Caldwell Banker Realtor in Reno looked back at her from the phone screen.

Ava placed the call.

"This is Yvonne. Can I get you into your dream house?"

"You can't, but I can pay you a hundred bucks if you can tell me if you had a husband who owned a Karmann Ghia."

The line went silent, and Ava worried that she'd overplayed her hand.

"My husband Garrett owned a seventy-four model. Some lawyer from California already called me about this. I've been away on a retreat and haven't had a chance to call him back. What's this about?"

"The said lawyer and I work together. I know your husband passed, and for that I'm sorry. But did you sell his car after he died?" Ava asked.

"My brother handled all that for me. I do know that he sold the car, and I got top price for it, but I can't remember who he sold it to. Let me call my brother Ethan, and I'll get back to you. Am I in some kind of trouble related to the car?"

"Not at all, Ms. Abbott. I appreciate your help."

FIFTY-ONE
Carly

Carly sped down the freeway in her rental car en route to the Whites' Malibu estate.

There was no logical reason behind her decision to return there, except she had nowhere else to go, and home was out of the question since that would be the police's next stop after not finding her at school.

She veered off the exit that would take her to the Whites' place and felt bruised again over Rebecca's masterclass in betrayal. Here, she was worried that Julien was going to dupe her, and under her very nose, her assistant did it instead, despite all the support and chances she'd given to Rebecca.

The rental car reached the top of the Whites' old street, and Carly parked it behind the familiar thicket of eucalyptus trees that would keep her hidden.

She ran along the tree line until she reached the gate and hid in the shadows.

Her cell phone buzzed in her pocket. An unfamiliar number left a text message.

I'm sorry if it seemed like I was stalking you at the beach on Friday. Please call me—Amelia Peterson.

Carly tried to make sense of her former student's message.

She dialed the number and prayed Amelia would answer.

"Miss Bennett, thank you so much for calling me back. I had your number from last year, and I hope it's OK that I contacted you by phone. I'm sorry to keep pestering you, but I wanted to apologize if it seemed like I was staring at you while you were on your date. I never meant to make you feel uncomfortable, and I know I did because you've been avoiding me. I'm not a stalker, I swear."

"You saw me at Zuma Beach last Friday?"

"I went for a run, and I saw you on the beach with a bearded man. I knew it was you right away, and I always thought you were so cool and a great teacher. I could tell that you were on a date, because I saw the man kiss your hand. He looked at me, and I knew you both realized I was staring at you. I didn't mean anything by it. I'm going to register for one of your classes next semester, and I wanted to be sure that was OK."

"That's more than OK. You can take any class of mine for the rest of your life."

After she ended the call, Carly planned to phone Ava with the great news she now had an airtight alibi for Russo's murder, but crouched down when gravel snapped behind her from an approaching car.

The automatic gate opened to make way for the vehicle, and Carly waited for it to pass before she came out of her hiding place.

In the driveway was a yellow convertible. Phillip Edwards exited and was greeted by the lady of the house.

Carly at first couldn't understand why Edwards was there, but then figured the most logical reason was that he bought the place after Christopher died, and the woman was his wife.

"That's her, the woman who was here before. She's standing at the gate."

She'd been made. Edwards and the woman approached as Carly ran to her car.

"Hold on," Edwards yelled.

Only steps away from her vehicle, Carly skidded on the loose gravel and lost her footing. By the time she scrambled to her feet, Edwards was already there, out of breath, but close enough to touch her.

"I told you to stay away," Edwards yelled.

He was in her face now, finger jutting the air to make his point and eyes wild with anger.

"Coming here was a mistake," Carly said.

She stepped back, wanting to defuse the situation, but Edwards grabbed her arm and squeezed.

"Let go!" Carly cried.

"I will when I've said my piece. You need to leave Chris

alone. Badgering a man on his deathbed isn't going to do you any good."

"Christopher is alive?"

"Of course, he is. Why on earth would you think otherwise?"

"Julien," Carly whispered.

FIFTY-TWO
Ava

Tired of waiting and now gunning for a confrontation, Ava was ready to knock on Rebecca's door, when a red VW Bug pulled out of the garage. Ava dropped three spots behind Rebecca's VW and followed it onto the freeway entrance toward Santa Monica.

She dialed Carly's number, but when it went straight to voicemail, she took an incoming call from Sean.

"You'd better not be calling to tell me the LAPD arrested Carly."

"Smith and Rodriguez tried to pick her up at school, but Carly had already fled the scene. I'm guessing you tipped her off. I know she's your friend, but I don't want my backdoor line to the cops drying up because of this."

"I have no idea what you're talking about, and you need to tell your secret sources that their colleagues are after the wrong woman. I'm following Carly's assistant right now. If I can get her to admit to her relationship with Russo, then the police might loosen their grip on Bennett. From where I'm standing, Rebecca Hunter had a rock-solid motive to kill Russo. His wife told me about a woman he was seeing at school, and apparently, Russo's chick had a vicious jealous streak. Russo cut off the relationship because he was worried all the drama was going to affect his recovery. Rebecca sees Russo paying a bunch of attention to Carly, she gets jealous, and offs him. The girl is an oddball. I thought she was harmless before, but with the weird ones, you can never be sure of their true intentions."

"What you've got is a juicy theory with no evidence and no confession, not to mention an uphill battle against cop mentality to pivot if they've already locked in on a suspect."

"I was starting to feel better about things, but now you've gone and ruined it."

"Sorry I dampened your mood, but I'm calling about another one of your urgent matters. My buddy who works patrol ran the plate you asked about. The owner of the Range Rover is Anthony DiMatteo."

"That's all you've got?"

Ava blew past a lagging car in front of her and shot back into the lane.

Rebecca's vehicle was still in sight.

"Of course not," Sean said. "I knew all the trouble I went through to get you a name wouldn't be good enough. Anthony is twenty-eight and studied pre-law at Chico State. He goes to St. Vincent de Paul for Mass most Sundays and currently works at the law firm of Nowak, Miller and Hawkin. It looks like he's a glorified paralegal secretary to the partners in the firm. I knew you'd want me to check his nasty sheet, but the only thing on the guy's record is a citation for being drunk at a college football game."

"Rah, rah Chico State."

"One more thing, I figured Anthony had some kind of connection to that Julien White character you asked me about. I did some digging, and it looks like Nowak, Miller and Hawkin is Julien White's law firm. And his father's too."

"That's past tense. Julien's dad is dead."

"You're wrong about that. I did a deep-dive check on Julien, because I knew you'd ask. Christopher White is alive and kicking, but apparently, he's got cancer and his prognosis isn't good."

"Ooh, that is a juicy tidbit you unearthed. As expected, Mr. White's lies begin to unravel. I owe you for this," Ava said.

"If Rebecca did kill Russo, then all your digging into Carly's stepbrother will be a waste of time. The only thing you'll know for sure is that Julien White is still a liar, and there's no crime in that."

"Not yet. By the way, I connected with Yvonne Abbott about the Karmann Ghia driven by the elusive Sebastian Foster. Her brother sold it after her husband passed, and Yvonne is tracking down the seller," Ava said.

"Nice work. Do you think the buyer was Julien?"

"I'd bet the house on that one, love."

Rebecca exited the freeway at Venice Beach.

Ava kept the tight tail until the VW parked next to a restaurant called The Butcher's Daughter.

Ava idled halfway down the block and, out of habit, took a few pictures when Rebecca exited her vehicle. A male dressed in a tie-dye T-shirt, olive-colored harem pants and Birkenstock sandals rushed over to Rebecca and enveloped her in a close embrace before the two entered the restaurant.

Rebecca's male companion complicated her plan, but with the police closing in on Carly, she needed to take a risk.

After parking a block away, Ava pulled on a baseball cap.

Inside the restaurant, Rebecca sat in a booth, facing the door. Across from Rebecca was her companion.

Ava could only see the man's back and his dark hair piled high in a dorky man bun.

She claimed an empty stool at the bar, shielded her face with a menu and ordered a coffee. Ava opened the camera icon on her phone and took a few discreet pictures of Rebecca and her hippy-looking friend.

Despite the collective din of the happy hour crowd, Ava was close enough to catch intermittent snatches from the pair's conversation, and from the bits and pieces she was picking up, it was clear Rebecca's friend was doing most of the talking.

"That's terrible."

"You did the right thing."

"Please don't give me even an ounce of credit. It was all your idea. You were the one who realized something was wrong, and you were brave enough to act."

"Stop blaming yourself. Sometimes a person's problems are so big, no one can help them. You went above and beyond, but you were never appreciated, not once."

Ava pretended to study the menu and wondered if Rebecca hired the man to help kill Russo.

"I'm sorry about what happened, but God, you look sexy as hell. You are way too beautiful to be sitting so far away from me."

His voice had a slight Southern twang, yet there was something familiar about it.

The man got up from his side of the booth and moved toward Rebecca.

He turned then. Ava's heart beat a jagged rhythm when the man's face was revealed.

Ava pulled down the bill of her baseball cap, put a ten down on the table to cover the coffee and did a smooth and easy walk to the exit.

Unable to help herself, she turned and shot one last picture.

When she reached her car, Ava scrolled through the photos until she came to the last frame.

"You son of a bitch."

She couldn't take her eyes off Julien wearing a fake scruffy beard and man bun.

Ava shuddered in disgust when she enlarged the picture. There was Julien giving Rebecca Hunter what was likely the most passionate kiss of her life.

FIFTY-THREE
Carly

Carly felt like she was in a parallel universe. Christopher was no longer the virile doctor who lorded over the wealthy Malibu set and ruled his household with an iron fist. This Christopher was all bones and hanging skin on a melting frame, a body ravaged by sickness and looking much older than his years.

Christopher inched his wheelchair forward on the porch and cupped a withered hand over his eyes as if to get a better look at his former stepdaughter.

"Chris is terminal. If you don't leave this minute, I'll call the police," Edwards warned.

"It's fine, Phillip. She can stay," Christopher said in a hoarse voice, and then turned to Carly. "I always knew you'd come back, but I didn't plan on having this conversation in the middle of the street when you did. Please, come inside."

The woman with the dark hair guided Christopher's wheelchair into the house.

"Bridgette, get me a blanket and take me to the deck. I'd like to see something pretty," Christopher said.

"You don't have to say anything to the girl, Chris," Edwards pleaded.

"Yes, I do. I need a few minutes with Carly without everyone hovering over me."

Carly followed her stepfather and the woman she now assumed was Christopher's caretaker into the house, and then out to the expansive deck that faced the rear of the estate and the ocean.

"That will be all, Bridgette, thank you. Make sure Phillip goes home."

Christopher waited until they were alone to continue.

"I imagine you don't like me very much, but say what you must because I deserve it."

"Julien told me you were dead."

"You spoke to him?"

"Julien showed up at my school. The last time I saw him was the day you and my mother kicked me out of here."

"I tried to protect you, but Julien must've found out somehow. This is important. I need to know exactly what my son told you about me."

"Julien said you'd been sick and recently passed away. Victor is under the same assumption. Julien told him that you died."

"You spoke to Victor?" When Christopher said his younger son's name, his voice cracked with emotion.

"We got back in touch recently. You should be very proud of him."

Christopher raised a hand, as if to dismiss the sentiment. "Did Julien hurt you?"

"He was never physical, if that's what you mean. He apologized and claimed he wanted to make amends."

"Don't believe it. You should be terrified of Julien. I know I am. It's a terrible thing to say about your own child, but Julien always scared me, even when he was a boy. That's why I first sent him to a psychiatrist, but I made a pact with him fifteen years ago. I sold my soul to him then, and I've regretted it ever since. Most people in my condition would do anything to get better, but part of me wants to die because that's the only way I'll ever be free of him."

Carly moved to the railing and looked at the Pacific Ocean, trying to summon the courage to tell another soul her secret.

"Julien said you were the one who found my mother's body. I left school the day she was killed and took a bus to Malibu. I've never told anyone this before. I planned to confront my mom and beg her to let me come home, but I was so nervous, and something bad happened to me earlier that day. Chatham used to give troubled girls pills to keep us quiet. I never took them, not even once, but I brought a stash with me, in case. I have no idea what they were, probably Prozac or something. When I got to the house, I was so nervous, I took a few of the pills to calm my nerves. I can't remember anything after that. All these years later, I always wondered if I witnessed my mom's murder, but didn't do anything to stop it."

Carly leaned against the railing and sobbed until she felt a comforting hand on her back.

She turned. Christopher looked even paler than when she'd first seen him, and his face was dewy with sweat from the obvious effort that it had taken him to wheel across the deck to her.

"You weren't there, Carly. That's one thing I'm sure of. We had security tapes all over the property, but I wiped them clean so the police wouldn't know they existed. The tapes showed you, hiding in the trees near the security gate, but you ran away, toward the main road. You never entered the house."

"I failed my mom then. I could've stopped her killer."

"If you'd gone into the house that night, you would've been murdered too. I know that as a fact. I was there."

Christopher's hands trembled when he recounted the story.

FIFTY-FOUR
Christopher

March 2010

Christopher pulled into his driveway and decided he'd forgive Emily for having an affair. He'd been in such a blind rage, believing Phillip was her lover, but later realized his mistake when his best friend explained what had occurred the day Christopher thought he'd caught them in the act.

Still, he knew his wife was seeing someone on the side. Emily had grown aloof after Carly left, and then she'd leave the house for hours at a time without explanation.

Christopher found his proof one night while Emily was in the shower. Despite his suspicions, Christopher felt out of his body when he discovered several sexually charged text messages on Emily's phone from an unknown sender.

He was never able to confirm the man's identity, which left him picturing the naked back of a man moving above his wife until she gasped in pleasure. Regardless of her infidelity, he would forgive Emily for this indiscretion, and only this once, would look the other way to save his marriage.

It wasn't exactly as though he was blameless. Christopher was in part responsible for driving Emily away and into the arms of another man. He liked Emily's girl at first, but Carly's constant acting out drove a wedge between him and his wife. Christopher continued to apply the pressure and insisted Carly would be better off at Chatham. The school was one of the most revered girls' institutions in the country, yet Carly never appreciated her good fortune, and her misery from being away from her mother ate away at Emily like a disease, until his wife started to resent him.

He and Emily could have a fresh start if his wife promised she'd never cheat on him again. He loved her enough to take her back. Some might think he was a lesser man for it, but Christopher didn't want to lose the vibrant, beautiful young woman he took as his wife.

When Christopher exited his car, it was after midnight. He left an hour early from his shift at the hospital to surprise Emily, and hoped she'd still be up, but was disappointed when he saw their bedroom light wasn't on.

Even if she were sleeping, he ached to see her. To feel the warmth of his wife's body and smell her perfume would be enough.

Christopher fit the key in the lock but paused when he heard movement on the roof and then a loud crash coming from the second story. He thought he heard a rustle in the trees behind him but rushed into the house and bound up the stairs to their bedroom.

"Emily?" Christopher called.

When he flicked on the light, there was Julien, straddling Emily on the bed with a pillow pressed down on her face.

"What are you doing?" Christopher screamed.

Julien looked blankly at his father and then went back to work.

"Get off her now!"

Christopher ran to his wife's side but stumbled over a lamp on the floor that had been knocked off Emily's nightstand. He picked up the lamp and smashed it over Julien's shoulders to get his son to stop.

Julien was unmoved.

Christopher pried the boy off his wife, and Julien bucked as father and son tumbled to the floor. Julien thrashed underneath his father like a rabid, vicious animal until Christopher punched his son in the nose to finish it.

"Get off me, you bastard," Julien said. "This is your fault. I hated her. I hated her so much, but you let her into our life, Emily and that stupid daughter of hers. Emily was a gold digger and a phony, but you were too dumb to see it. Everything was fine, but then she came along and spoiled all of it."

Christopher looked at his son with utter revulsion and then ran to Emily's side.

Her body was still warm.

"Hang on!" Christopher begged his wife, but then broke down when he couldn't get a pulse.

"Call 911," Christopher shouted.

"For what? She's dead. I made sure of it. If you bring your wife back, she's going to be a vegetable. Is that what you want? Have some mercy, old man. Let her go."

"Call the police," Christopher begged, but he knew it was too late.

He collapsed on the edge of the bed next to his wife's body, scooped her into his arms and held her.

"Emily was nothing but a nuisance. You would've grown tired of her eventually, like you did with my mother."

"Shut up. You're going to pay for this. I'm going to tell the police everything."

Julien rose from the floor and wiped his bloody nose with the back of his shirtsleeve.

It was then that Christopher saw the pair of black gloves Julien was wearing.

"Are you sure that's what you want to do? I think that will put you in a very tricky situation. Your DNA is all over your wife's body now, isn't it? Plenty of people will remember your outburst when you accused your wife and best friend of sleeping together behind your back. There were so many witnesses . . . me, the housekeeper, and your friend Phillip with the stupid car. You threatened to kill him, we all heard it."

"What are getting at?"

"It's simple. If you call the police, I'll tell them that I rushed home from a school trip when I called Emily to check in, and she told me the two of you got in a huge fight and she feared for her life."

"That's not true," Christopher said.

Julien looked at his watch and yawned, like murdering his stepmother was a tedious chore he'd just completed.

"I have phone records that prove I spoke with Emily earlier this evening. So, it's my word against yours. Even a smart police officer might need a nudge in the right direction to put two and two together that your first wife died under suspicious circumstances and so did wife number two. Police always suspect the husband first."

"You're going to tell the police I killed my wife?"

"Not in so many words, but I would lead them in that direction until they took the bait."

Christopher looked at his beautiful Emily and wanted vengeance for what Julien did to her. But he wouldn't last a day in prison.

"What do you want?" Christopher demanded.

"For you to roll up your sleeves and help me. We need to make this look like a robbery, but I need a promise from you. Swear you'll never tell anyone what happened."

Christopher swallowed and wondered if he'd be sick.

"Say it."

"I swear," Christopher said. "I'll never tell anyone what happened."

"Good, now hurry up. I've got a three-hour drive ahead of me, and I need to get back to the hotel before the chaperones notice I'm gone."

FIFTY-FIVE
Carly

Carly held onto her mother's ruby pendant as Christopher's cruel story settled in.

"Julien killed my mom out of jealousy, and you were too afraid to do the right thing," Carly accused.

"I'm ashamed of what I did, but the situation was complicated." Christopher's voice sounded whiny, like that of a petulant child.

"The truth isn't complicated. It's the people who twist themselves in the lie that make it complicated," Carly said. "There's one thing I don't understand. If Julien thought you were headed for a divorce, my mother wouldn't have been a problem for him anymore, so why did he murder her?"

"Julien planned to go to a class trip to San Diego. Right before he left, he came by my office to get some money. I told him I'd spoken with Emily, and she and I had agreed to try and work things out. I said we loved each other very much, and Emily was going to bring you home. Julien seemed pleased with the news. He told me how great it was that Emily and I were getting back together, and he'd been worried about you being alone at school. I believed him."

"You never told the police the truth," Carly said.

"I couldn't, but I've tried to make it right by you."

"I never wanted your money after my mother died."

"I wasn't referring to that, but it's better you didn't know."

"The police said you had an alibi the night my mother was killed."

"The doctor who was my supervisor at the hospital, he was a friend. I loaned him some money for a restaurant project. After Julien murdered Emily, the police questioned me. I needed an alibi to make up for the lost hours, and my friend covered for me. I told him I was stuck in traffic on the way home from work, and when I got home, Emily was dead. My friend backed up my story."

"But Phillip knew the truth. He's still trying to protect you."

"I never told Phillip specifics, only that there was more to the story. I think, deep down, he knew Julien was the killer, and I was covering for my son."

"I'm going to tell the police the truth," Carly said.

Christopher stared out at the ocean and nodded, as if resigned to his fate.

"Why did Julien resurface in my life?" Carly asked.

"I'll call a security firm to keep you safe."

"I can take care of myself. Is Victor in danger?" Carly asked.

"I don't know about Julien's intent toward his brother."

Christopher turned his wheelchair to face her then, and his eyes reflected stone-cold fear.

"There's one thing I know for sure. Julien wants you dead."

FIFTY-SIX

Ava

Ava lay on a thick branch of a tree in the backyard of the house that abutted the rear of Julien's home. Her camera was clipped to her side, and her gun was holstered underneath her jacket.

As she waited for Carly's stepbrother to arrive, Ava replayed the events she'd witnessed at the restaurant and what came after.

After her abrupt exit, Ava staked out The Butcher's Daughter until Rebecca and Julien emerged. The two left in separate cars but followed each other back to the city and Rebecca's duplex. Julien stayed at Rebecca's for exactly one hour, like he was timing it to the second, and left alone. Ava then followed Carly's stepbrother back to Silver Lake and settled in at her previous lookout post to try and catch Julien. But catch him at what? begged the million-dollar question.

It was clear to her that Julien had seduced Rebecca to get to Carly, but for what end? And there was no clear line that connected Carly's stepbrother and Ed Russo, unless Rebecca killed the janitor, and his death was separate from her relationship with Julien.

Still, with no Julien in sight, Ava did a search for Carly's bio page on the USC website. Up popped Carly's headshot, her curriculum vitae and class roster. Then, as Ava suspected, was the following: *To reach Miss Bennett, contact her assistant, Rebecca Hunter.*

Rebecca's phone number and e-mail address came next.

If Ava had been working a job and needed an "in" on a bail jumper, she would have snatched that low-hanging fruit and found Rebecca's whereabouts within minutes. Ava considered Julien was intelligent and would've done the same, but with an additional heavy dose of doting and compliments, which would've easily won over the insecure girl.

Still, she wasn't sure what was behind the lie about Christopher White being dead, or the connection to the law firm and the preppy, Anthony DiMatteo, whom Julien had seduced the day before.

Ava grabbed her camera when the lights came on inside Julien's house. Carly's stepbrother came into view. Still wearing his hippy getup from earlier, Julien moved past the living room to his kitchen, where he set a large brown paper bag on the counter.

Ava zoomed in on Julien, who pulled on a pair of black plastic gloves. He removed each item from the bag and arranged them in a neat row.

Ava snapped a picture of each: A container of Sleep Time Cookies, a single pill bottle, a jar of store-bought vanilla icing, and a small brown box.

Julien retrieved a glass bowl from a cabinet and filled it with water from the sink. He opened the box and pulled out several colorful balls, rolled them and dropped them into the water.

Next, he pulled out a larger, rectangular box, and then poured a teaspoon full of its contents inside the liquid mixture. Julien then opened the pill bottle onto a cutting board, and with a sharp knife, ground the white tablets against the blade until they were powder, and added it to the icing. With the careful precision of a skilled baker, he topped off the vanilla icing onto the cookies, closed the container, and placed a label on the package that read, "Healthy Life: David Ramsey Foods."

Ava tightened her focus on the pill bottle and the box, and nearly dropped the camera when she realized what Julien was doing.

She dropped from the tree, scaled the fence of the property and ran to her car.

FIFTY-SEVEN
Carly

On the drive to her house, Carly tried reaching Ava several times for a debrief about her alibi for Russo's murder and Christopher's confessional, but her calls went straight to voicemail.

Carly turned onto her block. Her house was dark except for a light that was on in her kitchen. She was certain she'd turned off each light before she left that morning, as she always did.

Christopher's warning rang in her head.

Carly parked on the street and crept along the side of her house, until she was underneath her kitchen window.

Standing on her tiptoes, Carly peered inside.

Rebecca stood at the kitchen island.

Carly ducked down and hurried from the window when she felt her cell phone vibrate in her pocket, alerting her to a new text message.

It was from Ava.

Julien and Rebecca are working together. They're slipping you ketamine and trying to poison you. Stay away from them and don't go home. Call me as soon as you get this.

Cheerful, hopelessly insecure Rebecca had been conspiring her downfall with Julien this entire time?

Carly couldn't let Rebecca get away with it. She raced to the backdoor and entered the kitchen.

Rebecca hid something in her purse when Carly came into view.

"Carly, you scared me! I didn't think you'd be home already."

"That's obvious. What are you doing here?"

"I came to drop off your key and leave you a note. I've been gutted since our fight. You were right about everything, and I overstepped my bounds. I idolize you so much, and I got carried away. I thought you didn't appreciate me. And then I slapped you. I feel sick to my stomach every time I remember what I did. I hope you can forgive me."

Carly kept moving closer to Rebecca until her assistant backed herself against the wall.

"You're a liar. You were the one who was making me sick. I thought there was something wrong with me, and I convinced myself I was losing my mind. You're a wonderful actress, Rebecca. I would've never guessed you of all people would try to kill me."

"I have no idea what you're talking about."

"You can give up your charade. I know you were poisoning me. That time I found myself at Moonshadows, and then the accident; I thought I was going crazy. But you and Julien were drugging me too. How long have you and Julien been working together?"

Rebecca seemed to fold into herself and cowered.

"Who's Julien? You're acting crazy again. I was only trying to help you, that's all I've ever done."

"I'm calling the police."

"I did everything for you, but you never once appreciated me. You took me for granted and ruined any good thing I had—our friendship, my career . . . My life was perfect, and I was becoming someone like you. Maybe even someone better than you. It's not fair, but I have someone who loves me now, and you can't take that away."

Rebecca stood up straight and reached into her bag, pulling out something silver and shiny.

The butt of a gun.

"Ava knows everything. If you kill me, she's going to come after you," Carly said.

"I wish you'd stop saying crazy things."

Rebecca's face fell. "I loved you, Carly."

In one swift motion, Rebecca's hand came out of her bag.

A gunshot rang out, sounding as loud and as powerful as a bomb exploding in the small space.

The second shot came fifteen seconds later.

FIFTY-EIGHT
Julien

Julien finished adding the crushed ketamine to the icing and infused the last of the flowered tea blossoms with the rat poison. He then assembled them carefully in a Tupperware dish to dry. He peeled off his gloves and scrubbed his hands and underneath his fingernails with hot, soapy water to ensure they were clean.

When he was done disinfecting himself, Julien poured a scotch and removed his hairpiece and the itchy fake beard that made him crazy every time he wore it. Sacrifices had to be made to win the endgame. His latest game would be over soon enough.

The floor-to-ceiling windows of the house clinched the property when he toured it two years earlier, and he admired the view they offered. Julien savored the scotch, when something appeared to dart across the yard of the vacant property behind his.

Julien flicked on floodlights, but whatever it was, dog, cat, or coyote, it was long gone.

He tilted the crystal tumbler to his mouth again, finished his drink, and decided Carly had some degree of luck going for her, despite her terrible childhood that he helped ruin without that much effort. Carly and her mother had been a colossal nuisance, two lowlife degenerates from the Valley, no less, infiltrating all that was his. When they were young, he liked Carly, and as such, picked her off first. Still, he'd let her down easy, considering what he'd done to Emily.

What an exhaustive process that had been.

Julien planted the seeds early with his father that Emily was cheating. And then there was his brilliant performance with his phony psychiatrist, Brian Whittaker.

"How are you feeling today, Julien?"

Whittaker was never clever enough to once come up with a better opening line.

Even as a teenager, Julien recognized Whittaker's skills as a shrink were basic at best, and it had been so easy to dupe him. During their last session, Julien pretended to be overcome with emotion, and insisted he had to call his stepsister.

Whittaker had handed over his personal cell phone to Julien without expressing a single concern.

Of course, Julien never had any intention of making the call. Instead, Julien pulled out a blank piece of paper from his pocket and then pretended to punch in the numbers to Carly's school, when in fact, he was texting Emily from Whittaker's phone.

Em, I can't stop thinking about what we did last night and how sexy you looked on top of me. I can still smell you on my skin. Call me when C isn't around.

Not exactly the stuff of Keats, but Julien got the point across. Christopher, who had become suspicious of Emily because of his son's prodding, got in the habit of looking at his wife's phone and found the racy message.

The only problem was that Whittaker's number showed up as unknown, so Julien couldn't ensnare him in the mess. He was so tired of being dragged to Whittaker's office every Saturday for his appointments. With the whole "unknown number" snafu, Julien decided to sabotage Whittaker in a different way, and told his dad the fake story about how his shrink came onto him. That was nearly the end of Dr. Whittaker.

Julien placed one last call to Whittaker the day he killed Emily, when he pretended to be near suicidal and claimed his father had misinterpreted his story about how Whittaker put his arm around him at their last session. During the conversation, Julien told Whittaker he was feeling increasingly unstable and begged his shrink to call Emily, since she might listen to him, unlike Christopher.

In case the police wouldn't buy into the theory that robbers killed Emily, Julien left a careful paper trail behind that would first link Christopher to the murder, and then Whittaker would be suspect number two. If Christopher felt cornered, he might shift the blame onto Whittaker, and say the psychiatrist was in love with his son and had grown incensed that the Whites had cut off sessions with the boy, so Whittaker had gone to the house to confront the couple and killed Emily when he found her there alone.

That would make perfect sense, since Whittaker called Emily shortly before she died.

But the cops ate up the robbery theory, and everything worked out as it should, plus Julien enjoyed the added bonus of never having to see Whittaker again.

He had fixed up that little mess quite nicely, but the latest situation was taking longer than he anticipated.

And then there was Victor to consider.

Julien paced the floor in frustration over the hanging, loose threads.

Carly should be dead by now. She had a cushy exit fifteen years earlier, but things had to be hard this time. She shouldn't take what didn't belong to her.

The change in Christopher's demeanor was what first tipped him off. His father was obviously ill, but it was the cool, clipped way Christopher spoke to him that first triggered Julien's concern. The sicker his father became, the less often Christopher returned his calls, and when radio silence followed, the next step became obvious.

His father was going to turn on him.

Lawrence, his lawyer, confirmed Christopher was in Europe getting a last-ditch alternative treatment. Julien took a thirteen-hour red-eye flight and stayed by his father's bedside, doting on him, fluffing his pillow, and reading to him like a goddamn nursemaid.

Julien wasn't too concerned his father was going to give the police a bedside confessional about his complicity in the cover-up of Emily's death. Christopher was too much of a slave to his lifestyle to man up to that. What was causing Julien to lose sleep was the thought of Christopher bilking him out of his rewards: the massive payday from his father's inheritance after his old man died. Julien could've killed him years ago, of course, but Julien took great enjoyment in owning his father due to their little secret about Emily's murder.

As payback, Christopher was going to cut off everyone and give all the money to Carly out of guilt and as a punishment to him and Vic.

While Julien was still in Europe, he waited to ask Christopher about the money and fussed over his father until the time was right. On his last day at the medical facility where Christopher was being treated, Julien pushed the living skeleton with the breath that now smelled like spoiled milk out in the garden, and only then did he say anything.

"You look so much better today. When you get back to the States, I'm sure you're going to make a full recovery," Julien said. "Still, with your illness, I've been thinking about what you'd like me to do with your money when the time comes. I think the most obvious choice would be a generous donation to a charity for pediatric patients, but, if you had other plans, I'll honor your wishes."

Julien knelt in front of his father's wheelchair and took the old man's hand.

Christopher didn't look at his son, but instead stared at a fixed point on the horizon.

"I don't want to talk anymore. I want to just be and look at something pretty," Christopher said.

To Julien, lying was a skill, a learned gift honed to perfection. And he had some coaching from the best in fine-tuning the art of the lie. At that moment, Christopher was lying. Who on earth would want to sit still and stare at a bunch of stupid flowers?

When Christopher refused to divulge the specifics of his inheritance, Julien's suspicions went full tilt. The only other obvious person to inherit the money was Carly. Even the *LA Times* had written about Victor's ascent without his daddy's money, since Christopher had long cut off his youngest son.

When he returned to the States, Julien paid a visit to his father's longtime driver, Bernie Washington. After a few beers at a dive bar that Julien knew the worker would like, Bernie revealed, for the past two months, he'd been driving Christopher to the English building on the USC campus, where they would wait until a pretty, tall blonde woman came out. Then Christopher would tell Bernie to take him home.

That sealed it. Julien had to make sure Carly was out of the picture, and if he were wrong about his father's intention, the worst that could come was that Carly would die.

But then came along the unexpected snag with his idiot lawyer. Despite his full court press, Lawrence refused to give him specifics about his father's will, leading Julien no choice but to seduce the preppy paralegal from the law office. After offering up a good bit of attention and the promise for sex, which Julien delivered, Anthony DiMatteo made a bootleg copy of Christopher's will, hid the document in his jacket when he left the office for the day and later hand-delivered it to his one-night stand.

Julien's suspicions were validated when he read the amended document. His father had not only changed his will in the last two months, but he was leaving all his fortune to Carly.

Julien and Vic were left holding an empty bag.

On the last page of Christopher White's Last Will and Testament was perhaps the biggest surprise of all. Lawrence, or anyone else at the firm, was never to make public that Carly was now the sole recipient of the entirety of his estate. Instead, the party line would be that Christopher left his entire fortune to charity. Looking through the gobs of legal jargon, the only way Julien would get his father's money was if Carly died.

Julien had to give it to his dad. Christopher knew his son was a killer, and if Julien found out about the change in the will, his boy would snuff out Carly in an instant.

Like sex, murder was a transaction to Julien, a necessary means to a desired end.

When Carly died, she would be his third kill, if you counted his own mother. Julien liked Lauren as much as he could ever like any other person, but when she fell deep into one of her moods, his mother had dragged him down.

A woman like that, with so many demons, was better off dead, and then she'd stop annoying him.

When he awoke on the day his mother would later take her own life, Julien found Lauren curled in a ball at the bottom of the bed.

Vic was standing there in the doorway, rubbing his eyes.

The poor kid had been up all night due to Lauren's latest crazy patch.

Victor whispered in Julien's ear, and then his younger brother returned to bed.

Julien had recently turned thirteen, and yes, it was time for him to take control of how he wanted his life to go forward.

"I upset you again, I know I did. I heard you and Victor knocking on the bathroom door last night, and I wanted to come out so you wouldn't worry, but I couldn't. I'm feeling much better today. I think we should be naughty. You boys can skip school. We'll fly to San Francisco and ride the cable cars."

Lauren's eyes were bright and shiny again, and she grabbed Julien's hands between hers, ready for the two of them to go set the world on fire.

Julien was having none of it. He was exhausted from a terrible night's sleep because of his mother and was angry at her for causing him to be so tired, especially since he had a calculus exam that morning. He did consider Lauren's proposition though. A San Francisco getaway would be fun, and he could make up the test later, but when they returned home, his mother's high would be over and then she'd come crashing down. With Christopher always being at work, Julien would be the one who'd have to deal with her spiral, as he always did, because he was the oldest.

Christopher said so.

Make sure your mother takes her medication today, Julien.

Keep an eye on her if she's in one of her moods, Julien.

He was a kid, for Christ's sake, and shouldn't have to be his mother's caretaker.

Victor with the big mouth and the big plans never had to do the dirty work.

"San Francisco sounds boring, and then you'll be in one of your moods again when we get back," Julien said.

"What should we do today instead?"

"No, Lauren, it's not what I should do but what you should do," Julien answered. "You should kill yourself and get it over with. You want to die, don't you?"

"Julien!" Lauren said, sounding surprised over her odd, lovely boy's suggestion.

"I was kidding around, but if that's something you decided to do one day, I wouldn't be mad. People get all wigged out when someone dies by suicide, but I say it's an individual person's choice."

Lauren nodded then, as if she completely understood, and climbed under the covers next to her boy.

He pouted a bit until he knew what he suggested had sunk in and fell asleep with his forehead pressed against his mother's.

Julien woke up once and saw Victor and Lauren in the hallway.

Victor was animated, feet bouncing side to side, chatting up Lauren, who was nodding her head in agreement. Good old, Vic.

Julien rolled over and fell back asleep.

Julien finished the scotch and was ready to call Rebecca when his phone buzzed.

The call was from an unfamiliar number with an LA area code.

He answered.

"Mr. White?"

"Yes, who is this?" Julien asked.

"Detective Dylan O'Rourke. I don't know if you remember me, but I worked Emily Bennett's case."

"Is there an update on my stepmother's case?" Julien asked.

"That's not why I'm calling. I believe you're a relative of Carly Bennett's."

Julien felt his heart soar. "Yes, has something happened to her?"

"I'm sorry for not breaking the news to you in person, but your stepsister is dead, along with another woman, Rebecca Hunter."

"Oh my God, I can't believe it. I saw Carly yesterday," Julien answered and made his voice thick with emotion. "Was it a car accident?"

"The crime scene is still fluid, but right now, it looks like a murder-suicide. It would be better if we can meet. I'd like to ask you a few questions about your stepsister's state of mind in recent days. Were you close?"

"We were estranged for a few years, but we reconnected recently."

"Were you familiar with Rebecca Hunter?"

"I have no idea who she is, and Carly never mentioned her," Julien answered, and paused for effect. "I'm sorry, I'm having a hard time accepting this. My sister was so young, and she had her whole life ahead of her. Do you think Carly murdered the other woman and then killed herself?"

"It's possible, or the situation could've been reversed. We've discovered some evidence that Ms. Hunter may have been responsible for the murder of a janitor at USC. We can talk more about this in person. Can you meet me at the station in about an hour?" the detective asked.

"I'll help you in any way I can, but I'm with patients right now. I'm a psychiatrist, and most of the people I treat are unstable with severe psychoses. As much as I'd like to offer my assistance right now, it's going to be disruptive for my patients if I cancel their appointments at the last minute. I'm sorry, considering the gravity of the situation, but I can meet you at ten tonight if that won't be too late."

"Ten is fine," O'Rourke answered.

When Julien ended the call, his smile was so wide, he felt he could disappear inside of it. Julien worked on his script for O'Rourke, in which he would tell the officer that—as a professional expert of human behavior—he should've seen the warning signs. Carly had been acting erratically, and was exhibiting delusional behavior.

As for Rebecca, while the scruffy beatnik David Ramsey had

been seen out with her only a handful of times, Julien White had a clean slate with the girl. He'd been meticulous, never once bringing her to his place, and he always used a burner phone when he called her.

Now Rebecca was dead too. Could his luck be any better?

Julien took a quick look at his watch. He had exactly three hours to drive to Malibu, complete the last bit of business, and return to the city in time to meet O'Rourke.

The win was in sight.

Julien scratched his chin that still felt itchy from the fake beard. He reserved a rental car and then called for a car service.

Time for the final act.

FIFTY-NINE
Julien

Julien left his rental car by the slip of his family's private beach and climbed the steep path that led to the rear of his family home.

He never cared much for the place. It was too gaudy, with its opulent fountains that made the driveway look like the entry to a Las Vegas hotel, more fitting to a lowlife lottery winner than for a Malibu doctor who came from family money.

His father's hired help, Bridgette, a lovely little nymph who likely wiped his dad's ass these days, would be gone for the evening, which offered a one-hour window before the night nurse arrived.

It was after eight, and sunset was chasing away the final memories of the day, leaving the sky a fluid streak of orange, magenta and gold, which reminded Julien of the multicolored Popsicles his mother gave him as a child.

The whole sob story he'd told Carly about Christopher hitting him with a belt wasn't true. He wanted Carly to think Christopher had a tendency toward violence. Seed planted.

Julien didn't believe for a minute that his simple, stuttering stepsister, who almost collapsed after a spin on the merry-go-round, would start digging around her mother's murder after all these years, but just in case, he needed to paint the picture for her of Christopher as the murderous villain.

His calves burned when he reached the sheerest point of the path and made the final ascent to the house. Julien strained to remember any fond father-and-son memories of his youth. The only vaguely pleasant moment he could recall was the time Christopher took him sailing off Catalina Island when he was ten. Victor was at some dumb theater camp, so it was only Christopher and him on a merry adventure.

"There you go, Julien. Nice work, son," Christopher had said. "Steer a little to the left."

The boating lesson lasted fifteen glorious minutes until Christopher insisted Julien let go of the wheel, but Julien refused.

Julien loved the rush of being in control. His father had to pry his son's small fingers away, leaving Julien red-faced and furious, damning Christopher to hell and pummeling his father with his fists. Christopher had held him at arm's length and looked at him like Julien was a rather queer little bird who was disturbing and a thing to fear.

Christopher's reaction taught Julien a valuable lesson: Never tip your hand to your true feelings. After that, if he ever needed a prompt on how to react to any given situation, Julien mimicked the respected adults he knew or the hero characters he saw on TV.

Julien's favorite role model was his literary hero, Holden Caulfield, the misunderstood, tragic demigod of youthful angst. Julien had picked the carousel at Griffith Park to meet Carly, since Holden Caulfield took his sister Phoebe to a similar spot in what was Julien's favorite scene in the book. He was disappointed Carly didn't pick up on that obvious cue, since the book was such a goddamn literary masterpiece.

Julien stuck to the shadows when the long-overgrown beach path ended, and he came to the rear of the property. From the cover of the trees, Julien spied the silhouette of his father on the deck. Christopher was wearing a brown wool hat and sat stooped in his wheelchair with a thick blanket over his legs.

His memories of the place came flooding back. All those years spent with Vic. Where was little brother at that moment?

Julien snapped on a pair of black plastic gloves and headed to the guest quarters, which offered a separate entry point to the deck. The estate was a good mile away from any neighbors, but it was wise to eliminate any risk of being noticed if he accessed the deck through the main house.

Julien rubbed the gloved fingers of one hand against the clear plastic bag in his pocket.

As expected, the guesthouse was silent when he went inside.

Julien climbed up its spiral staircase to the second story and opened the glass slider to the deck.

"There you are, Father, I brought you some food," Julien said.

He approached the old man from behind.

"I thought it would be a nice change for you to eat in the guesthouse. I know your doctor has you on a strict diet, but for tonight, you should indulge. I brought your favorite sandwich from Malibu Market and laid out a feast."

Christopher didn't respond.

He must be sleeping.

Julien moved toward his father, felt for the smooth plastic bag in his pocket and grazed his father's shoulder.

Christopher's body felt odd and stiff.

Maybe his father was already dead.

Julien did a quick pivot, so he was positioned in front of the wheelchair.

He took a step back in surprise.

In the wheelchair was a mannequin dressed in his father's clothes.

A familiar voice called his name. Carly stepped out of the shadows.

"Hello, Julien. I guess you weren't expecting me."

SIXTY
Ava

Two Hours Earlier

"Put your hands where I can see them."

Ava stood in the center of the kitchen, weapon drawn and pointed at Carly's assistant.

"Rebecca's armed."

"That's not true!" Rebecca pleaded.

"Don't play stupid with me," Ava said. "I know you and Julien were working together to make Carly sick. Julien was lacing that tea you were pushing with rat poison, and you were jacking Carly's food with some hallucinogenic shit."

"You made me think I was crazy. And you were trying to kill me," Carly said.

"I wasn't, I swear. I have no idea who this Julien person is, and I don't have a gun. You accused me of trying to poison you, so I reached into my bag to show you the tea from my boyfriend. David owns a health food company. I told him how stressed you've been, and he gave me the tea to help you relax."

"Your story is weak," Ava said. She combed through the contents of Rebecca's purse and pulled out a box with the logo "Nami Organic Tea" printed on the label.

"There's no gun, Carls."

"I told you!" Rebecca said. "I wasn't trying to hurt Carly."

"Why did you come back here after I fired you?" Carly asked.

"I was upset after our fight. It was eating me up, so I drove over here to apologize. When I didn't see your car, I decided to leave you a note. That's what I was doing when you walked in, I swear."

"Why didn't you tell anyone about your past relationship

with Ed Russo?" Ava asked. "It seems like an obvious thing to mention after your boss discovered the dead man in her office. Russo dumped you, and you hated the fact that he was paying Carly attention. So, you killed him and let Carly take the fall."

"I did date Ed a few years ago. I was lonely, and he was nice to me. The relationship lasted for about a month. I was upset when he ended things, but I didn't kill him. I didn't tell anyone because short janitors aren't exactly a catch. I didn't want people to think I was a loser."

"Even if that's true, it still doesn't explain your relationship with Julien," Ava said.

Ava holstered her gun and tapped the camera app on her phone.

She shoved her cell in front of Rebecca's face. On the screen was a picture of Julien wearing the fake man bun and the beard, sitting next to Rebecca at The Butcher's Daughter.

"This is your man?" Ava asked.

"That's David, not the Julien person."

"If you take away the hairpiece and the fake beard and put him in better clothes, this is what you get," Ava said.

She scrolled through her pictures again until Ava found the one that she wanted.

On the screen was a surveillance shot of Julien leaving his office building. He was dressed in a suit and tie.

Rebecca lifted her hand, as if to bat the phone away, but dropped her arm to her side when Ava let out a low, threatening growl.

"Don't be stupid, little girl."

"The picture must be from a few years ago. David told me he used to work in the corporate world until he couldn't take it anymore," Rebecca explained.

"I took that picture yesterday. The man in the suit is Julien White, Carly's stepbrother. If you don't believe me, this should change your mind."

Ava's index finger flicked across the screen, offering a slide-show of Julien's intimate moment with Anthony DiMatteo.

"I don't need to see anymore. I can't believe David did this to me."

A floorboard creaked in the hallway, and Ava reached for her gun.

"Drop it," a female voice shouted.

LAPD Detective Rodriguez and her partner rounded the corner.

"Easy, easy," Ava said.

She raised one hand at her side and slowly placed her weapon on the floor.

"The gun is registered, and I'm authorized to carry it," Ava said. "If you're here to arrest Carly for Ed Russo's murder, we're way beyond that."

"A former student can place me at Zuma Beach when Russo was killed," Carly said.

"It's too late for made-up alibis," Smith snapped. "You're under arrest for the murder of Ed Russo."

It was all Ava could do not to smack the smug look off Cop Junior's face.

When he approached Carly with handcuffs, Ava pointed her phone at Smith.

"This LAPD cop is dirty. He was just told the woman he's about to arrest has an alibi," Ava said. "Officer Zachary Smith set up this woman to take the fall for the murder of USC janitor, Ed Russo. Carly Bennett is innocent, but the LAPD doesn't care."

"Are you recording this?" Rodriguez asked.

"And I'm a second away from posting it to my socials."

"Hold on, Smith," Rodriguez said. "Ms. Bennett, give me the contact information for the student who can place you at Zuma Beach."

After Carly shared Amelia Peterson's phone number, Rodriguez went outside but returned within a minute.

"The student confirmed she could place Bennett at the beach when Russo was murdered," Rodriguez said.

"I'm not buying it," Smith answered. "If that's true, then who killed Russo?"

"You need to keep up, love," Ava said. She looked at Carly. "Are we thinking the same thing?"

Carly nodded. Ava's girl stood tall, looking like she got her swagger back.

"I think I know how to get my stepbrother to confess," Carly said to the officer. "But I'm going to need your help."

SIXTY-ONE
Carly

Carly prayed Julien wouldn't pick up on her fear, and cursed herself for assuming he would enter the estate from the main road.

Her memory of the layout of the property had dimmed after fifteen years, and Carly neglected to tell the authorities about the mile-long beach path that connected to the rear of the compound, not to mention the miscalculation the authorities made in believing Julien was still in the city.

When Carly revealed herself, Julien's face registered a flicker of surprise, but then he regained his composure.

Carly's chest constricted and she reached into her pocket for her inhaler.

Breathe in, breathe out, slow and easy.

"Where's my father?" Julien demanded. "Cat got your tongue? Speak, girl."

"He told me everything. I know that you were the one who killed my mom."

Carly's voice quivered, but at least she spoke the truth.

"You blackmailed your father to make sure he'd cover for you," Carly continued.

"Your summary is succinct, but you shouldn't believe my dad got a conscience at the eleventh hour."

Julien retook his position of power and moved closer to his stepsister.

Hoping to buy time for O'Rourke to surface, Carly tried to keep Julien talking.

"Why did you kill her?"

"Isn't it obvious? Why can't you be smart, Carly? You had potential until I ruined you. Em was a colossal drain on my life. Your mother didn't belong here, and neither did you. After my mother died, my father paid attention to me for once, but then you and Emily came along, and everything went back to the way it was between my father and me."

"If you care about your father so much, why were you willing to let him take the fall for you?"

"It wasn't a point of caring or not caring. You and your mother were taking away what was mine," Julien said. "You have some degree of luck about you. The tea should've killed you by now, but it's Rebecca's fault for not doing her job."

"Why did you murder Ed Russo?"

"Wrong place, wrong time. Rebecca kept your schedule on her phone, and I found out you were going to be at Nobu. Rebecca had a key to your office, so I had sex with her, and then when she was sleeping, which she always did after I screwed her, I looked at your schedule, took the key, and went to your office. Rebecca mentioned that she filled a prescription for your asthma at the pharmacy. She said you always kept a bottle in your office, in case you had an attack at school. I found the bottle in your desk drawer and was going to replace your medication with ketamine, but then Russo showed up. I had to improvise."

Julien shrugged, as if killing Russo were no big deal.

"Killing me was about money."

"That makes me sound predictable," Julien answered.

"Did you forge the letter from my mother?"

"No, that one was authentic. I found the note on the desk in her bedroom after I killed her. The necklace you have on, Em was wearing it that night. She put up a hell of a fight. After I was done, I took the necklace, since she scratched me, and I took the letter too. I gave them to you because I needed to bring you close. Look at you, shaking like a leaf. What was your plan, to try and bring me down on your own? You've got no police, no backup, Carly Bennett, the same dull-witted girl from the Valley who never realized her full potential because I ruined her."

Julien removed hands out of his pockets, revealing a silver knife in his hand.

"S–s–stop," Carly stuttered.

"Stupid stuttering, Carly. I bet you despise yourself every time you look in the mirror."

The tightening in her chest now felt like a block of granite was sitting on her lungs.

She coughed and reached for her inhaler, but when it fell from her hand, Julien snatched it and tossed it over the deck.

"What will you do without your crutch now, Carly? You're a weak girl, and I made you that way. One of my greatest satisfactions—beyond breaking your spirit—was when I snuffed the life out of your mother."

Still holding the knife, Julien dropped his hand to his side and laughed.

In that moment, the fifteen years of hurt and loss erupted to the surface.

"I'M. NOT. WEAK."

Carly's arm flew up and her fist connected against Julien's cheekbone.

Surprised, Julien fell backward, giving Carly the opening she needed. She raced toward the outdoor stairwell but stopped when Victor ascended the last step.

"He's got a knife!" Carly warned.

Victor's eyes darted between Carly and his brother.

"Finally," Julien said, clutching his injured cheek. "What took you so long?"

SIXTY-TWO

Ava

Ava's gut screamed at her that something was wrong.

A hammer of a headache started between her eyes as Ava turned to O'Rourke who was standing next to her in the driveway of the Whites' estate.

"I want to stick around. You can't have Carly upstairs without any cover," Ava said.

"We've got it under control. An LAPD unit is babysitting Mr. White's place. His car hasn't left the driveway, meaning our boy is still in the city. Rodriguez and Smith are ten minutes out, and my partner is at the gate. There's only one road up and down the mountain that leads to the house. My partner will radio me when he sees Mr. White's vehicle. Once Rodriguez and Smith get here, the three of us will get into position inside the house. We'll make sure nothing happens to Carly. She needs to get her stepbrother to confess to Ed Russo's and Emily Bennett's murders, and then it's over."

"Don't underestimate Julien, he's smarter than you think. What happens if he tries to hurt Carly?"

"Then we'll shut him down. You need to leave now and trust that we have it under control."

Future promises meant nothing. Right now, Carly was a sitting duck.

"I want to check in with her first."

"I took your word that you wouldn't bring your weapon here, but if you broke your promise, I hope that you aren't stupid enough to try and arm your friend before you leave. That wouldn't be protecting her."

"I'm not a liar, and you don't need to remind me about untrained gun users being lousy at self-defense. As for you, I'd tell your backup to haul their asses here immediately."

"I'm going to do a walk-and-talk with my partner. When I get back, I expect you to be gone. I appreciate your concern for your friend, but you need to let us do our jobs."

Ava waited until O'Rourke was halfway down the driveway to respond.

"Like hell."

She entered the house.

There's no way she'd leave her friend behind.

At the foot of the staircase, her phone vibrated against her hip.

Yvonne Abbott's name appeared on the screen. No time for that. Ava ran up one stair, then two, but something niggled inside her.

"Yvonne, you need to make this quick," Ava answered.

"You wanted to know who my brother sold my husband's car to, right?"

"I only need a name, and fast."

"He sold the Karmann Ghia to a Mr. White."

"Julien, right?" Ava said, annoyed that her usual spot-on instincts were so off this time.

"No, the car was sold to a Victor White, or the Paramount Pictures prop department, to be exact."

Ava ended the call and raced up the remaining stairs. When she reached the second-floor master bedroom, a loud crash came from the deck.

She grabbed the closest item she could find and sprinted toward the sound.

SIXTY-THREE

Carly

Victor strode the length of the deck and leaned against the side of the house with his arms folded across his chest. Cool and relaxed.

"Hi, Carly. It's nice to see you," Victor said. His smile was big, as if this were all a practical joke, but there was something mean and unfamiliar in his eyes.

"What do you want me to do now?" Julien asked.

"We clearly have a problem because you didn't do your job. Where the hell is Chris, and why isn't she dead?" Victor said and pointed at Carly.

"I don't know what happened," Julien answered.

A tidal wave of sound seemed to crash inside Carly's head as Victor's betrayal settled in. How had she been so stupid?

It was Victor who had masterminded her downfall. It had always been Victor.

"You two were working together the whole time, but you were the one calling the shots," Carly said to Victor.

"I'm glad you caught up to speed, and kudos for outwitting Jules. Vindication is a sweet ride, and all the sweeter when gained over time," Victor answered. "You'll need to please excuse me because I have unfinished business. Come here, bro."

Julien walked in Victor's direction, a priggish expression never leaving his face.

"This is a minor hiccup. I was a breath away from taking care of Carly before you arrived," Julien said.

Julien kept his confident stride across the deck toward his brother. At the halfway point, he stopped and took a surprised step back when Victor pulled a silver revolver from his jacket.

Victor snapped into ready stance and trained the gun at Julien.

"Stop playing around, Vic. We've got no time for your theatrics."

"Playtime is over. I haven't been this serious since I figured out a way to get Carly and her mom out of our lives when we were kids. I gave you a longer list of tasks this time, but you failed to complete them."

"Don't you dare speak to me that way. I did the heavy lifting on all of this," Julien said. "Seventy–thirty. That was our agreement on the inheritance cut. You made the plan, I did the lion's share of the work, I get most of the money. Maybe I didn't construct the plot, but I'm the executor, and nothing gets done without the executor. You know I'm right, Thunder."

Victor laughed.

"That childhood taunt doesn't hurt me anymore. But you're right. You did everything, which means all trails lead back to you."

Carly recoiled when a shot rang out, and Julien slumped to the ground.

"Sorry for the family drama," Victor said.

"Christopher knows what you did and so do the police," Carly bluffed.

She stared in shock at Julien. His body was limp, and a pool of blood was growing underneath him.

"You can do better than that two-bit lie. Your eyes were as wide as saucers when you realized I was the main player in the game. Not Jules. You're an interesting one, Carly Bennett. It's not self-deprecation that stops you from reaching your full potential. It's the fact that Julien and I were able to convince you that you were never worthy. You know it was us who made you sick when you were a kid? Or should I say, it was me. I told Jules to pour a little industrial cleaner in the tea he used to give you when you lived with us. I guess you could say I'm a little predictable having Jules run that route again fifteen years later, but it worked when we were kids, and it almost worked now. You must have one hell of a constitution."

"You're e–evil," Carly stammered.

"How does anyone take you seriously with that stutter?"

As Carly fought to regain her center, her eyes locked on the silver revolver still in Victor's gloved hands.

"That's the same gun you showed me at Paramount," Carly realized.

"You would've been a smarter partner than Jules. The gun isn't a prop, but a bona fide firearm, and your prints are all over it," Victor said.

"You set me up."

"Correct again," Victor answered.

"Sebastian Foster was your creation too."

"He was a struggling actor looking for work. I hired him for a side job, gave him a role to play and even a pretty cool ride for the evening. What he didn't know was that I planned to kill you that night. His job was to make you pull over at the Las Virgenes Road lookout, where I was waiting. When you didn't, I had to improvise. You're a lucky girl."

Victor moved in Carly's direction. His back faced away from the screen door of the house.

"What's your plan now?" Carly asked. "My prints are on the gun, so the police will think I killed Julien."

"Everyone knows how unstable you've been acting. Even Rebecca can attest to your erratic behavior, which got you suspended from your job. Jules filled me in on that latest development. Here's what the story will be. You killed Julien and then yourself."

"No one will believe that."

"No one?" Victor taunted.

"There's one person who won't."

From behind the bedroom's screen door, a light brown hand parted the curtain to the deck.

She had to warn Ava, and in a way that only her best friend would understand.

Her practice phrase that Ava had given her on Chatham's rooftop so many years before that cemented their friendship.

Carly cleared her mind and delivered it in a voice that was perfect and clear.

"The girl wore her hair in two braids, tied with two blue bows."

Victor cocked his head to the side. "You're a peculiar one . . ."

Before he could finish, Victor was knocked off his feet by Ava, a streaming blur of movement, who sacked him from behind and then struck him repeatedly with a long metal object.

Now that the power positions had shifted, Ava stood in dominance over Victor. She held a fireplace poker in one hand like a baseball bat, ready to take another swing.

Victor grinned up at Ava and raised his hands like he was signaling defeat.

"You must be Carly's friend. I predicted that you would tend toward violence. I'm afraid you've injured me," Victor said and winced when he rose to his feet.

"I was warming up. You take one step in Carly's direction, I'll finish you off," Ava warned. "Are you OK, Bennett?"

"I'm better now."

Still with the fireplace poker in hand, Ava retreated until she reached the deck's railing.

Victor followed, and Carly realized Ava's move was done on purpose to draw Victor away from her.

"You masterminded the plot to kill Emily Bennett, and now you've killed your brother. You'll get jammed up for being an accomplice in Ed Russo's death too," Ava said. "And you almost got away with it. And all for some green. How does it feel to be overpowered by two girls?"

"You make me sound small when you frame it like that. But it's all true."

"Thanks for the confessional, numbskull," Ava said. She reached behind her back and pulled out her phone, where she continued to record Victor's admission of guilt.

Something switched in Victor's expression. In an instant, he turned from the easy-going boy from childhood to a monster that let out a guttural roar before he charged her friend.

Ava, unmoved, held her ground, until Victor was inches away. A second before he attacked, Ava pivoted, and Victor, who was now off his feet and lunging mid-air at his target, cleared the railing, and fell four stories to the patio below.

Carly rushed to the edge of the deck and looked down.

Victor's body was splayed unnaturally on the cement. He blinked once, and his eyes seemed to focus in on Carly.

From behind her on the deck, she heard a light shuffle and then Julien whisper, "You won."

SIXTY-FOUR
Carly

Three months later

Carly sat barefoot on the sand on Zuma Beach and looked at the ocean.

Ava was by her side and admiring a different view of two shirtless men about their age who looked like they could be linebackers for the NFL, tossing a football a few feet away.

"The blondey boy with the spikey hair, I'm naming him 'Bicep Blake,' and the one with the buzz cut, let's call him 'Quadzilla.'"

"You're objectifying those men," Carly said.

"Oh please, they're putting on a show for us."

The football slipped through the fingers of the blond male and landed a few inches away from Carly and Ava.

"What a decoy move. He missed the ball on purpose," Ava said. She snatched up the football and nailed a perfect spiral back to the men.

"Nice arm. Do you and your friend want to join us?" the spiked-haired male asked.

"Thanks, but this is a girls' day only. But you boys have a lovely afternoon," Ava answered.

When the men jogged off after their play was shut down, Ava reached into her cooler.

"I've got water, lemonade, or iced tea. I'm guessing it's a hard no on the iced tea," Ava said.

"Iced tea will never touch my lips again," Carly answered, and gave Ava a playful flick on the arm with her finger.

Carly's phone buzzed in her bag, but when she tried to reach for it, Ava stopped her.

"Don't you dare. I've got this," Ava said. She looked at the number and answered the call. "Uh huh . . . I see . . . Good work . . . I'm glad they finally nailed the bastard."

"What happened?" Carly asked when Ava hung up.

"Nothing for you to worry about right now."

"Come on, Ava. I'm fine. I really am."

"It was Rebecca. She's at the courthouse. You did your time as a witness. I dragged you out here to relax after the trial, so how about we talk about this later?"

"Tell me what happened."

"Rebecca gave her victim impact statement during sentencing and the judge delivered his verdict. Julien got screwed seven ways until Sunday. It's a miracle he survived after Victor shot him, but at least he'll be held accountable for the rest of his life for his part in what he did to you and your mom. Are you happy, Bennett?"

"I'm glad it's over."

Carly closed her eyes and felt the warm sun on her skin. She envisioned her mother holding her hand as the two of them walked back to their little ranch house after Emily arrived home from work, as they had done so many years ago.

It was a simple memory that meant everything.

And no matter what happened for her ahead, Carly knew she would be OK this time, surrounded by people who loved her.

Carly walked down to the shore and thought about her future. It could be anything she wanted it to be.

She dove into the ocean and let herself drop deep into the black water. She stopped her descent and swam to the top and the shimmering blue light that awaited her on the surface.